REGIME CHANGE

■ She's the CIA's woman in North Africa, a fast-tracker with a brilliant career and an enviable counterterrorism record who suddenly finds her life threatened. Who among the players wants her dead and why?

■ Is it her mentor, who's running the biggest cyberwar operation in CIA history? And what about her estranged husband, whose ambitions would be boosted if he were the widower of a genuine heroine in the War on Terror?

■ The trick is to stay alive while she finds answers and reevaluates her life.

...Her vision compressed, focused down to a cone, her eyes seeing only what was within the headlights' beams. Karim and his gun were lost behind black blinders. A sound like a swarm of locusts drowned out anything he might be saying. ...The wall rushed towards her, growing in the headlights, shock absorbers protesting on the rough ground. She manhandled the wheel with her good hand. Would he pull the trigger? The wall seemed to mushroom. In seconds it would fill the universe, would block out the world. How much longer? Ten seconds. Nine. Eight. "Seven. Six." She cringed. She ticked the seconds aloud the way she'd once counted a horse's strides before hitting a take-off point for a high fence. Timing. Timing was everything.

PAT A. STUART

Pat A. Stuart, a veteran CIA operations officer, spent thirty-one years in the CIA's Directorate of Operations—the predecessor organization to the National Clandestine Service. *Regime Change*, her first espionage/suspense novel, draws on her years within an organization she feels deeply about and among people who are among the most hard-working, interesting, and dedicated that America has to offer.

ALSO BY
PAT A. STUART

Pockets of Magic
A Gathering of Grizzlies
Grizzly Memories

REGIME CHANGE

A NOVEL BY
PAT A. STUART

WYBAR HOUSE

The characters in this book are fictitious although it is impossible not to be influenced by acquaintance, experience, and the nature of the plot. Similarities to real persons, living or dead, however, is coincidental and not intended by the author.

Copyright © 2014 by Pat A. Stuart

All rights reserved. In accordance with the U.S. Copyright Act of 1976, the scanning, uploading, and electronic sharing of any part of this book without the permission of the publisher constitutes unlawful piracy and theft of the author's intellectual property. If you would like to use material from the book (other than for review purposes), prior written permission must be obtained by contacting the author at info@patstuart.com. Thank you for your support of the author's rights.

WYBAR HOUSE

978-0-9908727-0-2

Cover and interior design by ColorStone Design www.webportfolio.com

...we talked of Mu'ammar Qadhafi
and Cold War hopes, of
the Arab Spring
and Wall Street bulls.
"I'm an expensive friend,"
she said.

Then,
we walked in the garden
where dew
spangled flower petals
and shivered the hair of our arms
until
it was time for her to go

away with her
sleek image promising
change and fortune,
sated need; giving
revolution and death,
killing greed.

From ....*Drinking Wine with War*

AUTHOR'S NOTE

I began *Regime Change* in 2009 under the assumption that Libya's Mu'ammar Qadhafi had little time left and would not go easily. Some level of violence was inevitable. Looting, burning, and the rise of terrorist groups could easily be forecast along with a resulting interruption in oil supplies and cascading North African instability. No one in Washington would want that. But what type of preventive action could I imagine the U.S. Government might take that would lend itself to a good plot?

Cyberwar was in the news. The use of malware was always a possibility. Thus, the novel took shape. As I finished the first draft in early 2011, the expected happened in an unexpected way. Instead of a cataclysm in one country with minor ripple effects, the great magna chamber of Middle East unrest exploded ... beginning, quite literally, with a match lit in an obscure Tunisian town.

About that time news of a new kind of virus appeared in my morning reading. Semantic coding promised an undetectable means of by-passing firewalls. Since my draft needed a plot adjustment and rewriting, anyway ... .

And so to *Regime Change*. Enjoy.

To Robyn, who never let me lose faith

■ ■ ■

CHAPTER ONE
Bay of Tunis, Tunisia, February 18, 2011

The interior of the car was dark except for the glow of Karim's cigarette and light shining from a GPS-looking device mounted on the windshield. Its screen showed a ghostly night-vision video of an empty dirt lane.

She brought the car to a stop on a gravel hammock above a rocky shoreline and turned off the ignition. Next to her smoke escaped in strings from Mustafa Karim's mouth and nose, roughening his voice as he ranted at her from the passenger seat about how, "You people insult my intelligence and treat me like a dog in the street. There it is. You comprehend nothing, understand nothing. But me?"

Nearby, so close it seemed to be inside the car, a toad croaked an accompaniment for the man. A breeze wafted the foul-smelling Gauloise smoke out the open windows and whispered through reeds and coastal shrub, the sea grooming the beach beyond.

This meeting hadn't started well, but emergency meetings never did. He continued, "Now, I know everything. Every thing. Some times it is a thing of months for me to receive this intelligence, but always it comes to me. Some times ..." Through the windshield she could see rocks and sand and long lines of surf shuttling silver froth along the moon's path.

A case holding $500,000 jabbed the back of her legs. It'd taken the station's Intel Assistant hours to assemble. "You're going to let me do this by myself?" Gwen had feigned disbelief earlier in the afternoon when Regan left her and the office to drive out here to look around. It'd turned out to be an unnecessary precaution. Nothing in this stretch of undeveloped land along the Bay of Tunis had changed since the day, three months ago, that she'd last scouted it.

"If not because I have new sources, men I recruit and put in place only one month past," Karim jabbed his cigarette at her. "If not for them, the treachery you people make? Never will it come clear to ... ."

He'd been haranguing her since he'd eased his London bespoke suit, floor-length burnoose, and gold accessories into her car back at the pick-up site. But he would run down soon. She reached for her iPad with its encrypted note-taking app. Mustafa Karim was a conspiracy maven, having built his life on plots and machinations and prone to see an elaborate web of deceit behind the most innocent of events.

She read through her notes not having to look at her core instructions. **Terminate contact at earliest convenience. Pay him off. Having lost access to high-level information and ability to influence leadership thinking … .**

Simple enough instructions but, clearly, Karim had a bone or two or ten to pick with the CIA, and it might not be as easy to sever the connection as Langley would like to think.

The toad croaked. Karim vented, and a rotting pile of kelp tossed ashore in the last storm emitted an increasingly irritating stench.

"*Tu compris?*" he said. "These things I tell you so you will understand the situation in Libya. Your people are … ." And he was off again on another rant.

The iPad shut itself down and, for a moment, its last gleam of light seemed to bounce off the scrub growth half a mile or so to her right. There was another flash. Headlights? Couldn't be.

Karim's finger waggled. "… me to believe this massive lie—" A strong wash of surf rose to tug at the dead kelp.

Her eyes flicked to the GPS lookalike, and she saw them. So did Karim. A combination of indignation, anger, and self-righteousness had made his actions jerky, but now a new kind of tension stiffened his body. She felt it herself. Fear. Or maybe just trepidation.

"Who?" He tossed his cigarette out the window and hit the dashboard. "Do not wait to see. Go. This moment."

A second car passed the camera she'd mounted at the turn into this track. The video was not good, but the first car had held at least three men. The second? Two?

She started the Peugeot, saw a spark where Karim's Gauloise had landed. Said, "Son of a bitch!" And, "Get that cigarette."

His eyes flashed white, his breath hissed, but he did as she said, his embroidered gray burnoose flaring, as seemingly insubstantial as the vehicle images on the screen. Then, he was back in the car, the cigarette head glowing once before being mashed out.

She turned off the camera monitor and eased the car forward across a rocky bed lining the high-water mark.

"What are you doing?" He'd switched from Arabic to French, using the hard and impersonal 'vous'.

"My job." She saw no reason to explain further. There should be no cars. Not here. Since there were? It had to be Karim's fault; his carelessness. Had to be. He'd said something; not run a proper surveillance route; something.

Tires slipped and slid over loose rocks, the steering wheel twisted in her hands, the lion logo in its center blurring silver in the pale white light of moon and stars.

In seconds the first car would top the berm separating swamp from drained flatlands. More seconds would pass, seconds of blindness for their pursuers, a small period of grace for her. The Peugeot would be hard to see, its original dark blue paint lusterless with age. Only the windows might catch and reflect light, and they were dirty.

A brighter glow above the coastal scrub showed they were closer, very close. The Peugeot's right front tire dropped into a hole. Its tough frame, one made to survive African driving conditions, groaned and bounced out. How long? Less than a minute by a conservative estimate.

There. She saw the broken but still intact concrete ramp where once a French colon had run his boat down to the sea. Now, the house that had graced this place was mostly gone, its walls and contents recycled, the site marked only by a twisting iron staircase and the remains of a chimney rising from a heap of oleander.

The Peugeot rocked and bounced up the fractured ramp to settle on firm ground. She parked behind the old fireplace.

"Wait here." She switched off the engine and turned to rummage in her tote bag, pulling out a CIA-adapted Nikon and a black scarf. "I'm going to find out who the bastards are."

They could hear the cars now and see the glow of headlights above the thick vegetation that separated her parking place of moments earlier from here.

"Stop." Karim had a gun in his hand.

The rant. Now, a gun? But she had no time for this. "Put that away," she hissed, hearing car doors slam and flipping the scarf over her head. "You won't need that if you stay here and stay quiet. Whoever they are, they're not going to find us." She hoped.

"You remain here." The gun was aimed at her.

"Okay, Karim." She could feel a red-head's flush of anger spread across her face. "You go. You can crawl through the bushes to identify those bastards."

"We wait here until they go."

"Is there some reason you don't want me to see them?"

He said nothing, so she kept talking. "Then, I'm going, and if you shoot me, those men will be all over you. How many bullets in that gun? Or would you rather run and die in the swamp out there?" She didn't wait for an answer but slid out of the Peugeot, leaving the driver's door open behind her, the interior lights disabled, the car dark except for Karim's pale shadow.

Her skin crawled. Her black windbreaker and pants, black scarf and gloves gave her near invisibility but no protection against a bullet in the back. Predicting what Karim might do was impossible. From everything she'd learned, the Libyan was a state-enabled psychopath. Among other things, he'd been Qadhafi's Director of Prisons, meaning interrogating and warehousing Qadhafi's enemies, making them examples to the populace, his name used by mothers to frighten their children into obedience. Before that as a security service officer, he'd trained hundreds of terrorists in bomb-making and weapons, prepared them to go out and massacre innocents, to shred their bodies into lumps of unidentifiable flesh. Most recently, as head of the Libyan intelligence and security service, he'd become almost respectable, but … .

She inched the last few yards until the glow of light through the foliage resolved into the shapes of cars and men. Both cars faced the sea, their headlights aimed at the beach, the tires of the vehicle nearest to her almost where her Peugeot had parked. It was a Toyota. Five men stood in a semi-circle staring out at the bay as though looking for a boat. All were dark haired, swarthy-skinned, and bearded. All wore suit jackets over white shirts, reminding her of Mohammed Hamdan and his people. Where others of their ilk favored fatigues or native robes, he'd invariably dressed in a suit, and his men had followed his lead.

Maybe these people had nothing to do with her or Karim. Maybe they were smugglers and she'd stumbled upon a rendezvous site? What was perfect for her purposes could equally serve another type of covert activity.

She eased her body up to a sitting position, the litter under her rustling. Which didn't matter. The engines of the two cars still hummed and music blared from one of the radios, a bastard fusion of a minor key melody with a hard rock sound. Cross-legged, she propped her elbows on her knees. She was almost buried among the dense, low-hanging branches of some kind of oak, its lobate leaves providing excellent cover, its acorns bumpy under her. One jabbed her butt, and she shifted, bending her head to look through an old-style view finder. The camera's monitor screen was fully enclosed to render it light secure while the telescopic lens was recessed to prevent reflections

It took a few seconds to focus in on the first man's face. She snapped off a series of photos, the digital camera making no noise. She got a good full face and a good profile before going on to the next man. The camera seemed to bring his features almost up against her own. That nose. The eyes ... no. She shied backwards, almost dropped the camera.

"No," the word hissed on her lips, almost escaped. "No."

But it was. It was him.

Abdul-Ghaffar al-Din. She'd never forget that face or that thick, bulldog body. Last seen it had been laid out on a stretcher, blood soaking the right side of his shirt and the fabric of his pants. Bullet holes had told the story of his injuries if not the tale of how he came by them. She, though, knew. She'd been there, her own blood gathering in her right eyebrow and in the hair around her right ear, leaking from a gash in her hairline—made, possibly, by a bullet from al-Din's gun.

The memory made the scar, her souvenir of a hard-fought rendition operation, throb.

Not smugglers. No.

The camera weighed on her hands and wrists. Pictures. She needed pictures. This was her job. It was her life, too. She was sitting only thirty feet or so from a man who'd sworn to kill her.

She stared. That day three years earlier, CIA Air Branch contractors working with a Tunisian special forces unit had overrun what had been a terrorist training site deep inside Libya. The operation had bagged al-Salan's chief, Mohammed Hamdan. It had won her an intelligence medal. It had also led an obscure Sanusiya mullah to issue a fatwa condemning her to death.

But al-Din? He had been Hamdan's second-in-command, had spent six years with the Muj in Afghanistan, then had followed Hamdan back to Libya via Yemen and several spectacular terrorist incidents. He'd been captured and given to the Tunisians for interrogation, trial, and prison. Three years ago.

"Should still be in prison," she mouthed the words. "Should still be. Why isn't he?"

The answer was obvious—mass prison releases as a side effect of the Jasmine Revolution.

The man standing next to al-Din? Hadad Abdullah Juriy. Of course. Where al-Din went, so did Juriy. He'd been imprisoned in Tunisia with al-Din, had been his faithful lieutenant from the beginning.

Juriy was speaking, but whatever he had to say was lost to her. Between music, engines, and sea, she could hear nothing, just see the mouths moving.

The effect of the words on al-Din, though, was evident. He turned and walked back to the passenger door of the second car—one hidden from her by the Toyota. She switched to video function as he leaned down to the window.

So there were more than five men. Who else? She moved the camera, changed the focus, adjusted the zoom. Nothing worked. She could get no more than a vague form inside the second car. But it was one form. One person. Male or female? Not sure, but one only, not more.

She finished photographing the faces she could see, then went back to video, panning as the men returned to the open car doors. Al-Din was the last, taking a final look around. Then he returned to the open back seat door of the car nearest her, his mouth moving, apparently responding to something said by someone she still hadn't seen. The front doors of the other car slammed shut, cutting down on the music's volume, and al-Din's final words, spoken only feet from where she sat, came clear.

"... God's will if they do not come here. Speak to Him, not to me." He slid inside and closed his door. His Toyota backed and turned and drove off. The other car followed.

"... *if they* do not come ... ." She tried to make sense of the words while zooming in on the license plates. Then she did speak aloud, muttered, "Al-Din used English." Not Arabic or Maghrebi Arabic or French. English.

When their cars weren't even a glow on the horizon, she eased back through the oak's branches, then stood, her joints reluctant. She still had to deal with Karim and his gun.

A few minutes later she stood beside an empty Peugeot. Only Karim's gray burnoose showed he'd ever been there while the money case was gone. Paranoid. Karim was paranoid, but he hadn't lost sight of the important thing in his life: money.

Serve him right if she got inside and drove away without him. Not that he'd let her. Without doubt he was somewhere nearby with his gun trained on her.

"Olly, olly oxen, all in free," she called, disturbing the nocturnal creatures, quiet radiating out from her like ripples on a pond leaving only the soft wash of the sea and the whisper of leaves. It'd been a silly thing to say, but the childhood game call gave her an illusion of security, almost made her smile. Almost.

"What is this you speak? This 'olly'?" Karim's dark suit separated from the trunk of a tree. He carried the money case. The gun was nowhere in sight, and he sounded relaxed, safe.

"We still have a few things to do," she said. "And you may want a ride out of here."

"I saw these al-Salan men. They are employed by your CIA but, I think, it is you they want. It is you who they follow here. Not me. It is the fatwa that brings them."

She didn't argue the point. It was all too likely he was right—at least about the fatwa. "Load up," she said but couldn't resist adding, "and as I recall the al-Salan are all Harabi, as are you."

He grunted. Tribal affiliation among Libyans usually meant something. In this case, though, what? She let the topic go.

Instead she turned on the monitor and watched the two al-Salan cars depart the area via her concealed camera. Then she used another route out of the wasteland. Ten minutes later, the Peugeot bounced onto solid paving near the ruins of what had been a small store, the headlights illuminating a faded advertisement for Fanta on a broken wall—orange drink pictured dribbling from a tilted bottle. She accelerated and made two more turns before she began to relax, before her lungs expanded. She breathed deeply. Until then she'd been unaware of the tension that had tightened her muscles and increased her heartbeat.

But this wasn't over yet.

She tapped her ring finger against the steering wheel. Wedding diamonds, turned under, hit plastic in a reassuring way. Her thoughts didn't match. She had to finish up this meeting; get his signature on a receipt for the money; make it clear to him that there would be no more contact. As for the debrief she'd planned? Forget it. Get done and get out. Finish. End.

"There're just a few things left to cover," she said.

Karim lit a cigarette and exhaled. Smoke gagged her despite her lowered window, but she said nothing. They'd had the 'no smoking in the car' conversation a year ago. She'd lost.

"There is only one thing to finish, Madame," Karim said. "As I say before, you people steal from me, and I will have compensation. Not with the small sum you bring tonight. I require twenty millions of dollars, and I require it immediately."

She didn't answer. Had no answer he'd want to hear. The man had always been inventive and demanding. And now that he'd become about as welcome to the Agency as a flea on a dog?

The final crossroads before the coastal village of La Marsa came and went. Karim brooded and puffed smoke. Finally, Regan said, "I'll drop you off near the La Marsa Tennis Club. We'll complete our accountings there and say good-bye. Use your recontact number if you ever return to Libya. You understand? As for the twenty million? You'll have to take that up in Libya. When things stabilize, well … ."

She didn't finish either sentence. They had no endings. But Karim did. He was one man who'd never have another position of power or ever again be in a position to demand anything. He might never be able to return to Libya. For that matter, he'd be lucky if he survived his exile as tonight proved. Remember. Al-Din had said, 'they.' And, now that she'd had time to consider the matter?

If al-Din just wanted to kill her, he'd stake out her house or the embassy. No. For some reason—most likely for many reasons—al-Din was after both of them. Somehow he'd known they'd be together and where to find them. He'd not used a tracking device, obviously. Which left ... what? Karim couldn't have told them. Karim hadn't known where she planned to park.

She looked sideways, realizing the Libyan hadn't replied to her statement about the money and recontact. He glowered at her, tossed out his cigarette butt and lit another, said, "It comes clear to me, Madame. You think to save your twenty millions. You think your Agency can steal my facility and my algorithms without repercussion. This is why your CIA sends its killers."

The road brought them past a solitary house to the right and the ruins of what might have been a factory of some sort to their left. Widely spread eucalyptus bordered the way now, their leaves tattered and dry with winter and dust and pale as shrouds in the night. Behind them the walled compounds of more residential villas began to appear.

He continued, "But I have a gun and can defend myself, so you change your plan and now think to make me relaxed while you drive me to an ambush. You think I do not know all? Know your Arnie Walker spreads lies about me with my own government, forcing me to flee my own country. But this is not enough for him. He still fears me and must order me to be killed."

Gauloise smoke, unfiltered and rancid, puffed from his nose and mouth.

He had also gone completely off the rails. She sneezed, stayed focused on the broken edge of the road, using her right hand to grope at the lid of the center console where she kept her tissues. It opened easily, and she reached inside.

As her fingers touched a plastic wrapper, the lid smashed down. Pain shot up her arm. She yelped, an involuntary sound, and tried to jerk free. The car swerved violently, rocking back and forth, but Karim had her wrist trapped.

"Stop the car!" Karim's cigarette was clenched between his lips, and his body leaned on the console. The pain made thought difficult. Her throat seemed to have clogged. Everything in her chest felt like it was climbing upwards hoping to escape through her mouth. Then, the round bore of a gun barrel appeared less than a foot from her right eye, and her brain kicked into survival mode, realizing the car was swerving back and forth, veering wildly, bouncing every time a tire fell off the verge.

Sweat trickled out from under her scarf. She stood on the accelerator.

"Stop!" Karim's voice rose, the hand holding the lid of the console on her wrist pushed harder, but his head whipped back and forth, side to side, ash spilling from his cigarette. The RPM needle swung far to the right. Cylinders beat and the engine roared; the sound was of violence unleashed.

"Stop or I kill you!"

That's when she saw the rest of what could be. Her vision compressed, focused down to a cone, her eyes seeing only what was within the headlights' beams. Karim and his gun were lost behind black blinders. A sound like a swarm of locusts drowned out anything he might be saying. The Peugeot flew off the pavement and landed with groaning springs and screeching metal. She felt nothing from her trapped wrist, kept all of her weight on the gas pedal, and aimed the car at the cracked plaster of a garden wall a hundred yards ahead. One thing more. She licked her lips and forced the necessary words out of a constricted throat, "Throw the gun out."

The wall rushed towards her, growing in the headlights, shock absorbers protesting on the rough ground. She manhandled the wheel with her good hand. Would he pull the trigger? If he did, her body would fall forward against the wheel and, before he could move her, the car would crash. Would he think of that? The wall seemed to mushroom. In seconds it would fill the universe, would block out the world. How much longer? Ten seconds. Nine. Eight.

"Seven. Six." She cringed away from a feared shot but, still, she ticked the seconds aloud the way she'd once counted a horse's strides before hitting a take-off point for a high fence. Timing. Timing was everything.

■ ■ ■
CHAPTER TWO
Tunisia

The gun sailed away. Regan neither saw it nor heard it; but she knew when it was gone, felt her hand come free, heard Karim yelling something. She couldn't have said what language he used, but the gun was gone. For one additional second she did nothing, mesmerized by the enormity of the wall, seeing individual cracks and broken bits of plaster, hypnotized by the colors and the detail of the moment. It would be so easy to—

Shit! Shit! Shit! She turned the steering wheel hard over, foot jumping from accelerator to brakes. Again the silver lion flashed, but this time the car went into a skid. The fender missed the corner with all four tires skating sideways, Regan pumping the brakes. Next to her Karim held on with both hands, head thrown back. The trunk of a tree flashed by her window before the Peugeot went airborne, bouncing high out of a shallow ditch. With a sound of metallic anguish it came back to earth and landed on the roadway.

She brought them to a stop, good hand clinging to the wheel, breath pumping from a pounding chest, sweat soaking her hairline. Slowly her eyes dried and her vision and hearing returned, the world reassembling bit by bit. Next to her Karim opened his car door and fell sideways retching, the cigarette finally coming unglued from his lower lip and dropping to the ground.

There was no fight in the man now. She stabilized her breathing, cradled her injured wrist against her chest, unfastened her seat belt and got out.

Karim stayed where he was, a hunched and heaving shadow. Taking the car keys with her, unsteady on her feet, Regan walked toward the wall. It was dark now, a garden light shining on the far side making the concrete block surface loom blacker than the night, throwing the ground under it into a shadow so dense it seemed to grab at her legs. She scuffed along, stumbling but going back and forth until her feet found the gun—a Russian Tokarev. She ejected a bullet and released the magazine. It, too, was harmless now. The magazine and bullet went into her pocket. The gun stayed in her hand as she returned to the car.

Karim was outside, leaning against the hood, head down.

She got back in the driver's seat and restarted the engine, pain from her injured wrist both welcome and not. The adrenaline was draining away, and she'd have to deal with the aftermath of an overcharged body as well as the pain. "Damn," she said aloud, dropped the gun on the passenger seat, and gently massaged her wrist. Nothing broken, anyway. Not as far as she could tell, although with all those little bones in the wrist who could be sure. Anyway it was functional.

"Give me one of your cigarettes," she said. She hadn't smoked in ten years.

He stayed where he was.

"Listen to me, you bastard." Voice cold and hard and certain she said, "If my people were hunting you, you'd be dead. If it was my job to hunt you, you would be dead. Now call your bodyguards and tell them to pick you up in La Marsa at the tennis club and give me a God-damned cigarette."

He did, still standing outside but reaching in to her with a shaking hand, a fact that was not lost on him since he tossed her his lighter rather than try and fail to hold a light steady. She inhaled deeply and immediately felt dizzy and nauseous. Bad idea.

The cigarette glowed in the dark. The road behind them was empty, and no one appeared to check out the noise. Still it would be better to move sooner rather than later. "Let's go," she said. "I have a job to finish and that means taking you as far as your bodyguards to see you safe. After that … ?"

Karim might not have heard, had moved away talking on his cellphone. When he finished, he came around to her side of the car.

"I will drive," he said. "It is as they say. There is a reason why this Sanusiya mullah makes a fatwa on you for the al-Salan. Insane. You are both crazy and insane as they say. Also you are injured. I will not ride with you at the wheel."

For a moment Regan turned over possible responses to the crazy part—this from Karim—but gave it up and said, "No. My car. I drive." She threw the cigarette past him and watched it arc to bare dirt. Then she added, "This is not an argument you can win. Get in."

He drummed his fingers on the top of the car, then the sound stopped, and he walked around to put himself into the passenger seat, saying, as though finishing a previous thought, "You are stupid, too. A blind, stupid woman. I see it now. What has happened. You do not realize that together we are meant to die tonight."

■ ■ ■
CHAPTER THREE
Georgetown, District of Columbia, February 18, 2011

Arnie Walker sat in his usual place, dwarfed by an armchair that was shiny in places his body no longer reached. Low, somber voices came from the adjoining dining room where Doc Travis Meade and Junior Rachinsky had almost finished with Arnie's death certificate and other paperwork. Across the room, Craig Montrose, the CIA's Inspector General, stood looking out through long curtains at rain sluicing over two press vans and onto a brick-paved street. An occasional vehicle drove past, slowing to negotiate a lake of water in the intersection and to stare at the signature vans.

Craig shot a sleeve back to check his watch. "What's taking so long?" He didn't wait for an answer but strode to the hall door. His perfectly polished shoes made no sound on carpeting that was layered three or four rugs deep as though in a mosque. Smaller silk carpets hung on two of the room's paneled walls, radiating a soothing, jeweled glow that tried but failed to defeat the combined gloom of the winter day and the Inspector General's bad mood.

It certainly did nothing to improve his spirits. "I've got more to do than wait on these damn paper pushers," he muttered as he disappeared. His footsteps became audible on the hardwood floor of the center hall but then vanished as he entered the dining room.

Still seated in his big leather recliner, which sat like a belligerent hippo among the room's delicate, mother-of-pearl-inlaid furnishings, Arnie stared at the point where his friend's athletic form had been. Then, after several deep cleansing breaths, he shifted his eyes to a painting hung alongside the doorway. Craig wouldn't spoil his day. This was his moment, unique and transcendent, the end of what he had been, the beginning of what he would become. In this small box of time, he could savor what was and what would be—a gift of perspective given only to great men, to men like himself. Ones who altered history.

He focused on the original landscape by Albert Bierstadt. Its brilliant colors, a happy accompaniment to the prayer rugs below, made a fitting companion for his thoughts. Bierstadt's masterful use of pigments drew the eye to the soaring lines of mountain walls, hinting at infinite possibilities. A ribbon of water hurtled into an abyss masked by rising mist. A tiny figure stood in bottom left foreground, hands on hips, head tilted back, feet planted on a small ledge of rock. The man was dwarfed, but the viewer was left in no doubt. He was key to the painting. Only through the man's eyes did the magnificent landscape come alive. Without the man, the scenery was nothing.

Yes. Bierstadt was one who would appreciate this moment. When the German artist stood on a lip of Yellowstone canyon and stared into the vertiginous depths, he had transformed the experience into inspiration. Out of it came many of his greatest paintings, just as out of disease and suffering Arnie had wrung the seeds of his greatest idea, his own personal masterpiece. And it had led to this moment.

"Okay. That's it," he heard Craig's voice, muffled by walls but audible.

With a grunt of effort, Arnie levered himself out of his favorite chair for the last time and stared at his bony fingers and mottled skin. "It makes a perfect disguise," he'd told Craig. "All that radiation. All those drugs. Hell! Thanks to the doctors even my own mother wouldn't recognize me."

Well. Shit. He might not look great, but his old energy levels were back. He had a few more years. His best years.

Craig reappeared in the doorway, said, "Okay. Let's get this show on the road."

The contrast between the two men—both former athletes and once the same 6'3"—was stark. There'd been a time heads had turned when the two of them entered a room singly or side-by-side. Now? Arnie had shrunk, his shoulders had acquired a noticeable hump, and only wispy bits of white hair had grown back after the chemo. Craig, ten years younger, looked at least twenty and maybe as much as thirty years Arnie's junior. He'd kept his build the way it'd always been. Or, if there were changes, his tailor knew how to disguise them, to give Craig that camera-ready figure the press had loved during his confirmation hearings.

"Hollywood casting couldn't have done better," the *Washington News* had enthused about the White House nomination, but added, "The real question is just how well this walking advertisement for the spy trade will do policing his own kind." In recent follow-up coverage of Craig's three-year record, it'd concluded: "The jury's still out."

"Seems like I should've prepared a few comments for this moment," Arnie said, working to keep his tone light, to lift the atmosphere. Craig growled something under his breath. Arnie shrugged and took a last look around at twenty years of accumulation, pleased to be shut of it. What he valued—the carpets, the paintings, the furnishings—would go to Paris. From there, he'd fly them down to his villa in the Saharan compound. The rest ... .

He turned toward the mantle for a last look at another large oil painting. This one dominated the room the way Arnie, himself, once had. In a way it was a memorial to the boy he'd been, showed a young man leaping high in the air, football in hand, coming straight toward the viewer, seeming about to hurtle over the mantle and into the room.

Pulling on a belted raincoat, Craig broke Arnie's train of thought. "We can still postpone," he said. Do up another death certificate in a few weeks. Give you time to invent some appropriate comments. Better yet, give us a chance to see how this Libyan business shakes out." He stopped there.

Arnie hooked a thumb toward the front of the house. "Vultures," he said, meaning the news vans and people. "But there'll be cheers and toasts in Washington's newsrooms tonight."

The young man pictured leaping into the room wore a triumphant expression.

"It's now or never, buddy." Arnie added, shrugging into his coat, noting as he did that no one had been in today to clean the grate. Charred and twisted remnants of last night's fire remained on the hearth. But, hell. What difference did that make to him? He adjusted his collar. With any luck he'd never see this damn albatross of a house again. He was

Alex Wentworth now, taking damn-all little of Arnie Walker with him. Just his luck.

"A good case officer is a lucky case officer," he liked to say. "You do your homework, cross the i's and dot the t's, and pray for luck." Young officers always laughed, but they got the idea.

He'd always been lucky. Always.

A burly man wearing a white shirt, blue v-neck sweater, and tie under a brown tweed jacket appeared in the hall door. He had thinning brown hair, a nose enlarged and reddened by too many bottles of wine, and soft blue eyes. His lips were almost bloodless, his chin clefted, his tall figure running to fat around the middle, his expression one of worry. He was Travis Meade, the CIA's Chief of Medical Services.

"You got everything under control?" Arnie asked. "I'm well and truly dead?" He turned to Craig with his trademark, grin. "You know. The best part about this is going to be showing up as a ghostly guest on Doc's Montana ranch. I hear there's great fishing out there, and one of these days I intend to take advantage."

The doctor didn't respond but walked back into the hall, then returned carrying his coat.

"Shit, Doc," Arnie had straightened to something like his former height, found his gloves in a coat pocket and drew one on. "No point in getting your nose bent out of shape. Hell. Think of it this way. A lot of people've wanted me dead for a long time." He grinned. "And, you're making them happy."

Doc Meade just shook his head. He hadn't risen to the top of the Agency's medical profession by fighting barons like Craig Montrose and Arnie Walker. Yes. He'd had qualms about the scale of the lie Arnie had asked of him.

"For God's sake," he'd said when he'd heard. "You're expecting me to defraud the National Security Council, the Joint Chiefs of Staff, the Congress, the ... ."

"The President knows and approves," Arnie had said. "And that should be good enough for you."

Doc Meade had persisted. "And when I'm indicted? Who's going to pay my legal fees?"

"Don't be a God-damn drama queen," Arnie had grumbled.

Well, Doc had said what he'd had to say; had done what he'd been asked to do. Now, he just said, "Once you're gone, I'll go out and give the good news to the press."

Arnie's grin came back, and he clapped the doctor on his shoulder. "That'a boy. Good news, huh? Good news is exactly how half of Washington's going to take this."

"Good news? What good news?" The undertaker had just appeared, shrugging into his coat and putting on his hat.

"My death," Arnie said, still chuckling.

Junior Rachinsky, a man who was listed on the CIA's books as GDSTYX/1, smiled too. He had fabricated corpses before which, he fancied, made him a card-carrying member of the espionage community. He said, "This is the way I want my death to be. Painless and only on paper."

Arnie laughed again, as though Junior'd said something hilarious.

Junior nodded in the general direction of the press vans. "They'll want to interview me out there even though it's raining. But, don't worry. I'll just say I'm here to make the necessary arrangements, which is nothing more or less than the truth. The family, of course, is devastated but grateful to have had the last days with their loved one at home under hospice care instead of hooked to hospital machines. Blah, blah, blah." He walked over to Arnie to shake his hand. "Thank you for your service and good luck, Sir."

With a few more words about the charade—the phantom death and body pick-up scheduled for later in the day—the doctor and mortician left. Craig watched from the window as the two men worked their way through cameras and interviewers to reach their cars. The news people settled for only a few words, then they disappeared into the dry sanctuary of their vehicles. The drivers put their engines in gear and, within moments, the street was clear.

After all, spies come and go. And, while Arnie had been a particularly flamboyant chief of the CIA's National Clandestine Service, there would soon be another man in the job.

Inside, the house seemed extremely quiet.

Craig broke the silence. He had one last question for Arnie, "You got your papers?"

Arnie patted his breast pocket and walked toward the kitchen where his wife and twin adult daughters had retreated. "I'll just say good-bye to Mary and the girls." He waved at his surroundings as he entered the hallway. "It's a hell of a note, but my annual tax bill's now about the same as what I paid for this place."

Craig said nothing.

"Mary'll be glad to put it behind us. Besides, she's always wanted to live in Paris. Used to bug me about getting a tour there."

Craig heard the lie buttered as it was by truth, but he only shrugged. Mary wanted to stay in Georgetown and had agreed to go along with the sale of the house and Arnie's charade only after weeks of cajoling.

Trailing behind Arnie, careful to keep his stride short, Craig noticed the lack of light coming from the kitchen. Either the Walker women were sitting in the gloom of a rainy day or had left the house. Arnie had reached the same conclusion and stopped to call up the stairs. There was no answer.

"Well, hell," he said. "They were talking about some last minute shopping. I guess I'll see them in Paris."

The girls' gray-muzzled cocker spaniel, Jiggs, looked up from a bed in a corner but didn't move.

Arnie stared as though expecting something from the dog, then looked away, took an umbrella from a container, and opened the door to let in a gust of cold wet air and the sound of rain drumming on the porch roof.

The two men passed through the garden gate that joined their respective properties, then walked around a big, brick house that had been closed up since Regan had left for Tunisia and Craig had moved into his condo. Decomposing and sodden leaves stuck to their shoes then settled onto the floor of Craig's Porsche when they climbed in and drove in silence through a gate accessing a side street. Still not speaking, wipers making a steady slapping sound, the two men stared out at a gray-on-gray world as the Porsche swept toward Dulles Airport. Miles passed and they held their thoughts to themselves, their previous arguments as heavy between them as the rain on the windshield.

More miles rolled by. Office blocks occupied by Beltway Bandits appeared in scattered numbers, widely separated by sodden green fields and forests of dismal trees, their bare branches zebra-streaked with rain. Gradually, the remnants of Fairfax County's once lush and open countryside gave way to high barrier walls shielding tall hotels and geometrical buildings. A massive green overhead sign marked their approach to Dulles Airport.

Rain splatters turned mushy, became snow.

Arnie smiled. Almost there. One last new beginning. A sense of power and life unfelt since before the cancer diagnosis sent a tingle to the pads of his fingers. His hands wanted to carry a phone to his ear, tap out a message on a computer or cellphone, shape and mold his plans and give them life. Who would've thought he'd have such an opportunity again? By this time tomorrow, he'd be back where he belonged. On the streets. Speaking figuratively of course.

The board was set, the players ready. In a way the Libyan thing had been a blessing in disguise. He hadn't planned to begin regime changes there, but why not? He'd already stripped Qadhafi of his foreign bank accounts and emptied those monies into his own war chest. Well. Anna Comfort, his chief computer engineer, had. Richie Knowland, the officer he'd had running Hayburner, had identified a handful of men to form a provisional government under the leadership of a pliable Libyan colonel, and, thanks to help from the Tunisian government, the colonel'd be on his way to safe haven in Tunisia right now. Tomorrow. The next day at the latest, they'd announce the formation of a government-in-exile. Then, he'd put his computer viruses to work on the servers in the Libyan Army's command net. Yes. He was ready.

To the west on Arnie's side of the car, the clouds parted to let broad slabs of sunlight slant through the dense fall of wet snow. They illumed the low-lying Marriott Motor Inn behind its artificial lake and sent a fractured rainbow arcing over the airport.

He didn't believe in signs and didn't take this little interlude in the bad weather as more than it was. Still, he stared and enjoyed the sight as he might not have on a different day.

The strains of Beethoven's 5th and a notice on the Porsche's digital display announced an incoming call. Craig touched an icon labeled, "Answer." He then said, "Yeah? What is it?"

Both men listened as the duty officer said, "This name you flagged? Well. There's this report on Reuters and confirmation from the consulate."

"Read it," Craig said.

When the man finished, Arnie said, "Any other details?"

"No, Sir."

Craig disconnected in time to swing the Porsche up the departures ramp. He said, "God damn, poor bastard. They used a machete on him and put his head on top of a flagpole. What's that tell you?"

"That he's one colonel who won't be leading the new Libya."

Craig swung the Porsche into a spot just vacated by an old Land Rover. "I meant about what could happen to you."

CHAPTER FOUR
La Marsa, Tunisia

Three minutes after leaving Karim and the briefcase full of money, Regan hit 'send' on her iPad and extracted a bottle of aspirin from a bag in the back seat. She swallowed two dry.

La Marsa's well-lit beachfront esplanade was thronged with couples and families strolling and enjoying the sight of rolling white caps on the dark sea on one side and the colored glow of the village center on the other. Palms rattled overhead, sound effects to compliment the hum of tires on pavement, the murmur of the Mediterranean, and the pleasant voice of an Egyptian crooner blaring from a sound system meant to entertain the customers of an ice cream parlor across the boulevard.

Locking the Peugeot, she got out and crossed the street to join a line of Tunisians waiting to order their ice creams. Tables both inside and out were full of chattering, happy patrons. When she reached the head of the line, she summoned her most winning smile and asked for a plastic bag full of shaved ice, a cup of vanilla ice cream and a Gamarth Ice—a mix of caramel, chocolate, and peppermint flavors. The Gamarth should give her an energy boost if anything would. She'd tie the ice pack to her wrist. As for the vanilla cup?

That was special.

Weaving through the tables on the sidewalk and carrying her purchases in a bag, she rounded the corner alongside the parlor. Two large garbage containers flanked the parlor's back door while three young Tunisians lounged against the wall, smoking and talking. She'd seen them all before.

"*Le chat?*" she asked.

They all rolled their eyes and grinned. One pointed to a concrete block retaining wall. There, crouching, was a black and white cat with blue eyes. Regan approached it slowly and ever so cautiously reached up to set the cup on the wall. The cat didn't move. Regan backed away.

"You could buy me an ice," one of the boys, the son of the parlor's owner, laughed.

"When you grow up, I'll let you buy me one."

They all laughed. She patted the teen on the shoulder as she passed. "Would you throw the cup away when the cat is done, please?"

"But, of course, pretty lady."

She crossed back to her car. So at least one good thing had happened on this perfectly shitty day. She eased into the driver's seat and set about wrapping the ice bag in her scarf and tying it to her wrist with a bungee cord.

Every day, even though no one read them, she had the unwelcome chore of writing a situation report on what people were beginning to call Tunisia's Jasmine Revolution. But, like, who cared about such a small North African country? Few gave Tunisia a second thought even after mob violence persuaded President Ben Ali to flee the country. Only the most prescient realized the impact that would have on the Arab street.

So, Fouad Mebazaa had become Tunisia's interim President. And he tried, but the mob had tasted blood and wanted more. Even though you'd never know it in affluent suburbs like La Marsa, the Ministry of Interior in downtown Tunis was ringed by concertina wire and under siege. The Prime Minister felt exposed and, as she'd written that morning, would probably resign.

She'd been thinking about that when she hit the 'send' button on today's report, wondering why she bothered. Washington had ignored Tunisia's turmoil when it really had mattered and, now, it was focusing on spin-offs, like Libya—a typical case of ignoring the finger on the trigger and trying to stop the bullet.

In Washington, though, they'd be accusing her of 'localitis,' a common diplomatic disease.

But parts of her job really did make a difference. The sitrep on its way, she'd turned to work that could have a long term, positive impact on Tunisia's future. The new Tunisian president, groping for reform, had asked the CIA for recommendations on the shape of a new intelligence/security structure. In response, she'd pulled an all-nighter and banged out a one-page summary for what she called a National Intelligence Service. It would be independent of the Ministry of Interior, reporting to the president and the parliament. Mebazaa had responded immediately and positively, asking for a detailed plan.

She'd hoped to bring it all together today, but three sentences into a description of the separation of functions between military and civilian counterintelligence, she'd been interrupted by a call from a Gendarmerie lieutenant with news from Benghazi.

Before she could pass it along to Langley, another interruption had made the whole matter moot. It'd been Craig on a secure line from Headquarters telling her that Arnie had suffered a series of small strokes and, given his cancer-ravaged body, was unlikely to live out the day.

Then, Karim's signal arrived. It really had been a shitty day.

Regan leaned back in her seat and ate her ice cream. After a time the skin around her eyes softened and she found herself tasting the sea air, soothed by the sights and sounds, by the feel of her own arms and the comfort of the car. Would Karim have killed her? What would have happened if she hadn't thought to position a surveillance camera?

"Ambiguity," Arnie always said with his big laugh, as though it was all a joke. "It's the ambiguity that kills you."

Her cell bleated.

She set her ice cream cup on the dashboard and opened a text message from Mac.

Got here at 2010. Where R U, sweets? Shut it down and come home.

"Well," she said aloud. What a nice surprise. For a moment she imagined Mac on her terrace, sitting with a glass in his hand and a plate of some delicacy made by her housekeeper, Hadija, beside him.

How long would he wait for her? That was the question. Mac was not a solitary creature; had a very low tolerance for boredom, but he'd perk up when he heard about her evening. "Damn," she could hear him saying, "I miss the life."

When he heard ... oh, my God. Where was her brain! Al-Salan! Al-Salan on the hunt. Even if she hadn't been tonight's only target, al-Din and Juriy were in Tunis and on the hunt, and they had to know her address.

She tapped in a quick text. **OMG. Important. No joke. Take Hadija. Leave house asap. Go to Juniper hotel. Will meet u there in 30 to explain.** "Juniper" was the code name they'd used for the Abou Nawas Carthage Hotel during an exfiltration operation. Mac would remember.

Her cell bleated an almost immediate response. **OK. U heard? Arnie dead.**

So it'd happened. How like Mac to just dump such an announcement on her. Arnie. Why hadn't Craig called. He would've been with Arnie at the end. Why was she hearing this from Mac?

Why was she thinking about Arnie when she had work to do? The hell of it was, Arnie would've been really proud of her tonight. "You can't let the slimebags see you're afraid," is something he preached ... **was** something he'd preached.

She started the engine, then turned it off. No. There were other things she needed to do and best to do them right now before the hour got any later.

She retrieved her iPad, and used the interface with the Nikon to view tonight's photos, selecting a few of the better ones.

"You have to be stronger and tougher than anyone," Arnie often said. And tonight she had been. But he'd never know now. Maybe he was already in that Valhalla part of heaven reserved for strong, brave, flawed men and looking down at her. Maybe he'd met up with her father there.

It'd be nice if she could use a photo recognition program on the iPad, but no point in wishing. She did have access to the terrorist data base. She did have memorized lists of addressees for terrorist alerts.

Now ... .

First, she searched for and found al-Din's profile on the data base.

Her photos were better than the ones that stared up at her. She scanned down the known facts about his life, then drew a deep breath. The listing under 'Most Recent Known Employment?' Saharan Enterprises.

Saharan Enterprises. There could be two or more companies with the same name, of course, but it didn't matter. Saharan—the cover used by Arnie's Operation Hayburner—employed allegedly "former terrorists" as part of a much touted rehabilitation scheme. She knew that.

"It's a brilliant way to rehabilitate the bastards and use their skills," Arnie had crowed a year or so ago. "Brilliant, if I do say so myself." Not that it had been his idea. That honor had gone to Richie Knowland.

But al-Din? Juriy? Whose brain fart had put them on salary for a CIA proprietary?

For just a moment she wondered if she should get approval from Headquarters before sending out an alert. Could there be equities that needed protecting? Or asses that needed covering? But, no. Al-Din and Juriy had tracked 'them' tonight. They were back in the game.

She switched to another program and wrote the necessary text, dropping in the photos and bios of al-Din and Juriy. Next, she sent a one-liner to her liaison partners in the DGSE—the local intelligence service—and elsewhere in the Tunisian Ministry of Interior calling their attention to the alert and reminding all concerned of the connection between al-Salan and the men running a major security exercise scheduled for the morning. Now only hours away.

A final note went to another pre-formatted list, this of officers in the Tunisian Gendarmerie Nationale suggesting they raise the terrorist threat level and consider cancelling the morning exercise. If Al-Din and Juriy had come to Tunisia for revenge, she wasn't the only one on their shit list.

She didn't mention the Saharan Enterprise connection in any of her messages.

"For just an instant then she remembered Tiffany and a confrontation in her office. The young officer'd been seen in a pair of hugely expensive Stuart Weitzman heels. A gift from her Iraqi boyfriend, she'd confessed. A gift or payment for … ? No. That way led to true paranoia."

Finished, she slid the iPad down between the seats just as it signaled an incoming text.

■ ■ ■
CHAPTER FIVE
Carthage, Tunisia

As the CIA's acting chief of station in Tunis, Regan wore many hats. One of them, literally, was a black beret sporting the red, black, and white logo of the National Gendarmes' special paramilitary force—the *Unité*. The CIA was the Unit's primary source of funds. As a result, they occasionally participated in joint operations while she attended their exercises as a foreign observer, served at times as a judge, and participated when they needed live civilians. Today was one such event.

Regan woke in a dark, unfamiliar room at four a.m. after a few hours of blessedly dreamless sleep. She showered and dressed in clothes her housekeeper had thoughtfully packed for her and which she'd found waiting in the three-bedroom Abou Nawas Hotel bungalow where Mac had registered them all. Outside, she could hear the surf washing the giant rocks that formed a breakwater between the line of cottages and the Bay of Tunis. Little gusts of wind sent rain splattering against a set of curtained French doors. It was not a morning to be up and about.

Slowly, she wrapped her injured wrist in a stretch bandage she'd stopped to buy at an all-night pharmacy, forcing herself to focus on making each circuit of the wrap overlap the one before with perfection. Trepidation lay like mountain ridges around the edges of her expectations.

Too much imagination. Her grandmother always said too much imagination was bad for the soul. Or something like that.

Regan kissed Mac good-bye, lingering at the bedside. He didn't stir. His sun-streaked hair, worn clubbed back most of the time, framed bony features that spoke of character. For a moment she dawdled, admiring how a wash of fresh sunburn combined with lamplight to add authority to his already strong facial structure. A dream stirred his eyes under closed lids. He opened his mouth as though to speak then closed it, briefly giving her the scent of sleep-soured breath.

Regan leaned over to kiss him again, feeling weathered skin, inhaling a faint reminder of their late night lovemaking. Touching the tips of her fingers to his hair, she focused on the texture; let herself savor the sensuous tactile warmth that rose through her arm. The sensations were still new and fresh after six months—the time since Mac had resigned as Chief of Station Tunis. But how many times had they been together in six months? Seven? Eight?

No. She stepped away from the bed. He'd be gone in a few hours himself. In fact he'd be gone by eight taking Hadija with him thanks to a midnight call from Arnie's wife, Mary Walker.

It actually had been a bit of serendipity she and Mac had been together when the call came.

"Sorry," Mary began before Regan could voice her condolences, "I forgot the time difference. It's morning here."

Mary'd gone on to talk about funeral arrangements, sounding calm and collected, but she always had been a self-contained person. Also, her marriage to Arnie hadn't been the happiest. Still, Regan would have expected a tear-stained voice or sentences that trailed away into nothing or at least mild incoherence in a woman who'd lost her husband of thirty-four years only hours earlier.

"I know it's a lot to ask," Mary'd said after a few words about Arnie's "departure." That had been her way of describing his death. "He left us at two o'clock this afternoon. In fact he'd sent me and the girls off to do some shopping. But Craig was with him and Doc Travis Meade. They said he said something about it being time to go and he did."

She'd continued, "I know it's a lot to ask but would you consider opening your house and letting a few of Arnie's relatives stay there during the funeral. It'd just be for a couple of days, and the girls and I'll make sure it's clean and closed up afterwards." Her tone changed. "It's okay with Craig, if that matters to you."

"Oh, Mary," Regan felt overwhelmed by her friend's everyday normality, right down to the irony behind that last bit. But, of course, the woman had been living with this moment in mind for almost two years, never able to forget for a second that the cancer would win and this day would inevitably arrive. Maybe after so long it was even a relief. That was possible.

During the call, Mac had been standing next to her, listening and kneading her shoulders, no doubt feeling much as she did. Arnie had been his mentor, too—before his uncle'd died and he'd inherited the business.

Mac had listened to Mary's request and mouthed in Regan's free ear, "Send Hadija to open your house. She can do it, and I can take her as far as Paris and see that she gets on a direct flight to D.C."

Regan'd glanced at him with a sudden sense of rightness. Yes. This would get Hadija out of Tunisia and away from the danger the al-Salan men represented. And it would help Mary.

So, today Mac and Hadija would be headed for the Tunis airport. Mac would fly the housekeeper to Charles de Gaulle in the company plane he'd used to get to Tunis, would buy her a ticket to Dulles International, and he'd still have time to make an afternoon appointment in Palermo. Regan's day would be quite different.

"Better you than me, sweetheart," Mac had said. She'd smiled. And he didn't know the half of it.

Reluctantly, Regan pulled her cap low over her face, opened the bungalow door and ran for her car. Juriy and al-Din. Al-Din and Juriy. She hoped she was wrong. She hoped they had more sense than to try an attack against the *Unité*.

■ ■ ■
CHAPTER SIX
Abubahad Airbase, Tunisia

At six-thirty Regan drove through the gates of a generally closed and mostly abandoned World War II airfield. Two hours later the men role-playing as terrorists had wrapped their red and white-checked kefiyahs around their heads and readied their weapons aboard a Boeing 737, while their guests inside the aircraft—all role-playing hostages—were instructed to stay well down in their seats during the exercise. More guests were outside on a viewing platform set well back from the runway and well protected by massive panels of bullet-proof glass brought in from a nearby army base, while the new ministers of interior and defense were in the cockpit role-playing pilots.

As one of the judges, Regan had chosen a seat just behind the bulkhead separating tourist and first class sections. There, with a minimum of neck craning she could see the "terrorists" both fore and aft and would have a good vantage to watch their capture.

With a final admonition to the hostage/guests—reminders that the exercise could be dangerous—they began.

The commandos moved up on the wings and ladders, waiting patiently, a short chain of bodies linked by extended arms, free hands resting on shortened Tavor assault rifles loaded with blanks. The belts on their black fatigues were weighed down with gear. They had deployed in four groups of six each, two teams to take the rear doors and two for the mid-fuselage ones. No one would enter through the key front doors. The exercise scenario had these jammed by the hijackers. That meant double duty for the mid-fuselage teams

Most of the 'hostages' in the rear were VIPs, senior Tunisian functionaries wanting a close-up view of their *Unité*—an element of the *Gendarmerie Nationale* so elite that it needed no name. It was just the Unit, its members hand-picked, mentally tough, and physically superlative. Best of all, in a country where the police and security services were almost universally hated and were under attack every day, the men of the *Unité* remained unequivocal heroes.

Despite their black uniforms and the menacing balaclavas they wore under black berets, the Unit was widely known and loved for its history of rescuing disaster victims. Where floods or winds or man-made tragedies occurred, the familiar black berets would appear to carry children to safety or dig tirelessly for victims under debris. In happier times, the Unit marched in parades or did spectacular aerial sky-diving exercises, tracking colored smoke across the skies. But their primary function was counterterrorism, and their major duty was to keep their skills honed.

"*Dix, maintenant. Faites dix.*"

From a dozen practice sessions, Regan knew exactly where the assault teams were in the countdown. Not long now. Should be only seconds while the entry men finished priming the locks. If this had been a real takedown, the timing would have been different. They would be going in either during the pre-dawn hour or late at night, something they practiced monthly. But for this annual event consideration had been given to the ministers of defense and interior, their guests of honor.

"*Equipe Alpha, prêt.*"

Inside the aircraft Regan's heart thumped once, then the rhythm steadied. It was time. Earlier, eyes gritty, brain pumped with caffeine, she had participated in the situation room planning, working through the problem with the Unit commander and his staff. Now, she slid across the row of seats to the window, lifted the shade half an inch and peered out, could see the men waiting on the wing just as she'd imagined them. Could see ...

There was a lone man in the Unit's black uniform on the tarmac.

It took her brain a moment to process the fact. Everyone should be with their peleton. No Tavor. No sidearm. Was stout. Was walking slowly toward the forward ladder which led only to the door blocked by the exercise scenario. His head was tilted up, turning. Was he, like her, waiting for the sound of the midship's door being blown?

Oh, shit! She may have said the words aloud. Or not, because at that moment she heard not the poof of air and small bang that should have accompanied the mock blowing of the door locks, but the rattle of automatic weapons fire from the direction of the viewing stand.

She was out of her seat, knowing, grabbing the bulkhead frame, catapulting herself around it and up the aisle; past the empty first class seats to the comparatively wide area in front of the so-called jammed doors. They weren't, of course.

Ahead of her the cockpit door opened. A kefiyah-wrapped face, eyes wide with apprehension, appeared. It was Kadir Malak, a twenty-two-year-old who held a rank equivalent to corporal and today was designated a terrorist. He was capable, but she'd never seen him show an ounce of initiative.

"What—?" he started. His dark brown eyes seemed to be retreating into his head.

As big as it was, the aircraft was shaking now, the men on the wings running precariously toward their ladders, the role players inside rushing the nearest exits. Automatic weapon fire had been joined by the cough and snap of different caliber pistols.

She'd reached the outer door and threw her weight on the handle.

Everyone aboard, Kadir included, had been briefed on the presence of al-Salan terrorists in country and what to do in an emergency.

A second figure shoved Malak aside. He, too, wore a kefiyah, but the face under it had chiseled good features and a light tan complexion. The minister of interior's aide de camp. "Clear the way," was all he said, and she saw Suleiman Eschira, the new interior minister, right behind him. With a gesture from Regan, he hurried the minister down the aisle toward the back of the aircraft.

They'd all been briefed, all knew of al-Din's grudge against the Unit. Maybe worse, the fact that the Minister of Interior and the Minister of Defense were both present in one place, essentially locked into a tin can, made today's exercise an obvious target, one that should've been cancelled. Should've been.

The ladder was there; her ears rang with the ack-ack-ack, crack and pop of gunfire. Whose guns? She looked down. The man who'd been under the wing was in motion, running for the ladder. He must have intended to climb it during the confusion of the exercise. Then what? He didn't even seem to be armed.

A tall, blonde man loomed behind her.

Whoever the man below was. It was all wrong.

The Caucasian barely registered on her scope, her mind fully occupied now with angles and speeds. The man was almost below her. She dropped out the door backwards, grabbing for the ladder to break her fall. Her wrist screamed as her fingers closed around a rung. She swung, releasing her grip and grabbing the ladder's edges.

Her fingers burned; her wrist felt like it'd been smashed by a sledge hammer. The ladder's rungs bumped against her as she slid down. Five feet. Ten feet. The man below now aware of her presence, was reaching toward his waist. He was a blurred image as she kicked her legs and torso away from the ladder, swung outward as though she was on a parallel bar. He was looking up, a knife in one hand. She let go.

His eyes were dark holes in his black balaclava. The insignia on his beret was tipped toward her like a red, black, and white eye. His arm was up. His hand held a knife.

Then, her right boot slammed into his shoulder; her other boot collided with his head, and both gave way under her as she heard an "argh" of shock and pain and hit the ground, rolled free, jumped to her feet. Her right hand and wrist were useless, on fire. Her weight shifted back on her left leg, she rotated, looking for the knife, halfway into a kick.

Except, he wasn't moving. He was down. The knife had spun from his hand and lay a good five feet from his outstretched arm.

To her left men were in motion. The team that'd been on the starboard wing had made quick work of getting to the ground. A glance showed most of them rushing toward the viewing stand, but three men had peeled off. They pounded toward her, the rest continuing toward the edge of the runway and a chaos of shouting and milling bodies behind the glass walls. Had a terrorist gotten in there?

The rapid firing of automatic rifles was augmented by the boom of grenades.

Regan leaned over the man she'd dropped. His eyes were open; unfocused within the black knit balaclava. She ran her hand over his shirt, jerked it away, then eased off the man's hood.

The firing stopped, the pounding of running feet did, too, but not the harsh sound of men shouting. Again, there was a burst of rifle fire. One weapon first, then another and another.

A big man in balaclava and beret had stopped alongside her. He raised a hand to the other two. They stood back. They'd all shifted their Tavors, loaded only with blank rounds, to their backs and had drawn pistols holding live ammunition.

A vehicle started on the edge of the tarmac and roared toward them, passing barely twenty feet away before screeching to a stop near the aircraft's back stairs.

"He's dead, I think," Regan said.

The big man holstered his weapon, knelt, and ran his hands over the body.

"Don't—" Regan began, her breath catching, but the sergeant had already fingered open a button to expose a piece of vest and a corner of a plastic-looking brick.

Well, now they knew one thing. The bomb vest hadn't been wired to the shirt.

The sergeant snapped in Maghrebi Arabic. "Jabril. Get the bomb men here. Now."

More cars gathered around the tail of the aircraft. All firing seemed to have stopped but, now, it seemed everyone on the airbase was yelling at once, the sound interspersed with sirens and honking horns.

The sergeant was snapping orders into his radio. When he paused, she asked, "Do you know him?"

Through all of this, the downed man hadn't moved.

The features were unfamiliar. His face seemed squashed, the pieces too close together. Plus, the nose had been broken at some point and poorly reset. The hairline was low; the forehead abbreviated. Thick scar tissue divided his right cheek and forehead into two sides. A beard covered the lower face.

The sergeant answered the question she hadn't asked. "He is not of the Unit. That is certain. Are you ... ?"

"Hamid," she began to say something but then couldn't remember what because the runway seemed to be in motion, rippling like the surface of a giant trampoline. It was hard to keep her balance. Darkness ate away at her vision, narrowing a blurring world. She needed to sit down.

She did sit, the tarmac coming up to meet her, her wrist burning.

It'd happened before. She'd fainted before. She knew the symptoms. She knew the cure. In lieu of finding a paper bag, if there was one inside a ten-mile radius, she dropped her head between her legs, buried her nose in the folds of her pants, and took slow, steadying breaths.

Death was no stranger. Her grandmother had taken her hunting for the first time when she was eight. She'd killed her first deer the next year. After that she'd held, at the least, elk and deer licenses every season until she stopped having the time to go home in the Fall. Where she came from, wild game fed you through the winter. There you skinned, butchered, wrapped and froze the animals' useable parts. The tripe and poorer cuts of meat went to Cody Locker to be turned into sausage. The bones went to the dogs.

She'd read that life dims and the eyes show the moment life departs. It'd never been that nice to her. She'd look into a deer's open eyes and think that its heart still beat. A check of the pulse or a fly landing on the unblinking orb would tell her otherwise.

Death sometimes crept in like a deceitful prankster. Once, while they'd been bringing cows out of a river pasture, a moose had taken offense at a Jack Russell named Jasper, scooped the little guy up, and thrown him a good twenty feet. Jasper hadn't looked injured. There'd been no external sign of injuries. She'd thought he was still breathing and carried him home knowing that any second he would stir and squirm out of her arms. The dog had always been a clown. He was playing possum. It was all a joke to him. She'd sat down beside him on the front veranda, stroking his back, waiting. "How can you be sure," she'd protested when her grandmother said it was time to dig his grave. "You can't be sure." Not when it looked like he might lift his head at any moment and yap in his "Fooled you," way.

The thick smell of air filtered through denim gradually stabilized her and pushed the darkness back from her vision. She'd killed a man. But it wasn't that. Maybe guilt would come later, but now her problem was the sudden violence and the realization of what might've been.

"Cheated death one more time," she whispered the words to herself. She was alive. In the last few minutes she might have been killed in several different ways. So many things might have happened, but they hadn't.

When she looked up, she had to push hair back from her face with her good hand. She'd lost her baseball cap and her glasses in the drop off the ladder and her hair, masses of deep red hair, had flopped around her shoulders and over her face. She partially anchored one side behind an ear and saw that the bomb man hadn't moved. Well. Of course he hadn't. A crowd of men stood far back near the busses that were to return them to their vehicles.

The Unit's sergeant squatted next to her. "A medic comes," he said and patted her roughly on the shoulder. "But there are many injuries today. Some are shot. More fell or were trampled. The medics are very busy."

"No need," she said. "I'm fine. Tell them I'm fine."

He took her at her word and spoke into his radio. The body still hadn't moved.

Like Jasper, no injuries showed. Like Jasper, he was dead. She'd felt the neck snap, might even have heard the crack. It'd been like landing on a soccer ball—she remembered thinking that, but it'd been a head all right. His head had been back, of course. Way back. He'd been looking up, had his knife ready to skewer her. It'd been an unnatural angle for him, and … she looked down.

The inside of her right pant leg was ripped. She pulled it open to see a gouge in the boot leather. The sun warmed the top of her head.

She hugged her injured wrist against her chest.

If he hadn't thought he could deal with her and still get up the ladder to be sure of blowing up the entire aircraft? If he'd decided to do what damage he could and triggered the detonator on his vest when he'd first seen her? If he'd ... .

"Care for a hand?"

It was the blonde man from the aircraft. He had the sun at his back making his features indistinct. She blinked but gave it up. "I'm comfortable," she said, only then realizing the man had spoken in English with an English accent.

"I'm John Darnley," he said. "British Embassy, Tripoli. And you're Regan Grant, female spy extraordinaire." He held out a hand for her to shake or take, she wasn't sure which. In any event she ignored it.

There was a small breeze, and strands of her hair were getting in her teeth. "Would you have a pen or pencil?" she asked, squinting at him and removing hair from her mouth.

"I beg your pardon? Are you quite all right?" He leaned over.

She could see his features now, could see he was in his mid- to-late thirties with crow's feet around his eyes ... blue eyes ... with eyebrows that were the same pale blonde as his hair. His nose was long with a slight aquiline bump. He had high rounded cheek bones and a square jaw. Perhaps because of the way he stood above her, the angle elongating his head and the back-lighting washing out his hair color, she had the illusion that he wore an old medieval biggins—the ubiquitous cap used under helmets and hats and worn as nightcaps and just to keep the head and ears warm. It made her think of Renaissance portraits, of prelates with thin faces and long noses and ivory skin.

She pulled her own hair, now trying to tangle in her eyelashes, back. "A pencil?" she repeated.

He seemed to decide she really did want a writing implement and produced one. A lovely looking gold pen. All she really wanted was a plain old pencil.

She shook her head. "I'll need it until tomorrow."

"As you wish?" He didn't understand.

Did it matter? She grabbed as much hair as she could corral in her good hand and twisted, collecting most of what she'd missed in the process until she had all but a few stray strands. Then, after a final twist, moving very, very carefully to avoid adding screaming agony to the wrist's pain level, she took the pen from him and used it to pin her hair back more or less where it belonged.

When she looked up, Sergeant Hamid was standing next to the now squatting Englishman. "You are truly fine, Madame Regan? Your face. It is white. Very white."

"It's nothing. Nothing that an aspirin won't cure."

"Very good. It is that His Excellency the Minister of Interior wishes a word with you." Hamid gestured toward a cluster of men near the cars under the aircraft's tail.

"No problem." Regan reached her good hand toward Hamid, who pulled her upright. She patted the big man on the shoulder in thanks then spotted her hat and went to collect it, feeling only slightly dizzy leaning over. Which was when she saw her glasses. One of the lenses had popped out and the frame looked bent. That was the trouble with buying a cheap product.

Picking up the glasses, she remembered the Brit. He was on his feet.

"You'll get your pen back," she said. "Thanks."

He opened his mouth, then closed it and didn't answer. She shrugged as a line of ambulances approached along a service road, their blue lights flashing, their sirens screaming as though they might encounter traffic in this remote location. Apparently spotting the aircraft, the lead ambulance veered directly toward them, bouncing across a field and onto the runway.

Hamid waved them away, directing them toward what had been the viewing stand area. When he turned, he took a hard look at the Englishman, glanced at Regan, then said, "Monsieur. They will be worried you are not with the other guests. I think you do not wish to cause concern."

One by one the ambulances pulled to a stop some distance away and stilled their sirens.

Darnley seemed to wake up, said, "It's been interesting, Sergeant." To Regan he added, "You can buy me dinner one day soon ... to reimburse for the loan of a very valuable object."

Hamid saved her the need to answer, said, "Excuse us. My Minister is waiting as is your bus."

"Or I'll buy you dinner," Darnley said as they walked away, leaving him looking after them. Ahead, four of the big cars—all painted a khaki color—began to move away from the aircraft.

"That will be the Minister of Defense," Hamid said. For him, the subject of the Englishman was closed.

The cluster of men grouped near the other Mercedes, these all black, had seen their approach and turned to face them. "You don't have to escort me the rest of the way," she told Hamid.

"Good," he said and turned back toward the body on the tarmac.

The just-appointed minister of interior, Suleiman Eschira, stepped forward from the cluster of men that formed his entourage. Beyond him, broken tarmac and weeds marked the edge of the runway. Beyond that, the jagged ruins of what had once been a small building jutted through scrubby brush that had found a home in its cracks.

The Minister still held a Tunis Air hat he'd been given as a symbol of the role he'd been intended to play. He was a small man with a delicate bone structure under skin that looked lightly tanned rather than brown. His hair was combed back from a high forehead and held in place by some type of gel product, revealing small, tightly pinned ears. When she'd first met him several days earlier, Regan had thought of the word "tidy." Everything about him was tidy from his well manicured fingernails to his perfectly shined shoes. And nothing today changed that impression. He might have been hustled off the aircraft rather precipitously and had a near death experience, but she'd never know it by looking.

"Monsieur le Ministre," she said. With someone she knew better, she might have added, "Well, what do you think of the real world?" Eschira had been the one who'd insisted that morning that they continue with the exercise despite the excellent possibility that there would be some sort of attack connected to it.

"It seems," he said, "we have you to thank for dispatching this terrorist before he does major harm." He made no reference to her recommendation that he cancel this event. Which was probably something he'd rather forget.

"What happened to the men who attacked the viewing area?" she asked.

"One is dead. The others have fled, but we will find them."

"Injuries?" Regan asked.

"Minor." He made a sniff of disapproval. "Many but minor. Because of our precautions the area was well protected, but no one can guard people against themselves. It seems there was a panic among these guests. It seems fortunate that there were no necks broken there."

A careerist from the intelligence service came up behind the minister. "Madame. We are in your debt."

"Monsieur Abdul-Alim," she said as an acknowledgement, remembering his name, impressed that his hair was now immaculate.

Eschira said to Regan, "I have just said to Captain Udadram, and I wish to say to you, we must reschedule this event. I am still of the opinion that we must not let threats deter us from our programs."

She managed to not show either her surprise or her disapproval. Here was a man who would double his bets when he was losing. Not the kind of personality to be in a position to control all of Tunisia's civilian security forces.

"Also," he continued. "I wish to arrange for others in the cabinet to attend such an exercise. Being new to the government and to what is required to keep us safe will be a most enlightening experience."

He reached for her hand with the clear intention of shaking it then noticed the bandage and the way she clutched it against her chest. Tactfully, he moved his hand toward her left side, simply touching her hand when she raised it, adding, "The recommendations you're preparing for us? On the matter of reforms?"

"Yes."

"My new Minister Delegate will be reviewing them along with recommendations we are receiving from other services. As for me, I was impressed with your summary paper and your concept. The matter of parliamentary controls, however, will need considerable thought. We must sit down one day, and you will explain to me precisely what you have in mind."

Again, she nodded.

"Excellent," his small features lifted in a smile. "*Cher Madame*, a memorable experience." He turned toward the Mercedes, another aide jumping to open a rear door for him.

"Madame," Abdul-Alim half bowed. "What the Minister is saying? He wishes to see your recommendations before they go to the Minister Delegate." With another bow, he turned and strode after his master.

The senior DGSE liaison officer at the exercise, Mohammed Zayifi, had been standing alongside a second Mercedes and now came toward Regan. "*Bien fait,*" he said. "So now you are planning to reform us?" The words came with a slight smile on a face that was always weary.

"Is that possible?" Thanks to a year of monthly meetings, they'd developed a relationship that allowed a certain amount of needling.

"In these days? Perhaps anything is. Do you know, I no longer report to work at the Ministry? It is too difficult to negotiate the demonstrators and the barriers. But we continue to function, is this not so? The enemies of the people do not go away even when the people are unhappy and turn on us and mistake us for their true enemies."

"Hmmm," she murmured in acknowledgement. Zayifi was just venting and expected nothing more. But. She had a question she wanted to ask about the intelligence briefing his men had given that morning. The Tunisians had more information than she'd supplied. The source? If she asked, would he answer?

While she was thinking that over, he said, "No matter the organization, it is difficult, don't you agree?"

"Monsieur?"

"This business of ours." He wasn't talking about a potential reorganization or the suicide bomber or the aborted exercise.

Well. She could be cryptic, too. She said, "We do what we must do."

"*Bon.*" He was satisfied and changed the subject, seeming to assume that she knew what the subject had been. "Until next week, then? The Menzah IV apartment?"

"Of course," she said, "*A toute a l'heure.*" She turned to go in search of a medical kit and some kind of pain killer, wondering why she hadn't seen James Eckton, the local British MI-6 commander? He should've been here. He would've received an invitation—not that man from Tripoli, that man who should be back in Libya minding the store for MI-6.

■ ■ ■
CHAPTER SEVEN
Abubahad Airbase, Tunisia

Hours later, Regan checked her cell and found two text messages from Mac. He was home in Sicily after flying from Habib Bourguiba Airport to Paris, then Palermo, finally on to Catania. **Hadija made her flight. U owe me & I intend to collect. Fly with me to DC? Save a fare? Share a bed?**

That was Mac all over. He'd like nothing better than to monopolize her time during Arnie's funeral. He'd especially enjoy walking down the center aisle of the National Cathedral with her on his arm, thumbing his nose at her estranged husband and delighted at the idea of fueling the Agency's gossip mill. Without reading the second text, she sent a one-word reply to the first: **NO**.

Diesel fumes from a waiting bus tickled her nose as she read the second message. **Cancel that. Am off to Bangkok in a.m. Back whenever. Sorry to miss Arnie's funeral. Take care, sweetling.**

Returning the cell to her pocket, she took a minute to loosen the wrap on her wrist for the second time since she'd played Rambo. It looked horrible—swollen with ugly bruising—but nothing'd been broken, and it'd settled down to a dull throb. Icing it earlier had helped. The pain pills helped more.

She climbed aboard a waiting bus, following the last of the commandos up the stairs. Hamid waved her to an empty place—a few inches of bench next to his own bulk. She perched there.

With an awkward movement, an eyebrow twitching, he patted her good hand. "We are good. Yes? You smash this terrorist, and I am there to finish him. Next time, please, you will leave my job to me."

She gave him a tired smile. "Happily. Anyway, it was an accident. I'd intended to stop him long enough for the hero of the Unit to arrive, a man who was no doubt delayed by the need to ensure the safety of his men."

He chuckled. "You are right. The *Unité* is fortunate to have such a hero like I am." He was only partially joking. Hamid's ego was almost as big as his body and was largely justified, although not by good looks. His fat-cheeked and fleshy-jowled face, pitted by childhood acne and oversized like the rest of him, was not handsome. But it was the eyes that people remembered—they were dark and large and radiated confidence and character. People looked at Hamid, felt his strength and found it contagious. So was his ham-handed humor.

"This man," Hamid added. "This terrorist is crazy. Crazy. To kill our ministers and himself for his beliefs is crazy. To think. In Tunisia to find a suicide bomber even though he is Libyan. These times are not normal. It is something in the air. Crazy."

Which was about what the Unit's intelligence officer had said hours earlier, making the connection to the Sanusi Muslim sect and al-Salan and assuming, as everyone else had, that the two Tunisian ministers had been the target. "These radicals strike at important men in Tunisia, thinking to destabilize our democracy and radicalize our people, thinking to give extremists power where our people want only moderation and stability."

Thinking about the traces that had come back on Musa Khalik Mahomet, the dead man, her mind shifted to Saharan Enterprises. Mahomet, too, had a recent employment record at the CIA proprietary in Libya—not that anyone reading the traces had realized it. As far as they knew Saharan Enterprises was a well-respected non-profit organization with a senior staff and board of directors that read like a who's who in international development assistance—all of whom were heavily subsidized by Qadhafi as part of his reformed image. Even the use of former terrorists as guards was a do-gooders do-over dream, as Arnie had crowed. All part of the Hayburner cover.

That said, Richard Knowland, the man who'd dreamed up the idea of rehabilitating terrorists and who'd hired over thirty one-time al-Salanists for the proprietary, had warned there would be recidivism.

Well. He'd been right. Revenge and the fatwa had drawn al-Din and his buddies to Tunisia. Now, what? The repercussions should the CIA hand at Saharan ever be revealed and connected to terrorist activity could be huge.

How far would the Tunisian government dig into the Saharan connection? And what about the British? Arnie had briefed MI-6 on a highly restricted basis, and technically it wasn't their secret to reveal. Which didn't mean it wouldn't happen.

That fellow, Darnley? He knew.

Up front, the door to the bus wheezed shut. Captain Rafik Udadram, commander of the Unit, came up the aisle as the bus jolted into gear. He gestured that he wanted to talk to Regan and waved Hamid to the front of the bus. Regan stood to let the big man out before relaxing in the space he'd left behind. The captain sat down, leaving a respectable gap between them.

His thin, lined face had a grimy sheen, his black eyes under heavy eyebrows stared at something beyond her, but they always did. He never looked directly into her eyes. The Captain was a Berber from Kairouan who'd joined the Gendarmerie with only a grade school education. He'd risen through the ranks on sheer merit and an innate understanding of the Byzantine world of Gendarme politics. He knew he'd peaked out, but the fact didn't bother him. Subject only to approvals from his CIA funders and the Director General of the Gendarmerie, he ran his own show. The Unit, its men, facilities, and boy toys were his personal fiefdom.

And he'd keep them as long as he didn't screw up. Today, however, qualified as just that on a scale that could have been massive. As it was, he would now be known as the man who could've gotten two ministers and a host of second tier officials killed ... or saved them.

"I'm so sorry about what happened," she said in French.

"We were not truly prepared to defend against this type of enemy," he said, his eyes on the front of the bus. "But it is clear we must begin a new thinking and take new precautions. For the first change, we will never again have an exercise on ground we cannot protect. What was possible and normal before? It left us vulnerable today. It won't happen again.

"Also, I wish to thank you for your intervention today," he continued. "And tell you that I strongly disapprove. If you had been injured or killed, I am the one who would be blamed."

"Right." Considering another question, she shifted in her seat, thinking to put both her hands in her lap. The bus lurched, her wrist bumped against the wall of the bus, and she winced at the sudden flash of pain.

Rafik didn't notice or, if he did, he chose not to say anything. The man had no patience for physical weakness of any kind. In his world the strong deserved his time. Everyone else existed only to justify the Unit's mission. She'd learned this early on. Even though she'd led the joint exercise against al-Salan, which was where they'd first met, it hadn't been until she'd proven she could run his obstacle course, rappel off his rooftops, parachute with his commandos, and scuba with the divers that she'd gained his respect.

Taking a deep breath to steady her voice, she asked her question, one no one else in the Tunisian establishment would answer because of the third party rule which prohibited sharing information provided by one service with another. But Rafik owed her big time and that trumped any little moral cavils or international niceties. She said, "This morning, when we met to consider cancelling the operation?"

He nodded, alert, his eyes on the back of the head in front of him.

She continued, "There was more behind what I heard than just the terrorism alert I posted last night. The DGSE briefers already knew there was a strong possibility of an attack today."

Doing nothing to indicate affirmation or denial, he waited for her to ask her question.

She stopped there. His non-response was an answer, and there was no reason for her to continue. She would just burn up her credit with him and for what? The rest she could figure out for herself.

The Tunisians had indeed known more than what she'd told them. They'd had specific information about a direct threat to the

Unit's aircraft takedown exercise. And, why hadn't they shared that knowledge with her? If they'd developed the information themselves, she was sure they would have done just that. If they'd thought it essential that the CIA know, they would've found some way to alert her. But neither situation obviously applied.

The Englishman from Tripoli. He was the other clue. Darnley really had done what she'd thought he'd done. He'd developed information in Tripoli about an al-Salan attack on the Unit's exercise. He'd brought his information to Tunis in person rather than sending it through the MI-6 commander in Tunis. He hadn't shared it with the CIA at all—not with Headquarters and not with her.

And, when was the last time MI-6 had withheld anything from the Agency?

Wrong question. Not when, but 'under what circumstances.'

CHAPTER EIGHT
February 19, 2011, Western Libya

Arnie held the encrypted satellite phone away from his ear, not listening to Craig's complaints. He had his feet up on the desk of his fifth-floor office, his chair tilted back, and he was staring through one of the corner window walls at the Mediterranean. The sea should have been the incredibly intense blue he'd come to love on his first tour in the region but was masked instead by smoke of fires that burned just up the coast in the remains of what had been a military installation used by the Khamis Brigade.

It'd given him pause. If units led by Qadhafi's son, Khamis, would cut and run in the face of mobs of young men, well ... . On the other hand, they'd roared back and mounted a counter-offensive just after dawn, but the rebels or whatever you wanted to call them had finished looting and burning and been long gone. It had, Arnie'd been told, become a pattern.

"What?" he said aloud, hearing Craig come to the real reason for the call. He'd been expecting it.

Craig didn't repeat himself.

Arnie, responding to his friend's tone, spoke into the silence. "Watch it. You'll give yourself a heart attack."

"Billions. Not millions. Thirty-three billion."

"Oh, that." A smile crinkled the corners of his mouth. His own personal computer genius, Anna Comfort Rose, had cleaned out Qadhafi's American accounts. Left them nothing but shells.

Craig said, "Libya's going to have a legitimate government, and Uncle Sam's going to have to produce those billions one of these days. The God-damned U.S. Treasury's not going to make up the difference. Then there's Tunisia. I warned you."

"Go fuck yourself." The words rasped out on labored breath. Even inside an air-conditioned building the smoke was bothering him, but he'd be damned if he'd consider carrying an oxygen tank around.

"You don't sound good," Craig said.

Arnie was silent, only his breathing was audible. Finally, he said, "Consider it a loan. Believe me. As soon as Anna Comfort comes back, we'll restore it all. No one'll ever know it was gone."

"What'd you say? Where's Anna gone?"

"Evacuated." Briefly, Arnie described how the woman's Libyan husband had panicked when one of his hotels had been burned by rioters. "God damn shame," he concluded. "Half the business community here's packed to leave. The other half's already gone. But they'll all be back as soon things settle down."

Pausing for one of his labored breaths, Arnie changed the subject. "Myanmar ... Burma. Now listen. You're going to like this. We've accessed both police and military networks and ... the personal computers of half a dozen key government officials. The Hayburner virus is right where we need it."

"Fine. Great. And your computer wizard is gone, so your operation is dead in the water?" Despite the negative, Craig sounded interested. Craig was always interested when he could see an advantage, and he'd originally seen a big advantage to the regime change aspects of the Hayburner virus. He'd bought in completely to the concept once he'd realized that, with Hayburner in their arsenal, he could ride a tidal wave of success into the CIA director's chair which would position him for a run for the U.S. Senate after retirement.

"You let me worry about the operational end. That's why I'm here." Arnie put confidence in his voice, and he was confident. This rebellion couldn't last much longer. A few weeks and it'd be over. If not, if anything went wrong, he had his back-up plan. He continued, "You watch. It'll be the first of our imposed democracies. We'll have that Aung San Suu Kyi woman free and a liberal government in place within the year, damned if we don't. Faster if we could directly manipulate things, but this is probably surer. Anna Comfort thought so, anyway."

"Too bad you couldn't have done more in Libya. You could use some stability there."

"It was luck of the draw. The right programs didn't exist here, so the infection rate's been slow. But it'll happen. Just give me time." Arnie could see Craig staring across his office at the far wall and his Princeton oar hanging over a book case that incongruously featured a collection of belt buckles won as a bronc rider. Prize money and scholarships had taken Craig from the University of Wyoming to Princeton, from the rodeo circuit to sculling and on to military service and the Agency where guts, hard work, and the ability to ingratiate himself had all counted.

Arnie's own career hadn't been much different. He'd begun working in his father's Eugene, Oregon garage at the age of ten and spent summers and weekends as a grease monkey right through college. He'd skipped military service, which had been something of a mistake, but risen to the top of the Clandestine Service anyway by dint of better bullshit and bigger balls than anyone else and—not to forget—thanks to Craig moving aside for him.

Well. Hell. Craig wouldn't let him forget.

Craig said, "Now, Tunisia."

For an instant Arnie thought of feigning ignorance then changed his mind. "You're wrong. What you're thinking." He paused, then added, "Ah, hell. What could I do. These al-Salanists aren't pet monkeys, you know, and they've had one of those mullahs egging them on." He coughed. The smoke was a factor he hadn't considered. He hoped it wouldn't be a game changer.

"Richie had the right idea, though," he continued a moment later. "About putting those boys to work and channeling their training and talents into something constructive. Most of them are good types. Steady, you know. Plus, they're well-trained and fairly well-disciplined and make good guards. And that's all that really counts."

"Except now you managed to hire two former al-Salan leaders just out of a Tunisian jail, and I don't think you can reasonably claim they 'jumped the reservation.' They were never on the reservation."

Arnie cleared his throat but decided not to reply. Al-Din and Juriy, he'd learned, had indeed been hired by his HR people and had been here long enough to recruit a few of Richie's longer serving al-Salanists. Heads would roll over that, but it was his problem, not Craig's.

"It's that fatwa, isn't it," Craig continued. "But what I want to know is what you're doing to stop them."

"I'm trying. You've got to believe that. But I've got to be careful, too. Got to hang onto the al-Salanists I've got left, which is most of them. You can see that."

Arnie's breath came in quick gasps as he described the nearby attack of the night before. "God damn Khamis Brigade units. They've got a reputation for violence but not for fighting, which is why I think the rebels had a go at them. But so far? Well, hell. Everyone knows about our al-Salan boys' reputations, about what they did in Afghanistan and Iraq. It's why the rebels've been moving around us. It's what's keeping Hayburner safe."

Craig didn't acknowledge that, said, "The other thing you're overlooking? The Tunisians? This new government's fumbling, but our old friends in the security forces are still in place and smart as foxes. By now they'll have zeroed in on you, will be wondering why you hired men you couldn't control. Or asking themselves if, in fact, their terrorists are acting on your orders. One way or the other, they'll be on your doorstep in no time.

"So. I'll tell them the same thing I told you." Time to change the subject. Arnie had put his feet on the floor earlier in the conversation and swiveled around to face his desk to look at just one picture—a photo of Regan, her mouth was open in a wide grin, everything about her face inviting the viewer to join in with her good humor and pleasure.

Arnie scowled at the picture. He always told baby spies to religiously practice an old adage—keep your friends close and your enemies closer. Still focused on Regan, he said, "You know your wife's taken up with that gun runner. Good looking son of a bitch. This is a first, isn't it?"

"I heard."

"Ironic, isn't it," Arnie said, ignoring the implication. "You worrying about a woman who's screwing another man? And I think it's safe to predict that her next move will be to divorce your sorry ass." He kept his tone level. It wouldn't do to let his own anger cloud this moment. He was acting here in Craig's best interests. The fact was Craig couldn't afford to add another divorce to his record. Somehow he'd managed to maintain one marriage for a record-breaking period of ten years, seven of them spent on separated tours, three of those mostly estranged. But who was counting.

Who? Anyone who was considering Craig as a prospective CIA director, that's who. The White House, that's who. "He's failed with five marriages," they'd say. "Does that sound like a stable candidate to you?"

No. He'd be sorry if anything happened to Regan, but she'd made her own bed. And, hell, realistically it was like Richie said. Craig would be lucky if she was in her grave before her affair with Mac became serious or widely known.

Arnie struggled to his feet and walked over to his east-facing windows with their smoky view over the compound walls to the coastline beyond. His chest felt clogged; his throat tight. No one understood, but Regan's loss would affect him, too.

"Poor man," people would say of Craig. "Lost his wife in the war against terror. But there was a true heroine. Wonder if he'll ever recover."

No one would say a word to him.

"Keep your eye on the ball you old bastard," he said aloud. "Keep your eye on the ball."

It'd taken him two years to get this operation in place. What he was doing in Myanmar proved that it was bigger than any of them, was an operation for the centuries, and no one was going to derail it. Hayburner had to be protected at all costs.

And, on that thought, he returned to his desk, picked up the phone and dialed an old friend in Cairo. There was an abandoned World War II German-built base in the Western Desert he'd been offered. Well, tentatively offered. He could have it for the asking. And with $30 billion? Anything was possible.

■ ■ ■
CHAPTER NINE
Tunis, Tunisia

Regan slept on a cot in her office. An old dream of rocks and trees and a monster bear trailing blood and gore from an open wound woke her to the white glare of security lights penetrating layers of venetian blinds and curtains. Her legs and arms were heavy with fatigue making the act of sitting up difficult and the idea of standing seem unreasonable. Reaching out, she turned on a lamp then sat hunched until she noticed the shadow she cast. Outlined on the office wall was a seated bear with a grizzly's hump.

She stood, flicked on an overhead and went to make coffee. It would be dawn and a new day soon, and she didn't need the shadow's symbolism to tell her that she'd spooked herself. Still. The threat was real enough. A warning from her husband in an earlier call had reinforced her instincts and the available facts.

"Stay away from your house in Tunis," Craig had said. "Those damn al-Salanists are obviously using the fatwa to justify getting revenge. Vary your routines." He'd gone on to say a few words about Arnie's death and the funeral plans. "It'll be at the National Cathedral."

"I'll go with you, of course," she'd said then, a statement that'd been met with silence. So, she'd added, "You have a problem with that?"

"I do."

"You want to tell me why?"

"Well, hell, Regan. Tunisia's in crisis, you're filing daily sitreps, and you want to leave post just to attend a funeral?"

"Tunisia won't fall apart if I'm gone for a couple of days. And it's not just anyone's funeral. It's Arnie's. But if you don't want me to go with you, I'm sure Mac will be happy to take your place."

It'd been a stupid thing to say. Sitting in her desk chair she wrapped her wrist in its elastic bandage and sipped her first cup of coffee. What about going with Mac? Tongues would wag, but, "What's sauce for the goose is sauce for the gander," as her grandmother would say. How many affairs had Craig had? How many times had Agency tongues wagged and Agency eyes looked at her in pity—expressions that mirrored remarkably what she felt for herself? But then! Now that she'd found a lover to occasionally warm her bed? It's always different when it's the woman. People might not approve of Craig's constant philandering, but that wouldn't stop them from condemning her one affair.

Through the slatted venetian blinds the white glow of security lights gave the courtyard's grass and shrubbery an anemic tinge, but not for long. The compound's outer walls already showed the pink glow of an impending sunrise.

Al-Din and Juriy. She had to do something about them. She had to do more than that. They'd acted on information available only in the Emergency Meeting Plan segment of Karim's 201 file.

She called up the file on her computer and scanned the offending document. As she'd thought. It said nothing about what she might do if her meeting site was compromised. Said nothing because the waters in the bay had retreated a bit since she'd first scouted the area and the possibility of driving around to the old boat ramp hadn't existed.

The file was interesting in other respects, reminding her that she'd met Karim nineteen times without incident, listened to whatever he had to say, and accepted a flash drive from him to pass to Arnie. For the first year, she'd flown from her duty post in Nicosia to Tripoli for their encounters. Karim had driven out to the airport, spent a few minutes with her and left. She'd then climbed back on a return flight and been gone. Last summer he'd changed the arrangement, saying the encounters must be more discreet, and he'd rather meet her in Tunisia.

Arnie didn't give a damn where she met the Libyan as long as she met him. "But let's make this a little easier," he'd said and transferred her to Tunis as Deputy to Mac Masters. It'd been a promotion for her. More, it'd led to months of an awareness that Mac was someone she could feel strongly about if the circumstances were only different. "It's just not meant to be," she'd told herself at the time. "He's your boss and you're still married."

She'd remained married, but Mac's uncle had died, he'd inherited the family business, she'd been named Acting Chief of Station, and chemistry had done what chemistry does.

Not that there'd been much roiling passion with her mostly tied to her desk by political events and turning herself into a Cassandra, crying doom and gloom ... or hope and promise, depending on your point of view.

"Just as the U.S. became a hero in the Arab world when Kennedy abandoned France, when he took the high ground and supported Algeria in its war of independence, America could become a hero on the Arab street by expressing its unswerving opposition to the dictators and backing for reform. This would not entail boots on the ground but ... ."

She'd written those words and dozens of variations when she'd seen the improbable effects of the fever started by Mohammed Bouazizi's self-immolation and watched the same phenomena surface across the Middle East. She'd varied her words for her audience but banged away at her message. Washington had a huge opportunity if it would only get off its collective ass and get out in front of this thing. Like it or not, the fire had been lit, and it could be a game changer. How? That would depend on the policy makers actually surprising everyone and making a policy.

Like Cassandra, she'd been ignored at best. At worst? Arnie, for one, had told her to "tone it down." Craig had said, "Do yourself a favor. Can it."

She hadn't. She glanced at her office wall where a brand new, poster-sized framed cartoon commissioned by her staff held pride of place. It showed a overly feminine ant in a pants suit and red hair staggering along toward a desert oasis with a very large planet earth supported on her shoulders.

Sometimes she felt exactly like that. But back to al-Salan and the first thing she had to do.

She picked up her secure line, got the Agency operator, and was patched through to Richard Knowland's portable unit. "Hello, hello," he answered. "And what is it that brings a call from our beautiful neighbor this early in the morning?"

"I think you know," she said.

"Dreadful. Dreadful events," he acknowledged. "And you want to know what we're doing ... ."

She let him talk. Richie had a talent for words, an endless flow of them that seldom meant anything. But if she cut him off, he'd sulk, and she'd get nothing. Leaning down and reaching under her desk, she found a change of clothes in a bug-out bag—she would shower and change in the gym. And not to forget the Brit's gold pen. It went into an envelope which she addressed to James Eckton at the British Embassy. A piece of tape across the flap, and it was ready to go. She dropped it into her out box, then turned back to her computer monitor.

"... the way sociologists describe the phenomena seems entirely accurate, which is most unfortunate under the ... " Richie's voice reflected solid enthusiasm for the subject; his words implied his own profound understanding and expertise. How much longer should she pretend to listen?

The morning traffic queue was already a log jam of cables. She began scanning them, was on the second subject line when she forgot the queue; snapped her head up. "What?" she forgot to be polite. "You sent that bastard Fould here without consulting me?"

"Now Regan. Don't get your knickers in a twist and let me explain. Not that I want to throw stones, but this new man here. Wentworth? He's a contractor and ... well ... not to be critical, but he doesn't really know what he's doing. I told him he should at least talk to you, but he said, 'No. It's our problem. We've got to resolve it, and we need someone to liaise directly with the Tunisian security people on this.' I want you to know, Regan dear. I tried to..."

Her mouth had dropped open. For a moment she held the unit away from her ear and looked at it not believing what she'd heard. "Stop, right there," she cut off whatever Richie was saying. "You told someone like Nat Fould he could go around behind my back and talk to the DGSE? Without a word to me on the subject? Is that what you just said?"

"Pl...ease. Don't go killing the messenger. I told Wentworth it was a bad idea, but he'd known some of your security types years ago and said he thought an informal working arrangement with Nat ... who, after all, knows these al-Salanists personally ... would be beneficial to all and keep you from being tarred with that—"

Clicks from the cipher lock on the station door meant staff was beginning to arrive and the official day would soon begin. Her voice lowered and she interrupted again, "Listen to me, Richie. You retrieve your dog. You hear me? If I so much get a hint that he's operating on my turf, I'll be over there faster than you can blink, and I'll be holding you personally responsible ... not this Wentworth guy or some sociologist. You. And you won't like it." She paused a beat. "Now, is there anything else you want to tell me?"

"It makes me sad that you take that line, Regan. It's totally unnecessary and—"

"Good. I'll take that as a negative, and we can move on to another matter. I have evidence that someone's been digging in Agency files at Saharan and feeding information to al-Din."

"A leak? You're saying we have a leak? Oh, I don't think so, not that I'd dream of contradicting you but perhaps you'd like to—"

"I'd like you to investigate. That's what I'd like."

"Of course. Of course. I'll need whatever evidence you have, and there's no one I admire more than you, Regan dear. You know that, don't you? But really. Just give me some proof and I'll ... ." And he was off on another tangent.

When she hung up, she sat back. It was tempting to write Richie off. Tempting and wrong. And this 'new man?' Wentworth? He would've been hand-picked by Arnie and no dummy and no novice. As for Nat Fould. Richie's hatchet man who he'd installed at Saharan as Chief of Security? He was another matter altogether. Just thinking about having him messing in her liaison relationship, if there was any truth in Richie's allegation, gave her heartburn.

Outside, the sun was well above the horizon. The overhead lights had become unnecessary.

Every security officer and policeman in Tunisia was looking for al-Din and Juriy right now. Their photos would be on the front page of this morning's newspapers. They would be hiding out and inaccessible to everyone, including Nat Fould. Or … ? No. She wasn't going to start thinking like Mustafa Karim.

What she needed to do was flush al-Din and company into the open. And she needed proof of a computer compromise in order to force an investigation of the leak at Saharan.

Her eyes went to the time display on the bottom right corner of her monitor.

She'd had a surveillance team monitoring Karim's movements since he entered Tunisia, breaking them off the night of her meeting with Karim—the meeting being a matter they had no 'need to know' about—but putting them back on the job yesterday morning. They had orders to call the cops at the first glimpse of anyone in the al-Salan mug book.

She'd also alerted them to something Karim had confided—his intention of meeting his American partner today at a Hammamet restaurant.

That meeting. It was supposed to be secret from the Tunisians.

If she mentioned it in official CIA traffic, would the leaker pass the tidbit to al-Din? Maybe. But if she said that she was meeting Karim there?

She propped her feet on an open desk drawer and tilted her chair back as far as it would go. For several minutes she rocked it back and forth with elbows propped on the chair arms and her chin supported by her folded hands.

Abruptly, she dropped her feet to the floor and scooted toward the computer monitor.

"In for a penny, in for a pound," she said aloud and began typing.

TO: C/NE/MAG. ACOS PLANS MEET KARIM AT LA LUNE DE LA TUNISIE RESTAURANT IN HAMMAMET. That was the gist of the message. Next, she sent the chief of her surveillance team a short, encrypted message asking him to get someone down to Hammamet asap. She wanted quick plant audio devices in that restaurant.

The team, itself, would follow Karim.

Was she putting Karim and his partner, George Tendale, in unnecessary danger? Well. They were big boys, and they had their bodyguards.

■ ■ ■ ■ ■

Her watch said 11:05 when she eased into a turnout on a road just outside the beach-front resort village of Sousse which was where she knew she'd find Bashir Baralguiba. Sure enough. His battered old van was already parked there.

The young surveillance team leader had a smile on his face, a story to tell, and two discs to give her. Earlier in the morning he'd rented a donkey and a donkey cart, outfitted it with a signal booster and transmitter and set a young cousin to work selling rides to local children. The route the cart took just happened to circle the district holding the villa where Karim, his family and entourage were living.

"You understand, Madame Regan?" Bashir gloated. "It goes without saying that the DGSE will have bugs in this villa. This means they have a listening post nearby. *Eh, bien.* The DGSE equipment receives the signals from the villa. Our donkey cart goes by, catches the signal, boosts it, and sends it to a receiver in the business district. It is a storage shed of a pottery belonging to a man who is married to a cousin, so it is safe there."

She thought about Bashir's display of initiative, about the risks versus the gains. Hours and hours of work and bucketloads of money went into the technical side of mounting and exploiting any audio op. Almost always there were heavy risks involved in planting the bugs. And for what? People seldom said anything worth hearing.

Still this seemed very low risk and the cost was negligible so she congratulated Bashir on his initiative and brightened briefly as she considered how her message on the donkey cart operation would read at Langley. She was absolutely certain the cabled description would be passed around from hand to hand. Everyone loved a funny, neat, imaginative, tidy and—above all—cost-effective operation. A donkey cart, for heaven's sake! Good God. She could almost hear laughter erupting around tables in the food court and up in the executive dining room.

On that note and after reviewing with the team what she wanted during the afternoon, she put the first CD from the audio feed in the Peugeot's player and, listening, swung the car south. Bashir would bring the van along behind her while the team would follow Karim.

For February the day was lovely. Fair and sunny. As she drove, scrubby coastal growth on sand and rock scrolled past her windows, the sea on her left. It spread out like a flounced Navaho skirt, blue ruffles fading toward the distant horizon, white piping gathered along the shore's hemline, the whole sparkling with sequined sunlight. Overhead, seagulls made white polka dots on the sky.

From time to time, she pushed the fast forward function on her CD player, finding the bits of conversation sandwiched into vast hunks of ambient noise. Much of what she heard was inaudible. Some was garbled. Some bits made sense. There was nothing about Karim meeting with her. There was confirmation that Karim, as he'd told her, was now a refugee with a price on his head. Now she was hearing a new spin on the story.

"But I have investments here," he'd said to a visitor at the villa. "You know this man George Tendale. Together we have a big venture with the Tunisian government to market a revolutionary new operating system for computers. It will be a great success. And in Libya now? It is a good time to leave. The Leader does me a favor, you see."

On her west side scrubby coastal growth gave way to a string of buildings and walled compounds signaling the approach of another town. Ahead of her the road branched. To the right the highway ran on toward Hammamet's business district. Regan angled left, aiming at the massive walls of the old city and the Bay of Hammamet. Built by the Turks to withstand siege conditions, the city's high ramparts—once marked by the helmets and spears of Janissaries and mercenaries—now sprouted metal antenna branches and satellite dishes.

Just short of the city walls Regan pulled into a drive to a restaurant parking lot. She stopped under a row of eucalyptus trees, thin branches dangling scraps of listless, winter foliage. To one side of the driver's door, banana palms clicked their fronds like overgrown and rhythm-challenged marimbas. Dead, rotting vegetative material made ragged brown frames around the trees and fed a rich, earthy smell into the salty air.

With a flick of her fingers, she cut off the voices of three Libyan men, then turned off the engine and got out, hearing the hot engine ticking an accompaniment to the palms and adding one more sound to the wash of surf on the gravel beach across the road, to the swish of the sea breeze through the eucalyptus and, finally, to the minor key lute music coming from the restaurant's speaker system.

Beyond a low wall the restaurant's outdoor terrace was nearly empty, only a few tables occupied. The *Unité* captain and his sergeant, though, sat in their usual places. Both of them were in uniform black without insignia, their berets tucked into epaulets. Neither had noticed her arrival. From experience, she knew that the sound mix in this beach location masked activity in the car park.

The men hadn't waited lunch for her, either. While she'd called from the road to say she had to be in the area and thought she would be able to join them, sometimes she made it and sometimes didn't. They didn't seem to mind her erratic behavior.

"Welcome. You come," Captain Rafik Udadram said in English, rising when she walked up to them. His black eyes and thin lips smiled creating crinkles around the eyes and long crevices in the cheeks of his weathered face.

A bottle of wine and a big kettle of boiled seafood sat in the middle of the table while an empty place waited for her. The captain shook her hand and pulled back the free chair.

She shook hands with the sergeant, and they all sat.

"What did I interrupt?" she asked and settled down for an hour with two men whose company she enjoyed. Sometimes these lunches were simply pleasurable, an opportunity to expand her knowledge and understanding of two colleagues. But she'd come today for more than that and more than the fact that she was in the neighborhood with an hour to kill. This was a chance to get the Tunisian government's official position on what had happened at Abubahad.

Rafik was happy to oblige. After they'd covered the major points, he pulled a file on the suicide bomber from his briefcase. She shoved aside her plate, took another hunk of a fresh-baked baguette and flipped through the folder. He had been employed as a gardener at Saharan Enterprises in Libya. Overnight, DGSE analysts had contacted the Human Resources office at Saharan and received a complete copy of his personnel file. Reading it, Regan learned he was 23 years old, was a Sanussi Muslim, had studied engineering for two years before enlisting in the Libyan Army. They'd detailed him to a U.N. peacekeeping force, and he'd gone to the eastern Congo where he'd apparently become part of a radical Muslim group. A year later, his military service complete, he'd applied for and gotten a job at Saharan.

CHAPTER TEN
Hammamet, Tunisia

Regan's watch said 1:30 when she found a parking place for the Peugeot in a popular shopping street, replaced her low heels for a pair of sports shoes, slipped the surveillance CDs into a pocket, and wrapped a black scarf around her head for the walk to the alley where Bashir had left the van for her. Another ten-minute drive, this time in the van, took her to a south-side waterfront restaurant—the place Karim and the computer engineer, George Tendale, were scheduled to meet. She drove past, noting two men sitting at a table on an outdoor terrace. She recognized neither. A block further on she parked the van behind a tourist bus along the seawall.

The air was fresh but heavy with the salt smell of sea grass and algae. The day had remained cool but sunny. She propped a sun reflector across the inside of the windshield and climbed into the back to don headphones and turn on the receiver. No surprise. The quick plant audio devices Bashir's team had placed inside the restaurant were working, one transmitting a desultory conversation between two men who were arguing about whether the windows were due for washing, about who would do the work and who would pay for it. The voices were indistinct on the other device where a sound like running water dominated with an occasional clunk and clink of pottery or glass hitting metal.

Shifting to her radio she checked in with Bashir and listened to his report. He was staked out in a nearby hotel parking lot. His people were tailing Karim's vehicles and had orders to peel off and position themselves on each of the four approaches to the restaurant. They all had throw-away cells and would alert the police at the first confirmed sighting of an al-Salanist. Yes. Everyone had the license plate numbers Regan had given him.

"Good." She was satisfied. "Over."

"But there is one thing, Madame. The al-Salan is famous for the bombing in Yemen, yes? I wonder because of this about a big Mercedes that I see earlier. It has Yemeni diplomatic plates and is armored. Over."

"Occupants?"

"Impossible to tell. The windows are tinted dark. Over." Which was illegal in Tunisia but, of course, diplomats were exempt.

"Keep an eye out for it. Let me know. Over and out." She flipped open her laptop and booted it up. Yemen. Al-Din would have good ties there. Good enough to get the use of an embassy car? Good enough to get diplomatic protection? She stared at a street map of this Hammamet district.

Smoked windows. Obscure. Like this whole idea. Say, for the sake of argument, that al-Din was using a diplomatic vehicle. Would Hammamet's police force even consider stopping such a car?

At least she understood the Karim-Tendale partnership and the reason for today's meeting. Seen in hindsight, such an unlikely pairing of human specimens had been almost inevitable. George, after all, was the brains behind the theory that eventually became the Hayburner virus and had told the world about it—including Karim.

"The rest is history," Arnie had said … it must've been about October 2009. "Karim originally bought the algorithms from George. The theory was good but for some reason they just didn't work, so he hired Anna Comfort Rose to fix them and apply the virus to his pet programs which he still thinks she's going to do and which she's done except he doesn't know it. So here's where you come in. We can't just ignore the smarmy bastard … he's chief of the God-damned security service for Christ's sake … but we can divert him with a new operation and peel him away from Anna Comfort. Or vice versa. Double her against him. Put her to work for us while he still thinks she's working for him."

Arnie had stared at Regan with a disconcerting intensity. "You're going to be my potato peeler, lady. He's convinced we need Anna Comfort for a joint cyber op against North Korea, and I've let him persuade me that he's got to keep his anti-American credentials, meaning he doesn't meet with me or any other known CIA official. We pay him off. We get Anna Comfort. He thinks we're working on North Korea. Right? It's a shell game. We keep Karim's eyes on the money, give him something reasonable to believe, and he'll stay out of our way."

"And I'm a walking dead drop," she'd said.

"Just remember: I'm doing the heavy lifting here. Got it?"

She'd got it.

She'd also 'got it' when Karim had finally become convinced of what Arnie called 'the core lie'—that Anna Comfort would never make Tendale's algorithms work. Predictably, he'd gone to London to see if George could help him. There, he'd found the computer engineer struggling with his latest project—something he called Cumulus—and again in bad need of money. Karim had already lost a fortune investing in George's work and wasn't about to send good money after bad, but for a percentage of the Cumulus deal, he would broker it. This he did, eventually bringing in the Tunisian development people to banker it as a joint venture. As Karim wanted, he became a silent partner.

Regan stared out her peephole. This was not going to be Karim's lucky day. Not with al-Din and company in the neighborhood. Should she warn him? Had her cable triggered al-Din's presence?

A moment later the questions were moot as two Mercedes with Tunisian government plates pulled up to the curb near the restaurant's sign, its name—*La Lune de la Tunisie*—written in faded blue letters on a battered background that once had been white.

Men got out of the chase car to position themselves. Only when they signaled did Karim's aide descend from the lead car to open the back door for his boss. Karim stepped to the pavement, taking his time, his well-tailored suit showing no obvious bulge. His gun hadn't been apparent the night of her meeting with him, either.

One arm at a time, he shot the sleeves of his shirt a careful faction of an inch beyond his jacket sleeves before adjusting the white embroidered wool of a burnoose that hung down his back like a cape. Only then did he appear to glance around, his eyes roaming from the waters of the Gulf of Hammamet to the restaurant's dirty front windows, from peeling paint to the blackened doors of a garage next door where stacks of old tires partially hid the scabby plaster of the one-story building. Inland a maze of small streets, most of them dirt, housed many of Hammamet's working poor but half a mile away in either direction, what had once been plantations of oil palms now hosted upscale villas and a line of beach-front hotels.

Two women turned the corner and crossed the street to walk along the seawall. They wore traditional Tunisian *safsaris*, tablecloth-sized pieces of fabric wrapped around the body and over the head with the free corner carried between the teeth. These billowed out, giving the women the appearance of large-breasted pigeons trying to fly. The same breeze kicked up whitecaps beyond the low stone wall and narrow beach, ruffled a sleeping boy's hair where he lay in the sand, and blew through the cracked windows of Regan's van.

As the women sailed past Karim, both turned to appraise him, no doubt attracted by his operatic clothes and handsome features, not seeing the tightness of those lips, the calculation and coldness of the eyes, and a lump on each side of his jaw as though he might sprout horns from those unlikely locations. At that, they took care to avoid direct eye contact and, anyway, Karim didn't seem aware that he had their interest as, finished surveying his surroundings, he reached for a cigarette. One of his men jumped forward with a lighter cupped in his hands.

Regan had no doubt Karim'd taken in every detail of his surroundings, perhaps even identifying her van as a possible surveillance vehicle. She'd know for sure if one of the bodyguards came knocking on her door.

■ ■ ■ ■

Karim had noticed the way the wind had pinned the *safsaris* to the girls' bodies, had enjoyed the neat turn of calf and ankle, the painted toenails, and the way the kohl-accented eyes didn't quite make contact with his. Women were attracted to him. That was both a curse and a blessing and no fault of his own. He'd inherited his looks and love of sweets from his Italian mother; his height and bad teeth from the Harabi tribe of his father. The combination, his wife once liked to tell her mother and aunts, was deadly, making him a target of female attention. "But, poor soul," Amara would say in her teasing way, "he can not enjoy this because his teeth hurt him so much. And this is why we have no more than two children."

Some of this was true. His teeth did hurt, decaying one by one as though they wanted to torture him or as though he wanted to be tortured. For he could've had them all out. He could've had them replaced with implants or dentures. Instead, he'd felt and still felt a compulsion to hang onto the ones he could save, postponing root canals and filling as long as possible and, as a result, losing teeth. But every post was capped with gold. Each half-measure filling was gold, as well. That gave him a certain satisfaction even as periodontal rot continued to undermine the new glinting surfaces.

Two of Karim's men, ones he'd assigned to George Tendale, already had places at an outside table where they'd been enjoying the sun and nursing glasses of tea. They'd jumped to their feet when Karim's cars arrived and now remained respectfully standing as he passed, the breeze flaring his burnoose dramatically. Behind him two of the men from the chase car peeled off to join their colleagues on the terrace. Bodyguards now flanked the restaurant doors.

Inside, George Tendale waited at a square, battered metal table while the third of Karim's three bodyguards—ones he'd assigned to Tendale—sat at an equally decrepit table next to the windows. It was late for lunch and the restaurant was otherwise empty.

"There you are, dear boy," Tendale spoke first.

Karim didn't offer to shake hands. As for George Tendale, his right hand held a digital notepad and moved not toward Karim but at a leather pouch that hung over his shoulder and ran under the opposite arm. Abruptly, he seemed to change his mind and he set the device on the table. Then he used his right hand to smooth back his hair, tucking a few wisps behind his ears. The effect was somewhat bizarre, emphasizing an anomaly. The top of Tendale's head was nearly bald while his remaining hair had been allowed to grow and was held at the nape of his neck by a red polka-dotted scarf.

The rest of George's appearance was equally strange. His tall lanky body featured hairy and bony arms and legs which were exposed today by knee-length shorts and a shirt with sleeves buttoned up above the elbows. More buttons strained over his thick waist and a red sweater, probably selected to match the scarf, was draped over his shoulders.

Karim barely glanced at George but looked for the waiter and found him standing in a side door. It was the man with twine for a belt. *"Un café Arab,"* he said and sat gingerly, adjusting his burnoose, the chair rocking on battered legs. "We have much to discuss," he continued in French while looking around for a better seat. Ah, there was one, its metal legs not bent at all. He rose and signaled to one of his men who rushed over to swap out chairs for him.

Tendale picked up his water glass, lifting it in a casual greeting. "My dear friend, could you have found a more out of the way place? And, let me say, I adore your cape. The embroidery is truly splendid."

One of Karim's eyebrows twitched. He sat down and tapped the table with a well-manicured nail. He ignored the compliment and didn't bother correcting George. "We have things to discuss that I wish to keep from the ears of our Tunisian friends."

"Oh, really?" One eyebrow in Tendale's deeply lined face twitched. "Up to our old intrigues now are we?"

"Read this." Karim pulled several pages of paper from a pocket and pushed them across the table. "It is transcribed from a bug I place in the secure phone unit of Richard Knowland at this Saharan Enterprises place. There is no doubt."

Tendale lips twitched, and a hand hovered around his mouth to cover a smile.

"Here is what happens," Karim said. "Before I am forced to leave my country and my people, I infiltrate men to watch what this Knowland dog does there ... and here is the information that finally comes to me." He paused to be sure Tendale was listening. "What I learn is they intend to kill both of us. What I learn is that they have made the computer virus work, the one I purchase from you. Also, I learn you know about this in great detail and have kept secret from me."

Tendale raised an eyebrow in exaggerated amazement. "Oh, my. You do make it sound like I'm a central figure in a great conspiracy. Such drama. And I'm supposed to take any of this seriously?"

"Twice," Karim leaned forward. "Twice in the last two days they try to kill me. Yes. I would say 'seriously' is the correct word. They send al-Salan killers here. Do you believe me? No. But you will believe this."

Tendale's pink-rimmed eyes flickered around the restaurant then fell to the offered paper. Karim watched the American as he read an English-language transcript dated 0800 17 February of a call between Richard Knowland and a man named Alex Wentworth in Washington, D.C.

Karim tapped the paper. "I'm their primary target, of course. These men. I spit on them. They are the spawn of she-camels, they are shit-eating dogs, the evil faces of a rotten culture. But they do not know the caliber of man they attack. They do not know their own actions will bring disaster on their own heads."

He'd approved Walker's idea of a joint operation, he'd approved building the compound they called Saharan Enterprises and even obtained use of the old munitions storage base for them. Incredible as it seemed now, he'd been flattered when the great Arnold Walker confided that the CIA had surveyed the possible successors to Qadhafi and had hand-picked him for the job.

"In three years ... four at the most," Walker had said, "If you play ball with us, we'll have a very successful joint operation to prove to the White House that you are a friend of America. We'll set the stage to remove Qadhafi and his family and put you in his place. The plan's already in the works, my friend. You'll be the next Leader of Libya."

Lies. It had all been lies. Instead Walker had stolen from him and conspired to first ruin him and then kill him.

Now Walker was dead, and it was too late to extract a deserved revenge, but ... . He had a plan. He tapped the table again. "Listen to me, George. We will teach them a lesson they will never forget. We will do two things. First we will use their virus against them to destroy them with their own people. Second we will hijack the virus itself." Across from him Tendale was shaking his head. Karim's voice rose, "We will steal it right out from under their hands."

"You're using the wrong pronoun. There's no 'we' here." Tendale gave his head a final negative shake.

"Are we not partners and do not partners help each other? But rest easy. The bulk of the work I, Mustafa Karim, will do myself. Also, I know courage is not your most notable of traits. I understand this and do not think to put you in the way of harm. Why else would I give you such first class bodyguards? No. I wish to mention now only the outline of my plan."

"Courage, dear boy," Tendale again lifted a hand to his mouth, partially covering it. "Of course I have courage. The courage to keep away from dangerous ideas. But … please. Be my guest and do what you want. In any event, the whole question of the virus is moot." He dropped his hand and tossed his hair back, then leaned forward to whisper. "Because, when you have brains you don't need courage. Listen, my friend. Once Cumulus is operational all will change. Cumulus will corrupt the blueprint that pulls together the semantic virus. You see? The virus they're using will no longer be able to spread. It'll be useless. The people who cheated you will be left with nothing."

Karim closed his eyes in an obvious effort to keep his temper. He knew how the virus worked, how an innocuous bit of coding acted as a blueprint, pulling bits and pieces of existing code together behind a computer's firewalls. Without the blueprint? Without it, a lot of people would lose a lot of money and influence. He opened his eyes and said, "*Ecoutez*. This is no secret. Do you not think the CIA dogs know that? Why do you think they plan to kill you? They tested Cumulus for you. Even I know that. You see? This man Walker can not allow Cumulus to survive. This Walker will kill you to destroy it. You—"

George interrupted. "You seem not to know … it's Walker who's dead."

Karim didn't bother acknowledging the interjection. Walker's demise was already old news and not germane. "And," he said, "this Richard Knowland replaces him at the CIA. This is why Knowland was promoted and why he travels often to Washington to brief your White House and your Congress. It was all in the transcripts I receive from the telephone tap. Walker arranges it all before he dies." Karim left one hand on the table and leaned back in his rickety chair. "What is important for you to remember? It is Knowland who hires these al-Salan thugs. Besides, his motive is identical to Walker's."

George dismissed the thought with a wave. "Richie? Dangerous? Trust me, sweetheart, I know him. But, even if it's true, you've surrounded us with protection. We're safe as churches here." He used another wave to gesture at the bodyguards. "The thing we must do is get

Cumulus on the market as fast as possible."

Karim stared at the brilliant, irritating cretin that fate had made his partner. He lifted his eyes to the fly-specked ceiling and mentally recited a sura from the Koran to calm himself. It wouldn't pay to lose his temper. Instead, he would move along to his next agenda item. Later. Later when he got Tendale back to London, they'd return to the subject. He'd learned with Tendale that you just had to put him in a computer lab, tell him that something had never before been done, and the man wouldn't stir until he'd done it. He was monomaniacal to the nth degree. Although he wasn't easily led to a challenge, there were ways to present this one ... something like, "You may have come up with a virus and a virus killer, but no one could possibly hijack a virus." No. That wouldn't do, but he'd think of something when the time came.

Shoving the transcript to one side, Karim replaced it with another document. This one was in legal format, festooned with seals and stamps. "Now we turn back to the subject of marketing Cumulus," he said. "Now that we can see it will one day reach market, my lawyers tell me we must plan for the possibility that one of us could die. Which is why I need you to sign this agreement."

Tendale smirked as though Karim had made a social gaffe before putting a hand back over his mouth.

Karim continued. "There are no survivor benefits in our arrangement. That was an oversight we must correct."

George dropped his hand to the notepad he'd left on the table. He didn't even glance at Karim's document. "Well," he said. "You see here's the thing. I've got no plans to die any time soon. I mean. Look around. I've never been so protected. As for Cumulus? Do you have any idea how unique it is? Do you know what it means to the world of technology?"

Karim lips compressed before he opened them to answer. "I have twenty million reasons to know what it means ... reasons that are covered by our partnership arrangement but not in the contract with the Tunisians. If you die ... ."

George held up his hand. "It's your turn to listen to me. Thanks to me there's about to be a quantum jump in computing. Do you know what that means? Well, it was nothing compared to what's coming. That's the reason the CIA agreed to test Cumulus at the Saharan data center. And that's why MI-6 decided to work with me on more field testing. And in the unlikely event that I die, it'll be my name that's remembered, and it'll be my next of kin, my life partner, who makes sure that happens."

■ ■ ■ ■ ■

Down the street from the restaurant, the interior of the van had grown uncomfortably warm. A trickle of sweat had formed on Regan's forehead, and she reached up to wipe it away. The tension between the two men was almost palpable. She keyed her radio.

"No sign of the Toyota or either license plate? Over."

"That is an affirmative. Over."

"And what about the Yemeni car?"

"It leaves the hotel but stops for petrol," Bashir said. "The driver gets out but he wears a ghutra and agal which makes it difficult to see his face. Over."

"A thobe, too? Over." She referred to the robe worn on the Arabian peninsula that went with the scarf and the cord that attached it to the head. Traditional dress would tend to confirm that the driver, at least, was Yemeni. Certainly, not Libyan.

"That is also an affirmative. Over and out."

The sound of giggling and girl voices came from outside the van. She glanced out the peephole to see uniformed schoolgirls walking past, arm in arm, seemingly headed toward the bus parked in front of the van. They couldn't see her, but still ... .

It was time to move. She removed her headset leaving the recorder running to tape the conversation in the restaurant. Next she pocketed her handheld radio before checking that her scarf was in place and moving forward and into the driver's seat to remove the sun protector from the windshield. The radio stayed in her pocket where a brushing encounter with the side of the driver's seat turned a green light to red.

Across town Bashir repeated a call to Regan several times before setting his own handheld unit in its holder. He would try again in a few minutes.

CHAPTER ELEVEN
The Control Van

Regan had parked behind a furniture maker's shop, the fragrance of freshly cut wood strong and refreshing, a heap of unfinished chairs just outside the driver's window. She rolled up the glass and locked the doors before climbing into the back to catch up on what was going on inside the restaurant. Only then did she notice the red light on her radio, switch it back on, and ask for an update.

The Mercedes was on the move, Bashir told her. He was following. They were on a line to possibly approach the restaurant. She flicked on the circuit transmitting from quick plant #1 and heard Tendale talking about his new operating system.

Her new position was about two blocks from the restaurant, at the outside range of the quick plants and the quality of the sound was not as good as it'd been when she'd been closer. They weren't saying anything of interest, anyway, although the earlier exchange about Richie Knowland made the audio op worthwhile by itself. No surprise that he'd said nothing to her about returning to Langley or such a fantastic job opportunity.

No surprise. She'd met the man twice under circumstances she preferred to forget. The first time he'd groped her. Come close to attempted rape. After that? There were rumors.

Like Craig's story about his friend, Jack Martinsen, Knowland's first chief of station—an officer who'd seemed destined for great things until Jack, treating Knowland more like a son than an employee, promoted him and made him his deputy. Two months later a counterintelligence scandal ended Jack's ambitions and left Knowland in charge of the station. A subsequent CI study of the event, which had claimed the life of one agent and put still another in jail, traced the trouble to a careless comment made to the local intelligence service by none other than Richie Knowland. But Jack had already been demoted and moved to another operating division and Knowland had kept the station. Three months later he'd received another promotion ... that'd been a case of bureaucracy in action.

"Unit One calling Control," the radio interrupted. "Mercedes coming to you. Do I call police? Over."

Regan glanced at her laptop map, then out the window. Diplomatic plates. She said, "No sign of the Toyota or the numbered plates I gave you?"

"No, Madame."

"Return to your original position. Everyone else stay where you are. Over and out."

She looked at her watch, then again outside at the intersection ahead. Her cell beeped.

She reached for it just as noise erupted through the one earphone she'd kept in place. From inside the restaurant came the sounds of gunshots, of metal tables and chairs crashing against tile floors, and of men yelling. She dropped the radio, ignored her cell, and grabbed the other earphone. Even with the poor quality of the reception she heard, "My arm. My arm. They shot me." The voice was Tendale's. The words were in English.

If George Tendale said anything else, it was lost in the nearby blasting of handguns. Karim and his bodyguards were fighting back. The sound escalated, grew until it sounded like a war raging.

George had been hit but only in the arm. Who else? What else? She keyed her radio. "Call police. Gunshots fired. Now."

Even without Bashir's call, the police would arrive in minutes.

The sound of shots ceased. She thought she heard the squeal of tires. The Mercedes leaving?

Karim's and Tendale's bodyguards would whisk them away. Her team was okay. Karim would take George to the DGSE, and they'd see to it that he got medical attention ... if he got out of there alive.

She picked up her radio. "All cars. Clear the area. Do not attempt to follow the Yemen car or the rabbit." She meant Karim. "Copy? Break off. Do not follow. Over." She wasn't going to have her people shot at or run the risk of being identified by Karim's DGSE friends.

"*Cinq cinq.* Over and out." The acknowledgements came in.

Inside the restaurant, the sound of gunshots stopped had been replaced by excited yelling. She listened, aware finally that her mouth hung open. She closed it. Then came silence. No sound. They'd all left.

She'd accomplished nothing, but she had a fair idea that al-Din and friends would go to earth in the Yemeni embassy.

In the meantime her quick plants were still in the restaurant and, when the dust settled and the police arrived there, they'd certainly find them. Well, she'd known this was the risky part—the result of following a last minute sketch of a plan, the result of wishful thinking, too. Now, she had to retrieve the devices.

"God looks after fools and idiots," she muttered to herself as she dropped into the driver's seat, jerked the sun protector off the dash and stomped on the gas pedal.

A Volvo skidded out of the alley behind the restaurant, swerved to miss her on the narrow street, scraped along the edge of a house, and passed at speed. John Darnley. Her foot came off the gas pedal, and she looked in the rear view mirror, watching him going away.

Her lips moved. "Son of a bitch." What in the hell was going on!

■ ■ ■
CHAPTER TWELVE
Libya

For John Darnley, nothing had gone right since he'd first called his counterpart in Tunis, James Eckton. All he'd had in mind was to pass along a fragmentary piece of information. Even as he'd put the call through, though, he'd had doubts about the wisdom of it all. The thing was, this spy business was strange and new to him. Already he'd sensed unwritten rules and noted the undefined culture, its internal politics and old boy networks. To make matters worse his personal relationship with his chief of service meant whispers of nepotism and "he's not quite one of us" and subtle exclusionism. If he was just a new boy, he could cope. He'd clawed his way up the ranks in the Special Air Service and no amount of hazing by the starched shirts in MI-6 could ever equal that.

Or so he told himself.

"I'm inserting you near the bottom of the ladder," his cousin had said six months earlier, just after John had finished his training at the Fort. "Nothing's happening or likely to happen in Libya. Go. Perfect your Arabic. Get your feet wet. Wrap your brain around the business."

Then Libya had erupted in violence, and he'd found himself not only in the eye of a storm—that he could handle—but eyebrow deep in a muck that even lifelong Arabists were having trouble deciphering. Plus there had been that one operational imperative from his cousin.

"Keep a weather eye out on what the Yanks are up to at Saharan Enterprises, young John. Go visit with them; make nice. It's delicate but I want weekly reports."

"To what end might that be?" he'd asked.

"A word to the wise," was his cousin's only answer. "When you meet Arnie Walker, keep one hand on your wallet and regard anything he says with a healthy skepticism. He's got so-called ex-terrorists and something he terms 'smart viruses' there. Either one of those things, when in Arnie

Walker's tender grasp, is sufficient to give me nightmares."

After six months John was beginning to understand. He'd watched the completion of a large office block, of a batch of apartments, of luxury villas—all within the American compound. He knew that a complex system of tunnels and levels allegedly crammed with a data center underlay the site—a place the Libyan army had once owned and that Qadhafi had given the Americans for what was supposed to be a joint operation. He knew a lot and yet, he sensed, he understood no more about Saharan Enterprises than he did about the customs and mores of his recently adopted employer.

Hence his discomfort with the call to Eckton in Tunis. Maybe he should've sent a back-channel note instead. Maybe he should just forget the whole thing. Talking person-to-person with someone who'd been around as long as James Eckton could be tricky.

"Ah, John," James came on the circuit closing off the possibility of disconnecting. "Hanging on by your fingernails over there, are you?"

"Day by day. Thanks for asking."

"Need help? Anything I can do?"

"Quite the contrary. I've picked up a small nugget that might interest you. Nothing worth putting in official traffic. Just a whisper from a new source. He thinks al-Salan might have an operation planned to coincide with some Tunisian Gendarmerie unit's exercise."

"Sounds like it ought to be reported. Can you give me more details?"

"Aye. There's the rub."

"I trust this has nothing to do with dreams?" James jumped on the Hamlet reference. "Can you provide details or not?"

"You've read no doubt about the Americans trying to rehabilitate these old al-Salan cadres?"

"Go on."

"And you know no one at Langley will want to hear a word against them, particularly if the word in question is 'terrorism.' You see the problem? What I have is a source of unknown reliability who heard about this from his wife who got it from a friend who's a maid at Saharan."

"Or someone's using plausibility to put the wind up you, John."

The point was too bloody likely to dispute. John didn't try. "On the subject of wind," he said. "Whatever's in the wind, if anything, and if you care to share with the Tunisians, please do."

"I'd say you'd better put this in official traffic. Just caveat it with source unreliability. And do it quickly. There's a big Gendarmerie exercise planned for ... . Well. I'm not sure, but it's coming up soon. Now, if there's nothing else, I have an appointment."

"One sec more. I'm wondering if this information isn't too closely tied to the cousins for comfort and much too close to put in an official message the Yanks will read."

"I'd trust they would read it." James' voice turned indignant, then he grumbled something about the politically ambitious and excesses of caution before John could hear the man clearly again. "All right. What did you say? A Gendarmerie unit? Could your source have meant the *Unité*?"

John's French was serviceable and for a moment he was confused. Unit? *Unité*? The words were the same. But "the *Unité*? He said to clarify, "You mean there's a unit that's called just a unit?"

"Hmm," James said. "The exercise I mentioned is hosted by the *Unité*. Got an invitation here somewhere. It's an annual affair and the guest list always reads like a who's who in the Tunisian intelligence and security communities. Given the political climate, though, they may decide to cancel it. I would."

"So, then it'll all be a non-event and no problem. Just drop a word in the appropriate ear in case there's some truth to the report, would you? I'll ring off now. Remember you and Janet are welcome anytime you care to stop by, not that I'd recommend Tripoli, and I'd definitely recommend against coming via a land route. Our esteemed Leader seems to be losing control of the situation and we're looking at exit strategies."

"Seriously?" James' tone changed. "Evacuation?"

"An imminent possibility. You'll have traffic on it later today after 'his nibs,' our much admired ambassador, sorts out his prose. Well. I'll let you know if I get anything more concrete."

"Hold on. We need more information on this so-called threat, particularly since it involves an Islamic group, and we've got our own Islamic resurgence here. Didn't your source say anything else? Anything at all? Where does the maid work? How did she hear this?"

The answers were: no, I don't know, and I don't know. That should've been the end of it. For several hours John went about his affairs blissfully unaware that Eckton had contacted their mutual section chief in London who had recognized a political hot potato when he saw one. He'd lost no time in sending it along to the counterterrorism gurus who had collateral information and who had bucked their conclusions up the ladder to their chiefs who kicked it straight onto the desk of their ultimate master, Lord Raymond Kendrick.

Kendrick called John Darnley. ""Listen carefully," he said. "Nothing is to be committed to paper or fed into a computer. Are you quite clear on this point? You're not in the uniformed branches any longer, John, and we don't work as they do."

"Do tell," John replied and refrained from pointing out that the matter was not on paper now only because his instincts had told him it might cause trouble. Apparently he was learning. Apparently, too, he'd get no credit for it from the man who was not just his employer but his third cousin through one family line and a second cousin through another.

Lord K. obviously did not appreciate what John had thought a restrained reaction under the circumstances and said, "Please refrain from sarcasm, John. It's unbefitting and unattractive in a subordinate."

"Indeed," he agreed. "Then I'll get back to shredding files. We're preparing to evacuate, you know."

"Shredding paper should be below your pay grade. The fact that this doesn't seem to be the case indicates to me that you need either to be broken in rank or find substantive employment, and I have just the thing in mind."

Which is how John Darnley received his orders to take his just-formed and inadequately trained surveillance unit—the only such British team in the Maghreb—to Tunisia. They were to proceed to Ben Gardane in Tunisia and camp on the crossroads where the routes from the two Tunisian-Libyan border crossings met. They were to memorize the faces in the al-Salan mug book and to alert John if they identified even one such face.

One day later, he'd gotten the call. "The one with the very bad scar and four others we think we recognize are here now."

"Follow them," he'd said. "I'll join you as quickly as I can."

To John Darnley's surprise, his surveillants had done a credible job. They'd actually stayed on the al-Salanist's trail as far as Gabes, where John—who'd hired a helicopter—joined them. There, in the town of some 116,000 people, the al-Salanists had disappeared.

"When in doubt," a training officer had once told Darnley, "stake it out." Accordingly, Darnley had sent his men north to the Skhira crossroads where the coastal route and the direct road north to Tunis diverge. Two hours later, watching from a vantage alongside a raised stone ditch that irrigated a patch of oil palms, he'd seen a strange convoy. First came one Mercedes, then another, and another. Two furniture vans belching smoke followed. A collection of lesser vehicles brought up the tail end, their drivers jockeying for position, passing each other to the right or the left as road and shoulder conditions allowed.

His surveillants had told him about seeing this group of vehicles at Ben Gardane, laughing as they'd described it. Even as worried as he was about reacquiring the al-Salanists, Darnley had smiled and aimed his binoculars on the cars. Almost immediately he'd recognized a passenger looking out a rear window of the second Mercedes. Mustafa Karim. There'd been rumors, and apparently they'd been true. One of Libya's most powerful men was on the run or had jumped ship or whatever.

"Well, well, well," he'd said to himself. No matter Karim's motivation, he'd left Libya, and London would be interested.

He'd had another thought, too. Karim was Harabi. Al-Din was Harabi. John had learned one lesson well—in Libya's tribal society this was important. He'd put two and two together and reached a resounding twenty-two. He couldn't have been more wrong, but how was he to have known? At any rate he'd done the right thing. Despite the fact that the Karim convoy proceeded not via the Tunis road but took the coastal route, he'd summoned his team and they'd followed, ending up in Sousse. He'd been certain that either al-Din and his fellows were buried in the convoy or that Karim would contact them.

Which was before he'd spotted the Tunisian DGSE connection.

He'd called Eckton from Sousse. "You see, don't you?" he'd asked. "This changes the entire dimension of the situation. We have to ask ourselves whether al-Salan's plans aren't being orchestrated by someone else, whether we haven't stumbled over a much more serious conspiracy."

"Such as?" Eckton had sounded dubious.

"God knows. Libyan intelligence might be behind this ... Karim's departure could be just a cover for an operation. The Libyans could be planning to knock off their counterparts in Tunisia and from what I hear it sure as God wouldn't be the first such effort. Perhaps there's some kind of unholy alliance between the Libyan JSO, the Tunisian DGSE, al-Salan and Annahda."

Eckton snorted. "Annahda may be an Islamic party, but ties with terrorists? Not a chance."

"Or Karim," John persisted, not having an answer, "might be acting on behalf of one of the rebel groups in eastern Libya. It'd be to their benefit to destabilize Tunisia. With most of North Africa in an uproar, they might just get us, the French, and the Americans to put boots on the ground to help them. Or perhaps it's something else entirely. It may be far-fetched but the Tunisian DGSE could be using the Libyans to conspire with Annahda against their own government. I doubt there's much love lost between the old boys from Ben Ali's regime and the civilians of the new government."

"I see a very active imagination but no credible motive in any of your scenarios."

"Right." He said at last, "Of course, I'm just guessing."

"Well. When you figure it out, give me a jingle. Now you're running out of time. London says to pass your fragment to the Tunisians tonight even if you've learned nothing more. I'm to do it verbally and without informing the cousins although I can't for the life of me understand the rationale for that type of restraint. This is a terrorism matter."

"Perhaps because London understands the connection to Saharan Enterprises?"

"I shouldn't be surprised. But it still leaves me on the hot seat with our local lady."

John didn't understand what James meant. Nor did he care enough to ask. He had his own problems and, as James had just said, he'd better get on with the chore of resolving them.

"Back to the business at hand," James continued. "I can give you until ... say ... twenty hundred hours. No later. I'm not going to be put in the position of explaining why I'm getting people out of bed when we've had the information for several days. I hope you understand. Eight o'clock. Not a minute later."

So John had staked out the villa which he learned belonged to the DGSE and had been put at the disposal of Karim and his entourage. He'd watched as a team of workers unloaded the trucks, disgorging a stream of ornate furniture. The trucks had left and a caterer's van had arrived. Food went inside. Flowers went inside. A car belonging to a computer service with "Le Monde des Ordinatures" painted on its side was admitted. Shortly after that a sedan parked outside the gates. Four men in dark suits got out and were ushered through with much bowing and scraping. They left after only ten minutes.

For the next half an hour nothing happened. Not a hint of an al-Salanist in sight.

Darnley had been about to give up when Karim emerged with his bodyguards. It was seven-o-five, 1905 hours. Darnley and his team followed them.

At 1930, Karim vanished. Darnley had been at the rear in the rotational he'd worked out with his surveillants, had been avoiding looking at his watch and, otherwise, yawning from a day in the car, hoping something would happen soon. It did. His man with the 'eye' had radioed, "They were here. Then they weren't."

Karim had disappeared. To meet with al-Din?

At twenty-one hundred hours on February 19, John Darnley found himself in the Tunisian Ministry of Interior building, one opening on the riot-scarred Avenue Habib Bourguiba in downtown Tunis. He faced three impassive Tunisians dressed in black suits, white shirts, and dark ties. The tallest of them was improbably introduced as Mohammed Ali. He was a new man brought in to implement reforms, James Eckton had explained earlier, and the name was a likely work alias. His suit was of much finer quality than those of his two colleagues, one of whom presented a very rumpled appearance. He was introduced as Mohammed Zayifi.

Mohammed Ali opened the meeting after an exchange of pleasantries, "So, my friends, are we to understand that you and the Americans believe the *Unité* exercise is threatened by these al-Salanists?"

"The exercise? It's possible, of course, but I'm not sure the Americans ... ," Eckton looked at John.

"Yes, well ... ," he began, temporarily at a loss for words, still processing Zayifi's presence. The man had been one of those in suits he'd seen entering Karim's Sousse villa. Which meant? What? Was there a conspiracy here? Could Zayifi be plotting with the al-Salanists and the Libyan JSO? What about ... ?

"John?" Eckton prompted.

So, he'd shut down his suspicions and focused on a broken slat in one set of closed and dusty venetian blinds behind Mohammed Ali and said that to the best of his knowledge neither Washington nor their Tunis Station had yet received his report. "... given its fragmentary nature and pending some confirmatory information ..." was the way he put it, adding, "and its time sensitive nature, so we came straight to you."

After a long moment's pause, Mohammed Ali turned to his colleagues and the three exchanged a few words in Maghrebi Arabic. From it, John understood that the two colleagues planned to attend the exercise and their rapid exchange had to do with extraordinary measures already taken to protect the attendees.

Mohammed Zayifi, at a nod from his new boss, changed to French and spoke to Eckton. "But you've seen the American's report, yes? From earlier this evening? You are on the distribution."

Eckton had allowed that he hadn't been in the office.

Zayifi picked up a red dispatch folder and handed it to Eckton. He read, flipping through pages and photographs, then passed the folder to John.

The CIA woman had written a concise note, attaching stock CIA documents on al-Salan and its dissolution plus file photographs and biographies on two al-Salanists she'd identified as in Tunisia. Her note included the information that both of them had been jailed in Tunisia after being captured in a joint CIA-Gendarmerie exercise, concluding with a conjecture that they might carry a grudge and that the Gendarmerie exercise the next day might be a target.

"Well done," he said aloud. "It seems we've been wasting your time."

"Not at all," Mohammed Ali said, his tone a shade too polite. "But if you learn anything further ... ."

Later, when they were in James' car driving toward his house in Gammarth where John would overnight, James said, "Nothing much escapes Regan, and you can see she's ahead of us on this, no thanks to you. I've said it before and I'll say it again, London is wrong, ordering us to bypass the Americans, but that doesn't matter."

"You certainly won't get an argument from me, but this Grant woman. There was no sourcing on her report. Where and how do you think she got that information?"

The car's headlights were lost under the rows of streetlights as they took the coast road. The sea was no more than a dark wall paralleling their route. James said, "You're questioning the veracity of her report?"

"No."

"Well, don't. At least not in front of our Tunisian colleagues. Just keep in mind that Grant's been their friend while their world's been falling apart around them. Now, I hear she's come up with an outline for a reorganization that means most of them'll keep their jobs. Plus, she's decorative, smart, and makes them laugh. Best of all she's the source of a steady flow of counter-terrorism assistance. You get the picture."

"Right." John cleared his throat. "The ideal woman. The mind quails."

"Whatever your mind does is your problem," but James smiled. "Now, enough said. I've arranged for you to attend the *Unité* exercise tomorrow, so you'd best get some sleep. As for me, I'm putting a great deal of distance between myself and this affair. I smell a very big rat somewhere."

"Remind me to follow your example in the future," he replied.

It was his last good moment for some time. Under other circumstances he might've found pleasure in encountering the highly decorative Grant and loaning her a pen that'd been a gift from his first wife—Gwendolyn's way of kissing him off before divorcing him and marrying up.

So, he'd gone back to tailing Karim.

In fact Karim had led him to al-Din. Karim had also led him back to Grant, who was ahead of him one more time at the Hammamet restaurant. He'd watched her park her van and wondered what she was doing. A directional mic? Something else? Then, she'd left, and he'd entered the rear of the restaurant thinking he might do a bit of eavesdropping. He'd been just in time to bless the fact that the walls were concrete block and stopped bullets.

He hadn't seen the shooters. He didn't know why al-Din would want to kill Karim, but ...

He'd hoped to catch up with the shooters as they left the front of the restaurant and had run for his Volvo, thrown it into gear and spun its tires getting it moving. He'd also almost run into Regan Grant. He'd looked up in time to see her turn into the alley that he'd just left. Why? He'd almost gone back but had been recalled to his own problems by radio chatter from his own men who had heard the shots and scattered, frightened they would be detained by nervous police and security officers.

"Regrettably, we lost al-Din again," he'd said to Eckton later. "But I'd like to know what that woman's game is."

Eckton wasn't interested, said, "Now you're telling me these al-Salanists have multiple targets, are after Karim, too."

"It seems eminently possible."

"Right." All in all, Eckton had seemed to take the news rather well, Darnley had thought.

He'd just begun to relax when the Tunis MI-6 commander added, "Then explain to me, old sod, why would al-Salan come all the way to Tunisia to kill that JSO bastard when they could've done it at any time inside Libya."

Looking back John would wonder at his own obtuseness. Even though he'd known the American spies on the joint Libyan project headquartered at Saharan Enterprises had hired a few former and much touted "reformed" terrorists and even though his own primary reason for being in Libya was to watch them. And even though the reason he'd formed a surveillance team in the first place was to keep an eye on senior Saharan Enterprises' officers, he didn't make the connection. Not until he accompanied his new DGSE friends to what seemed to be a riot and he saw one particular occupant of an armored Mercedes speeding away.

■ ■ ■
CHAPTER THIRTEEN
La Cité, Tunisia

Looking through a stack of children's books, Regan ate a carry-in dinner in a tenth-floor safehouse apartment high over the Menzah IV district of Tunis. Across from her, lights of the city shone indistinctly beyond sliding glass doors and a doghouse-sized balcony. Out there the chill of night had merged with the day's quota of warmth in an impromptu and misty marriage, veiling the bottoms of the higher buildings and lying like a shroud over miles of flat-topped houses.

She'd had no difficulty retrieving the quick plants but had been on her way out the back when a black Fiat with flashers and two armed men in suits arrived. The DGSE. A minute longer and they would've have seen her. Or they would've seen a woman in a safsari, anyway. And she wouldn't have moved as fast as she had if she hadn't spotted a collection of electronics tucked into an overturned planter. Obviously, the DGSE had been eavesdropping, too.

Something else to think about.

The books were gifts she'd ordered and planned to give at tonight's meeting, one she'd wanted to postpone but then thought better of it. It was a once a month affair held with the Baralguiba patriarch, Bashir's uncle, the man at the heart of her operational support structure, the man without whom she would have no support structure.

At 1915 hours, she dropped the books into a bag that already held a box of chocolates for the Baralguiba women. Then, she descended to a garage under the building where a Peugeot—the one she'd used for the Karim meeting—waited. It now had a different license plate.

Forty-five minutes later she completed a surveillance detection route, having seen nothing and not expecting she would. Why would anyone follow her when they knew where she'd be? Or was she wrong about that? Better to do the route and be sure.

Surveillance-free and with ten minutes to spare she reached the nightly throng of trucks and busses clogging the road fronting the massive Tunis dump. Cook fires, strings of fairy lights, and lamps of every type lit the scene. Horribly overloaded conveyances crowned with ungainly bundles of plastic-wrapped goods lurched and inched through the traffic, imminent disaster only a strong wind away. Polyglot peoples with skins of white and black and every shade in between milled on the road and off. The smell of singed meat and of great pots of vegetables and couscous mixed with wood smoke and rotting garbage.

Finding a gap in the traffic, she pulled off the clogged highway, nosing the old Peugeot into an opening between two stalls, negotiating her way around to the back, coming to a stop behind a decrepit truck with a broken driver's door window.

She got out. A Palestinian kefiyah covered her head, make-up darkened her skin, and black-rimmed glasses hid her eyes. Under a shirt and suit jacket showing worn spots and wrinkles, she wore a tight breast cloth. A fraying pair of jeans and dirty sneakers completed her disguise, a familiar one to the Baralguibas. Carrying only a small cellphone, she circled the truck and made herself comfortable leaning against its shoulder-high bumper.

She tried not to smell the acrid odor of charred wood and burned rubber, a tangible reminder of a demonstration that'd gotten out of hand here a few weeks earlier. The remains of several trucks and a food stand had been bulldozed back into the dump. The evidence was gone, the market was back to normal, but the reek still lingered.

Coals glowed and small flames flickered only feet away and gave off a much more pleasant smell. Headlights shocked the darkness as a driver started his vehicle and swung onto the road. Being

February and night, the men who moved within her vision wore ground-sweeping burnooses of brown camel's hair, their high-peaked hoods mostly lying flat on their backs, or they sported old suit jackets like Regan's. Thick, pile bathrobes seemed popular as makeshift coats among the women, blue the common color. Sometimes a *safsari* covered these fashion statements, sometimes not. A few women wore the hijab, scarves folded across the forehead in the Egyptian way—a style of increasing popularity promoted by Islamists and Egyptian sitcoms.

Regan checked her watch. Bashir should be along soon. She levered herself into an upright position.

That's as far as she went. How long had it been here? Didn't matter. There it was. A bullet-scarred Mercedes, a conspicuous vehicle in any neighborhood, was easing through the throngs on the paved part of the road. She resumed her lounging stance but now aiming her cell at the Mercedes. As she took photos, the driver twice passed the nearly invisible alley that led to the track into the Baralguiba family compound.

Her phone registered the time on the last photo as 8:01. 2001 hours. Two men got out. She clicked off another photo. 2002 hours.

So far, she couldn't see their faces. One wearing a blue jacket stopped to speak to a man changing a tire on his car. A moment later blue jacket moved on.

The air stirred next to her, and she smelled what Bashir's wife called his *"eau de vehicle"* odor. Obviously, he'd been back to the garage this evening.

"They are here?" Bashir asked. "The Libyan pigs?"

"Your uncle is ready for them?"

"My uncle knows what he does."

"You see the Mercedes with the scarred sides?" She spoke quietly in French. "And, there. The blue windbreaker at ten o'clock? I think he's asking how to find your uncle's place, but it doesn't look like anyone's saying. I think the Libyans have been given an approximate location but that's all, and this place is a maze."

"Very normal type men," Bashir said.

"Don't let them fool you. So, what's your uncle's plan?"

Bashir grinned, his teeth golden in the firelight. "You will be happy. Now, I think to climb to the top of this truck and get some good pictures."

Across the road blue jacket had disappeared behind a food stall.

And Bashir, too, vanished. One minute he was next to her looking like a manual laborer and the next he was gone.

Four long minutes passed. Another three went by. The crowds shifted and eddied. Bashir did not rematerialize.

Until she smelled him and looked down to see a figure squatting below the grill of the truck she'd been using as a prop. "Bashir?"

"One minute." He had his head almost buried in the interior of a canvas bag and she noticed a faint gleam of white light escaping its sides—his camera monitor. Or his 3G cell?

She waited. When the light went out, he looked up, his face in shadows, the glow of the nearby fire reflecting from his eyes. "I have good photos. It is the terrorist, al-Din. It is definite."

Regan said, "You've told your uncle?"

Still squatting, he nodded. "This is big error for the Libyan pigs. Big error."

She hoped he was right but said nothing. This was Daud's territory and his call.

Bashir added, "Not to worry. My uncle will speak to these men, using language they can understand and arranging for their departure from Tunisia. You will not see them again because ... and this is a fact perhaps they do not consider ... they cross a very wide line when they come to this place."

The young man's crisp dark hair bent back to the interior of his bag. Regan considered saying something, something cogent and pithy, because these particular Libyans would not be amenable to listening. They would not just pick up their marbles and go home. These were a different breed than any who had crossed paths with the Baralguiba clan in the past. Bashir and his people came from

Tunisia's Saharan south—an area that straddled the Tunisian-Libyan border. They were comfortable with business sharks, government thugs, and desert rats but simply had no experience dealing with Afghan-bloodied terrorists or terrorism.

Across the road the man in the blue jacket straightened and spoke quickly to a boy who'd been seated next to a small fire but had gotten to his feet. The boy was pointing. The blue jacket said something into a cellphone or it might have been a radio. The Mercedes nosed in his direction. The second man came out of a crowd to open a rear passenger door. Blue jacket pushed through a crowd around a food shack. In a moment they'd all be inside the car. And, clearly, it was armored.

Once there, small arms wouldn't stop them. The Mercedes could easily crash through the compound's old gates. Automatic rifles of the sort these same men had used in Hammamet would kill everyone inside. Expecting her to be among the women and children, even they would not be spared. And the terrorists would be as safe as they had been in the Hammamet firefight. Except here there would be no expectation of a police arrival and, thus, no reason to hurry or to leave prematurely. This time they would finish their business.

Now it made sense. The reason they hadn't ditched the bullet-pocked Mercedes. They needed it badly enough to run the risk of being spotted. After clearing the compound, though, they'd ditch it and find new rides.

"Bashir," Regan said with urgency.

"We must wait for my uncle." But the young man was on his toes, neck craning.

Blue jacket had reached the door, had his hand on the handle. He couldn't be allowed to disappear inside the protection of that armored vehicle, and those inside had to be lured out.

Regan reached up and jerked off her checked kefiyah, shaking out her red hair as she did. She climbed up onto the high bumper next to her, screaming over the surrounding tumult and waving her arms, "Al-Din, you bastard. Al-Din. Come out."

Her hair would catch light from the night fires, would stand out like a banner. The harsh and foreign English words would cut through the night and its sibilant sounds. Even if the Libyans couldn't actually hear the words, the sound and her hair would get their attention.

The result was spectacular and frightening. Terrifying in fact. First one of the Mercedes' doors opened. Next the other three doors sprung wide. Men spilled out with guns in hands and a sound like a sigh went through the crowded market, a wave of sound spiraling outward, trailed by a heartbeat of silent. Then, pandemonium. The first bullet slammed into the lorry's hood as she dropped to the ground, passing just inches from her head.

Shock had kept her rigid a moment too long. It hadn't crossed her mind that they would use guns in this busy, crowded place. She'd thought they'd come after her. She'd thought ... .

Wrong.

Bashir pulled her to the ground.

Around her was a vision of hell illuminated by fires and the lights of vehicles all jumbled together with cars and people moving in conflicting directions, but all trying to get away, the scene punctuated by the crack and bang of different caliber weapons, by women and men screaming and children crying. Then a fire overturned in a food stall; the cooking oil erupting with a whoosh of sound and a flash of light.

"This way," Bashir shouted in her ear, bullets clanging into metal above them. "We can't stay here."

She couldn't have agreed more. Any doubts she might have had disappeared. Tonight she was the target. Al-Salan had known where she would be and had come for her. Not anyone else. Just her. No ambiguity now.

"Split up!" she screamed at Bashir. "Split up."

Using knees and elbows she scurried around and behind the temporary cover of a small truck. Wiggling forward she saw Bashir still with her. She snaked under a big transport parked next to their first shelter. Above her that vehicle's driver started his engine.

It bellowed and belched smoke. "Go back toward the wall," she hissed in Bashir's ear.

"No. I stay with you." His eyes glinted.

Hers glared.

"No," Bashir repeated.

There was no time for this. They had the protection of a huge set of double tires. But for how long? Regan looked back and saw blue jacket running their direction, an automatic weapon held in firing position.

They had to find better cover. Crouching and running, dropping to use elbows and knees, they moved. Elbows and knees. Fear drove her onward and under the drive train of another truck. Elbows and knees. Fear plus elbows and knees had saved her more than once. The first time—or the first time she remembered—elbows and knees had carried her into a snow-covered, tangled interior of a windfall with fifteen hundred pounds of infuriated moose after her, his enormous rack had cracked like thunder, terrifyingly, as he'd used those spade-like, hooked horns to root in the branches above her. An eye, huge, had come close and promised death. His massive nose, cartoonish when seen at a distance, had pushed almost up to her ball of a body.

That same moose had killed her little dog Jasper. And all of it had happened within sight of the ranch house at Highwinds with her screaming for help from her grandmother. Even then she'd known that danger is no respecter of place and that the proximity of those who love you and who should keep you safe means little. "God helps those who help themselves," her grandmother always said to reinforce the lesson.

Shit! The gearshift engaging in the truck above them was all the warning they got.

"*On y va. Vite.*" She grabbed a handhold on the outer frame with her good hand, pulled, found a place to wedge a heel, used an elbow and scrambled up the side of the truck. It was rolling. Pain lanced up her arm. Bashir was alongside her, climbing as she was up ropes holding a massive stack of chicken crates in place. The smell and sound of chicken shit and terrified birds was overwhelming, and neither of them noticed.

They clambered onto the top of the truck's load just as the driver stood on the brakes.

CHAPTER FOURTEEN
La Cité, Tunisia

The view from their high heap of chicken crates was excellent even surrounded as they were by vehicles cramming both highway and verges. Bashir pointed. "Look."

Al-Din had disappeared, replaced by a solid mass of milling, shouting men. Where the Mercedes had been parked there was a dense crowd visible as a dark patch of black hair and burnoose hoods. The Mercedes, itself, was in motion, for a moment coming straight toward her before careening sideways and crashing through a stall selling rough pottery. Neither clay nor wood framing slowed it down. Instead it gathered speed. As it twisted around the pod of stalled trucks where Regan lay, she caught a clear view of a white face pressed against the back passenger side window.

Instinctively, she rose up on her knees to see better. But the Mercedes had completed a U-turn, presenting its back to her and was notable only as a phenomenon in flight, trying to find a clear passage, crashing through stalls and across fires, anything that could move leaping to safety from its path. When it cleared the traffic-jammed section of road in the direction of Tunis, it rocked back onto the highway and was almost immediately lost around a curve and behind buildings.

Regan didn't see it disappear. Her attention was fixed on a familiar figure. Mohammed Zayifi. The DGSE officer stood well back from the densely packed but surging crowd of people as his men worked at trying to break up the scrum. His stoop-shouldered shape, his round, lined face and his graying hair gave him a grandfatherly look, one he cultivated with a generally sad cast to his mouth and dark, sympathetic eyes. It may even have fooled a person or two.

Regan dropped back below the level of the topmost chicken crates but popped up again. It couldn't be. But it was. The tall, blonde unmistakable figure of the Brit ... Darnley. Darnley with Zayifi? She ducked back, quickly wrapping the kefiyah around her hair. She should've done it earlier. Had Zayifi seen her? Had the Brit? Or his men who must be saturating this place?

"Look," Bashir began laughing. He pounded on her shoulder, hooting with a pure release of nervous energy. She slid out from under his fist, as gales of laughter shook his body. It wasn't everyday someone shot at him. In fact it was probably the first time in his life, and he apparently found the fact of his survival hilarious. Everything was funny. "Look," he said when he could talk, pointing at a cluster of scuffling men. "My uncle comes and talks to these men in a language they understand. I think they have now left this land. Did I not say this would happen?"

■ ■ ■ ■ ■

At least fifteen minutes passed before Regan could risk leaving cover, even with her disguise, to work her way back to the old Peugeot. She couldn't be certain the DGSE men hadn't seen her strip off the kefiyah and scream at al-Din. In fact she had to assume they'd had a tip on the Mercedes. So, what would they think now?

But maybe not. In the event she reached the Peugeot without being stopped and drove it along a rutted track and into a grove of eucalyptus. There she sat, watching again for any indication that she was being followed or under any form of scrutiny. Seeing nothing but the passage of several darkened cars she knew belonged to family members, she got out, found an observation point on a lower tree branch near the edge of the grove, and watched the chaos of the market gradually subside as the DGSE cars nosed their way back to Tunis and the police investigators arrived. A TV crew appeared and was sent away. By then all that was left of what had been a thriving market were empty stalls and overturned oil drums, all starkly clear in portable police floodlights.

Eventually she talked herself into believing the coast was clear, that she'd either escaped notice or that those who might be interested in her had better things to do with their time than search for her. Probably she'd hear from the DGSE tomorrow.

She dropped to the ground, returned to her car, and drove back onto the track, following its rutted, ungraded length to and through an open gate in a high wall. No one challenged her as she came to a stop in an unlit flagstone yard.

Other cars—visible as shadows—were parked there, and a dog barked nearby. She pulled up alongside an ancient van and got out in time to see vague, almost ghostly figures bundling two inert and awkward shapes from the back of a car into the van. Bashir was with them. Before joining them, she pulled the kefiyah from her head and used a flexible wire to tie up her hair.

"What happened?" she asked, stopping alongside Bashir.

"It is one of the Libyans, the one named Juriy. There is another one from the photos you gave us. One named Badr."

She didn't ask if they were dead. That was obvious. "The security people?"

"They do not see what happens. When they finally disperse the mob and come to the place, even the blood on the ground is gone. We take care of our own problems here. It is as I told you."

Regan asked no more questions, wanted no more information. The two al-Salan men caught by the mob had been knifed and stomped and beaten, their remains passed through the crowd. It was enough to know. More than enough. A shiver passed down her spine. She said, "I must meet with your uncle now. Is he here?"

Bashir nodded. "He waits for you."

She turned, got her bag from the car, and walked across the courtyard toward a passage leading beyond the outer court to the main part of the compound. Effluence, the distinctive and nose-wrinkling smell of concentrated garbage mixed with the more powerful and pungent odor of horse droppings tickled her nose. She had never been quite sure if this compound was part of the city dump or an adjoining property. Except for the air quality, it didn't matter.

Behind her the outer gate hinges creaked, and she heard a primitive engine clatter to life. One of its cylinders sounding permanently ill, it rattled and belched its way out the gate. There was a clunk as a bar dropped into its slots. The outer gates were closed, the same gates she'd feared the Mercedes might smash through.

She continued along an arched passage lined with stalls where hooves whispered in straw and a horse nickered. In the near dark she stuck carefully to the middle of the way, staying well clear of the half doors of the stable block. They were all stallions here with centuries of warrior breeding behind them, were natural attack weapons with none of the tractability of the horses Regan knew. A head and neck could snake out to grab a careless passer-by in the flash of a moment. But even these fierce creatures would have been defenseless against automatic weapons fire.

A few steps further on, Regan emerged into another courtyard. In its center was a metal table with two chairs, one of them occupied by a man known to the CIA as PLMAJOR/1—true name Daud Baralguiba. A storm lantern holding a single candle illuminated his face. A cigarette glowed in his right hand. Smoke curled around the flame, climbing with it, seeming to carry the golden reds up into the branches of an overhanging tamarind where it brushed the underside of pinnate leaves with a diffused palate of oranges and yellows.

"*Miss'air-el kheer,*" she said and started to say more, but the man lifted a hand to stop her. He stood, his brown burnoose flaring dramatically as he did.

Daud made her think of a long, thick piece of flexible pipe. Draw a line from the outer edge of each shoulder and it would graze the waist, hips, thighs and ankle. And none of the width was fat. Waving Regan into a chair with his own words of greeting, Daud gestured and a woman emerged from the dark carrying a tray with two tea glasses which she placed on the table. Before sitting, he put his two hands up, palms together and bowed slightly.

"On behalf of myself and my family, we apologize for the events of tonight," Daud said, speaking in French, the words formal as always. "You are inconvenienced in an area where I am the guarantee of your safety. This desolates me. I cannot express sufficiently my chagrin and sorrow for this."

"It is I who must apologize," Regan said. "I obviously acted precipitously. It is you who have resolved a very dangerous situation with a minimal loss of life."

For the next several minutes they exchanged these individual assumptions of blame and giving of credit.

"I suspect, now," Daud brought the obligatory *politess* to a close, "these remaining al-Salan pigs will not return."

"Not here," she agreed. A shudder started up her spine and she had to clench her fists to control her reaction. No. The al-Salanists would not be back. Not here. But it wasn't al-Salan that concerned her now, or not as more than a weapon, a tool. Al-Salan was not the source of her problems. The veil had been lifted, the ambiguity was gone, had disappeared the minute she'd identified the face in the Mercedes' window.

She changed the subject. She had a job to do here of which the night's events were only a part.

More of the polite banalities that formed a sort of glue for this strange relationship followed. Thank God she'd remembered to bring her tote bag with its load of presents from the car. Completing the formalities, Regan handed over her gifts to a woman who materialized to accept them. *"Pour les enfants,"* she said and was proud that only a small tremor remained of the shakes she'd been fighting. What a difference a change of scene can make. Ritual and routine are to emotion what water is to fire.

She received a quiet, *"Merci, Madame.* Perhaps you will have time to read to the children one day."

"It is devoutly to be hoped," she replied with complete sincerity. And, perhaps, one day she could.

When the woman withdrew and after she and Daud had sipped their tea and exchanged news of their respective families, she returned to business, "One thing I must know. Will there be repercussions for you? From the DGSE or the police?"

"These Libyan dogs will cause no more difficulty in our country. Clearly the security men were hunting them and will continue to hunt those who escaped, but neither dogs nor men will return here. As for others? Already people are talking of this spontaneous political demonstration that briefly turned violent. But, *Hamdulillah,* they say only a few were injured and none killed. No deaths will be reported. You need not trouble yourself further. Now we will speak of more pleasant things. Yes? You are agreed? Yes? Tell me how my nephew and his team performed this afternoon? Am I to be proud of him?"

And so, with this breath-takingly casual dismissal of the night's bloody events, another routine meeting with the family began. One after another she talked to Daud's relatives. Some of them, PLMAJOR/8 for example, had been the first to spot al-Din this afternoon and to realize the al-Salanists had changed vehicles. Then there was PLMAJOR/2, Daud's wife, who'd served the tea and taken the gifts. She kept track of the information—more gossip really—collected by members of the family working as guards, clericals, drivers, and coffee carriers in a variety of key offices and organizations. Their contributions rarely resulted in hard intelligence but were useful as background.

Regan had run clearances on and given cryptonyms to almost all of the Baralguiba family or, rather, those living in Tunis. There were twenty-two of them here, not counting children. When she recruited Daud, like it or not, she got the entire northern branch of a clan of Berbers and had been expected to put them to work and pay them. Which was fine with her and with the CIA. The family had proven themselves more than useful, but clearly it had put them in an unanticipated type of danger.

Thinking about that, her mind weighing what she'd learned and the source of the threat, Regan felt a slow throb of anger building and heard an edge form on her words. She accepted more tea and tried to keep her focus on the mundane details that needed resolution.

The meeting was longer than usual because of the many reports family members had obtained of conditions in western Libya. It was all interesting stuff, exciting even, but overt in nature. She'd pass it along to the Embassy political officers who could use it in their sit reps—their situation reports.

At the end, Regan returned to the night's events. "Daud. These men." She told him about their background. She told him that traces had shown their most recent employment as guards at an American-owned company in Libya. She said nothing of the white face and the man's identity, but she also had no doubt he'd been told. Still, she didn't want to say too much and only just slid the name 'Saharan Enterprises' into the exchange, burying it in the narrative.

When she fell silent, he zeroed in on the Saharan connection, said, "We have heard of this place, this Saharan Enterprises. There is much talk and resentment in the surrounding area because they bring in these Harabi Salafists dogs from eastern Libya. How long will they stay working for these Americans? Are they there because it is a convenient platform from which to launch terrorist attacks into Tunisia? We do not know."

She said nothing.

"Today," Daud continued, "there are big riots in Zumara, the Libyan town nearest the American compound. The people of Zumara join their brothers in the east and decide to fight for their freedom and to eliminate the corrupt dictator. Two days ago they destroy an army base near the compound. Perhaps it will not be long before they attack the American place, too."

Sensing Regan's discomfort, possibly fearing she'd lie to him if he pressed her, he didn't ask more questions about the compound or voice the obvious ones about why an American company would employ terrorists and why the American government didn't do something about it.

She considered Daud's reticence. But, of course, Daud assumed the al-Salanists ... men he'd referred to as Salafists probably because he knew little about the Sanussi sect ... had acted independently from their American employers, had been motivated tonight by the fatwa.

Daud had paused. Now, he asked, "What do your analysts say? Can those in Zumara and the other western coastal towns break away from Tripoli? Will the Qadhafi government collapse?"

Her answer was a shrug. "They would want to ask you, who know the region better than others. As for the men who came tonight? It is certain they will bother you no more."

"This is in my mind," Daud replied and leaned forward to peer directly into her eyes, a rare occurrence. "Some things, you understand, one must arrange for one's honor. These men and those who direct them make themselves our concern."

"I—"

"Understand me. When a scorpion tries to bite, the scorpion is ground to a pulp under the sole of a shoe. When a scorpion scuttles for safety, the escape is blocked and the bug killed lest it return. To block the escape and kill the bug is a pleasure." He sat back, his tone again genial. He lifted a hand for more tea and added, "What we learn in the process, my friend, we will be happy to share. But in the meantime, you must take great care for we are not the only ones who hunt. The men who fled tonight will blame you for losing their comrades."

"Yes," she said.

"I fear you do not take this threat with enough seriousness. While there was the fatwa, it was an impersonal thing … only words in the mouth of a far-away mullah. You were only a woman and only one of the Americans who capture their leader. You understand? Now, because of tonight, it will be personal for many Harabi. You understand? You will be blamed personally for what has happened this night."

CHAPTER FIFTEEN
Tunis Station

Hayburner was a snake pit that Arnie had pulled her into, but Arnie was dead, and now something very nasty had happened ... was happening ... in Libya. She had seen for herself. The Hayburner Director of Security Nat Fould, a CIA staff employee, had come to Tunisia with at least four killers and with at least two agendas. Three men were dead. Fould and al-Din, possibly others, had gotten away.

She walked across the stair landing outside her office. The night grill was in place, blocking access to the one and only entrance to the station's large suite. She reached into the cipher box and tapped the correct number sequence. The grill's lock clicked open.

Everything went back to Hayburner and ... Arnie's death?

She turned on the lights in her office, crossed to the safe and worked its combination. For the next few minutes she went through the routine of booting up computers and security systems. While she waited for the equipment to ready itself, she checked for text messages. Among them was one from Craig.

Would he move back to the Georgetown house to be with her while she was there? Or since Mary wanted the bedrooms, maybe he'd suggest she stay with him?

Her cheeks held a flush of anticipation as she keyed the message, then it faded as she read: **DODO just called w/news. Need a full update via 'Eyes Only' channels. Nothing to be put into intel format until advised.**

Not a word of caring. The "DODO" was the old acronym for the Directorate of Operations Duty Officer, an affectionate bit of terminology that had survived the demise of the DO and its renaming as the "Clandestine Service."

Think of something else. Forget Craig. Except he was on the

Hayburner bigot list, would be one of the few who was kept informed about the operation. What did he know about ... ? No. That way led to paranoia.

Karim? Think about him.

She'd never finished her paperwork on their meeting. Never looked at the flash drive he'd given her to pass on to Arnie Walker. She leaned over to rummage in the bottom drawer of the two-drawer Diebold safe, shoving aside a box of nine millimeter ammunition. An envelope that had been supported by the ammo box fell over and a sheaf of rubles slid out. She pushed them after the ammo box and propped a locks and picks kit against the side of the drawer. That left a pair of gloves. The flash drive was under them.

She stuck it into a USB port, brought up the decryption program she'd used on all Karim's other drives and asked it to open this one. Sorry, her computer said. It didn't recognize the language. She sat back, surprised, as another notice came on the screen. Did she want to open the files in Drive E?

Yes.

The computer responded, and there on her screen as a directory with one file. No encryption? Was that possible? Had Karim just been careless?

She scanned down through a few of the 459 documents listed on the drive's menu. Each one of them was in a familiar format. The first was labeled: **Arnie Walker**. Well. He'd never get a chance to read it now. She clicked on it. The format was .txt. No extra encryption. No salutation. She read:

Your time is up. I now have immediate need for the $20 million you promise to reimburse for the virus development. Or you give me working virus codes. Otherwise, I will find it necessary to find a buyer for the documents on this drive and make known that they come from Saharan computers, that they are ones your man Richard Knowland steals for you from CIA computers.

In the next half an hour, she verified that the drive was full of Clandestine Service cables. They came in different priorities and were on various subjects, none of which would've excited her interest if she'd found them in her own computer or in any computer in any CIA station ... or at Headquarters, for that matter.

Shit. She remembered what Karim had said about planting his own agents at Saharan. Was this what it was all about? She stood up and walked into the Station's common room to run a glass of water out of the dispenser. Drinking it, she felt the flush in her face subside.

She returned to her desk and went back through the cables, checking to see if any of them held operational information from her own station and on her activities. None did.

But face it. Face the facts. Richie Knowland hadn't stolen CIA traffic. Arnie'd set up Hayburner to be within the CIA network, which meant the man in charge of Hayburner was reading any traffic he wanted—hers included. That's how Nat Fould and his assassins had managed to show up in such a timely way for each attack. Four times now. It didn't have to be a virus, but it had to concern Hayburner.

Her hands and arms felt weak. Under its bandage her wrist ached—a reminder of fresh traumas. The computer's screensaver was back, this time with a photo of Mac in the cockpit of an old Hercules transport plane he'd just bought. "You can drop this baby down almost anywhere," he'd said. She hadn't asked why he would want to fly a large transport to 'almost anywhere.' She hadn't needed to, because that's what men in the gray arms market did.

There had been four attacks. She'd been at three locations but, possibly, expected at the fourth. The Unit had definitely been the target of one, her presence probably no more than frosting on the cake. Karim had been at two.

All directed by Nat Fould? It seemed a safe assumption.

The heating system came on. Cold air rushed from the ducts, stirring dust off the shelves and ruffling the edges of an arrangement of peacock feathers, their iridescent colors glimmering even under the office's florescent lighting.

Finally, Regan swiveled her chair around. Her arms lifted themselves, her fingers went to work. From a dropdown menu she selected the template for intelligence reports and chose the slugs that would guarantee the widest possible distribution. Craig had said to use 'Eyes Only' for her report on the airfield attack. But Craig wasn't in her direct chain of command and, besides, this concerned another matter. Sort of.

At the 'Subject' prompt she wrote: FORMER AL-SALAN OPERATIVES INVOLVED IN TUNISIAN SHOOTING.

After this, the text flowed from her fingers. WORKING UNDER THE GUIDANCE OF AN AS YET UNIDENTIFIED WESTERNER, FORMER AL-SALAN TERRORIST OPERATIVES WERE POSITIVELY IDENTIFIED AS THE ... .

Four paragraphs later, she stopped, reread what she'd written and hit the 'Send' button. Next she prepared an operational message to go along with the intelligence report. Its distribution would be restricted within her own service. She'd like to spread it all over Washington, but the rules prohibited that kind of dissemination for this type of report. Still, given the sexy subject matter, she knew copies would pass from hand to hand. Everyone at Langley would want to have seen it. Terrorists. Car crashes. Death. A female officer. A fatwa. Secret night meetings. It was all there, and even the dry official language she had to use could not disguise the story line.

She finished the only slightly varnished tale with: THE CAR USED BY THE LIBYAN TERRORISTS OF AL-SALAN, WHO ARE DEFINITELY BACK IN BUSINESS, WAS PHOTOGRAPHED BY BRITISH AND TUNISIAN INTELLIGENCE OFFICERS AT THE SCENE. STATION SOON HOPES TO OBTAIN POSITIVE ID ON THE UNIDENTIFIED WESTERNER.

That should give Fould something to think about. She hadn't mentioned Bashir's photography. He probably had a picture of Fould, but if she claimed any such thing, no one would be sure she hadn't photoshopped it. No. They had to think she had photography from an independent and unimpeachable source. She shivered. Anyway, it was the threat and not a photo that was important.

She felt cold. She felt sick. She needed a glass of water, maybe a glass of scotch. She rose to find water. Stretching to relieve cramped muscles, she heard the sound of someone working the cipher lock. A moment later metal grated on metal as the station door opened.

She froze. Fould was a staff officer. Worse. He was a staff security officer, and all of her combinations were on file in the Office of Security. Shit! What was she thinking. Fould could get her combinations.

The realization that she wasn't safe in her own station hit her like the blast from a shotgun. Fould could be coming through the door with a real shotgun. Christ! She dropped to her knees and pulled out the bottom drawer of her safe. She was reaching for the Browning she kept there when she heard Chance Norris' voice. "Hello? Anyone home?"

Good God! She sank back onto the floor. Above her the heating system, at full power now, blew down on her. "In here," her voice croaked.

"Wondered who was around. Saw the light." Chance appeared in her doorway. "What're you doing on the floor?"

Regan looked up and around. Could Chance be part of Fould and Knowland's conspiracy? How far did it extend? How big was it?

Chance Norris was a burly man dressed tonight in a short-sleeved white shirt, a tie pulled open. His dark blue slacks were belted firmly around his overlarge waist. His skin was tanned to a near mahogany and wrinkled around blue eyes as he grinned at her.

"Great party at the Greeks," he said. "Tiffany and that Iraqi dip were there. Still very tight, the two of them," he said of the station's junior case officer. "Even after your chat with her. Which is something we need to talk about. So where were you? People asked."

"Had a meeting with the MAJORs," she said. "And al-Salan had another try." She sketched what had happened during the afternoon and evening, leaving out the part about Fould and the dead al-Salanists.

"You're going to have to do something about those damn terrorists, too," he said. "Let me know if you need help. I'd be glad to ride shotgun." He added, "And how did our favorite tribe of troglodytes behave under pressure?"

"Swimmingly well," she said of her Berbers—their sobriquet derived from their former custom of building underground desert houses.

Chance dropped into one of her client chairs and looked down at her. "Haven't you had enough of late nights? What're you doing here at this hour?"

Rising and sliding into the second client chair, she said, "Thought I'd bang out a couple of reports while the place is quiet. And you?"

"Washington wants more information on what the Tunisian army's likely to do about Ennadha, if anything. Sam's still convinced that General Ammar will behave exactly as the Algerian military leaders did when the FIS looked like it would control Algeria."

"Which he could still do." They were talking about the Tunisian army chief and how their division chief, Sam Brannigan, saw him, and the lessons that Headquarters had taken from the Algerian civil war, the FIS being the Algerian Islamic Front. Like Sam, Regan thought it was early days. Who knew how Ammar and the Tunisian army would jump if it looked like they'd be ruled by Islamic law and Islamic government forms ... a la Iran.

Chance disagreed. "I know the man," he said, and let the subject drop.

Chance was one of the station's three case officers, his job primarily to conduct liaison with local military intelligence, which meant working closely with the U.S. defense attaché's office and with military personnel assigned to other embassies. He loved field work, refused to take a Washington tour or an administrative job and, as a result, had been stuck at the GS-14 level for the past ten years. Because of this and despite the discrepancy in their ages and experience and seniority, Regan was acting chief of station and his immediate boss. Chance seemed to like it that way.

Now, he said, "Any news from Langley? I heard the director called an executive committee meeting today. You think Craig got Arnie's job?"

It was a good question. She moved around to sit in front of her computer where she pulled up a new menu. Incredibly, she'd forgotten all about Arnie's empty chair. And, in a way, Craig would be a logical candidate to fill it. No wonder he hadn't returned her calls today.

He should've gotten the job five years earlier, but things had changed since then."

She'd been there the night Arnie had paced about the living room of Craig's condo in Adams Morgan laying out all the reasons Craig should withdraw as a candidate for the empty top spy position and recommend his best friend for the job.

"I'm older and more experienced," Arnie had said. "Okay. So I have a temper. Most of our really good chiefs had short fuses." He'd gone on in that vein for some time before concluding, "Okay. The big thing is that I'm older than you. I'll retire in a couple of years and then you can have the job. But if you take it now, I'll never get a crack at running the service."

Craig, of course, had done as Arnie'd asked and had a chat with the then director, taking himself out of competition and recommending his friend. Craig almost always did what Arnie asked.

Now, as Regan scanned subject lines on the evening's traffic, Chance kept talking. "I'd be glad to see Craig take charge even though I suppose that would mean you'd go back to D.C. He'd be an improvement on Arnie which is something I say only because I never knew where I was with that man. I liked him, though. Hell. It was impossible not to like him."

"I don't see anything here," she said. "No announcement yet. But I think Craig's got his eyes on other things now and probably doesn't want the job." She swiveled her chair away from the monitor and looked at Chance. "But what did you mean? You suppose I'd go back to D.C.?"

"Well," he laid an ankle across a knee and picked a bit of lint off a sock. "Just a thought."

She blinked. "A thought?" she repeated.

"It might be a good solution." Without looking at her, he added, "Things are getting a bit awkward here." His fingers worked on his sock.

"Say what you have on your mind, Chance."

His fingers continued to graze over the sock. "Well. I guess it does have to be said, and I've been down the same road a few times. I know what it's like … ."

"You're referring to … ?"

"Marriage. Relationships. Whatever."

She waited, still not sure where this was headed.

Chance said, "Here's how the story's supposed to be scripted. No one likes it, but at a certain point when things aren't going well, you either do the marriage counseling thing and get back together or you break up. You split. You get on with your life. That's normal. That's healthy. That's—"

"None of your business." Time to end this. Maybe Chance did have her best interests at heart, but it was her problem. Not his.

"Except," he ignored her. He also didn't look at her. "Except when it gets in the road of business." He lifted his head, staring at a point over one of her shoulders. "Which brings us to Tiffany. I don't need to tell you that after what I saw tonight? It's too late to rein her in. You're going to have to send her home."

He was right about Tiffany, and she appreciated the change of subject. Having seen Tiffany and that Iraqi together and knowing about Regan's talk with her, he was right in saying something.

"Don't get me wrong," Chance said. "But Tiffany knows about Mac and thinks if you can screw around, so can she. She doesn't get the fact that her sleeping with an Iraqi is a security problem. They're both young and single, she says to herself, so why not? Especially when she sees you, a married woman, in bed with your former boss. How bad does that look? The thing is, Regan—"

"That's enough," she snapped, feeling a red head's flush blooming in her cheeks. "My relationship with Mac is entirely my business and Mac's. Maybe Craig's. Not yours. And sure as hell, not Tiffany's."

"Another thing while we're speaking our minds."

"We?"

He ignored her, but now his blue and slightly bloodshot eyes came sideways and up to meet hers full on. "This is a Muslim country, Regan. So, wake up. You can live apart from your husband or he from you, which is how most people here see it. But when word gets around that you, a married woman, are sleeping with another man? That's going to put the fox in the hen house with the Tunisians. Your credibility will be gone. Maybe they don't stone adulteresses to death here, but the double standard is alive and well. Your contacts in the government ... much as they like you ... will close their doors, and our work will be affected."

Lips set in a flat line, her cheeks bright with color, she broke eye contact, swiveled her chair around and said, "I think you've said enough." She clamped her lips together. Chance probably had had one too many drinks tonight. He'd regret this tomorrow.

"Worse," he continued. "This undermines all of us, not just you. Craig loses face. Since he's our IG, the Agency loses face. Since we're working for you, we lose face. You get it?"

"Are you through yet?"

"Just drop Mac or divorce Craig." Chance stood up and walked to the door where he turned and added, "What earthly difference would divorce make to your relationship with Craig, anyway? It's a piece of paper. A simple solution. Think of it as a career move." On that note he left.

For long moments she stared at nothing. Fragments of things she should've said to Chance swam through her mind. Sensible arguments. Angry retorts. Chance was wrong. Dead wrong. He hadn't looked drunk, but he probably was. And you can't argue with alcohol.

Besides, everyone knew Craig was a womanizer. He'd had dozens of affairs ... well, maybe not that many. But, she was being castigated for one? And, no one ever blamed him for his affairs. And no one understood why she hadn't divorced him. "Great guy," they'd say. "Good officer. But not marital material. So dump him, Regan. Find someone else."

Her secure phone rang. She glanced at the caller ID and wasn't surprised to see it was Craig. Think of the devil, and he calls. Her eyes moved up to the clock over the door. It was twenty minutes past midnight. That made it just after close of business in Washington.

She took a deep breath, then lifted the receiver. "Hi," she said, the one word sounding normal enough.

"Figured you'd still be in the office."

"You're calling about the cable I just sent?"

"Yeah. Sort of. I thought I'd better tell you that Hadija's here. I took her grocery shopping then dropped her in Georgetown. You should know, Mary wants her to stick around a few days after the funeral to help her pack. I said that'd be okay."

"What packing? Mary's going somewhere?"

"That's another story. I want to talk about your cable. This Westerner you mentioned? You got an ID on him, yet?"

When she didn't answer immediately, he said, "Regan? Did you hear me? I hope you're not playing games here. You know, I'm seriously thinking about having you recalled. For your own safety. But we'll talk about that when you get here."

It wasn't often that she couldn't figure out something to say, but so many thoughts vied for attention within her brain that she sat silent.

"Regan?"

She stood up. Looking at the peacock feathers, she told him about the night. A safe drawer clanged shut in the next office.

Craig said nothing for several moments. "You know who that Brit is, don't you? And he was with the DGSE men? You're sure they all recognized Fould?"

"Let me spell this out for you," her mind had cleared. She no longer felt she was talking to her husband but was on the record. "The al-Salanists, whose employment history includes Saharan Enterprises and who were in the market tonight with Nat Fould, attacked a viewing stand full of senior Tunisian officials two days ago and tried to blow up a couple of government ministers. You think that's not going to blow back on Hayburner? There were seven injured in the aircraft attack. Two were serious, and one of those worst hurt belonged to the Ministry of Interior. He's likely going to lose a leg."

"I—"

"Plus this afternoon a group of thugs in the same car that was used tonight shot up a restaurant in Hammamet and wounded George Tendale. Remember? He's the golden boy who's bringing the world of high tech to Tunisia? The local cops are going to assume that all of the men in the photos they took tonight were involved in both attacks, and they'll be moving on it in their own way. Your pet terrorists from Saharan have hit the Tunisians hard, and you can bet they'll hit back. Worse. When they identify your Nat Fould, they're going to be on my doorstep."

"Well," he said, then added, "I guess I better get back to you. I suppose you'll be putting all this in the official traffic?"

"When I hear from the DGSE. Probably early tomorrow. It's not something I can sit on. Not once the Tunisians start broadcasting it."

Footsteps from outside her office made Regan look up just as Chance appeared in her door. "I'm on my way," he said.

"See you tomorrow," she covered the phone's pick-up.

"Any news on our new chief?" Chance nodded at the phone.

She dropped her hand from the secure handset and said, "Chance is here and asked about a new D/NCS. Do we have one?"

"Yes and no," Craig said. "Tell him no."

She did, and, with a wave of his hand, Chance left.

"So?" she asked Craig. "What did you mean? Yes and no?"

"Exactly." He sighed audibly, and she wondered how an encryption system managed to take the sound of air escaping from a mouth, encrypt it, send it half way around the world, de-encrypt it, and faithfully reproduce it for her ear. After a long pause Craig told her.

Earlier in the day, Director Thomas had honored what he called 'Arnie Walker's dying wish' and selected Richard Knowland as Arnie's replacement, citing not just Walker's exceptional ability to find and promote talent but Knowland's record developing and running the Agency's most successful operation—one Thomas termed the "better than the famous Berlin Tunnel Operation."

His tone hard and precise, Craig returned to the Fould/al-Salan mess. "I'm trusting you on this, Regan. Now, I better start getting people out of bed. As for you. Watch your ass." He paused, then added, "I suppose you're still coming for the funeral?"

"Suppose?"

The desktop computer went to its screensaver, a photo looking down on her real home—the Highwinds' ranch buildings tucked into their Wyoming mountain fastness. Her own reflection on the screen overlay the scene like a ghost hovering over her family home.

CHAPTER SIXTEEN
Georgetown, D.C.

Arnie's family and select colleagues gathered at the Walker residence after the funeral service just as Arnie had planned.

"I want everyone to get drunk," he'd said. "And I want to hear exactly what they say about me." To that end he'd bugged his own house, setting up video cameras and feeds via Agency satellite links to his villa on the Saharan Enterprises compound.

Craig moved around, participating as small groups formed, reminisced, then broke up and reformed in new combinations. Arnie's big recliner, though, was the unacknowledged focus of everyone's attention and of Craig's ire.

It was the timing, and it was Arnie's fault. He'd insisted on an elaborate blow-out even though at least a third of the guests—those under cover—shouldn't be here. They shouldn't have gone to the funeral, either. Those were the Near East hands, everyone from the chief of the division, Sam Brannigan, on down. Plus half a dozen chiefs of station who'd flown in for the funeral. Among the latter was his own wife. It was her station, for God's sake, that was the epicenter of the problems spreading across the Middle East.

He looked at his watch, begrudging the time. Demonstrations continued in Tunis. Terrorists were mixing with rebels in Libya and Tunisia. Al-Salan, that beacon of hope, that grand experiment in reforming terrorists, had morphed into a case study of what not to do with one-time terrorists. Attacking a group of freshly minted, pro-democracy Tunisians officials? Then yesterday, the important Libyan city of Misrata had fallen to rebels while the town closest to Saharan, Zuwara, had also been taken over by rebels. More, the Zuwara rebels were threatening Saharan. Now, the trouble in Egypt. Unrest in the Gulf. What next?

Regan had been preaching through the cable traffic since Tunisia's president fled that Arabs elsewhere would look at how easy it'd been for the Tunisians to rid themselves of a dictator and would be encouraged to do likewise.

Okay, had been the response. You might be right, but what do you expect us to do about it?

One of the "whats" became apparent almost immediately when Qadhafi refused to follow Ben Ali's lead. He wasn't going quietly. He wasn't going at all, and it was his example that would become the rule.

Regime change. Arnie had been right about the beauty of an operation that could initiate regime change in a peaceful and seamless way. But Hayburner wasn't ready. There just weren't enough infected computers and, even if there were, the Agency didn't have the right infrastructure in place to exploit use of the viruses. Witness what had happened to Arnie's hand-picked successor to Qahdafi.

Mary Walker touched Craig's arm. He looked around. As always, every hair on Mary's graying blonde head was where it belonged, and her make-up hid any signs of grief. Not that she actually had anything to grieve about.

Reading Craig's mind, Mary said, "You try living through what I've had to these past days and see how you manage."

"I wasn't—" he started to say. "Actually, I was thinking that most of the people here should be at their desks. This so-called wake is a travesty. That's what I was thinking."

"Nevermind. You're as bad as Arnie about ignoring your domestic situation. He gets away with it, but you won't. Or at least not much longer." She nodded toward an archway to their left. "I'm just surprised she didn't bring Mac with her today. I invited him, you know."

He hadn't known. He didn't really care. Mary had a valid complaint about Arnie, but she'd long ago become a one-issue person and a bore.

Mary was still talking, "When she divorces you, Thomas will blame you. Not her." She pointed at CIA Director Thomas and his wife in the entry hall. They were deep in discussion with Regan. Like Mary, Regan's hair had been carefully combed and wrapped into a knot at the nape of her neck. In her case a chandelier softened the severe style, highlighting shades of red that ranged from a deep crimson to a rich chestnut. Beneath the spectrum of color, her strong features looked almost soft, reminding Craig of moments of shared enjoyment, stirring him momentarily.

He quashed the feeling and said to Mary, "Mind your own business."

She laughed, but the sound had a bitter overtone. How long had it been since she'd been anything except bitter? Too long, but there was nothing to do about it. She hadn't liked any part of Arnie's scheme and had said so repeatedly. Not that Arnie had listened or accommodated to her objections. "You'll love living in Paris," he'd said. "Besides, I'll finally have the money to buy you all the things you missed when we were younger. I want our last years together to be really happy ones."

Craig had been in their kitchen during this exchange and remembered Mary's reply. "With you in Tripoli most of the time?" The words had been ladened with sarcasm. "What you really want, Arnie, is to play your spy games and carry on your affairs right up until the moment you die. What you don't want is to have to worry about me or your daughters."

It was the truth, and it had shut Arnie up for the moment. Craig had cleared his throat, then, thinking he'd say something about getting on home. Anything to transition himself out of the Walker's domestic problems. But calling attention to himself had been a mistake.

Mary had turned on him. "And, you. If anything you're worse. At least Arnie calls a spade a spade. At least I know where I stand with him. You. You've got the staying power of a butterfly, and you're a lousy influence on Arnie. There's that poor wife of your's thinking someday you'll want her back, thinking she can hang on to you with a sham marriage when all she's doing is giving you a license to philander. There's ... ." Mary had gone on in that vein. Gone on way too long. Craig didn't want to remember the rest of what she'd said.

He looked down at her now. If only he could just walk away, but she'd been so badly treated in this whole affair. Pity held him in place; pity which she saw and hated so much that she clearly wanted him gone even more than he wished to leave—the two of them bound by the iron-strong strands of Arnie's will and their own sick senses of guilt, duty, and that cesspool of pity. He said, "Peace. This'll be over shortly. In the meantime is there anything I can do?"

She shook her head. "But the man, himself, wants to talk to you.

There's a secure line upstairs. He wants you to call."

Craig knew Arnie could well have just overheard the exchange between himself and Mary, depending on which of the many microphones and video feeds he had switched on. He shrugged and a moment later made his way up the stairs to Arnie's study.

The packers hadn't been in it yet, and the room still had both the smell and the feel of its previous owner. The walnut table that served as a working surface, though, gleamed with polish, its usual stacks of papers gone. Only the secure telephone unit remained, sitting in an open aluminum case.

Beyond the windows, across a narrow bit of garden and a six-foot high brick wall, Regan's house shone with light and gleamed through curtains shrouding the windows of the bedroom he had once shared with her. To the right were the windows of what would have been a nursery if Regan had had her way. They were dark.

Craig shut the door and checked to be sure the sound-masking system was turned on. Then he sat down in one of the four captain's chairs and called Arnie.

"Enjoying yourself, are you?" Craig said when his friend answered. "Zuwara's fallen to the rebels. You haven't evacuated, and you're likely to be overrun at any moment, but you have time to listen in on your own wake?"

There was no response.

"Arnie?" he said after a moment.

"I'm here," the voice belonged to an old man. "Just getting the end of a conversation. There's more lies being bandied about in my living room than I'd thought humanly possible. God damn but this was a good idea."

"Well. Record them all. You can listen at your leisure when you're back in Paris."

Arnie cleared his throat. "How'd things go at the Cathedral? I gather from what people're saying that it was a good turnout ... even had a bunch of those bastards from the Pentagon come to pay their last respects."

"Actually I think they wanted to make sure you were dead."

"Oh. Well. You're right about that. Too bad for them that the funeral was no more than false confirmation." Arnie changed the subject. "You should be listening to what I've been hearing. Director Thomas's been quizzing Regan about your marriage. Not that I'm complaining."

"Regan's—"

"On that subject, before you say something you'll regret, I want you to know that we knew nothing about what that son of a bitch al-Din was up to, and I did my best to stop him ... almost got Nat Fould killed in the process."

"What?"

Arnie's voice almost purred. "Well. You said to do something. Don't be so surprised that I did. Nat took a suitcase full of money to buy al-Din off, but it didn't work. Al-Din kept the money and sent us a ransom demand for Fould. I paid it, too. Still, I got to tell you. Regan would've made a great martyr. She'd have been remembered as a heroine in the frontline of the War on Terror, and it would've done a lot for your career. It was a win-win situation. Instead, I'm out a ton of cash and Nat's a fugitive because the Tunisians got Interpol to put out a warrant on him. A misinterpretation of the facts." Arnie paused. "I'd say that was your fault. Wouldn't you?"

Craig looked at the blank computer screen that had been pushed to the right side of the desk and wished he could see Arnie's face. But he had to believe him. The alternative? It was ludicrous to even think that Arnie would wish to harm Regan.

He changed the subject. "Another thing about the Tunisians."

"What about them?"

"There's a new Economic Development team in Tunis."

"There's a new everything team in Tunis, and none of them know which way is up."

"Cumulus," Craig refused to be side-tracked. "They've been briefed on Cumulus, and it's become a handy focus of attention."

"They've been listening to Mustafa Karim is what they've been doing. And that ungrateful son of a bitch is out to destroy my reputation ... spreading stories about how I plotted to take control of Tendale's Cumulus system to strip it of its anti-viral properties. Dozens of emails and phone calls. Incredible how many people don't know I'm dead. What I'd say is that George Tendale should be more careful about the company he keeps. Anyway, I can handle the—"

"Listen to me, Arnie," Craig interrupted. "The analysts give you maybe a couple of days before Qadhafi mops up your local rebels. Then, if the rebels don't overrun you first, Qadhafi's troops will either bomb or occupy your compound or both. We've heard that from the Italians who've still got a man in the Bab al-Azizia. Seems Qadhafi's blaming you for the local rebellions. Whatever." Craig kept his eyes on a grandfather clock across the room from him. In addition to its normal mechanical functions, a cluster of carved roses along one side of the casing concealed a miniature audio/video feed.

Staring at the man he couldn't see, he continued, "Maritime Branch have got a freighter docked in Malta you can have. It'll be on its way to you sometime this afternoon, as soon as they top off their fuel tanks ... you'll get a cable from them. Be ready to leave when it arrives."

Craig swung his chair around, presenting its back to the wooden rose as he asked, "How much of Hayburner can you pack and haul off with you?"

Arnie might not have heard, said, "Thomas is on his way out. Did he tell you he's thinking about resigning? And you're going to be the White House candidate of choice to replace him. They like you downtown. Hell! They even like you at the Pentagon, and the SecDef will say so."

Craig wheeled around and stared at the clock. With an effort he didn't say, "What?" Or, "Say that again." He swiveled his chair back around in time to see a figure appear briefly in a downstairs window of Regan's house. Thomas resign? Thomas downstairs talking to Regan. Thomas moving out of his seventh floor office at Langley. Craig moving in. Thomas leaving his big corner office at the Executive Office Building. Craig having a daily view of the White House and dealing directly with the world's problems, like Libya, like ... .

He said, "Don't change the subject. I'm firm on this, Arnie. You've got to get all your expats out asap."

"Look. What about a simple thank you? I even made a point of having a personal chat with the President. You're going to be D/CIA, old buddy. I'd think that was something worth celebrating." He paused. "Okay. Okay. You're pissed that I got Thomas to finger Richie for the NCS seat. Sure. But I owed Richie that much, and Thomas had to make a very obvious blunder ... sort of a final kick in the butt at a strategic moment. I wouldn't have wanted him to have a last-minute change of mind about resigning. And he fell for it."

"And, what if I'd let Richie's appointment stand?"

"What if? There'd be worse selections. As I said to Thomas, Richie may be an ass-licker, but he's our ass-licker and highly capable to boot. Well. What the hell."

"Listen to me, you old bastard. We're talking about evacuating your people from Libya. You keep them there, and you'll get them killed." Craig stared at the clock. "I mean it. Buck me on this, and I'll make sure Hayburner dies a sudden death."

Arnie laughed. The sound was a weak version of his signature belly laugh, the one that once had been heard up and down the Langley corridors, one that had echoed through his seventh floor offices. He said, "Go screw yourself." He laughed again but this time the sound was bitter. "Power's gone to your head, old buddy. Time to climb down off your high horse and face a few facts. Fact numbers one through ten. You can't stop this. Try and I'll expose you as the author of a fraud."

A siren whooped a few streets away. A breeze bent the gray arms of a tulip poplar in Regan's side yard. Several plump sparrows flew down onto the thickly mossed top of the brick wall separating the two houses.

When Craig said nothing, Arnie continued. "Let me spell this out. You're the one who made all the arrangements to fake my death. You're the one who signed all the Hayburner documents. You're the one who approved the operation and set up the operational controls. Me? I'm just a poor old man who's facing death and going along with his good buddy, trying to be a good soldier and a patriotic American to the end. And that, old friend, is how it will play out if you get in my way."

A ray of sunshine glowed off the bricks of Regan's house and shone through a window onto a row of stuffed toys. There was a white unicorn with a golden horn, a brown koala bear with large glass eyes, and a Raggedy-Ann doll with yarn for hair. Gay, red and white curtains hanging on either side of the window gave them a cheerful frame, but only added to the sense of depression left by Arnie's threat.

Regan had insisted on the nursery and on furnishing it.

Arnie had insisted on Hayburner and ... . Futile. So futile. So senseless.

Regan had tried to get pregnant behind the three bedroom windows immediately across from him. Arnie had sat in this chair plotting Hayburner and his own death. Arnie ... sitting in this chair, watching the house as he was now.

At the Libyan end of the line a woman's voice, faint but audible, said, "Arnie. Cut it short. Lunch's ready." Craig recognized Arnie's longtime secretary, Lori Jacobson's, voice.

As for Arnie's threats? Craig felt his head moving back and forth in a form of denial. Was Regan right? "You look at Arnie and you see yourself, but you're wrong," she'd said and said frequently. "He's not like you."

Through the phone, Craig heard Arnie say to Lori, "Give me five." To Craig he said, "Lobster and champagne for lunch today ... to celebrate my surviving my own funeral. Now. Where were we?"

Craig said nothing.

"Well, hell," Arnie said. "Let's jack this down a level or two. First, we're evacuating. I'd planned to send the ex-pats out by air in the next few days, but you'll save me a bundle with your freighter. So consider that done. As for Hayburner, we'll follow the emergency plan. I've already had the key equipment, programs, and data packed. It's ready to go. The data center can be sealed off. We'll leave guards on the perimeter with orders to evacuate themselves if it looks like they'll be overrun. And, well, hell! If it comes to it, I'll just blow the data center up. We've got the money now to start over someplace else."

"Easy come. Easy go?" Craig heard a querulous tone in his voice. Could it really be so easy? Him. The next D/CIA.

"Hey," Arnie was off on another tangent. "Could you put a bee in the MI-6 bonnet for me? I need George Tendale back here. The SOB flew in to make sure I hadn't done anything to his precious new operating system, then he took off again despite the fact that I needed his help. Ungrateful little queer. I let him use our facilities. So what's he do? Takes advantage of us. Uses his access to the working virus to teach the artificial intelligence element of Cumulus to recognize the Hayburner coding. The little prick. And to add insult to injury, I've got that crazy Karim on my back. Well. That's another story. In the meantime I need George here. Do it, Buddy. Now, I gotta go."

CHAPTER SEVENTEEN
Langley, Virginia

The diamonds on Regan's left hand sparkled above newly manicured nails.

"Lose the glasses and you'd look smashing," Craig said when he picked her up at her Georgetown house. The sun, rising earlier every day now, had begun to burn the frost off the grass running down the broad medium of the George Washington Parkway. With such normality it was hard for her to believe bad things could happen, that not forty-eight hours earlier she'd been belly down on Tunisian earth under a truck, fearing bullets, remembering a moose charge. Bad things do happen and they can happen anywhere. It paid not to forget the fact.

"Richie will get the news today," Craig said. "Apologies from Thomas and all that, but he'd had to rethink the nomination." His hands, covered in black leather driving gloves, lay relaxed and competent on the steering wheel. In a plaid beret driving cap and his wonderfully tailored black wool coat, he was the picture of a man in control. After a brief pause when she said nothing, he continued, "We'll be relocating Hayburner to a warehouse at Quantico temporarily, and Richie and this contractor we brought in will continue to run it. The cover company employees will go into evacuation mode, standing by in case we can reopen the Saharan facility which is way too valuable to abandon if we don't have to."

Ahead of them brake lights flared in a cascading format for no reason Regan could see. But that was commuter traffic for you.

"And listen to me, Regan," Craig continued. "About Fould. I talked to him. He claims those al-Salanists kidnapped him. Says he was handcuffed and helpless all afternoon and evening."

"He didn't look—"

"Be that as it may," Craig didn't let her finish. "As soon as we can, we'll bring him back for questioning. Okay." His gloved hands rolled on the steering wheel, leather on leather making a soft sound audible over the engine and traffic. He continued using a tone that sent his subordinates into a 'saluting the flag' mode. "One last thing. We've sent Chance in to talk to the Tunisian DGSE and offer full support in tracking down what's left of that rogue group of al-Salanists. If they're even still inside Tunisia. The rest of it you have no need to know."

Before she could protest, he added. "Don't misunderstand. We're grateful for the part of the puzzle you brought us. That flash drive ... the Libyan's demands ... they really drove home the point. No one's happy with Arnie's management over the last months of his life, and there will be consequences. But that's none of your business. As far as you're concerned? Like I said last night, your need to know just got pulled. So. I think you'll have enough time today to finish your consultations and can head back to Tunis whenever you want to go."

He seemed engrossed in his driving, his gloved hands still caressing the wheel, his eyes on the road ahead. She leaned against the chill of the side window. That's what it came down to for him. He'd sweep Hayburner under a carpet, and he'd get her out of Washington as fast as possible so he could get back to his twin ambitions of scoring more pussy than any other man in town. Oh, not to forget ... and clawing his way up the political ladder.

But she wasn't being fair. Craig wasn't an indiscriminate philanderer. With every woman that'd entered his life she'd worry that this one might replace her, might persuade Craig to seek a divorce. Every time, so far, his affairs had lasted between six months and a year. Then that one would be over, and he'd show up on her doorstep again, seeking reconciliation, seeking something from her that she apparently couldn't deliver because their reconciliations never lasted. "Cut your losses," she'd tell herself, but didn't.

"Men don't change," her grandmother had warned her years ago. "And with Viagra on the shelf now, even age doesn't help." And Liza liked Craig. She just didn't like him as her granddaughter's husband.

Remembering, Regan waited for her pulse to steady before she said, "Is there a rush? About my leaving?"

Ahead of them brake lights stuttered to life, then died, a sort of Morse Code of dots and dashes signaling to beware. Watch out.

Obediently, Craig down-shifted, the transmission slowing them. The Porsche would not flash its brake lights until the last minute, would not be part of the general alert being sent down the highway.

The lines of red lights steadied and the heavy morning traffic on the GW Parkway came to a stop. Craig finally looked over at her. *Men don't change.*

She turned sideways to meet his eyes, taking in the strength of his image, knowing the weaknesses it hid. His blue eyes were as clear as ever. But there was change in the mass of fine wrinkles winging out from the outer corners of his eyes, in the lines cutting down the sides of his chin, in the coarsening of his skin. He was getting older, but he hadn't changed.

She hadn't, either. She reached across the center levers to touch his cheek and let her fingers stray down to the curve of his chin. Her wrist didn't protest, but she felt a tensing in his jaw.

Behind them a car honked. The red brake lights had gone out, and traffic had begun to move. Craig eased his foot off the clutch.

Her hand dropped back to her lap. Her mouth opened to say words she'd rehearsed hundreds of times but had always balked at voicing. "I'll leave after I see my lawyer and after we go over the terms of our divorce. I shouldn't imagine it'll be difficult. You keep your condo. I keep my house. We'll sell our joint assets and split the money. No alimony. And that'll be it."

They'd picked up speed, were passing one of the overlook areas along the parkway. Virginia grape hung thickly from trees flanking a straight drop down to the Potomac and framing a view of thickly packed nude vegetation on the District shore. Only impressionist blurs of color and form hinted at houses and stores, roads and vehicles masked by a dense network of branches and trunks.

"Is this about Mac?" Craig said at last. He took his hand off the gear shift and reached out to rest it lightly on her bandaged wrist. "Look," he continued. "I'll admit I was unhappy when I heard. Not because I had any grounds to be upset except, I mean, it made me look bad. That sounds pathetic, doesn't it? But it's the truth."

She picked his hand up and set it back on the steering wheel.

"Then, you're angry because I filled the condo with guys who came in for the funeral from overseas instead of saving it for us?" He needed his hand to shift into high. The speedometer needle moved up to sixty. "I shouldn't have to explain that Mary asked me to help out with them."

He'd done it again, an old trick of his. The lie dressed in truth.

Tears came to her eyes, and she turned to stare at the side of the road. Were they tears of anger or pain, of self-pity or futility?

He saw her pull out a tissue and said, "Okay. I'll agree to a divorce. But not right now. There're things going on, and ... . Well. Leave it at that, but let's just postpone this until, say, this summer?"

Inexplicably, brake lights flashed ahead, this time coming on and staying on. This time Craig stepped on his own brakes. The tail of the van just ahead rushed at them; the speedometer needle flopped to the left. They came to a stop, sandwiched between the van and an SUV, flanked on the right by a mini-bus.

Craig stared at the back of the van.

She said, "My relationship with Mac makes you look bad? Can you imagine how your various women affect me? People used to feel sorry for me, which was bad enough. Now I'm the butt of their jokes." It was true and it was deserved. Pretty sad. Pretty funny. She could face down terrorists, but she couldn't manage her own personal life.

■ ■ ■
CHAPTER EIGHTEEN
Georgetown, District of Columbia

She'd needed R&R. Which was why she'd accepted Craig's suggestion that they spend a day at Harper's Ferry. "We both should get away from Langley and its problems," he'd said. "And it'll give us a chance to talk through this divorce thing."

And what a day it'd been with never a false note and nothing said to hurt or disturb. Even the undercurrents of tension so manifest at Arnie's house and in the drive to work had failed to materialize. It was as though by voicing the word 'divorce' she'd freed the two of them from some dark spell.

The weather, too, had cooperated, being one of those late winter days when you can almost see the buds popping out on branches and daffodils pushing their way out of the ground. They'd walked through the town, feeling the eyes of strangers turning to stare at them, maybe with envy. They'd picnicked in a bed of sunshine along the river, talking of friends and how her grandmother Liza was faring in her campaign to secure the future of Highwinds. When they'd disagreed, it'd been over the best flavor of ice cream, compromising by ordering cones with a scoop of each. Then, to work off the calories they'd rented a kayak. Once on the water their strokes had come effortlessly in unison, the water whispering, the sound as quiet as a conspirator's wink.

Only the shadow of time lay over the day, the knowledge that it would not last, and all too soon the two of them would return to their corners.

It was three in the afternoon when the Porsche's tires bumped over the driveway bricks. He brought the little car to a stop in its old parking place alongside the kitchen door, turned off the engine, and reached across the center console, his hand tanned, palm open. "Where're your keys?"

She gave them to him and got out.

The day remained comfortably cool and cloudless. Feathery shadows cast by the maze of bare branches and twigs moved lazily in a light breeze and sent shadows chasing over the yard. A cluster of crocus blades speckled the ground alongside the kitchen porch, a thickening at their apex indicating the presence of nascent buds.

Craig unfolded from the car, continuing a story he'd begun as they crossed Key Bridge, pausing only to find the kitchen door key on her keychain. He inserted it, opened the door, and stood back to let her enter.

She did, turning to retrieve her keys. He almost ran into her. Regan found her face about an inch from his neck, her eyes getting a close-up view of his chin, so close she could see the beginning of a stubble. Embarrassed, she stepped away.

"But that's not the end of the story," he said. "How about a cup of coffee and I'll tell you the rest." He strode toward the refrigerator where they'd always kept the coffee beans. "In fact, I'll make it. Any of the funeral guests still in residence?"

"Last of them left yesterday," she said. "And, I don't think I want coffee."

"Tea?"

"There're scones in the bread box if you want some," she said, unwrapping the scarf she'd worn. "It's been a great day," she added, and stepped over to peck Craig's cheek, turning what had been an awkward moment into casual friendship. "Like the way it used to be. I'm glad I went. Sometimes I forget why we ever got married, forget how much fun you can be."

The last word trailed away as Craig turned away from the refrigerator and put his hands on her shoulders. His thumbs bracketed her neck and moved up to her hairline. Her redhead's flush rose with them, staining her skin.

■ ■ ■ ■ ■

She was a willing participant in her own victimization, a happy collaborator who needed only one drink to be back on the bottle. But this was worse than alcoholism. This was a sort of psychological master-victim thing sometimes lodged under the Stockholm syndrome umbrella. If all she had to resist was the oblivion of alcohol, of something set before her, she would do it—one drink at a time. But Craig was smarter than that. He ignored her. He enjoyed the company of other women and found stimulation a long way from her. He made her work hard for the smallest hint of approval so that, when he turned to her with a smile or a touch, she melted into a malleable puddle at his feet.

She lay quietly knowing this wouldn't last but still savoring the moment. Shadows of bare tree branches moved like graceful dancers across her bedroom ceiling. The perspiration coating her body, sticking her skin to his gave her a delicious sense of oneness that mirrored penetration the way a blurred film muted an image and created a kind of beauty quite different than the original. For this instant in time he was hers.

Except even that was only an illusion born of sexual satisfaction. He wasn't hers. If anything, she was his with no reciprocity worked into the equation. She had just proven it to him ... one more time.

She didn't even have an excuse. One minute it seemed they had been standing in the kitchen, the next Craig had lifted her up and the rest was history. Their history. Something that she still believed had begun as a good history.

Passion between them in the first year of their marriage was a constant, like the pilot light on a water heater. It never went out, was always there with them as a tingling of skin, the soft beat of the heart. Not invasive. Pervasive. Just there beneath the surface where the slightest breeze could fan it into a flare of activity, often at the most unexpected times.

He shifted next to her, the flesh of his hip parting from hers with a small sucking sound, the warmth of contact replaced by a sudden chill. Above her, tree shadows swayed and shifted, figures merging and separating, a metaphor for their relationship and just as mindless.

With a slow caution she turned her head, wanting to see Craig's face but the movement was too much. His eyes snapped opened, his head tilted toward hers and he kissed her, his lips soft, almost spongy. In so many ways Craig had been the ideal husband.

Always he was interesting, exciting, a good conversationalist, and a perceptive lover. He set the bar so high she had never met anyone who had tempted her for more than a passing moment. Except for Mac.

She rolled against the man who was still her husband, wanting more from him. This was when they once had shared their most intimate thoughts. Now was the time to begin a conversation. Just a sort of tentative probing to find out what he was thinking. He had, after all, been the one to initiate everything that had happened today. He had invited her on the outing. He'd spent the day evading any references to divorce. And, this. She'd done nothing to prompt it. Had she?

Perhaps he did want a reconciliation. Even Craig, who Arnie had sometimes described as having "the sexual self-control of an alley cat," would not have made love to her just to stop divorce proceedings or at least not such passionate yet tender love. Surely he had felt what she had.

Through her nose, pressed against the base of his neck, she could feel the throb of pulse, smell the lingering odor of aftershave and sex. The skin there, less than an inch from her eyes, had aged, had roughened since she'd last done this. She reached up to touch the flesh along his jaw line, feeling how it had begun to sag. He would soon develop jowls, a reminder that with age might come wisdom or at least a change of focus. Her grandmother could be wrong. Maybe there really was a future to think about.

She could take a Washington-based job. Craig could move back here, rent out the condo. In fact, if he did, Craig could use the rental income on his condo to pay for a place in Wyoming. He'd said he was thinking of reestablishing residency in Wyoming's income tax-free environment. A home in central Wyoming was far from her own preference, but Casper was where he'd grown up and still had ties. Plus there was his idea of retiring and going into politics. A nice cabin could be a home base and a permanent residence. The Georgetown house could become a second home. Perhaps it would prove a good investment after all.

Craig eased his arm out from under her head. Air touched more of her damp skin, chilling it. A reminder of reality. Craig would give up his bachelor pad condo when hell froze over. The future together? Only in her dreams.

She opened her mouth as he held his wrist above their heads and consulted his watch. "Christ, look at the time! We both have early hours tomorrow, which means I'm going to have to get moving. Want to share a shower first? God, it's hot in here." He swung his feet and legs off the bed, sitting up, shaking his arm to restore circulation. "You've got a damn heavy head, woman. Must be you've been working your brain muscles."

Regan closed her eyes. She heard the impersonality of his words. They could have been aimed at anyone. Were meant to restore distance. She recognized the tone and the intent. Craig wanted to file this afternoon under the heading of "impulsive behavior." Bitterness clogged her chest. Bile rose in her throat. If she were lucky, he'd term it a "farewell fuck" and leave her alone in the future.

Christ. She turned her head toward the window to hide her burning cheeks. What if she'd been dumb enough, naïve enough to voice even one of her thoughts? Or had Craig guessed them? Really. It was just sex, he'd say. Don't build Rome on a mouse turd, he'd say.

She tried to swallow the acid, but her throat held a lump of disappointment. Even her mouth burned. She had to blink. Indifference was the key.

"You generated the heat, my friend," she managed a chuckle, wondering if he could smell the bile on her breath, turning her head away to keep the smell from him and to hide the tell-tale flush. See? Her tone was exactly right. She could play this game. "Anyway, the thermostat's haywire. That's what happens when you shut up a place. Things go wrong."

"Tell Hadija. She'll get a repairman in."

"Right." She sat up, thrusting her legs over her side of the bed, taking deep breaths until her complexion returned to normal, then followed him into the bathroom and let him soap her back. She focused on the signs of aging in his body. Craig was going to turn into one of those pathetic elderly Lotharios and could kiss goodbye to hopes of a post-CIA political career. The Wyoming voters with their bone-deep conservatism might conceivably overlook Craig's marital record but not his continued womanizing.

Regan's secure phone rang, a traditional ring, ring, ring sound that easily penetrated the shower noise. It had to be the duty officer. It had to be a crisis to warrant a Sunday call. Saved by the bell. She stepped out of the shower and grabbed one of her oversized towels.

■ ■ ■ ■ ■

Craig watched her go before closing the shower door, enjoying the way her long legs moved under her tight butt. Elegant, but looks were subjective.

Sometimes it surprised him how many people considered her beautiful.

Which didn't change anything. She wasn't. She was striking. She was stunning. Those eyes above high, flat model's cheeks. Well, she didn't have much for breasts, had an athlete's figure, was really too tall.

He lifted his chest to the spray and rinsed off the accumulated suds.

As much as he appreciated her, admired her professional competence, and even loved her, he didn't want a reconciliation. What he wanted was the appearance of one. He wanted the word to spread of husband and wife sharing quality time together before their separate careers sent them in different directions one more time. Through the steamy glass, he could see Regan's outline as she pulled on a bathrobe.

The ethics of the situation might be a bit hazy, but he'd been right. There was really no reason why he shouldn't enjoy Regan until she went back to Tunisia. One had to deplore the circumstances, yet it wouldn't pay to give people the impression that he lacked stability, and a divorce action would definitely remind everyone of his marital history. Who knew. It could be the make-or-break factor when the White House looked at D/CIA candidates. And it wouldn't be for long, plus it wouldn't hurt Regan.

Water streamed over his head, straightening the curls in his hair, drawing it into strings over his forehead. The sex had been good proving just how much a little deceit adds to a relationship. Gives it that ounce of tension and uncertainty. Makes it more interesting and let him forget the core truth that Regan would never admit ... but she had a version of an Electra thing going. She'd married him to get a father as well as a lover.

He rolled his shoulders. She'd never divorce him of her own free will any more than she'd think of divorcing her own father. If hers had lived.

Nice that the water straightened out his mind as easily as it straightened his hair.

He reached for the hot water tap and raised the level. Hot.

Hot. That's what Arnie had said early this morning, "God damn hot here," meaning both the weather and the climate of violence. Craig had caught him in the midst of the evacuation. In a few words, Arnie had informed Craig that they'd packed up the essential Hayburner hardware and programs after working a deal with the Egyptians. He'd be setting up a temporary shop at an unidentified location in the Western Desert. The only fly in the ointment from Arnie's point of view was one Craig could solve for him. "I'm working with Egyptian military intelligence," he'd said, "and they want a formal agreement with the Agency before they'll do more than let me across the border. That means I need Thomas' signature, and I need it on Monday."

"Egypt? What in the hell are you talking about. We agreed you'd come back here."

"Plans change."

"Not mine. Have you talked to Thomas?"

"Stubborn son of a bitch. He's on his way out but won't budge an inch. Even with his resignation practically on the President's desk, he says he wants Hayburner in Washington. But it's not a problem. By Monday ..." The call had been interrupted by static, then cut off.

Craig turned off the water and stepped out. He didn't need to hear more. It'd been obvious to him for months that Arnie intended to ease control of Hayburner out of Washington's hands and solely into his own. Now Arnie was going to gamble everything by removing the essential elements from the system and transporting them to what he considered a safe haven in Egypt—safe because of his own relationship with the Egyptian intelligence services. Once the situation in Libya stabilized, he would return. He had to. He needed the data center.

The temptation was to let Arnie play the game out then step in and grab Hayburner back. The danger was the system's vulnerability while away from its protected compound. Arnie would be gambling on secrecy as his best defense … secrecy and, possibly, his old networks in Egypt where he'd been chief of station once upon a time. But Arnie'd proved his judgment was impaired.

Steam hadn't fogged up the mirrors, and Craig could see his reflection from several angles. He didn't look bad considering he'd turned fifty-four on his last birthday. Retirement age if he wanted it. Still. Good muscle tone. Flat belly. Bronze skin.

He reached for a towel. No. If he was going to run the CIA, he had new priorities. He'd have to stop thinking of Alex Wentworth as his friend, as invincible. Alex Wentworth was some sort of unrecognizable creation possibly with psychopathic tendencies. Someone—namely one Craig Montrose—had let Arnie's cancer-ridden brain run away with both of them and would have to put an end to it. Or, maybe, that'd be a job for Regan. Keep this all in the family. Under wraps. Who else could he trust? She could … . No. The Brits were the answer, but he'd have to go to London, himself, to be sure of getting them on board. Afterwards he'd run down to Cairo and retrieve both Hayburner and Arnie. Not tomorrow. The White House meetings came first. But Tuesday.

The door opened. Regan stood there, fully dressed. She had a backpack over one shoulder. Her words were quick and almost disjointed. "I've got to go. A problem in Tunis. Help yourself to anything you need. I'll talk to Hadija on my way out. She can fly back when things are a bit more settled there. Would you drive her to the airport when the time comes?"

"Sure but—"

"Got to go, buddy." She came close, gave him a quick kiss on the cheek and left.

"God damn it," he said to the empty doorway. "God damn it to hell!"

CHAPTER NINETEEN
Tunis

The familiar dual-lane highway led from Habib Bourguiba airport past sprawling compounds and high-rise apartment blocks with glimpses of the lake beyond. White walls showed as rain-shrouded specters behind rows of winter-tattered eucalyptus and bougainvillea. Despite the weather and the suicidal traffic, Regan relaxed into the familiarity of the drive. Traffic thinned where the road turned toward the coast and took her on and past Carthage's Roman ruins and French villas with their daily quota of tourist buses and street-side vendors until, ahead, she could see the Bay of Tunis beyond more ruins and villas. Out there on the water mini-rainstorms randomly chased among white caps and along noisy rows of waves.

Her destination was La Marsa and an automotive garage that the Baralguibas had opened with CIA money as a cover for surveillance activities. She needed to talk to Bashir before facing her official problems. Because the killing hadn't stopped as she'd learned at Frankfurt airport. A copy of the *Herald Tribune* she'd picked up stuck out of her tote now, open to an article on a terrorist bombing of a Thames houseboat. George Tendale was dead.

George. He'd come into the station after the Hammamet shooting, but she hadn't been there. And their last email exchange had been about his digital notepad. Now where would she send it? To his executor?

Not his partner ... Lionel something ... who'd been killed with him. Not his business partner, Mustafa Karim. But the Libyan'd be wanting his share of whatever George had left. As would the Tunisians who'd be putting their lawyers to work to make sure they got full control of that Cumulus project.

She drove on and in short order was sipping a cup of coffee and listening to Bashir's report on events during her absence.

He'd had surveillance on Mustafa Karim but had nothing of any particular interest to report except there'd been a flurry of calls and messages from Karim's villa to Libya that morning—content unknown.

As for al-Salan sightings? She'd given Bashir the entire CIA mugbook on al-Salan, but no one looking like the people pictured in the book had been sighted around either Karim's villa in Sousse or her Sidi Bou Said home. Bashir did have confirmation that Abdul-Ghaffar al-Din had been wounded and had disappeared off the radar, was probably back in Libya, maybe heading for Benghazi to get a piece of the action there.

Also, Bashir's Uncle Daud wanted to see her. There was important information from Libya she would want to see immediately.

"Tomorrow," she said. "Today is impossible. But, ask him to put the Libyan information together and send it via steganography. Okay?"

She left La Marsa reluctantly, her mood having nothing to do with the weather which seemed to be settling down to a steady rainfall, the vagrant storm clouds having closed ranks and settled down on the metropolitan area.

Chance Norris appeared in her office door before she had time to take off her rain gear.

He closed the door behind her and, without greeting said, "I didn't sign up to handle hysterical women or provide advice to the lovelorn. Which is why you're the God-damned acting chief of station ... not me. They don't have enough money to pay me to do your job. But, here I am."

"How was your meeting with the Tunisians on the Saharan business?"

"Ever try spitting into the wind?"

"Not fun, huh?" She sat down behind her desk and fired up her computer.

"I'm well into my spiel ... you know. What Headquarters said to say ... about how there's bound to be recidivism when you try something as tough as reforming committed mujahidin, and how we were reliably informed that they'd kidnapped the Saharan chief of security ... and, ah, shit." His voice wandered away into nothing, and he dropped his bulk into an aluminum-framed chair. He just fit.

"And?" She typed in her password at the prompt.

"And they had photos of this guy who's supposed to have been kidnapped standing next to this bullet-pocked Mercedes, an automatic rifle over his shoulder."

"Hmm."

"Yeah. I didn't have anything to say, either." He'd been staring at his hands. Now, he looked up at her. "So? You read my report about Tiffany?"

"This report?" She picked up a single piece of paper that sat in the middle of her desk. Under it was a second paper with a blue "Immediate" precedence sticker attached. She glanced at both and said, "I just sat down. So. No. Obviously, I haven't."

"Well. Read it." Placing a hand on each of the chair arms, he hefted himself up and, without another word, opened the door and lumbered out. Heavy footfalls continued across the common room, ending with the sound of his office door closing.

But how bad could it be?

A young woman had succumbed to the charms of a handsome foreigner and ... shock and horror ... discovered he was interested in more than sex and her scintillating personality. Disillusion and a broken heart followed. A lesson had been learned—the hard way.

■ ■ ■ ■ ■

Regan picked up the report. She already knew the plot line. Here was the story of one of the most common ways a woman could screw up a life and the worst way to destroy a clandestine career.

No one wakes up one morning deciding to trash their jobs and betray the trust of friends and colleagues. No one. But add the cliché of sexual passion and the equation changed.

Regan began to read.

It took less than four seconds for her eyes to stop and her lips to move. Aloud, she said, "Oh, no." She reread, and words that weren't on the page pushed through those that were—words like compromise, betrayal, and treason. Rain dripped off the overhang beyond her window. A burst of laughter came from the common room beyond her office. Her station had been compromised; she'd been blindsided. Outside her office, someone worked the cypher on the station's main door, the click of numbers loud. Finally, fingers nerveless, she let the paper fall.

No wonder Chance's short message to Washington had contained only a sketchy outline of the problem and a suggestion that Regan return to post. No wonder he hadn't waited while she read his report. This was a CIA station chief's worst nightmare. Chance's closed office door spoke volumes.

The station's intelligence assistant, Dawn Mason, was at her desk in the big room that served as the station's reception area and lounge. The space held a high counter behind which Dawn labored plus several comfortable chairs, a coffee table covered with a week's worth of local newspapers, and a shelf holding coffee-making materials. Large, curtained windows filled the wall behind Dawn's desk while the other walls sported framed copies of Western masterpieces by Remington and Moran—prints Regan had hung as replacements for travel posters.

Millie Benson, a tall and regal-looking reports officer, sat on a couch under a Moran painting of an erupting geyser. Dawn leaned against the counter that shielded her desk. Both held cups of coffee and looked up when Regan appeared in her doorway.

"Well? What's the verdict?" Millie asked. There was no question as to what she meant. The entire station—Dawn, the Ops Support Assistant, Millie Benson, the communicators, and the case officers—would all have heard about the contents of the single-page report right down to the last punctuation mark.

"She's pulled us all into deep shit," Dawn said. "Hasn't she."

Regan looked from one to the other.

Millie said, "Listen. I had dinner at the Italian military attaché's place last night, and everyone there knew about the elopement. There was a lot of guessing thanks to—"

"Talk," Dawn finished Millie's thought, her tone agitated. "Thanks to the fact that Tiffany likes to talk, so the whole dip community has heard about the affair. You get a lot of snide comments, because Tiffany's cover's never been very good. She likes to be known as a spy. And that Iraqi? You should hear what they say about him."

"We'll discuss this later." Regan looked from one woman to the other, then said to Dawn, "Get Tiffany. In my office."

"The thing is," Dawn said and set her coffee cup on the counter behind her, some of the liquid slopping out. "I need to know, Regan." Her round face usually wore a smile. "Tiff's in denial, but the rest of us understand." Now, there were white spots alongside her nose and her lips were turned down. "I brought my kids to Tunisia when it was a nice safe post. We stayed through the revolution. But this? That's what we were just talking about. If Tiff told that Iraqi asshole what my job is here? I could have every crazy in Tunisia stalking me and my kids. I've been thinking I ought to pull Maddy and Justin out of school. At least until we know what's what."

Dawn had once been an attractive, pixie-like woman, but after an unhappy divorce she'd started packing on the weight. Now, topping out at 186 pounds on a 5'4" frame, she looked more blocky than obese, treating her weight like armor. Sex, she'd told Regan, was what happened to other people. It wasn't going to foul up her life again.

"It's not just Dawn and her kids," Millie picked up where Dawn had stopped. "I mean we don't even get danger pay, and no one's talking about it even now, even though al-Salan's got a cell here and they've actually attacked you. But at least risks go with your job. Me? I'm an analyst and I write. I use my brain, and my brain tells me we might wake up to find not just al-Salan but other mainstream al-Qaeda elements targeting all of us ... thanks to Tiffany. What's wrong with her, anyway." It wasn't a question but a condemnation.

She added. "You've got to get her out of here. In fact, we've been thinking you should send all the dependents home until we know what's what."

Dawn said, "We're glad you're here. I'm not going to criticize Chance, but you've got to get us in front of this. Which brings up that Immediate. I tell you, frankly. If you're leaving, I'm leaving."

"Right," Regan said in a tone of finality. Millie and Dawn were talking themselves into a panic and trying their best to pull her in with them. Behind Millie's head, the Moran geyser shot scalding water into a blue sky until the spume disintegrated in clouds of steam.

Appropriate.

Which wasn't to say that the women didn't have legitimate grounds for concern. But just how worried should they be? They didn't know. Neither did she. Not yet.

She continued, "After I talk to Tiffany, we'll have a staff meeting, and we'll work this out together. Until then, let's just take a deep breath and step back. We have time. I guarantee it."

■ ■ ■ ■ ■

Two minutes more or less later, Tiffany Borgstrand knocked on Regan's open door. "Glad you're back. You wanted to see me?" Her voice sounded as though she'd dropped by for a social visit.

"Come in and close the door."

Regan said nothing more until the twenty-five-year-old woman had seated herself, positioning her feet together, pulling her skirt over her knees. She clasped her hands and lay them in her lap; held her back straight and her head erect. Besides looking whip thin, young and attractive and slightly defiant, she'd clearly taken pains with her appearance. The blonde hair, which often fell down her back in long straggly lines, was tied up in a knot at the base of her neck in imitation of the style Regan normally wore. Her blue eyes were clear, her lids brushed with a violet tone, her pale eyebrows and lashes darkened. She'd added a bit of blush to her cheeks to give her pale face some color and the illusion of more width. Finally, she'd used a gloss to fatten her thin lips.

"I'm hoping you'll understand what happened. I've learned my lesson," Tiffany said.

Regan leaned forward, wanting to feel some sympathy, perhaps because they shared so much of the same background. Both of them were from the Rocky Mountain west. Both had gone east to college—Regan to the University of Virginia, Tiffany to Columbia. Both had passed through the Agency's endless batteries of psychological and physical testing and survived the polygraph and intensive security scrutiny. They'd endured the crucible of tradecraft and associated training and done interim assignments at Langley.

Tiffany had come straight to Tunis after that and, here they were, six months later. It'd taken the girl five months and one week to lie down and wallow in that most classic of espionage tricks—the honey trap. Right out of the gate, essentially, she'd been caught up in a situation as old as the hills and as ancient as the profession. As Millie had said, "What's wrong with her?"

It hadn't started badly. Tiffany had reported meeting an Iraqi diplomat—one Regan knew to be American-educated and too handsome for his own good. The station's mug book of local diplomats and routine trace queries to Headquarters and Baghdad revealed nothing negative. The young man appeared to be exactly what the Iraqi Embassy said he was, a junior economics officer. An inquiry of the American Embassy economics section produced only a shrug. "Not too smart but an asset at parties," one of the econ officers said.

"No one's interested in recruiting Iraqi dips," Regan remembered telling Tiffany. "Move on to something else. He's a waste of time."

Then the girl had appeared in the Stuart Weitzman shoes, and the truth about the affair had come out, and there'd been that earlier confrontation—the day of Arnie's death. Tiffany's hair had lain in untidy straggles down her back then and, Regan also remembered, Tiffany'd tangled her fingers in a long strand as she spat out her defense, then flipped them free in a way that drew the eye.

Now with rain splattering against the windows Regan bridged her hands and rested her chin on them. Tiffany had ignored what advice Regan had given her. Worse, she'd violated Agency protocol on attachments to foreign nationals, guidance embodied in the Code of Conduct. It had been part of her terms of employment and, like everyone else, she'd sworn to abide by it. Instead?

"I mean," Tiffany's words rushed now. Her voice came a bit louder than it might have if the wind hadn't come up, rolling rain sideways across the Lac de Tunis and slamming it into the buildings along the shore. "I mean I did wonder when I first met Mahfouz if he might be an intelligence officer, maybe, but that wouldn't have been a conflict, would it? I mean we organized the INIS ... Iraqi intelligence. They're like practically part of the Agency, aren't they? Of course, they're Sunnis and Mahfouz is Shiite, so that's why I didn't worry about an intelligence connection. Not really. I mean I knew about the MOS, but it's so small no one pays it much attention, do they? They're just a bunch of Shiite amateurs playing at spy games."

Outside the noise softened as the wind shifted.

"Well ... ." Tiffany glanced at Regan's face, then her eyes flicked away. She stared at the curtains as though she could see through them and the rain to the lake beyond. She knew the cardinal rule of intelligence work. *There is no such thing as a friendly foreign intelligence service.* And it's corollary: *Never underestimate the enemy.* The CIA often trained other services, helped other services, and worked closely with them. Alliances and fruitful collaboration were important, but rarely was anyone in the business stupid enough to lose sight of the fact that other countries have other priorities and a friend one day could be an enemy the next.

Regan waited, wanting Tiffany to admit that her justifications were ludicrous.

"Well ... you know what I mean." Tears flooded Tiffany's eyes, enlarging them. "It was so horrible," she rushed to change the subject. "And it had seemed so wonderful. We went sailing. We cycled. We flew to Algiers for lunch one day. It was so romantic I had to say yes when he proposed even though we had to keep it secret because of his family, but we decided to fly to Prague and have a civil ceremony then drive to

Switzerland for our honeymoon. After that we'd come back here as man and wife and face our respective embassies."

"And you had to do this immediately because …?"

"He didn't stampede me, if that's what you're implying," the girl flared back, reminding Regan of her attitude during their last meeting. Was this all a waste of time?

Catching herself, Tiffany said. "Well, maybe he did. A little. He said he was being recalled to Baghdad, and if we didn't marry right then we might never have the chance again, but once we were married everyone would have to accept it."

The heat kicked on with a muffled roar, pushing air through vents. The peacock feathers stirred. The temperature outside would be falling with the rain and the approaching night. Regan got up to turn on the overhead lights. After returning to her chair, she said, "I know I wasn't here during much of this whirlwind romance, but you failed to do the mandatory reporting to Headquarters. You deliberately violated the Code of Conduct. You didn't have to talk to Chance, but you could have. You could have gone to him with this and asked his advice."

"Oh, really," Tiffany's eyes dried. She wiped her cheeks with a hand. Her voice said she found Regan's suggestion ridiculous. "You know he doesn't like to be bothered about personnel things and, besides, I knew we'd be back before anyone missed us and started to worry. I thought you'd all be mad you weren't invited to the wedding and that you'd be losing an officer because of course I'd return to Iraq with him but otherwise—"

Regan held up a hand. As with Tiffany's comment about the INIS being 'practically part of the Agency' or the MOS being so small it must be harmless, this was pure blather.

Regan tapped the report in front of her, "Let's get back to the Shiite thing. When did he tell you about his MOS employment?"

"Oh, God, Regan. I couldn't have been more shocked when he said he wanted me to prove my love for him by coming back to Tunis, not resigning but working in place for his service. It was at our wedding breakfast. My world came apart over the newspapers, coffee and croissants. Isn't that just so unbelievable?"

"Unbelievable."

"I hoped he meant we should both work for the INIS, at first, and said that was silly. Why should I? Our organizations are allies. We're both working for the same things and have the same goals. There'd be no problem about my continuing my own career, I said, if he just wanted us to stay in Tunis.

"But, no, and that's when he told me. MOS, he said. Not INIS. He said the CIA had an unjustified grudge against the MOS because it was an independent intelligence service and was Shiite where the INIS is Sunni and completely under the thumb of the CIA. He said by working together and working secretly we could change that and bring our two services and governments closer together on much more meaningful levels. A couple of years of this here in Tunis, and we would live happily ever after. The thing was, besides being the right thing to do, we had no choice because he had no money of his own." Dramatic tears spilled down her cheeks.

"He'd borrowed everything he'd spent on me, he said, and done it because he loved me, but now we'd have to pay it back. He said we had no choice." She found a tissue and dabbed at her cheeks.

"Oh, Regan," she wailed. "One of my classmates used almost exactly the same words in a recruitment pitch for his final exercise at the Farm. He'd set up the same kind of scenario. It was like déjà vu. Except déjà vu in a nightmare. A nightmare over coffee and croissants. I couldn't believe it was happening to me. In real life." She raised the tissue to dab around her eyes, then stared at the mascara on the tissue as though the black smudges were letters that spelled out a different ending to her story.

Her thin lips worked over the next words before they came out. Gradually, she told the rest. There would be no honeymoon. Instead they would fly to Baghdad for a few days of training.

"What happened then?"

More of the story dribbled out. Tiffany had then made an excuse to leave the table, went out the back door, caught a cab to the airport, and flew back to Tunis where she'd spent the night in the Embassy.

"Good." Regan said. The girl had clearly left out a lot, but what she had said provided a framework and a place to begin.

Obviously encouraged by Regan's one word, Tiffany said, "I learned a huge lesson, Regan. Not that I ever did anything any other woman of my age wouldn't do, and I got out before it went too far. I really did nothing really wrong. Really. Actually, I'm thinking we might be able to turn the tables on the MOS."

"Oh?"

Tiffany responded to the negative sound of the 'Oh.' She leaned forward and rushed on, all enthusiasm now, a saleswoman making a pitch. "I know better than to let them think they recruited me. But we could string them along, get them to send people to Tunis to talk to me, find out what they want. I mean I already know some of this, but ... well ... I could continue to be with Mahfouz, and he might even be persuaded to work for us. Not as an agent, of course, but if he left the MOS he could be a consultant or something. I've got more ideas, too."

And there they were. The girl's face beamed. Her eyes held hope.

She must've spent the last twenty-four hours justifying and rewriting what had happened until it didn't seem so bad. Whatever had really occurred, though, had scared the shit out of her.

A pen Regan had just picked up fell from her fingers. It hit the edge of her desk with a click, teetered, then went over, landing on the carpet with a little plop. There it lay. Whatever had occurred during that breakfast had put the fear of God into her. So much so she'd run for the airport without even returning to her room for her things. A girl like Tiffany loved her things—those Stuart Weitzman pumps, for example.

Nothing she'd said so far even began to explain that. Nor did it explain what had changed. One minute she was afraid, yet now she wanted to roll back time, find a way to continue the relationship.

Regan let a hand fall on Chance's report and looked away, angry with the girl's vulnerability but fighting pity for her naiveté and understanding all too well the dynamics that had made it possible.

Someone—Dawn, probably—turned on the station sound

system and the gentle, introductory notes of Resphigi's "Pines of Rome" came faintly through a pair of speakers. The rain seemed to have stopped for the moment. At least it wasn't splattering against the windows.

"Let's back up and talk about what happened before you got to Vienna," Regan said after a long pause. "You said something about thinking you've done nothing wrong."

"I really didn't, you know."

Regan ran a finger down Chance's brief report. "If I'm reading this right," she said and read aloud.

Tiffany had done nothing but gossip about station personnel with her lover, naming names. She'd done nothing but talk about her work because she and her lover "shared common goals." While sharing, she'd compromised classified information. Who knew how much.

"Here's the bottom line," Regan said. "Your Iraqi? I understand that you invested a lot in the relationship, but you'll have to come to grips with a core truth here. He developed you just like your classmate at the farm developed his target. Whatever you think Mahfouz might feel for you and whatever you see in him, it's over. He treated you like a commodity, the way you would treat an agent candidate."

"You can't pretend to know—"

"Tiffany. Grow up. We're not in kindergarten here," Regan snapped the words, suddenly out of patience. "This isn't corporate America. You're part of a war effort, the war against terror. You're in your country's service, and you're under orders. First order is, you can't see your Iraqi again. Not now. Not ever. You'll have to go back to Washington and face a review board and possible legal action. Your little affair may seem innocent to you, but it's going to cost and cost us a lot. We'll have to bring in people on temporary duty to meet your agents. We'll probably be moving some staffers around. Think about how this is going to affect Dawn and Millie and—."

The expression on the girl's face hardened, became willful and determined. Streaks of mascara, which might have seemed comical under other circumstances, aged her and made her appear threatening. She interrupted. "I told you. None of this is my fault," she snapped, her lips visibly stretching and thinning under the lip gloss. With no break at all, her words rushed on. "I acted in good faith. If there's fault here and if anyone should face a review board, it's you. Everyone says so. I'm young, and you should have helped me. You were supposed to give me guidance. You should've told me to stop seeing him. If you'd told me not to go to dinner with him, I wouldn't've. But you're never here. You're always out. Even George said that you could spend more time in the station. Besides that you set a bad example." The girl's voice rose; her cheeks were bright red but her eyes were dry. "I mean who do you think you are, preaching at me, acting all holy as though you're the Virgin Mary and not an adulte... ." Her voice trailed away as she realized she had gone too far.

Regan smothered her surprise—shock, actually—at the transformation and the attack. Blackmail now? What the woman was actually saying was: 'Report the extent of what happened, and I'll take you down with me.' Even now Tiffany didn't understand the train of events her actions had set in motion, had no conception that Regan had no latitude here. She ... .

Just a minute. What had the girl said? George? George who?

Regan's eyes dropped to the newspaper sticking out of her shoulder bag. She could see the words, **Thames Bombing**. She leaned forward and examined Tiffany's narrow face, looked into the big blue eyes, and said, "George who?"

Tiffany blinked. She stared at the curtains again. One hand rose and fluttered about until it reached the wrap on her neck. Even then it didn't settle. Tears returned to spill down her cheeks. She said, her voice choked now, a hint of fear there. "None of this is my fault. I told you. I did the right thing. I've reported everything that happened."

"Everything? You met George Tendale, didn't you?" Regan hoped she was wrong. Her hands clenched into fists, her wrist complained, and she prayed there wouldn't be a connection. Yet, she knew from Tiffany's reaction that there was.

"No. Absolutely not."

"You met George and told your lover about him. Isn't that so?"

"I can't believe this. It's worse than a nightmare. I didn't come back to Tunis to be interrogated. What I should've done is go straight back to Langley. Even Chance understood me. But you know you're at fault." Tiffany was sobbing again. "That's why you're beating up on me."

"Who is George?"

"You should've been there for me. Even now, you're just jealous. You can't see that this could all be made to be a really important operation. You think you're such big stuff with your intelligence medal, your lousy one-off operation to capture that terrorist, but you don't want to let anyone else shine."

"Actually," Regan said, not listening to all this obfuscation. Her heartbeat had accelerated. She could smell the girl's fear. She reached down and pulled her copy of the *Herald Tribune* out of her bag and slapped it down on the desk. She said. "You told your friend Mahfouz about meeting George Tendale, didn't you? You told him all about how George was the Agency's best cyberwar contractor. Then George was murdered. His house boat blew up and he and his partner with it."

"I didn't know—" The girl spoke without even looking at the newspaper. She'd already read the article. She knew the content.

Regan said, "This was the newspaper Mahfouz was reading during your wedding breakfast. You talked about it. That's why you ran away from him. You thought the Iraqis killed George because of something you told them. You thought you'd become an accessory to murder. You thought they'd kill you, too, if you didn't do what they said. You were scared to death, Tiffany."

Regan brought her hand down hard on the newspaper. "Time to come clean, Tiffany. What did your lover want to know about George? And what about my meetings with Karim? What'd you say about them?"

Tiffany stood up so fast her chair tipped and threatened to fall over backwards. "I don't have to sit here and be insulted by you.

You're a lousy supervisor and not a fit person to lecture me on my morals. Everyone knows you're having an affair with a gun runner, so don't you dare presume to tell me what I should and should not do and I'm leaving." Her arms were stiff at her sides, her fists clenched, her eyes glistening but no longer with tears.

Regan sighed and sat back. God! Had the Iraqi MOS gotten wind of Hayburner? And maybe Tiffany was right. Maybe the MOS did kill George. Until Tiffany opened up, she wouldn't know. And what else had the young woman precipitated? But Karim and al-Salan? No. Any connection would be indirect.

Tiffany had the door open.

Regan said, "Chance was right. The MOS lost you, and they'll want to reclaim you if only for what could prove a fatal interrogation."

"That's ridicu—"

Regan tapped the cable with the blue sticker that sat next to Chance's report on Tiffany's problems. She said, "Headquarters has no clue about the extent of your problems, but they want both of us at Langley. We'll take separate flights. That said, I'd like to be sure you arrive in one piece, so you'll travel either with a federal marshal or an embassy security officer."

"I won't—"

"If you cooperate, you won't return to Tunis. Your household effects will be packed and shipped for you, and we'll pay your airfare. Once in Washington, if you do return there, you'll face a formal hearing. Depending on those results you may be charged in Federal court. Right now, I couldn't say which because I have no way of assessing the damage you've caused."

"That's—" Tiffany's eyes had grown huge. This time the tears that poured over her cheeks and into her mouth were not pretty and all too obviously real.

"That's called treason, Tiffany. Now, let's look at what happens if you walk out that door. First, your employment will cease as of today, your salary and allowances pro-rated, and you will be asked to vacate the house you now occupy. Second, your diplomatic status will end; your diplomatic passport cancelled. I think you can assume the Tunisians will ask you to leave country. But, if it's any consolation, I don't think you'll have to worry about any such thing because, before the Tunisians kick you out, the MOS will pick you up and ship you to some hole in Iraq. After that ... ." Regan shrugged.

"But I didn't—"

"But. Come back, sit down and tell me absolutely every word spoken between you and your MOS lover. Afterwards, if I'm satisfied you've told me the truth. Then, we'll see."

■ ■ ■
CHAPTER TWENTY
Sidi Bou Said, Tunisia

Long strands of Tiffany's hair had come free and fell over her face, partially obscuring smeared mascara which several tissues had failed to remove.

Regan felt drained and near despair at what she'd heard in the past hour, but they still had a long way to go. Shifting in her chair, she propped her elbows next to a digital recorder that would transmit their exchange direct to a variety of recipients at Langley.

There, they would listen to how Tiffany had built what would become her own private hell with her own two hands. From the beginning the junior officer had known that the world she'd chosen to inhabit was fraught with dangers and filled with people who would chew her up and spit her out just because they could. She'd known her love life would be necessarily limited and selective and ringed with peril.

It would've been bad enough that she'd just walked herself into a recruitment pitch, but her gullibility, willfulness, and self-centered actions had compromised her colleagues and people she called friends. In the name of "love" and "sharing," she'd committed a long list of offenses Regan could never forgive.

"But I never, ever mentioned anything about my agents," Tiffany said now, pulling on a hank of hair. "You believe me, don't you? That counts for something, doesn't it? And I was never, ever under surveillance. I ran good SDR's. I know."

"Let's talk about your last meeting with RZFINDER," Regan turned back to her computer monitor and keyed for Tiffany's contact report on the meeting. "It says here that you … ," and she began another round of questions. Once Tiffany was back in Washington, she would be questioned intensively. Right now, Regan needed a broad picture of the damage she'd have to cauterize.

Two hours later, Regan still didn't believe much of what Tiffany said. "Your contact report says you'd parked your station car in the garage of the Menzah apartment building before getting it for that last meeting, but now you say—"

"You can't hold me to details," the girl flared back, interrupting. "You've confused me. I'm just so tired. Can't we stop now?"

"Soon. We'll stop soon. Let's go back to where you picked up … ."

The sound of the door opening made both of them look around. Gwen stood there. "It's getting late, Regan, and everyone's waiting to hear what's going to happen next. Are you about to wrap this up or can you take a break and talk to us?"

Tiffany jumped to her feet, slid past Gwen, and disappeared.

"Well," Gwen said, watching her go. "I guessed I screwed that up, didn't I."

"No." Regan pushed herself to her feet. She could hear the sound of multiple voices coming from the common room. "Is everyone here?"

Gwen nodded.

"Then, let's get to it."

Tiffany had confessed to talking freely about her station colleagues with her lover, and the people she'd compromised needed to know it. "I was sure he would keep my confidences," Tiffany wept. In essence she'd gifted the anti-American, Iranian-supported Iraqis with a who's who of the CIA presence in Tunis. She might as well have sent the information direct to Teheran. She might as well have proclaimed those same names to al-Qaeda and Hizballah and every other terrorist and radical Islamic organization operating in the Middle East.

"It wasn't on purpose," Tiffany had rallied to defend herself. "I just talked about people I worked with. That's what people do. They talk about their colleagues and friends. Well. My friends are my colleagues."

George Tendale had been neither friend nor colleague, but Tiffany had talked about him, too.

Holding her wrist against her chest, Regan walked out of her office to be met by a smattering of applause. "Now, we'll find out what's going on," someone said.

Regan took a second to gather herself before facing a room full of worried people. More than just a set of co-workers, they were a family, roped together by bonds of trust, by secrecy, and by the restrictions and limitations of their work. Only with each other could they be themselves, could they talk freely, could they obtain understanding and sympathy.

They would all feel betrayed, uncertain, perhaps afraid.

How to deal with it? How to keep them from overreacting? God. She needed to keep herself from overreacting. It'd be so easy to do.

They were all in their places, sitting in a semi-circle in the same spots they occupied during staff meetings. All except for Tiffany, that was. She usually lounged in a comfortable chair next to the coffee table, twining hair around a finger. Today her seat been taken by Mark Rodher, a gray-haired communicator. His fingers were moving over an iPad screen, probably playing a video game.

The room was as silent as it could be. "Well," Regan began. "It's not been the best day in the world for us."

That understatement was met with a cascade of nervous sound. "You could say so," Joe Marquez muttered. His job was logistics; his territory was regional. Of all of them, thanks to his frequent travel, he might face the most danger from Tiffany's revelations.

"But," Regan plowed on, "it could've been so very much worse if Tiffany hadn't had the courage to face her mistakes and come back to confess them."

No one reacted to that. They waited. So, she summarized what had happened, occasionally looking at Tiffany, who stood alongside the corridor door as though not sure whether to stay and listen or retreat to her cubicle.

Millie, too, had noted Tiffany's presence. When Regan paused, she said, "Why not let Tiffany tell us what she did?"

Everyone turned to stare at the girl. Their faces were not friendly.

Regan thought about it. Tiffany remained silent. Several voices rose in agreement, but there was one audible, "Why? She'd just lie." The voice belonged to Chance. He'd rolled his desk chair into the common room, positioning it where he always did—directly across from Regan.

What was different was the way he looked. The normally taciturn, good-natured man she knew was gone. His arms were tightly crossed over his chest. His chin stuck out. His eyes were hard, his lips so taut they made white marks on the surrounding skin. Did he feel a degree of guilt that he hadn't done more to head this off?

Regan said, "I see the value in your idea, Millie. But we're not at a 'truth and reconciliation' phase here. Our job is to cauterize the damage and move on while Tiffany will go back to Washington. Tomorrow."

She waited to see nods of agreement before going on to practical matters. "This isn't rocket science," she said. "The circumstances have changed for all of us. Tunis was a nice, safe post when you all signed up. Then came the Jasmine Revolution which gave us a new set of security problems. Next, al-Salan showed up, but I think we've got that under control and, anyway, they were just interested in me ... a distinction I could've done without. Now? Well, the MOS will hang us all out there as potential targets for every crazy in the Middle East. If they haven't already. Myself, I'd recommend that those of you with families to protect get out. If you do, I'll make sure that none of you suffer for it. We'll handle it as an emergency evacuation and arrange onward assignments to a safer part of the world as soon as possible."

"Christ!" Chance muttered. "If I had kids, I'd go. But I don't and, anyway, al-Qaeda's probably got my name already. Along with the names of every one of our declared officers in every country in this cotton-pickin' world. I stay."

"I want to stay here, too," Tiffany said. "I'll go back and do penance in Washington or whatever, but I want to finish my tour."

"Oh, shut up and grow up!" Millie snapped. She was on her feet, her eyes angry, her mouth as tight as Chance's. "You'll be lucky if you stay out of jail, which is where I'd put you."

"Millie ... ," Gwen began, but Chance interrupted.

"Millie's right," he said. "And, Regan, with all due respect what you said earlier? About Tiffany deserving credit for coming back? You're full of shit. What she's done to us may not be as bad as it could be, but ... by God ... it's bad enough. You give me a length of rope, and I'd personally—"

Tiffany's eyes almost bulged. With a small shriek, she vanished down the hallway.

Regan held up a hand for silence as everyone seemed to have something to say at once, voices rising over other voices until it seemed every person there was shouting. Her heart pounded in sympathy with the overt anger. She was mad as hell. She, too, wanted to strike out. Yet, this was what she'd feared, this instinct to strike back.

"Please." She stood and banged on Gwen's counter with a stapler.

They stilled, habits of rationality reasserting themselves.

She said, "Yes. We all want to vent. Me, too. But we don't have time. We have decisions to make, and they'll affect every one of you. These aren't easy decisions, but it has to be done."

"Sorry," Chance muttered. He'd jumped to his feet and had remained there during the furor. "It's all so damn stupid." He folded his arms, again, and sat down, rigid still.

"Well, it happened," Millie said, "and we've got to cope. I hope Tiff thinks those damn expensive shoes were worth it."

Dawn shook her head. "I'm not coping. I'm not staying. This's been a great place to work, but ... ." She and her children would be on an aircraft in the morning.

Lennie Johnson, one of the younger communicators and a divorced man whose children were due to visit him for the summer, spoke up then. He, too, had decided to go. "Having the summer with my kids and not having to worry the whole time? Well. I like Tunis and all, but maybe it's time I try someplace else."

No one else volunteered a decision.

The meeting then moved on to a review of personal security, to decide that Mark, the game-playing communicator, should move into the compound—his current house had never been given a security upgrade.

"Guns," Chance said. "We need blanket approval to carry guns."

"Not me," Millie snapped.

"I'll have to think about that," Regan said to Chance. There was a reason that gun-totting approval was given sparingly.

"And danger pay." That suggestion came from Jeff Probst, a swarthy-skinned, slightly effete Reports Officer.

Regan agreed, "I'll ask for a six-month period, then we'll see where we are."

Otherwise, there wasn't much they could do ... except for Mark's house, they'd already implemented all the security upgrades recommended for high risk posts.

Finally, Chance said, "What about you, Regan? We all saw that 'immediate' from Sam ordering you back to Langley. But, I'll tell you in front of everyone here, you shouldn't go. Not only will they scapegoat you over Tiffany, but we need you here to handle the fallout. What we don't need is them sending in someone to run the place who doesn't know squat about us. It's going to be bad enough with the counterintelligence teams we'll have crawling all over us. Right?" He glared around the room.

Regan cut off the chorus of agreement. "I'll talk to Sam," she said.

By now their division chief would've received the digital record of the Tiffany interview. He'd be livid, worried, and ready to chew someone's head off—most likely hers. Like Tiffany, he would see much of what had happened as a management failure. And, when he heard about the station's personnel changes and her promises to staff, he'd be even more angry, if that was possible.

■ ■ ■ ■

She didn't call Sam. She did remain overtime for private meetings with those who wanted to talk to her, discussing their individual decisions and their careers.

Altogether, the day had exhausted her. She wanted to drive mindlessly home but that wasn't possible. She had her own security to consider, nevermind the normal hazards of driving in Tunis. So, she made sure the PLMAJORs were on duty at her house, watched for possible vehicular surveillance, and fought traffic and weather with her windshield wipers turned to their highest setting.

As the Peugeot's headlights swept around the back of the Sidi Bou Said hill, the rain stopped and—almost at the same moment—a PLMAJOR car intercepted her, flashing its lights.

"Good God, what now," she muttered aloud, pulled over, and went back to talk to a pair of Baralguiba cousins. "A Libyan gentleman, Madame," one of them said. "He sits in a government car outside your house. Because it is a government car, we can do nothing but tell you he is there."

"Nothing is good," she said. "You've done exactly the right thing."

It was as the cousins said. A few minutes later she drove past a black Mercedes with a government license plate parked on the street opposite her gate. The windows were tinted, the interior invisible, the body work unscathed. She stopped in front of the gate and honked.

The cousins had followed her up the hill. Now they parked behind the Mercedes and turned off their headlights.

With the usual grinding and shrieking of aged iron fittings, the gates in her courtyard wall swung open, the night guard appearing in the gap. As he did, Mustafa Karim got out of the Mercedes and approached her car.

She rolled down her window, wet air and the smell of seaweed hitting her in the face, "What?"

"We must speak, you and I," he said. If he was put off by her tone, he didn't show it.

The cousins were out of their car, leaning against its wet sides.

The night guard marched to one side of the open gate and waited, back ramrod straight. He was an elderly man whose sole purpose in life, beyond opening and closing gates for the three families that shared the courtyard, was to raise the alarm should there be a burglary attempt.

"This is serious, Regan." Karim had dropped his usual "Madame Regan."

"What is it?"

"There are three things." He didn't lean over to speak but stood as stiff and erect as the guard, his head well above the car's roof, his words spoken to the damp air. Regan had to strain to hear.

"What three things?"

"These are best spoken in private, but we can sit in my vehicle if you will not invite me into your house."

She could smell his signature bad breath and just wanted him gone. Other people did the right thing. When contact was broken, it stayed broken. But not this man. He wouldn't go away. She said, "What do you have on your mind, Mustafa?"

"I do not think you want these things spoken in the street where anyone can hear."

She gripped the steering wheel and stared at the courtyard beyond the open gates. Gas lights flared under their glass covers. A Volvo and a Fiat belonging to her neighbors sat in the vehicle shed that jutted out from one wall. She wanted to park her Volvo next to them. She wanted to go inside, lock her doors, pour a glass of wine, and forget the hours of arrangements for Tiffany's travel and protection, for getting Dawn and her children on their way to Paris in the morning, for writing reports and cables. She would drink her glass of wine in peace, make herself some dinner, and sit at her piano and let her brain relax and, hopefully, develop reasonable courses of action to resolve her problems and her station's problems.

Karim's belt—alligator skin—was at her eye level. He said, "One of these things is the death of my partner, George Tendale, who is killed by your CIA people. Perhaps you do not know this. I can give you names and proofs. The second is that I've heard of your problems with the Iraqi peoples. You will want to learn what is being said, I am sure. The final thing is my virus. I would remind you that it belongs to me. It was my money that developed this weapon. The one you and your Arnold Walker steal from me. Now, the computers that control it have been moved, and we both risk them falling into other hands."

Her chin lifted. An eyebrow rose. The gas lights flickered. The night guard waited. Finally, she spoke to Karim's belt, "The money you keep harping on wasn't yours in the first place but was misappropriated from official Libyan accounts. Even so, Arnie paid you some five million dollars for your cooperation with us. That's a net profit to you of five million. Now, is that all?"

He tilted his head back and stared at the sky.

She put the Peugeot in gear.

"Regan. Madame. Wait." He finally bent down to speak directly to her, and his bad breath hit her square in the nostrils. "About the present location of my virus."

She shied backwards, "Location?"

He stepped away from the car.

She turned off the ignition and got out.

"You do not wish to have me in your home," he said, drawing a pack of cigarettes from an inside pocket of his suit jacket. "You think I am one of Qadhafi's thugs. But this is not so. I only do what is necessary for me and my family to survive." In the light of the lamps set on either side of the gate and a streetlight many yards down the hill, his eyes seemed blacker than usual, his nose straighter, his lips firmer. She was reminded that he was a very handsome man. He lit a cigarette and blew smoke away from her.

She crossed her arms over her chest against the chill of the wet evening air and waited. Craig would want to know what Karim claimed, no matter how preposterous the story. So, she would listen. "You were saying?"

"You want informations from a man you do not respect. But since we are being crass and blunt, I will remind you that no matter how I obtained the twenty millions, they were mine. As for the five millions, I earned these monies. Now, I expect your organization to honor its debts."

All of this was so typically Mustafa Karim. Bait and switch. Make a provocative statement, then demand money. She turned to get back in her car.

He spoke quickly, said, "Your people have stolen my virus. They try to kill me. I have proofs of both of these things. Now, they kill my partner, and with his death I will lose my claim to an interest in the Cumulus project. Cumulus, too, may be lost forever."

"You'll have to see your Tunisian partners about that. Anyway, why're you talking to me?"

"These Tunisians? They have nothing but a new campus, a new

data center, and the people they hire as staff. Without the Cumulus codes, the sensors and other hardware that are manufactured and ready to market are useless. Already, I am called in to explain what they are to do with this massive investment if there will be no codes. Already, they are angry and blame me, as though this is my fault. No, Madame. It is not my fault, and all I want from you is what your people owe me. I want Cumulus codes and my twenty millions." He took a deep drag on his cigarette.

"Right. You want twenty million. I want a good night's sleep." She put her hand on the car's door handle.

She opened the door and started to step into the car.

He put a hand on her arm to stop her, said, "Who else am I to trust, Madame." She froze, whipped her head around, and glared at him.

He pulled his hand back, threw his cigarette away, and spread both hands. Behind him, the end of the cigarette glowed red for a moment against the wet pavement, then went out.

He said, "Always we have difficulties, Madame. If it is not because I wish to smoke in your car as a man is entitled to do, it is because you think I would shoot you. In truth I would not have done so. In truth I am your great admirer and wish only that we can make an alliance."

"Right," she said and got into the driver's seat.

"Madame. We have common enemies."

"You were going to tell me about the computers, the ones you claim were moved," she said and started the car.

"It was the American CIA man who tries to kill us. You and me. And who does kill George Tendale. It is the American named Fould who comes to Tunisia with al-Din. Perhaps he is a renegade. This is what I believe. He steals the computers from Saharan after the evacuation and flees to Cairo. Many know this. Now, we make common cause, Madame. You arrange to pay my twenty millions, and I will deliver this traitor and … ."

She stared up at the Libyan for a moment. Did he realize how incredible his allegations sounded even larded, as they were, with elements of truth? Enough was enough. She drove forward and missed whatever else he might have said. The guard hurried to close the gate behind her.

As she parked the Peugeot, the big gates screeched and clanged together. Next, with a final grinding and clunk, the bolt shot home.

Nat Fould stealing computers from Saharan and fleeing to Cairo? Nat Fould who'd made the terrorism watch list? But Nat Fould had led the attack on the Hammamet restaurant. Was it so far-fetched to think he'd gone to London to kill George? Or back to Saharan to steal computers?

The Peugeot's engine ticked, cooling off. One thing she could say about Karim's visit. It'd taken her mind off Tiffany, had put the girl and the station's problems in a whole new perspective.

She went inside, dropped the bag she'd carried from Washington in the bedroom where she kicked off her shoes. After that, she lit a fire in her study's brazier and poured a glass of wine. The house was quiet ... too quiet. She retrieved her iPod from her purse, set it to an album of Mozart piano concertos, then placed it in a Bose cradle. The intricacies of Mozart filled the house.

Settling into a deep, cushioned chair, her heels propped on the carved wood that railed the brazier, the fire warming her feet and her spirit, she postponed a decision on whether or not to report what Karim had said. Instead, she considered her own situation.

First, al-Din and Fould were still at large and active—witness George's death. She had to assume the two still considered her a target. Second, once Langley learned the extent of Tiffany's betrayal, the search for a scapegoat would begin, and she'd be the most likely candidate. If she returned to Washington as Sam demanded, she'd be relatively safe from al-Din ... maybe ... but the fall-out from the Tiffany affair would keep her there. And that would be the end of her career plans which relied on her having at least another two overseas tours after Tunis. Third, Craig and a divorce.

Better she should consider what needed doing here. This evening's meeting with station personnel had only begun to scratch the surface of putting Tunis station back into a fully operational mode. There were agents to be relocated or, at least, shifted to new handlers and new security routines. She'd needed a deputy for a long time, and she could no longer take "as soon as possible" for an answer—look where that had led. Someone would have to replace Tiffany—this time an experienced officer. Those were the biggies. As for station morale … ? Well, that would improve with full staffing and a few successes.

She drank off half her glass of wine, slouched lower in her chair, and let the rich cabernet rest on her tongue. The fire crackled bringing out gold and orange highlights around the wide lip of the brazier, warming her toes almost to the point of discomfort.

Back to Hayburner and Karim. What if he'd told the truth? What if…, "Oh, hell." She said the words aloud and picked up her cellphone.

■ ■ ■

CHAPTER TWENTY-ONE
Sidi Bou Said, Tunisia

Given the time difference, her call caught Craig in his office. "For God's sake, Regan," he said. "What's going on there? Sam tells me you may have given us another Sharon Scranage case."

"I like the way you put that, as though I did it on purpose ... like a gift I'd thought out and presented on a silver platter. And, to think. Here I called to do you an actual favor."

He almost laughed, the sound a cross between a bull's bellow and a choke. "So? How bad is this girl's situation?"

"Let me put it this way. The Iraqis came close to eating our lunch but gagged on the hors d'oeuvres. Read what I sent Sam; listen to her interview, but do it later. The girl, as you call her, will keep. Another matter won't."

He waited.

Speaking in their own personal code, she told him what Karim had said. As she was talking, her land line phone rang, the caller ID that of a cellphone she'd given Bashir for use in emergencies. "Hold one," she said to Craig and answered it.

One of the Baralguiba cousins stationed outside her house spoke. "Madame. Your American friend who is here before. We let him pass? This is good?"

"Thanks," she said. "That's fine."

"Fine," he repeated the English word and disconnected.

"Okay. That's all I know. Now, I'm going to have to go," she said to Craig. Mac had neither called nor texted. She hadn't heard from him in days, but here he was. How typical.

"Listen to me," Craig stopped her. "Karim told you the truth. At least about Fould taking the computers to Cairo. He did it under orders from that contractor we sent to head up Saharan."

"Then, if you know about this ... ? If that's true ... ?"

"Mitch tracked them down for me. To Zamalek."

"How did you ... ?" Mitch was her opposite number in Cairo. Zamalek was the diplomatic district of Cairo. She knew that much, but the rest? Frowning in concentration, she walked to the outside door and opened it. Mac stood there with his mouth and arms spreading wide to both roar a greeting and sweep her off her feet. Before he could do either, she waved him to silence and backed away, pointing a finger to the cell, then to her lips.

"Thanks to the riots," Craig was saying, "That area's full of empty houses ... the owners deciding this is a good time to be elsewhere. Mitch got the use of one right across the street and is keeping an eye on things for me."

In the courtyard torchlight, Mac's hair shone with reds and golds. He'd clubbed it back over the collar of an aviator's leather jacket which emphasized the breadth of his shoulders and the fine line of his waist. His narrow hips were clad in jeans, and a pair of cowboy boots added to his already substantial height, making her look up at the flat, clean planes of his face.

Craig was saying, "Listen, Regan. The situation there is a mess. I told you. I want those computers down at Quantico. Right now? It's like your source said, they're vulnerable, and we can't expect help from the Egyptians. They've got their hands full. So does Mitch."

She gestured to Mac to bring his duffle bag and close the door, then turned to cross the atrium.

Craig was saying, "This is serious, sweetheart. I've got a meeting at the White House in the morning that I can't blow off, but after that I'm heading to London, then on to Cairo. But in the meantime, I'd like you there. In Cairo. Just to keep an eye on things. Make sure no one does anything stupid."

"I can't help," she said. "Sam's ordered me back to D.C." Behind her, Mac's boot heels clicked crossing the atrium. He made no effort to walk softly.

"Screw Sam," Craig said.

She led Mac into the study, where the fire munched softly in its shallow brazier, and waved him toward a chair. He picked up the open wine bottle and poured himself a glass.

"I think I've said this before," Regan said to Craig. "But 'screw Sam' is easy for you to say. Me? He's my boss."

"And it's very likely that I'll be his boss very shortly."

She dropped into the chair across from Mac. Sam's boss? That meant ... . "Are you serious?"

"Hard to be sure, but we're talking seventh floor, center office. It could happen, which is why I can't go anywhere right now. Listen, Regan. I'm going to send you something I want you to read. Then I want you to turn the problem of getting that girl back to DC over to Chance and get your ass on a plane."

Mac took a long swallow of wine, sat down, and put his feet up on the carved teak of the fender around the brazier.

"Mitch?" Regan said, asking with the one word if he'd bothered to consult Cairo's chief of station and how he might feel about having an interloper invade his turf.

"I told you. Mitch's got his hands full with what could blow up into a full-scale civil war. Call him. He'll be happy to have you take this problem off his hands ... at least until I can get there. Now I gotta go." He hung up.

Slowly, she slid her cell into a pocket and looked across the brazier at Mac. He started to smile at her but read her expression and said, "I gather that call means you're going to be busy tonight."

"I don't suppose you could fly me to Cairo?"

"Now?"

"If I have to wait until tomorrow, I can fly commercial."

He saluted her with his glass, then stared across its lip, his expression hidden by the cabernet' rich red. "Home is the hunter; home from the hills ... . And what does he get? A kiss. A hug? A warm bed? No. The lady wants to go to Cairo."

"I thought you were in Indonesia or Hong Kong or someplace. They don't have communications from those places?"

"Which has to do with what?" One of his eyebrows rose.

"I'm glad you're here. Really."

"What's going on? What's in Cairo? Something more than street violence, I gather."

She made a hurumping sound, not so much an affirmative as saying, "That's a stupid question."

Mac continued, "You can get killed in Cairo these days."

"You can get killed almost anywhere these days."

"Yeah. I heard about the suicide bomber thing with the Unit and the ministers, and sorry I couldn't get back to D.C. for the funeral. I would've if I could've."

"I know." She changed the subject. "You've been inside the Saharan Enterprises compound in Libya, haven't you?"

He lifted an eyebrow and his wine glass, setting the ruby cabernet to sloshing gently from side to side. "Where'd you get that idea?"

She smiled.

"I did some business there. Arnie needed to arm his guards. I needed the business." His expression hardened. "What's the question?"

"The work there—"

A ringing sound came from her safe. She got up. A minute later she had the safe open, had removed the case holding her secure satellite receiver and hooked it up to her desk monitor. A few seconds after that she was looking at a document labeled TOP SECRET and EYES ONLY and at a string of code words she didn't recognize. Next came a series of NSA intercepts of encoded communications between an Egyptian military intelligence officer and a number at Saharan Enterprises.

She read through the entries, then glanced over her monitor. Mac had put down his wine glass and was working his thumbs over his cellphone, sending someone a message.

She reached under her desk to flip a switch that turned on a white noise system. This room and the house were swept for bugs on a regular basis, but that was no guarantee that they weren't here and operating. A small red light embedded into the top right edge of her desk came on indicating that the system was active. Mac had finished with his call.

"You knew what was going on at Saharan," she said, getting up and walking back to her chair.

He rose, picked up a poker, and stirred the coals in the brazier.

They gleamed bright red or glowed a brilliant orange in response, a few sending small flames licking an inch or so into the air. He said, "Which is relevant, why?"

She said, "Because the guts of that operation have been removed from the facility and are in transit ... somewhere. Langley wants them at Quantico."

"No surprise," he grumbled. "An operation of that nature should never have been set up outside the U.S. And now you think the valuable stuff's in Cairo."

She nodded. NSA had intercepted, deciphered and translated negotiations between a man named Wentworth on behalf of the CIA and an Egyptian army intelligence officer for the exclusive use of a small Egyptian base. The exchanges boiled down to arrangements for four Americans and ten Libyans to enter Egypt with eight hundred pounds of sealed and unidentified equipment and to proceed to the base where they would be given perimeter protection.

"The final message from the Egyptian," Regan finished summarizing for Mac, "says that due to 'circumstances beyond his control,' the American CIA party will have to wait in Cairo until he can get his hands on personnel and vehicles to transport them to this base ... personnel and vehicles having been diverted from his command to be on stand-by for riot control."

Mac had resumed his seat and recrossed his arms. "And people wonder," he said, "why I resigned. What a goat fuck."

"You made money off this particular goat fuck," she snapped. "And did so thanks to your CIA connections."

He snorted but, then, grinned. "So I did. So I did." He got up, came around to her, and drew her to her feet, cupping her jaw in one of his hands. He leaned down to kiss her, his lips warm, his tongue probing softly.

After a moment he straightened and drew back. "What the hell happened at that funeral, anyway? You and Craig have another reconciliation?"

She put her hand with its still bandaged wrist on his bicep, feeling the strength of him through the supple leather jacket he'd yet to remove.

Her own failure to respond to his kiss had surprised her as much as it'd disturbed him.

"I really don't know," she said, not of the reconciliation but of how she felt about him. She added, "My mind's kind of occupied just now."

"It's not your mind I'm interested in."

She waved that away as the hackneyed expression it was.

He shrugged. "Well. It's not that either of us swore to love and honor forever and ever. But a little friendly fuck never hurt anyone."

She heard the pain behind the coarse expression, behind the attempt at a light tone.

A portrait of a big Dutch horse Regan had owned during her two years in Rome hung on the wall behind Mac's head. She'd painted it using rich splashes of color and wide brush strokes. And, even though she'd used a very impressionistic style, the horse's one visible eye—large, staring, and wary—made him seem alive.

She said, "A friendly fuck won't keep those eight hundred pounds of sensitive equipment from falling into hostile hands. But you and me? We might."

He blinked. He turned away to poke the fire again. Then, he laughed, looked around at her, laughed again and said, "By God, Regan Grant. Someone ought to lock you up as hazardous to my health." He put the poker back in its holder. "So, what the hell do you want from me? Exactly."

CHAPTER TWENTY-TWO
Sidi Bou Said, Tunisia

Using the secure link in the satellite unit she'd laid out on her desk, Regan reached the chief of station in Cairo, Mitch Jenkins.

"Hi, good buddy," he said. "What a surprise to hear from you. Now, let me guess what's on your mind." The edge to his tone said he was about out of patience with something. He went on, his voice rimmed with sarcasm, "Perhaps another round of Libyan terrorism? No? Perhaps Qadhafi's seeking asylum, and the Tunisians want custody? Of course not." She heard him snap his fingers. "I've got it. It must have something to do with George Tendale's death, and this group from something called Saharan Enterprises."

"I know you need this like a hole in the head," she said the obvious.

"You could say that. Egypt's in the midst of the biggest hoorah since Cleopatra kissed an asp, and Headquarters says, 'Drop everything. We have something more important.' Hell! I'm talking to your husband, and I can hear the roar of the rioting on Tahir Square. I say, 'Did you know that Habib el-Adly's been detained and our liaison partners are going crazy?' Craig says, 'Nevermind that right now.' I say, 'Listen to the sound of mobs,' and hold the phone out."

"He's right about el-Adly," she said of the former Interior Minister who'd been the strong arm of the Mubarek administration and who'd also been a good friend of Arnie Walker's. The one time she'd met the Egyptian, in fact, had been at a dinner at the Walker's.

Mitch didn't seem to have heard her. His voice rose, "Nevermind? I've done nothing all day but listen to Headquarters ... sons of bitches all. Where are you anyway? Craig tells me you'll take this mess of my hands, but Sam says you're on your way home."

"Sam's going to have to wait."

"His loss. How soon can you be here?"

"In about three hours."

"Good. You'll make it before curfew. Call me when you land."

■ ■ ■ ■ ■

Regan and Mac dined on Hadija's meat pastries heated in a toaster oven and served on gold-rimmed china in the cabin of a Lear 25B with one of Mac's Sicilian cousins manning the controls and eating his share in the cockpit. While they cleaned their plates, the small, sleek aircraft ate up the night sky, its speed and power plus the luxury of the cabin attesting to the profitability of Mac's arms trading deals. Did that include smuggling?

The fact that he owned this particular model of aircraft argued that he did. This Lear could land on dirt strips and short strips. It could out fly all but the most sophisticated fighter jets. And it carried enough fuel to make refueling stops few and far between. At the least, he must use it to visit customers whose circumstances were such that they couldn't be seen in places with conventional airfields.

She let the subject alone but picked Mac's brain clean of everything he knew about Saharan Enterprises and the compound it'd occupied in Libya.

"You said they're out of there," Mac had protested at one point. "So what difference does it make what the place looks like? By the time anyone sees it again, the rebels and the looters will have blown up what they couldn't haul off. Or maybe Qadhafi's loyalists will reclaim it. Either way, it's history."

Arguing the point didn't seem worthwhile. But everything Mac said confirmed her in the belief that Craig would make an effort to strip the compound before the looters got anywhere close. As Mac had said, there was a fortune in equipment in the underground vaults. What she didn't know was if Hayburner could be operated without its support mechanism and what it would take to build another one. What she didn't know was what Craig would need to make Hayburner operational again under his own control.

The soft tan leather of the big executive chairs in the cabin glowed under the spot lights built into the cabin's bulkheads. Thick insulation suppressed the worst of the jet engines' noise. A faint smell of fine leather mingled with the spicy aroma of Hadija's cooking—Regan having raided the freezer and filled a picnic hamper with provisions to get them to Cairo.

Through the portholes a string of coastal lights like tiny breadcrumbs marked their path, arrowing toward their destination. On either size of the light zone lay blackness relieved by random pinpricks that could have been reflections of bright stars but were, in fact, large ships or small villages.

By the time they'd demolished the contents of the picnic basket, they were approaching Cairo International, and Mac left her to take the copilot's seat in the cockpit as they began their descent. Regan used the time and Mac's fancy satellite communications system to call Mitch.

"Looks like they're buttoned up for the night," he said of the Zamalek house. "Lights are out. The guards have all settled down. I've got two men who'll do shifts through the rest of the night and call if there's any activity."

"Okay."

"I've also left a curfew pass for you. The customs people know you're coming and will see that you get it. What I'd suggest is that you find a hotel room near here and get a good night's sleep."

"The Four Seasons," she said.

"The Intercon's closer, and I can get you a rate."

"I've already reserved a room. The manager's a friend of a friend."

"Whatever. We'll get together first thing tomorrow. After that, it's all yours."

CHAPTER TWENTY-THREE
Cairo, Egypt

She reached the Four Seasons just before the midnight curfew came down and dropped her backpack, happy she didn't have to spend the night in Mitch's observation post. She could sleep in a bed for the first time in forty-eight hours. Actually, she would sleep in a very large bed in one of the hotel's executive suites thanks to the friend of a friend and to the fact that the hotel was largely empty.

The grand night view outside a window wall drew her onto a wide balcony. She'd seen it before when Cairo was brimming with life and not cowed by violence and a police/army crackdown. Even so, the night sky reflected the city, its color ranged from a brilliant, smog-induced orange to a fading black. Below her, the waters of the Nile acted as a more accurate mirror, reproducing the illumined hotel facade and vast hunks of the electrified city.

The Nile was wide here, but just to her left it was broken by an island piled with luxury buildings and sports fields. That was Cairo's diplomatic enclave, the Zamalek district. From its midst rose the Cairo Tower—a golden obelisk, a beacon in the night. Brilliant colors—vivid reds, greens, and yellows—replaced unseen stars and shone back from the river's surface. Looking down, she could see a restaurant boat gay with fairy lights and potted palms tied up below her balcony, the whistling, evocative sound of a single flute playing in a minor key drifted up from it.

Eye candy with background music, and it brought a smile of appreciation to her lips. But out there, behind the pretty lights and the elegant, tranquil façade, the city simmered with anger and fear, with hate and frustration. There were buildings spotted through the city where interrogations would be taking place, where pain and suffering were being inflicted. In other buildings, men plotted while women eavesdropped or prayed.

She looked north toward Tahir Square, but the dome of the National Museum marking the south side of the square was out of sight around the side of the hotel. Even if she did have a view in that direction, though, the bulk of the Intercontinental Hotel would have blocked her line of sight.

Visible or not, tomorrow ... today now ... this morning demonstrators would be marching to Tahir, again. Arrests would continue even though the jails and detention centers were already full and many of the Mubarek ministers had been replaced. All the things that hadn't happened in Tunisia, because Ben Ali had abdicated peacefully and because Tunisia had a large and prosperous middle class, would happen here. The old regime had made it clear they would not go easily or peacefully. The younger generations and Islamists, the huge mass of unemployed and unemployable, would not give up easily. They'd seen what could happen. They'd die to make it happen. She didn't need to be an expert analyst or have a crystal ball to figure that out.

The flute music died away. There wasn't a moving car to be seen on the Corniche below or on the bridge nearest her. Which didn't mean an absence of people. She didn't have binoculars and she didn't need them to see a group of soldiers lounging around an Army jeep and a troop transport. There to keep mobs away from the luxury hotels?

Enough. She went inside, moved a flower arrangement to one side of a desk and fired up her laptop. Moments later she was connected to the hotel internet service and could scan her latest emails. There was one from her grandmother talking about conservation easements they both wanted to see put in place and one from her cousin, Jill, saying that another cousin, Charlie, was spearheading an effort to prevent any such move. There was an email from the realtor who'd sold her the Georgetown house noting that the sale of the Walker house had brought a group of buyers to the area and she could sell Regan's house in a heartbeat if Regan had any interest in turning a large profit.

Nothing else on her email menu caught her eye as of immediate interest, so she sent the realtor a "No," wrote Jill a "Thanks for the heads up," and tapped out a "Great work," to her grandmother. Then, she called up Google and typed in: Maghrebi Transport Companies. There were 28,600 hits, but the first ten included an entry for Transport en Afrique de Nord.

She opened the site, inserted a flash drive, and copied the home page to it. Next, she disconnected from the hotel internet before accessing an Agency specific program, hit a button labeled "Identify" and added a password. She was immediately rewarded. A period on the home page turned red, became a miniscule bit of color, marked the location of a microdot. That was it. Another program moved the microdot to a third program. It magnified the text on the dot and deciphered it.

She'd forgotten about the reports she'd asked for from Daud Baralguiba until she'd been en route to Cairo. She'd also forgotten she'd promised to see him tomorrow. Clearly, that was now impossible, but she owed him an explanation.

The microdot held several messages from Daud. She'd asked him to provide situation reports from as many of the towns and villages in western Libya as he could, and she found a paragraph or more on at least seven locations. Before moving on, Regan copied these into another program and sent it to a Tunis Station computer for forwarding to Langley.

The next report concerned developments around the Saharan compound. What she read now confirmed what she'd already learned. A freighter had arrived on Sunday, and a large number of people had boarded. Shortly after the freighter's departure for Rome, late Sunday night, a fancy yacht had arrived. Three white people—two men and a woman—had left on it along with ten al-Salan guards and a stack of boxes and suitcases.

The room around her seemed unnaturally quiet, so much so that it was a distraction. She got up and walked across the deep plush carpet to a credenza, opened it to find a large television and turned it on. After by-passing a 'Welcome to the Four Seasons' notice, she found the music channels and an opera performing, appropriately, *Aida*. The remote tuned into it just in time to get the beginning of the "Grand March."

Stepping in time to the truly grand music, she returned to her computer and opened the next message that Daud had included in his steganographic communication. Translated into English it read:

Elders wish to speak to you about recent events in Tunis. They understand that such things are outside your control but it would be good if you could come to a gathering on 2nd at family home outside Zarzis. Advise arrival time and I will meet you at Jerba Airport.

She set the laptop aside and stood up. "It would be good if you could come … ." Daud was saying that if she didn't come her arrangements with the Baralguiba family might be threatened?

Daud had sounded so very much in command with his talk of scorpions, but now she was hearing about "elders?" So Daud wasn't as all-powerful in the family as she'd thought.

She pushed open a set of glass doors and walked back out onto the suite's long balcony, the end of Verdi's Grand March following her. Below her the restaurant boat, closed for the night and lit only by a few ghostly bulbs, swayed at its moorings. Somewhere the flute again played in its minor key, a mournful counterpoint to the victorious crash of Egypt's armies on the television. The Nile made a rippling black mirror for the jeweled patterns of the city along its banks.

Her hands, resting on the balcony railing, trembled slightly from fatigue. More than anything, she needed sleep. She turned away from Cairo and went back inside. She couldn't be bothered with the Baralguibas right now.

■ ■ ■ ■ ■

The wake-up smell of coffee and croissants greeted her at eight, long after she'd expected to be up. The big bed with its acres of smooth sheets and firm support held her sprawled on her belly, arms and legs extended. Lifting her head with effort, she found the bedside clock. It said eight. She had adjusted her watch to Cairo time. It really was eight!

That brought her to her feet. She hadn't closed the curtains the night before, and the big room was flooded with light which spilled over a plush seating group upholstered in a warm gold. Through the window glass she could see a daybed, a table and two chairs on the balcony. The open door to the sitting room showed her more of the gold carpet, a coffee table, and a long couch colorful with pillows.

She stretched, then went to shower and change into the one set of clothes she'd brought along—widely flared black pants, a high-necked shirt with long, bell-shaped sleeves, and low-heeled black boots. Hair tied into a tight chignon, her face bare of make-up, she was ready to go.

A call to Mitch said that he wasn't. "I'm tied up in meetings until ten," he said. "But, not to worry. Everything's quiet as churches in the target house."

"I could just go along to the OP and introduce myself," she suggested.

"Better to wait for me."

The smell of coffee told her not to argue. A bit of breakfast wouldn't hurt her. Neither would the time to do more homework.

After a few more words with Mitch, she settled down with a cup of coffee, still hot in its thermos, a bowl of sliced peaches and strawberries, and a buttered croissant—all of which had been left on a credenza in the suite's hallway. The tray had included a note from the 'friend of a friend' saying he hoped they'd have a chance to meet during her 'visit' at the Four Seasons and to please feel at home. "If there is anything my staff can do to make your visit more comfortable ... ." Blah, blah, blah.

But that did remind her. Swallowing a mouthful of croissant, she picked up the phone and punched in the concierge's number.

"Yes, Madame," she heard. The Mini she'd asked for as a rental was in the hotel garage and could be brought around to the front whenever Madame wished.

She wished for 9:45, expecting traffic to be light, and checked her watch.

She had an hour, which she used studying Google Earth, then going through a computer file of the al-Salan mug book. She wanted to be able not just to identify the Libyans that had come with the Hayburner parts but to have memorized the bio data that went with the photos. As she worked to make associations between dates and names and places, to tie educational and family data to those same names and faces, she wondered about the three whites who'd come to Cairo.

Last she'd heard, Richie Knowland had gone to Washington, thinking he'd be the next head of the clandestine service. But hadn't Craig said something about his return to Saharan? Anna Comfort Rose, of course, was in the United States with her husband. The new man, Wentworth, would be in Cairo, though. Craig had said so. Fould, if Karim had told the truth at all, would be another. The woman? A wife? Girlfriend? Another computer engineer?

When she turned back to the computer, her monitor had gone to screen-saver mode and displayed a photo of a cow moose silhouetted against a snow bank in front of the wide veranda of the big house at Highwinds Ranch. The next picture was of a stunted, wind-tortured cedar, its roots, like talons, clinging to an overhanging cliff up on Boulder Ridge. That's where she had stopped to catch her breath and snap some other photos of the valley and Highwinds, of its buildings spread out a thousand feet below her.

Even sitting in a Cairo hotel, a million miles and a cultural gap the size of outer space away, she felt the pull of the place, as though she were still standing on those high rocks. From her eagle's vantage what looked like dotted lines in the snow was actually sawbuck fencing. Fatter dots represented cattle and horses, deer and big horn sheep—maybe some were elk and moose, as well—all foraging in the river pastures.

The pictures seemed to suck her in. Which in reality was what the family all thought Highwinds would do—sooner or later. And the draw strengthened at times like this.

Enough! She was running out of time. Impatient, she hit a key to bring up her desktop, and was instantly back in Cairo, a more ambiguous world, its edges and colors muted, its distances shortened by the opaqueness of the humid, polluted air.

Using her passwords, Regan again accessed the steganography program sequence. Having told Daud that she'd do her best to reach Jerba the next day and would signal him with a time, she wrote a text to Chance. She'd called him before she'd left Sidi Bou, and he knew what to do. **Advise when package is en route home. Anticipate return in 24 hours. Thanks.**

She hit the 'send' icon. By 'package' Chance would read 'Tiffany.'

Time to go. She went back to the bedroom for a long black scarf which she wrapped turban style around her head, letting the tail fall down her back. The mirror told her she would look at home in the Four Seasons lobby, while the scarf could later be used to make a hijab

As promised, a black Mini was waiting for her in the drive-through. It was the smallest and most nondescript of vehicles, and it was all by itself.

Regan dropped her laptop and bag inside, checked to be sure that her curfew permit was in the bag in case it might be needed, and tipped the attendant. Next, she checked the map on the car's GPS before nosing the Mini down the drive. She didn't worry about surveillance. "There will be no surveillance," Mitch had said. "No one has time to worry about foreign diplomats. Just use normal caution around roadblocks and turn tail at the faintest hint you might be driving into a demonstration."

She'd been right about the traffic. It bore no resemblance to her previous experiences in Cairo, which was a welcome change. But cops or soldiers on every corner?

The day was clear, or as clear as any winter day in Cairo, and chilly. The high towers of Cairo's biggest hotels rose along the river. Regan took the first of the Gezira bridges, carefully negotiating the access while watching the clusters of police and army vehicles and personnel that guarded the island. The Gezira end of the bridge was similarly thronged, but she'd put the curfew pass in her windshield. Even though curfew had ended at six am, the card said she was not a threat, and no one stopped her. She drove through the lower end of the island, passed within a block of the Tunisian embassy, and pushed on to the upper end of the island, admiring the facades of embassies, palaces, and apartment blocks.

Trees overhung the streets; few people were in the streets here. Cairenes, even the diplomats, were staying close to home.

"We've taken a ground-floor apartment," Mitch had said, "In a building with underground parking. She found the driveway right where Mitch had said it would be, its entrance guarded by a pole. She tapped in the appropriate numbers and watched the pole rise while several yards further on a garage door rolled up.

Inside she parked next to an Opel.

"That you, Regan?" A male voice called down a stairwell as she climbed out.

"None other."

"Damn well time."

Her watch said it was three minute to ten.

Mitch met her with a hug and a kiss on a cheek. He'd been a frequent visitor in her Rome apartment having been chief of station in Cyprus during that period. More tellingly, he and Craig along with eight other officers had shared a home room and living space during their six months of tradecraft training. Then they had gone on to other courses as a group. All in all, they'd been together for the most intensive year of their lives.

Now Mitch led her into a large kitchen and slid onto a bar stool that sat on one side of a cooking island. A case holding a secure commo package was open in front of him, a keyboard and monitor waiting to be used. Mitch made her think of a plumber's wrench. His body was tall and stiffly straight, his head typically jutting forward, his large teeth often bared in a wide, smiling mouth. When she'd first met him, he'd habitually kept a cigar clutched between rubbery-looking lips. While he'd given up smoking, he still had a tendency to emphasize his words by curling the corners of his mouth around a cigar only he could see.

"Well," he growled. "Pull up a stool. And what in the hell are you dressed for? Halloween?"

She unwrapped the scarf. "It's a disguise. I'm trying to blend in."

"Even your own mother wouldn't recognize you, I suppose."

"Actually, she probably wouldn't."

"Ah, hell." He got up and put an arm around her in a brief hug. "I'm sorry, Regan. I wasn't thinking." Then, he socked her arm and said, "I'm glad to see you, even if you do look like a character out of a Goth movie."

"Thanks. Don't you ever sleep? You've got bags under your eyes."

"Hell. Sleep?" His lips curled in their well-remembered way. "That sounds like a definition for boredom. Not something you're much in danger of here. Now. Am I going to be happy I let you come or not?"

She had no answer to that nor was one expected.

"It's Craig's nickel. What have you heard from him?"

"Watch and report. That's what he tells me he wants done until he can get here."

"Which will be?" She put her bag and scarf on a granite counter. The kitchen was right out of *Good Housekeeping* with fashionable hardwood floors, rich looking cabinets in some dark mahogany stain, and stainless steel appliances. A breakfast nook at one end sat just inside large paned windows that looked out on the bare branches of a tree. Beyond were the outlines of several brick structures.

Even with the light coming through the windows, Mitch had the overheads on. They hummed and they were needed.

"Mitch?" Regan prompted.

He was back on his stool, his torso jutting forward over a keyboard.

"What? Oh." He looked up. "Not soon enough."

"Indeed. Who's in the house now?"

"At least six of the Libyans plus the woman and that asshole, Fould. An old man—one of the contractors, a fellow named Alexander Wentworth—left after curfew. Surveillance tagged him to the airport where right now he's in the private terminal having a cup of coffee."

"Waiting for?"

"Time will tell. Now, I want you to earn your keep. Come take a look at this."

She walked over to stand behind him.

"Pull up a stool," he ordered and slid the monitor sideways. She sat down to peer at a video surveillance clip showing a wrought-iron gate overhung by a tree and several cars. Two men stood outside the gate in close conversation. The camera zoomed in on the faces.

"The one on the right," Mitch said, "is Barak Aziz Fawzi."

"I remember him."

"And on the left?"

Regan straightened. "That, my friend, is one Yuri Ayyub Haniff." She swiveled her stool away and looked through the windows at the end of the room. A tan and black crow jutted its head in her direction from a branch of the tree, probably checking his image in the reflective glass.

"Don't know as I've ever heard the name," Mitch was saying. "Who is he?"

"Part of the reason I'm here." She swiveled back around, stopped the video, and told Mitch about the half-Russian, half-Libyan who'd attached himself to Mustafa Karim some twenty years earlier and been his one friend, chief bodyguard, butler, and general dogsbody ever since.

Mitch didn't ask what Haniff might be doing talking to Fawzi, the senior al-Salanist in the contingent that had come from Saharan. Instead he clamped his teeth shut and twisted his mobile lips in thought.

Regan went back to watching the video, fast-forwarding and noting the time/date group flash through its numbers. At 0730 hours, Haniff clasped Fawzi on the shoulder in a brotherly way, then the two men shook hands and Haniff left.

"Ideas?" Mitch asked.

She pulled the keyboard over, minimized the video which continued to film the gate after Fawzi went back inside. A moment later, she'd accessed a Headquarters data base and found the 201- file on Haniff, a file that had first been opened in 1988 when he'd come to Agency attention as a student on a KGB-funded scholarship at Moscow University.

"Okay," she said aloud and began reading key points out loud.

In 1991 Haniff had returned to Libya and got a job working for Libyan intelligence, initially training Qadhafi clients in bomb making. His first JSO boss was Mustafa Karim. The Agency presumed he was either a Russian plant or involved in some kind of joint Russian-Libyan operation.

CHAPTER TWENTY-FOUR
Cairo, Egypt

Several minutes later Mitch led her into a spacious front parlor where two long French casement windows shrouded with sheers and flanked by green brocade drapes looked out on a narrow front garden and a row of trees that bordered the street. The garden's sidewalk fence had a brick base topped with wrought iron stakes rising to a height of about eight feet, providing easy viewing of the street and the property opposite.

A very tall male figure stood just back and to one side of the window, binoculars held to his eyes. Four cameras on tripods, green operating lights twinkling, filmed the exterior field of view through slits in the brocade.

The tall man looked around.

Mitch said, "Regan. This here's Robert Barrister, better known as Butter Barrister. Don't think you know him. Butter. The lady here is Regan Grant who's over from Tunis."

"Hey Regan," the man lifted a hand slightly but stayed where he was. The sheers made it unlikely that anyone inside could be distinguished from the street, but the less movement the better. This apartment, presumably, was supposed to be empty.

"Pleasure," she said wanting to ask how anyone could end up being called "Butter," but this was not the time.

Mitch said to Butter, "The man you spotted talking outside the gate earlier? Turns out he's closely associated with that no-goodnik who used to run Libyan intelligence. They're co-tribalists."

"Are those apartments over there or what?" Regan had focused on the target building which was a four-story structure of some kind of gray stone with a rather grand entrance. A flight of six broad stairs connected large double doors with a shallow semi-circular drive marked on their street ends with gateposts. The windows in the façade were set into deep embrasures and heavily curtained. Two cars were parked along the drive. Otherwise, the only sign of life was an armed and uniformed man lounging alongside each of the gates.

Mitch held up a hand to stop Butter from answering, said, "I'll let you two hash over the details here, but right now I've got to get my ass on the road." He looked at Butter. "You've got the schedule? Ray should be here at noon to spell you. Then, you're back on duty at six. I'll come by about then. The lady here'll make her own schedule. She's in charge ... within reason. You have questions, call me."

"Sure, Boss," Butter said. With a wave, a twist of his lips, and a toothy smile for Regan, Mitch left.

"So?" she said, only now noticing how dusty the room was. "What's over there?"

"Here's what I know," Butter began. He stood a good six foot six inches tall and was dressed in shades of yellow with a lemon-colored polo shirt over mustard-hued slacks. Long, stringy muscles stood out on the arms that projected from the polo's short sleeves. His face was narrow, his head domed under pale blonde hair, his complexion deeply tanned, his eyebrows almost invisible over small blue eyes set close alongside a blade of a nose.

In the next few minutes Regan learned from the loquacious Butter that the house belonged to the Sanussi Muslim sect and was used for religious retreats. He concluded, "We think those religious nuts cancelled their schedules and went elsewhere. Which left it available for the al-Salanists. I hear tell that almost all of them are Sanussi, themselves. So it figures."

"Anybody else living there? A caretaker?"

"It's possible. We didn't see this lot move in. Actually, the only people we've seen are those al-Salanists, and I'm told there's ten of them although I've only spotted three. And there's supposed to be three European types, but none of them have shown themselves since I've been here ... except. Sorry. I'm forgetting that old man, Wentworth, who left right after I got here."

A car drove past and turned at the end of the block. A boy with four dogs on leashes came down the sidewalk, the dogs pulling in different direction, stopping to sniff and pee, and tangling their leashes.

"No back entrance?"

"Yeah. See that driveway over to the right? It goes to the back door. Anyone coming out of it's gotta exit on this street where we can see them."

The dog boy, who looked to be in his early teens, didn't seem to mind his straining charges. He drifted along with the dogs, occasionally sorting out the leashes, until they disappeared out of sight. One of the guards lit a cigarette. A cat materialized, jumped up on the low wall in front of their windows, expertly negotiated the bars to drop down behind an oleander bush.

Butter talked about himself. Regan picked up a pair of binoculars and began a window by window examination of the building.

In the process she learned that Butter was an ex-Army ranger with two tours in Afghanistan. Since the Agency hired him, he'd done one tour in Pakistan before coming here. "I speak pretty good Arabic, some Farsi, and fair Dari which means no one's going to send me to any peace-loving place. But Egypt? It sounded pretty soft like ... you know ... a holiday tour. I thought I was coming to a post where I'd get away from, like, another war ... you know?"

She knew.

"I've been lucky, so far," he told her. "Only one purple heart and that ... knock on wood ... was just because a bullet sliced my arm." He held out the limb in question so she could admire his scar. "No roadside bombs. No mines. No IED's. I don't even have PTSD. Sleep well at night and all that. I credit my wife and kids for that bit. They're solid as rocks."

"You've been lucky," she agreed.

He shrugged. "Except now my folks back home ... I'm from Oklahoma ... been laying bets if I'll get out of Cairo in one piece. What'd you think?"

He didn't seem to expect an answer; she didn't have one.

"This is pretty good duty here," he went on. "If I hadn't been tapped for this surveillance job, the Boss'd have me out in Tahir

Square wandering around and talking to people, doing a one-man Gallup poll. And as tall as I am? Even if I put on a wig and whiskers to try to blend in? I mean I talk the lingo real good, and I got the customs down cold. But does that matter a good God damn? My head pokes up above even the tallest Egyptian. It's like wearing a target. Anyone wants to take a pot shot? There's my head."

Another car, a green Porsche, came by. "Is it slowing?" Regan asked. For a moment she thought it might be intending to turn into the drive across from her, but then it continued on. Butter said, "That's a Tunisian dip plate."

He looked at her, a speculative glance that said he might talk like running fountain, but he was no man's fool and didn't like the coincidence of an officer from Tunisia—Regan—showing up at approximately the same time as a diplomatically-plated Tunisian car.

"Their embassy's on the island," Regan said. But she wondered, too, and added. "Would you show me how to bring the video footage up on the computer monitor. I'll take a closer look at the Porsche driver. Maybe I can get an ID on him.

"Yeah." He edged across the room, staying against the far wall, then followed her to the kitchen. "No one really has to be in the front of the building," he said, folding his big body down onto the stool Mitch had occupied. "No one really needs to be in this house, in point of fact, except to fix the cameras if they stop for any reason. If we'd put a satellite dish on the roof, we could've set this up to do the monitoring in the office. But the Boss figured it'd be better for one of us to be here, this being ordered by the bigwigs and all."

Regan guessed no one had told him that she was the wife of the bigwig in question.

Butter chatted on even after he'd shown her how to turn the computer screen into a real-time monitor for each of the cameras or to display them all at once or to scroll through earlier frames.

He found the Porsche for her, froze the best shot of the driver, and enlarged it.

"Anyone you know?" he asked.

She shook her head. "You got a facial recognition program on this thing?"

He did, but it didn't help. The mystery driver of the Porsche remained a mystery.

"Oh well," she said. "If he has the money to own a Porsche, he probably lives on the island and goes this way to get to work."

But she didn't believe it.

CHAPTER TWENTY-FIVE
Cairo International Airport

"You're Arnold S. Walker?" an Egyptian officer dressed in Army drab with lieutenant's bars asked Arnie.

The funny thing was, the use of his true name didn't startle him. Maybe he was getting old. Years ago, when he was traveling in alias, if someone had approached using his real name, he would've gone into a major defensive mode. But here? Of course. He'd used his true name with the Egyptian military. He'd had to in order to pull in favors owed.

"Mr. Walker?"

"Yes," he said. "Yes. I'm Walker. What can I do for you?"

"You're waiting for a private flight from Dulles to arrive?"

"That's right. Has it landed?"

"Would you come with me?"

He thought about that for a moment, then said, "Can you tell me what this is about?" Something had gone wrong. The officer's tone and demeanor, his lack of courtesy, all told him so.

"Come with me," the man repeated. No use of 'Sir.' No, 'please.'

"Well," he started to equivocate, then felt something clog in his chest, as though he'd swallowed a hunk of gristle and it'd lodged not in his throat but in his lungs. He felt his breathing turn hard and shallow, and all the time his mind refused to acknowledge his body, kept conjuring up all the ways things could have gone wrong, all the reasons this lieutenant had come for him. Could this have something to do with Richie? Richie, the twelve-hour wonder, his rise to fame and fortune terminated abruptly because Craig didn't like him. Or was this about Mubarek's people. Were they out and new people in? The way things were going—the effect the events in Tahrir Square were having—that could be it. His old friends, once so powerful, could be in jail or dead. Had he tarred himself with the same brush?

His throat had constricted. He couldn't breathe. The lieutenant was reaching down to speed him along, to take his arm. With a heave, he tried standing, but he gasped and fell backwards. Pain burned in his chest.

"Wait," he fumbled behind his chair for the rolling bag that held his air canisters and his pills. Thank God, he'd brought them with him.

Time compressed after that until, finally, he could breathe freely again. By then, he'd been lifted into a wheel chair and rolled into a small lounge. A doctor had came shortly thereafter and suggested he be checked into a medical facility, at the same time noting that Cairo's hospitals were crammed with casualties from the rioting, and he couldn't be sure that the doctors there would be able to find time for him.

He declined medical help ... well, hell! He knew what was wrong. After that, and still not knowing what was going on, he fell asleep.

When next he awoke, Richard Knowland was shaking his shoulder. "There," Richie said, "Are you back with us?"

He blinked, trying to figure out where he was and why.

Richie sat down across from him, picked up a paper cup of coffee and took a drink.

Arnie straightened, swallowed, and licked his lips. He lifted his arms and stretched. "I could use one of those," he said of the coffee. He ripped the nose tubes out. Stale air rasped in his throat, but it went into his lungs just fine. "What's happened?" He'd already noticed two men by the door. Airport security, not Army.

Richie put his cup down. His boyish smile and deferential expression, the default look that Arnie had come to know well, were gone. Instead, the shoulders slumped aggressively forward; the downward sloping lips and dark eyes held contempt. "We tried this one your way," he said. "Big mistake. The first decision I let you make, and here we are. I should've known better. Now, we're going to put you back up on your pedestal, and you're going to sit there like a good little figurehead. Which is all you've ever been. This has been my operation since the first for all your strutting and posturing, and it'll be my operation from now on out." The tone was bitter. Richie stood and walked away, pulling out his cellphone.

Arnie understood. Richie felt betrayed. He'd counted on being the next head of the National Clandestine Service. "You'll take over Hayburner and shape the greatest operation of all time," Richie'd said back then. "You'll be able to create a heritage that no one will ever forget. While I'll go back to Washington and run the store for you."

He'd made his part sound dull and boring. Arnie'd known better. Richie would kill for the job.

Air congested in his chest, he reached for the oxygen tubes and reinserted them. Gradually, his breathing cleared. Across the room, Richie's smooth, young-sounding voice was explaining something, apparently failing to convince, and asking to speak to a higher authority.

Richie had been humiliated in Washington. In a way, what had happened had been much worse than never having been considered for the job. Well, Richie'd just have to get over it.

As for Hayburner, if what he was beginning to understand was true, he might just need to go along with Craig and move it to Quantico. Would that be so bad? It'd be the end of his hopes of full control, but he was running out of options. And, Craig would leave him in charge. Richie? Craig would cut him out, would probably fire him.

Jack Martinsen. Now he remembered the name. Jack'd been Craig's friend, Richie's first chief of station, Richie's first victim. Craig had a long memory.

"Richie. Listen." Arnie's voice sounded weak to his own ears. Richie didn't even look around, had someone else on the phone, was saying, "Yes, of course, I understand. But there's been misunderstanding. Of course, I had authorized use of the aircraft.

If you'd just contact ... ."

It seemed unlikely that Richie had commandeered an Agency plane, but ... . Well, obviously, someone at Langley had contacted the Egyptian Air Ministry. No wonder there were two security guards at the door. Unauthorized use of an aircraft? Some might consider that grand theft ... a major felony?

"Richie. Listen," Arnie managed something like his normally booming voice. He'd have to iron this out. For all of Richie's vainglory and pathetic efforts at manipulation, he'd screwed up one more time. How many other times had that happened in the past two years.

■ ■ ■ ■ ■

It had all begun because of the cancer. "Would you rather I just fade away or go out in a blaze of glory," he'd asked Lori one day. The question had been rhetorical. But his time was limited, and he knew he had no more than one last chance to win a place in history. What he'd needed was one big blowout of an operation. But what? So, he'd asked for ideas.

Responses came in. Paper piled up on a round table in his office where three bright young things poured over dozens of proposals. From time to time Arnie looked over their shoulders and scanned the summaries.

Then, and he could see them now, two people had showed up in his office with "the idea" for the operation he eventually called HAYBURNER. He'd never deluded himself that the idea was actually his own, but the operation, itself? He'd developed it. Hadn't he? He'd made the decisions. Well. Richie had made suggestions, some of which he'd adopted. And, some of those had even been core decisions. Some, not. Like the name, for God's sake. Richie'd decided to name the operation Hayburner after Anna Comfort's name for the virus. Strawmen.

That said, he'd almost refused to hear Richie's proposal, mainly because he didn't like cyber ops. The Agency's forays into the field had been spectacularly promising and mostly just as unsuccessful. So on that June day, he'd stared at Richard Knowland's handsome, smooth olive-tinted skin. It was absolutely unlined, showing neither character nor experience. It was a blank slate just waiting for someone like him to superimpose their own thoughts. He'd known that about Richie, known his straight and sharp nose, his rounded chin and high forehead were deceptive in their innocence. More revealing was his hair. Although cut to the scalp and visible only as a dark sheen, it still grew close to his features and shadowed them like a hood.

Not that the forty-five-year-old GS-15 chief of station wasn't a capable officer. He was. He'd also left a trail of bodies behind in his rise through the ranks of the Clandestine Service. Which was why, a year earlier, Arnie'd assigned him to Tripoli. The post might be in a backwater but Libya was one of the world's biggest oil producers with a bloodthirsty government and a history of state-supported terrorism. Staffing it had given Arnie two choices—send a mediocre to poor officer who would sit on his thumbs and cause no trouble or one with the instincts of a killer who could out-think and out-maneuver Qadhafi's thugs. Arnie'd thought Richie, for all his appearance of just having stepped out of a junior military academy, might do the latter.

He also might be the kind of man who'd find the holy grail of operations.

So, he'd listened, hearing how several years earlier a computer engineer and occasional CIA contractor named George Tendale had written an entirely new type of virus—a brief blueprint of a virus, actually. One that had no problem sneaking under defensive computer radar systems to embed itself behind firewalls. There it went to work building itself into a full-fledged virus.

Except George's algorithms hadn't actually worked. Even so he'd written the code into every program he touched thereafter—more because he was a son-of-a-bitch than for any other reason. There was no secret about this. George, not being prone to hide his light, touted his coding among a select few of his peers as revolutionary and as ahead of its time. Or would be with a few tweaks. The idea, itself, had stimulated some interest and had triggered several well-publicized stabs at getting it right but, as Richie said to Arnie, "No one was passing out cigars."

Then a Libyan named Mustafa Karim attended a futures conference where he met Tendale and became interested. On Tendale's recommendation ... George by then was working in England for British intelligence ... Karim had hired Anna Comfort Rose to work on the bugs in the code.

At this point in Richie's presentation, Arnie had turned to the woman Richie had brought with him, now understanding why she was here. "Well?" he'd said.

Face impassive and using words Arnie made no effort to understand, Anna Comfort'd told how she'd ironed out the problem. Her voice had been as colorless as her skin, her hands lying perfectly sculpted and lifeless in her lap.

Arnie hadn't tried to understand and stopped listening until Richie said, "George called it the Strawman Virus."

Anna Comfort didn't miss a beat but kept talking, now describing her search for viable strawman coding. She made Arnie think of life-sized dolls, mannequins—the kind that sat in glass booths at carnivals and handed out fortunes to the gullible. Even her black, almond-shaped eyes seldom shifted and, for most of the time, remained fixed on a point over Arnie's head. He'd never seen anyone stay quite so still for so long.

What would such an impassive woman be like in bed? Either completely lifeless or a tiger, probably. He didn't think this woman, who had specified she be called Anna Comfort—not Anna or Ms. Rose, would be one for half-measures.

"I'd hoped to find one or two strawmen," Anna Comfort concluded, her change of tone refocusing Arnie's attention to what she was saying. "Instead I found thousands. The few pieces of code George'd written could rewrite themselves and had spread. And I could talk to them."

Technically, she went on to say, her work belonged to Libyan intelligence or, maybe, to Karim. He'd put up millions for the huge numbers of servers she'd needed, millions she'd thought he might've embezzled.

"These are not nice people," she'd said to Richie Knowland.

"Look, chief," Richie, in turn, had said to him. "We're talking about really smart coding here. It learns and changes every time it lands in a new computer, rearranging itself to escape detection by whatever defenses the computer has. We do the same thing with words ... we can arrange the same words in new ways to make different meanings. It's semantics. It's what political spin doctors do, which is why the geeks call this type of code 'semantics.' It looks simple, straight-forward and innocuous but once it's behind the computer or the system's firewall, it acts as a blueprint, finding and adapting bits of benign code and assembling them into a virus. And there we are. We can contact the virus and put it to work behind the host system's defenses."

"Cut to the chase," Arnie remembered saying.

"You're the one man with the vision to use this virus. With it you can change history."

He'd known that was just Richie bullshit, but ... .

Richie had gone, filling Arnie's brain with images. One person with control of the right computer system could bring down governments or dispatch grain ships to feed the hungry during famines or fire a barrage of missiles or stop oil flowing through a pipeline or... The possibilities were endless. One person.

The hook had been well and truly set; the virus had a candy store attraction. Yes.

"Maybe you should talk to George Tendale," Richie had suggested, then laid out other thoughts...two years of them as the operation came together and Arnie had struggled with his cancer.

Still. "Lori," he'd shouted through the door his visitors had left open. "I want to talk to that damn George Tendale ... not on the phone but in person and tomorrow. Get what's-her-name, Lord Kendrick's secretary whatever-she's-called, on the phone and tell her to fly him over as a personal favor for me." MI-6, he'd known, would grouse but they'd do it.

He'd leaned back in his chair then, lifted his feet to the low box that covered the heating and cooling system and followed the base of his window wall, and stared out over the rolling, forested scene spread before him. A large part of Washington, D.C. lay under that tree canopy. The locus of world power lurked there—hidden under the spreading branches of tall oak and poplar, locust and chestnut—camouflaged and potent. How could he, America's spymaster, not love a city that might have been crafted by his own mind.

Talk about hubris.

CHAPTER TWENTY-SIX
Cairo, Egypt

Craig called around noon with news that the old man, Wentworth, and Richie were stuck at the Cairo Airport and would be until he gave the Egyptians word to release them. It seemed that Richie had forged orders for use of an Agency plane and used it to fly to Cairo. "I don't think he'll do that again," Craig said, his tone dry. Also, he was in London and would be along either late in the evening or early the next morning. "Just keep an eye on things," he said.

Butter had been replaced at noon by a quiet and impressive young man named John Breckenham. Regan learned he had a law degree from Tulane, was married to a former beauty queen pageant winner, and expected to spend six more years in the National Clandestine Service. After that, he would parlay his experience, family connections, and law degree into a political career. She liked the man's quiet, confident voice and his assured manner. There was nothing brash about him, and she found herself believing he'd do exactly what he planned ... unless someone talked him into staying at the Agency or moving up elsewhere in the Executive Branch.

At six John left and Butter returned.

By seven Mitch still hadn't shown up. Neither had Richie Knowland or the old man. Neither had anyone else. The al-Salan outside guards had changed at six, indicating they were doing twelve-hour shifts. But where were the rest of them?

Regan had spent hours browsing through the surveillance footage, finding nothing. The heavy curtains on the windows hid whatever was going on inside the house. How much longer could they or should they have Wentworth and Knowland detained? Until Craig arrived, they decided.

At five past seven, Regan was in the front room when a van drove up and parked near the east end of the drive in front of the target house.

It had Tunisian diplomatic plates. The guard on that gate walked up to talk to the driver. He stood there for several minute, lighting a cigarette, smoking, and talking.

Finally, he flicked the cigarette away and returned to his post. The other guard wandered over and the two stood there, eyeing the van, lighting more cigarettes. Regan wondered about the lung cancer rates in North Africa, not for the first time. But here and among these particular men? They were more likely to die of more proximate causes—like a bullet.

"What's going on?" Mitch's voice made her jump. She turned and made out his dim form in the hall door. There were no lights on in the house, the sun had set, and the street lights had come on, their glow reaching into the room.

"Don't know," she said. "It looks, though, that the Tunisians are taking a hand in this game. That's their van."

"Hey, Butter," Mitch greeted the tall man.

"Boss," Butter acknowledged.

"What're you talking about," Mitch asked Regan, crossing to stand beside her and peer outside. She told him what they'd seen, smelling second-hand cigarette smoke and sweat coming off his clothes plus something that reminded her of … .

Tahir Square. "What's going on in Tahir?" she asked when she finished. The smell was tear gas.

"More of the same. Demonstrations. Counter-demonstrations. Billy clubs, rubber bullets, and tear gas. Don't have a body count, yet. Now what would the Tunisian Embassy be doing playing footsie with a group of al-Salanists?"

She told him. This was Karim's doing.

"What in the hell are they up to?" Butter muttered. As he spoke, Regan saw the same thing he had. The side doors on the van had slid open and four armed men had gotten out and were standing in the street.

"Regan," Mitch handed her the glasses. "Earn your berth. Tell me who those bastards are."

"It's like High Noon in Dodge," Butter muttered.

"I'll be damned," she said, staring through the glasses. They weren't Tunisian at all. "Karim's bodyguards. And, there's Yuri Haniff getting out of the front passenger seat. What an unholy alliance. Karim, the Tunisians, and maybe the Russians. Yup. And there's the man, himself." Mustafa Karim had stepped out of a side door, and stood there adjusting his shirt cuffs.

She handed Mitch the glasses. "See. The one wearing what looks like an Armani suit? That's Mustafa Karim."

Yuri and the bodyguards grouped themselves around Karim, and they all strode through the nearest gate, the two gate guards closing in behind them, the van starting up, going to the end of the block, then swinging around to come back and follow the group of men up to the front door of the house.

"Looks like the Libyan JSO type recruited the al-Salan house guards." This from Butter. "Which explains why Yuri and Barak had their heads together."

"Bought off, you mean." This from Mitch.

"You bet, Boss. Bought off."

Regan said nothing. She knew what they were watching, but never had she expected such a blatant scenario from the Tunisians. Hayburner was not just under the protection of the Egyptian MOD but of the Sanussi and al-Salan. Any or all of those three, she'd thought, might have been enlisted by Karim to have a go at taking over the computers. But add in the Tunisians and make it a DGSE operation. So simple. Buy off the guards. Stroll into the house. Load up the computers and drive away protected by diplomatic immunity. The computers would be put under diplomatic seal and be flown straight to Tunis.

Quickly, she explained to Mitch and Butter.

"And we've got a ringside seat to it all," Mitch said taking Regan the binoculars from her.

Butter spoke up. "They've all gone into the house. Even the gate guards."

Regan felt her heart thump once and speed up. There wasn't going to be much time.

"Here's what we're going to do," Regan said. "Butter. You get over there and steal the distributor cap from that van. Maybe let the air out of its tires while you're at it. Mitch. You call your contacts in the Mukharabat and get them on their way here." She was talking about the Mukhabarat al-Aama otherwise known as the General Intelligence Service. "Tell them a robbery of diplomatic-protected equipment's in progress. Then, take the back door. I'll take the front, and we'll make sure no one leaves that house until your Muk friends get here."

Neither man moved. "Craig said … ," Mitch started.

"I have my orders. Craig sent me here in case this kind of thing happe—"

"As for keeping them locked up in the house?" Mitch cut her off. "In case you haven't noticed there's three of us and at least seven of them, maybe as many as fourteen. All have automatic rifles. What do you have? Besides Muk headquarters is surrounded by mobs and has other things to deal with. Like will they even be around in another few days? Like … ."

His brain had gone into a default negative place. Regan could see it and opened her mouth to try a new spin on what needed to be done.

"No, Regan." Mitch stopped her. "Craig's orders to me were to keep an eye on the Hayburner boxes and people. I'll put a tracker on that Tunisian van, and I'll get a surveillance team here to follow them. But that's all. Anything else? We'd risk embarrassing our friends plus cause a major diplomatic incident. Now, don't make me regret letting you come to the party."

"Listen." She had to make him understand. "Why do you think we're standing here? Why do you think you got orders to personally put eyes on that house? Why do you think Craig's on his way here? If he'd had any idea anyone could move as fast as Karim and the Tunisians have, he'd be here by now even if he had to sprout a pair of wings. You've got to believe me, Mitch. The equipment in that house can't be allowed to just slip away."

Mitch shoved the binoculars into her hand and started back toward the kitchen, speaking over his shoulder. "I won't waste time arguing with you about this. What I will do is call Craig right now. If he says do something, we'll try. But as much as I like you, Regan, I'm not committing suicide or creating an international incident on your say so."

"Where're you going?"

"Satphone's in the kitchen. Plus I'll have to get our own people moving. We'll need a tracker and a team here asap ... God. I really don't need this kind of grief right now."

"Look! Smoke!" Butter's voice interrupted. His words were accompanied by the faint sound of a shot and the distant crash of a window breaking.

Regan bolted out the door, racing into the kitchen. Mitch wasn't going to do a God-damned thing, but something was going on over there that would serve as a distraction. Confusion. Who knew what kind of opening she might get. This was a chance. She grabbed her scarf and a Glock that was lying on a counter, taking a second longer to make sure the pistol held a full clip and to shove it into her belt. Mitch, coming into the kitchen behind her, did nothing to stop her.

Wrapping the scarf back into a hijab, she jerked open the door and pulling its tail across her lower face and tucking it into place she crossed the deserted street on the run, the gun hidden by her loose shirt. She could hear shouts through the open front door of the house.

She almost ran into the two uniformed guards in a large, marble-floored entry, recognizing them by their uniforms and kefiyahs. One of them had a cellphone out and was cursing into it. Using her best Arabic, learned from the ubiquitous Egyptian sitcoms, she lowered her head and choked out, "My mistress. My mistress. I must find my mistress."

"Upstairs," the other pointed and added, "Maybe you can get the gun away from her."

"Gun?"

"Upstairs," he said again and ran toward the stairs. She rushed after him, passing the man on the cellphone. The veiled face, the long-sleeved, flowing black garments, hidden hands, the hijab and bent head all meant she was a religiously observant woman and just what she seemed—a servant.

The entry hall was wide and long, illumined only by outside light coming through the open front door and side windows. A formal staircase bisected the hall's center and disappeared into darkness above. A cart holding a stack of boxes sat at the foot of the staircase.

She took the stairs into the darkness to the first floor two at a time, keeping one hand on the railing as a guide going up toward a faint glow. On the next landing a door opened into a well-lit room, her view partially blocked by the figures of two large men carrying a wooden crate, the barrels of rifles jutting up behind their heads. They came onto the landing, one of them cursing about the lack of stairwell lights. She stopped and stood aside, shrinking into the shadows.

Hayburner parts? Most likely. She should stop them. How? The gun was in her hand but hidden by her shirt. Was she going to shoot them? There was the armed man just ahead of her. The two crate-handlers had their weapons slung on their backs. She could kill the two and the crate would plummet to the bottom of the stairs, likely destroying its contents. In the meantime the other men—one below and one above— would shoot her.

The crate handlers didn't seem to notice her as they passed, cursing and muttering at each other in Arabic. "Don't go so fast." "Watch what you're doing." "Careful there. Are you trying to kill me."

From above came the sounds of an argument. Regan went up toward the dispute, hearing the distinct syllables of American English but unable to make out the words. And there was the smell and now the sight of smoke as a beam of writhing, moving light coming through the open door. Another shot cracked the air. The shouting stopped. For a moment all human sound ceased. Even the men with the crate paused to listen.

Then feet pounded on the stairs and a man, his form a black silhouette, stopped just above her. Another figure emerged from the dimness beyond a doorway to stand beside him. Their rigid outlines showed guns, like sinister dark lines, pointing up the stairs toward the third floor landing. One of them yelled. Another shout answered and with a clattering of feet the shapes of two more men appeared above them. One bulked large with what looked like a carton in front of his body. The other had a heavy canvas bag over a shoulder. The armed men stood aside to let them pass.

"Crazy," one said as they clattered past Regan. "Claims the American tried to rape her."

The gun hung useless in her hand.

"Is why women should be veiled. Even I am tempted ... ."

The exchange became incomprehensible, the men reaching the area lighted by the open front door. They were outside now, and she'd done nothing to stop them. Why have a gun if not to use it?

What had happened up there? Besides attempted rape and the crazy woman thing. Something else about throwing a lamp and shooting? The wall was hard against her back. She coughed into the folds of her veil, beginning to feel the effects of the smoke.

Crazy woman? Maybe that was the way Mitch would be describing her to Craig. She could hear his voice punctuated by clicking teeth saying, "She ran out of here like some crazy woman and took my gun. God knows. She's probably going to get her ass killed."

He'd be right if he said exactly that. She'd been operating on automatic, not thinking, just running toward the obvious source of trouble and hoping some brilliant idea would occur to her or some glaring opportunity would open up. But even thinking about shooting men who were doing nothing worse than carrying boxes out of a burning building? That was a non-starter. She might consider it as an intellectual exercise or, more likely, as a sort of gut-level possibility, but she'd never do it.

If only Mitch would get the distributor cap from the unguarded Tunisian van. Or? Why hadn't she done it? Because she had no idea what a distributor cap looked like. That was why.

She could've let the air out of the van's tires, though.

And they could've driven on its rims or called for a replacement. Delays would work only if there were cavalry troops on the way, and if the Muk was as besieged as Mitch had indicated, there was no cavalry. Certainly, Mitch would get no help from military intelligence. The Mukhabarat al-Khabaya or MEK was working hand in glove with this Wentworth man. That'd been clear from the intercepts and the events of the day. In fact, if anyone showed up, that's who it would be.

Tucking the Glock into her belt, she edged on up the stairs, one hand on the wall. As she did a woman's voice shouted in English, "Stop! You God damn bastards." There was another shot, and a bullet whizzed past Regan's cheek, close enough to stir the folds of her hijab. Regan dropped down and clung to the wall, a riser gouging one hip. From below she heard a clunk and the high-pitched sound of a ricochet.

Then a man hurtled out of the smoke up above shouting something in Arabic about calling 180 for fire trucks and not to shoot. One of his shoes hit her shoulder, and he would have fallen if he hadn't had a hand on the bannister. As it was, his feet scraped and slid, he cussed and bad breath reached Regan's nose before he got himself rebalanced and clattered on down the stairs. She looked after him still smelling halitosis. Karim. Of course.

Too bad he hadn't killed himself. His shadow melded into the dark below. As it did, there was another shot and a beam from a flashlight played down the staircase, exploring the area above her. It picked out the two guards in their kefiyahs, showing them pressed flat against the wall, their guns aimed upwards, but they didn't shoot at the light source. It found Regan on the stairs. It probed through air that looked thick enough to cut. The smoke was no longer dancing but filling the hall and getting heavier by the moment.

"You two," the woman half-shrieked through a fit of coughing, presumably addressing the men on the landing. "Get down there and stop them. They're thieves." She hacked and wheezed and now Regan could see that she held a pistol of some sort in her right hand. Her voice screeched, "Get them!"

Accentuated by the flashlight beam, the whites of the men's eyes looked red, looked frightened. One side had bought them off. The other side paid their salaries, but their eyes, caught in the light and faced with a woman holding a gun, said all they wanted was to survive.

"Go." The woman's order was a snarl of anger now and sounded familiar. Regan tilted her head to hear better. Had Wentworth brought a female assistant from Headquarters? If so, this might be a lucky break. The woman wanted Hayburner back. Regan didn't want Karim or the Tunisians walking off with it. They were on the same side for the moment.

The men may not have understood the woman's English, but they certainly got her meaning. They went. The flashlight followed them, then came to an abrupt stop on Regan's shrouded figure. Regan blinked but more because they'd begun to burn than from the glare.

"Who're you?" the woman said, coming down the stairs, coughing.

"Good God," Regan spoke aloud, realizing who it was. Pulling the end of her scarf free she said, "Lori. It's me. It's Regan." She coughed on the word. "God, I'm glad to see you." She started to stand up. "I'll help you. We've got to get down there to stop them."

Lori didn't lower the flashlight … kept Regan pinned in its beam. "Well," she said, "Regan Grant. I should've known you'd be skulking around sooner or later." The words came out through a smoke-roughened throat as a garble.

"Lori?" Even allowing for distortion, the words didn't match the woman Regan knew. Lori had come to her wedding. They'd shared lunches and dinners and attended each other's parties. But Lori hadn't been at Arnie's funeral or the reception … . Why? She'd thought it'd been tact, but Lori had never been one for the social niceties where Arnie was concerned. So …?

Lori bent over, coughing yet again. When she could talk, she said, "A jackal. I always knew you were a jackal nosing around Arnie and following Craig trying to pick up his scraps." The muzzle of her pistol, clearly visible in the flashlight's beam, was pointed straight at Regan who'd gotten only as far as a sitting position and decided to stay where she was. This didn't make sense.

The smoke stirred and thinned. Someone had opened a door or a window, which was helping for the moment but would also fan the fire. They had to get out. Lori said in her strangled voice, "I should've realized you'd turn up. Ar … Alex said so. He said you'd figured out about Hayburner. He called you the 'wild card in the deck.' A 'discard,' is what he meant. That's all you are. A discard."

"Right." Something terrible must've happened to Lori. Could Arnie's death have unhinged her? She'd been in love with him forever. Or smoke inhalation? That could alter the mind. Or drugs for depression? Must be drugs and stress and fear … and smoke. They had to get out of the smoke. Very slowly Regan raised her left hand, "Give me the gun, Lori. You don't need it now. Give it to me."

A hunched shape very like that of the bear of her nightmares loomed out of the smoke above them. Regan's eyes burned. She blinked. What was she seeing?

"I should shoot you." Lori was having a hard time getting the words out, and Regan wasn't sure she was understanding. "Even Craig would thank me. If your body's found here? No one would know it was me—"

The big shape above Lori seemed to slip, thumped hard as it bounced off the wall and began to roll down the stairs. Lori heard and turned; then screamed and fired. The shape, discernible now with arms and legs, slammed into her.

Shrieking, Lori fell backwards, a final shot banging from her pistol, her body tumbling toward Regan.

Before Regan could do more than brace herself, Lori's angular form crashed into her. Regan reached to grab her and got her hands wrapped into heavy wads of fabric just as something hard struck her head. Something else grabbed her sleeve, almost pulling her over backwards before slipping off.

For just an instant, too, Lori's face hung only inches from Regan's, the eyes wide and bloodshot and full of shock, the mouth open in surprise and heavily ringed with dark red lipstick, the jaw sagging into a wrinkled neck where tendons stood out in a scream.

"Re...gan," the apparition shrieked, but the fabric ripped from Regan's hands, then Lori and the other body were gone. The sound of wood splintering and a final scream of "Re ... gan" was muffled by the blanket of smoke and a new sound—the crackling of flames.

Regan edged forward to down the stairwell but could see nothing in the hall below. Her heart seemed to have climbed into her head, pounding against her ear drums, throbbing on her palate. For a moment she lay there. Then she pulled her scarf back over her nose and went down the stairs on her butt, unwilling to risk a fall and knowing at some point on the descent she'd find the railing had broken away. She breathed shallowly and kept her eyes closed to slits and counted the stairs—not because she knew how many there were but just as a way of convincing herself that she was progressing.

■ ■ ■
CHAPTER TWENTY-SEVEN
Cairo to Djerba

Dressed in fresh clothing from a shop in the Four Seasons, recharged from a nap and a soaking, drowsing bath, Regan felt a bit of optimism as she boarded a direct flight between Cairo and Djerba.

Thought you might find this interesting, Mitch had emailed, his language a bit convoluted to avoid using true names or compromising security. Learned from a dead man's cell that the lady who built the computer system flew out of Libya before the evacuation, leaving no one who knew how to manipulate its special properties. Which seems to make finding the boxes your local friends carried out of the Cairo house questionable. Do yourself a favor and let them play with what they stole to their hearts' content. Whatever's there is useless without the computer lady and maybe even with her.

Figured this might save you some time and trouble.

Several more bits of news. C. was here. He's got a swelled head ... you may not have heard that the top dog quit and C.'s got the job? That's the good news.

On the negative side, C.'s pissed about your absence. He wanted to take you home with him. But that's between you two.

Also, Richie got a triple whammy. Lost his computers. Booted out by the Egyptians. Fired by C. For sure today wasn't his day. He's out of a job, shit out of luck and presumably heading back into Libya.

One more thing. That contractor? He had some kind of medical emergency at the airport which seems to be why the Egyptians just booted the pair of them out rather than arresting them for stealing an aircraft. Lots of drama, obviously. God bless. Mitch

Craig had wanted to take her home. Probably it had to do with his getting the D/CIA appointment. And what would that mean for their relationship? He'd want it to appear stable ... at least until he got Senate confirmation.

Her Tunis Air flight roared to life, raced down the desert runway to leave the brown earth behind. She watched the barren Egyptian coastline run invisibly into Libyan beaches, eventually spotting the peninsula and the walls of Saharan Enterprises, recognizing them from her explorations via Google Earth. For a time afterwards there was nothing to see except water until the olive-tree speckled, sandy island of Djerba appeared ahead. She set her watch back an hour—turning the two hour flight into one—as the aircraft began its descent.

She'd been warned in Cairo that the Djerba airport was a mess, but she wasn't prepared for the sight from the air. The little airport—surrounded by olive groves and palms and graced by a multi-domed terminal—had been built to accommodate the million-plus tourists who vacationed annually on the island. Now its bright white roof arches rose above a seething black mass that extended out of the parking lots and back down the road to the mainland, looking like a horror film rendition of army ants consuming a citadel. These were guest workers fleeing Libya. They would be exhausted and hungry after days if not weeks of frantic effort to reach safety. They would be desperate for places on the jumbo jets squatting on the aprons—aircraft sent by India and Pakistan, South Africa and China among other countries—to carry them home.

She spotted the policeman at the foot of the stairs before she'd cleared the aircraft's exit door. He was a tall, straight-bodied man like all of the Baralguiba clan, and she suspected he was waiting for her even though he seemed fully engaged, flirting with one of the air hostesses. Only when she came within two steps from the tarmac did he look up, his eyes glinting with leftover sexual promise. They sobered quickly. "Madame Regan?"

She moved out of the way of the two other passengers who'd been on her flight and said, "That's me."

"I come. Drive you." His English was halting. "Please to come." He gestured toward a police car, the blue light on its top flashing. She hiked her backpack higher up on her shoulder and went.

"Road very bad, Madame," he told her, holding the front passenger door open. "Bad because there are these many peoples. We go into boat. Me? I call myself Abdul Mujib." His uniform was clean and pressed, his face recently shaven, his teeth white and even, his black hair slicked to the back. She guessed his age to be around twenty-six or seven. His car did not make such a good impression, the interior showing years of hard use and inadequate cleaning with a smell of dust, grime, old sweat and oil. An open and much-used telephone directory with dog-eared and torn pages lay on the floor among discarded bottles and cans.

She dropped her backpack onto the directory and climbed in.

A passenger bus that had obstructed her view of the terminal drove away, and the Tunis Air pilot cut his engines. She'd been told that this aircraft was one of many being pressed into service to ferry people off the island. Tunis Air flights were dead-heading into Djerba from surrounding countries and carrying refugees out. The United Nations was paying the freight.

Now she could both hear and see the scope of this human disaster, could identify the rumbling roar of the mobs, could see armed frontier police reinforcing existing fencing with barbed wire. Inside the terminal, clearly visible through glass walls, the bright signs of car rental and tour companies, of money exchange booths and airline counters rose over the dismal sight of more heaving crowds.

They drove past the terminal to park alongside a concrete block structure badly in need of a coat of paint. "You wait," Abdul Mujib said and took her passport and entry card into the building. A mini-bus pulled up next to her, and a flight crew in Singapore Air uniforms climbed out, the women beautiful in their colorful sarong kebayas. Next, a Mercedes arrived carrying a family of Saudis—one woman in a tight silk dress and matching spike heels, the other in abaya and niqab with two boys in shorts and shirts.

Abdul Mujib returned with her passport properly stamped. Back in the driver's seat, he took a paved if badly worn road around the airport perimeter. Weeds grew up between wide cracks and ate at the edges of the macadam. The road, though, led them to a back gate. Abdul Mujib produced a key which opened it. About a mile later, he drove into an olive grove and a minute on stopped by a small domed shrine. A tall man, who'd been seated reading a newspaper on its white-washed front step, stood up and brushed off the back of his camel's hair burnoose. It was Daud Baralguiba.

"I wish to be certain you arrive safely." Daud shook hands through her open window before climbing into the back seat. Abdul Mujib put his vehicle in gear and resumed the drive.

"How is—" Regan meant to ask about the family, expecting the usual ritual formalities, but Daud cut her off, saying, "We will talk later." He leaned his head against the side of the car and closed his eyes.

Okay. Regan faced forward. They'd cleared the olive grove where Daud had waited and were on a narrow but paved road. White road markers passed as did small houses behind beaten earth yards. She saw an occasional goat tethered by a leg and one scrawny horse in a pen fenced with cactus.

Abdul Mujib said nothing. The wheels hummed and the road was empty. It was as though the tragedy spilling out of Libya had sucked all of humanity into its vortex leaving this part of the island deserted.

With little to see, she pulled out her cell, changed the sim card, and checked her email. There was a message from Sam Brannigan. It repeated what Mitch had told her about Craig's big news, then said:

You must know you're in major trouble over the T. affair. This is the biggest staff officer compromise since Ames and the fur is flying. The first victims have already fallen--it was the excuse the director used to let Richie go and the final nail in his own coffin. He's resigned rather than deal with it.

But about T. As you would expect, the people who hired, vetted, and trained her and did so at great expense have Teflon hides. I've ducked the bullet, too, which leaves you as the next designated scapegoat. It may not be fair but that's how it is. I'm in no position to help you and Craig will have to be holier than the pope. In short, get your ass back here, as ordered, and defend yourself. I'd also hire a good lawyer if I were you.

Take my word for it. The longer you avoid returning the worse it looks for you. Sorry, but there's no good news here.

Regan read the message three times without assimilating the reality. She'd expected something but not this blunt "hire a good lawyer." For God's sake! For all her negative thoughts, it couldn't be that bad. And, "The final nail in … ." What were the other nails?

Well. There was nothing she could do from this little island. She scanned down her menu of other emails, finding one from Chance saying he'd driven by her house and seen a government Mercedes sitting out front. There was another from the DGSE chief, summoning her to his presence. That didn't surprise her. Even though she'd avoided customs and immigration, somehow they'd learned she was on the Cairo-Djerba flight, assumed she'd be driving to Tunis.

She glanced over at Abdul-Mujib. Him? Using Maghrebi Arabic, she said, "The DGSE knows I am here."

"This is so," he said with a sideways glance. "They watch all entries to our country."

"And they think you drive me, why?" She wanted to know just how exposed the Baralguibas were.

"I am off-duty. My cousin in Tunis is chauffeur for you there. He calls to say you need a car and help exiting the airport and you pay very well." Abdul-Mujib grinned. "I tell this to security man. You do pay very well, is this not so?"

It was so. It was no cover at all. It was the best cover they'd have. She leaned her head back and closed her eyes. Behind her Daud slept. The air in the car was warm and stuffy and she was tired … so tired. She nodded off, waking to find Abdul-Mujib had parked alongside a decrepit garage that stood just above a sandy beach. To her right the blue of the sea was broken by a long pier that had seen much better days. A speedboat of some seventeen to twenty feet with a small cabin and twin outboard motors sat alongside it.

"Here we are," Daud was already out of the car.

Half-asleep, she negotiated the rotten wood and ladder, dropping onto what by comparison seemed a very solid and sturdy boat deck. Daud and Abdul-Mujib stood on the pier above, talking, the sound of their voices a comforting rumble through which she could hear a few words. "Your mother will… when next … the garden … dress … ." She gathered Abdul-Mujib was about to be married, and they were discussing a few last minute details.

If her relationship with the clan survived the next few hours, she'd have to remember to send him a generous wedding present.

The boat rocked soporifically under her feet. Through the open door of a small cabin she could see two cushioned benches. Just what she needed. She stretched out on one and went back to sleep, not waking again when the boat's twin engines fired up or when their roar ceased.

"Madame Regan," Daud's hand on her shoulder brought her back from a dream of falling down a well. She opened her eyes to find the boat rocking at a new mooring.

Groggy, she fumbled for her sunglasses, which had slipped off her head while she slept, hefted her knapsack, and followed Daud up the ladder of a short pier—this one well-maintained. Beyond, a sandy beach ran up to scrub grass and a two-story, square, concrete-block villa painted white and backed by olive trees. Both north and south and at irregular intervals similar houses spotted the coastline. The town of Zarzis was a dark smudge on the horizon. The sun was a benign source of warmth and light having none of its summer glare, just glittering playfully off waves and windows and creating deep shadows under vegetation.

Still only half-awake and adjusting her sunglasses, Regan stepped from the little pier. Sand shifted under her feet and blood seemed to drain from her head. The breeze changed directions, and she was assaulted with the smell of smoke and stewing meat. She swayed a little, reached out to stabilize herself against a post, blinking. For a moment the blending of sea and sky made everything look upside down, distorted, like she was holding a mirror at waist height and staring into it, the sky at her feet. She had the sense of being drawn into an indefinite world of blue, into an optical illusion.

Zarzis

"The women prepare a meal," Daud said of the aroma. He led the way to the house. The bout of dizziness had passed, and Regan followed retying a scarlet and gold Hermès scarf around her neck. She'd found it at the Four Seasons' shop and had fingered the fabric, remembering an identical one Craig had given her early in their marriage, a reminder of a happy period. So happy and so long ago.

Eleven years now. It'd been the Upperville Horse and Pony Show the summer before she was due to get her master's degree. Her mount—a Highwinds-bred Appendix Quarter Horse—had done very well, and word had circulated about the "horse from Wyoming." This tall man had come over to take a look and introduced himself as "from Wyoming. From Casper to be precise." They'd seemed to have so much in common and he was so handsome that the differences in ages had been inconsequential and, by the time she learned he was married, it was too late. She was captivated.

During her last semester of grad school, he'd obtained a divorce and they'd married a week after graduation, her family cramming into the main rooms of the Highwinds ranch house and spilling out onto the verandas, the day sparkling with high-altitude Wyoming sun. Boulder Ridge towered 2,000 feet vertically over it all, a backdrop of shifting color. There'd been a herd of elk in the barn pasture. Arnie had been the best man, of course.

Two weeks later, after a honeymoon week in the Tetons, she and Craig had flown to Rome where Craig had taken up his duties as the new chief of station.

Well. She'd decorated their spacious Roman apartment, worked with their cook, entertained and been entertained. Craig hadn't objected when she'd bought two horses so that they could ride together, which they actually did on some weekends. He had encouraged her art classes and her participation in philanthropic work with the other wives of the diplomatic community.

Children. She had expected to get pregnant. Craig had been ambivalent but not actually negative. So? She'd tried, anyway, and tried and tried and consulted fertility doctors and been disappointed. No reason. No children, either. It happened. Life happened, but she could take fertility treatments, try new technologies or they could always adopt. "Of course, darling," Craig had said. "Whatever you want but not now. Someday. When we settle in one place."

Arnie had visited about once a month through those years, dropping in unexpectedly, making a pass at her once, another time deliberately cupping his hand around her butt while walking into a restaurant with Craig at her side, Arnie trailing. It'd been such a shock, such an insult, she'd thought she must be mistaken, but then he'd followed it with a distinct pat, as though they now shared a secret and she'd been a good girl. Somehow she'd repressed her outrage and hadn't followed through on an instinct to turn and slap the hell out of his big face, one she'd known would wear a conspiratorial smile. Instead, she'd stepped back and planted a spike heel square on his instep. Then hearing his involuntary grunt of pain, she'd turned. It had been her turn to smile.

Craig hadn't noticed a thing.

Nor had the incident discouraged Arnie's visits, but he left her alone except for barbed comments about her lifestyle. "Good God, Regan," he would roar across a dinner table in a voice designed to be half-teasing, half-serious and for everyone to hear. "Are you still wasting your time with those music appreciation classes? That's pretty much like dry masturbation, isn't it?" And on the subject of her charity work, "Two thousand cotton-pickin' dollars? Congratulations. You ladies worked on that event for how long? What's that average out at, anyway? A penny an hour? Good job, but maybe next time you should consider waiting tables and donating your tips."

One June day, two months before she and Craig were due to leave Rome, their tour over, Arnie had arrived with a bombshell in his pocket.

"Here," he'd said after dropping his suitcase in their guestroom.

She'd opened the letter he handed her, had seen the lack of letterhead and two short paragraphs of type. **You have been accepted for the career training program and will be expected to report to Rm. 1001 OHB on 3 January ...**

"Of course, you'll do it," Arnie had said. OHB was the Langley acronym for Old Headquarters Building. "Take the training, at least. It'll improve your marriage. I always say mine would've been a lot more comfortable if Mary understood my job better. Besides, kiddo, you were born for this business even if you've yet to realize it."

"Up to you," had been Craig's reaction. "But it wouldn't hurt for you to get a little insider orientation. As Arnie says, it'll help you understand our work."

The letter had been an even more egregious pass than the hand on the butt. The words spelled 'separation.' She'd looked at Arnie and seen a smirk. Craig had called it differently. "He's just pleased at having done us a good deed," Craig had said later, cutting the ground out from under her.

"You want me to do this?"

"If you want it, I want it," he'd said. They'd gotten to that point in their marriage, the place where circular responses are the norm.

"I don't want it, then."

Which, of course, had not been the last of the matter. She'd gone for the training and found her marriage revived. Time at the Farm had made the time they spent together more interesting and exciting ... for the first year, anyway. And she found she loved the work and was good at it. Every day presented new challenges with a constant parade of fascinating people and situations. It'd been addictive. Training had led to an interim assignment which had led to a series of quick trips overseas to ... . Seduction? Arnie'd planned it all.

"Madame Regan!"

The cry jerked Regan into the present. Fadila Baralguiba had thrown open the villa's kitchen door and stood in front of it, her arms spread wide. She was a woman of broad shoulders, a high forehead and wide-set intelligent eyes. Her hands were toughened by work, her knuckles large, her nails blunt and clean. She was dressed in a calf-length skirt over thick stockings. Her blouse had a scoop neck and long sleeves. Her hair, the black threaded with silver, fell in a long thick braid down her back. Within the CIA she had been encrypted PLMAJOR/11.

Regan stepped forward to be met with a hug and a kiss for each cheek. Where Daud had been reserved, Fadila was her usual effusive self.

"We are most very pleased to see you," Fadila Baralguiba said, using French. "You are most welcome, Lilla Regan. We are happy to have you as a guest here in Zarzis. Long have we wished for you to see our home and our life in the south which offers the best of Tunisia and is the heart of our country."

Daud stepped past the women and disappeared through the door.

Fadila continued, "We are wishing you will stay for a very long time. Many of our family have come to greet you."

A chicken pecked close to the concrete stoop. Fadila's eyes focused on the bird, then moved off into the distance. She used her fingers to tuck a strand of hair back into the braid and turned her head to snap something at a child inside the house. She'd been an early advocate of the relationship. She'd also developed a personal friendship with Regan based on the hours they'd spent together discussing the similarities between their big families, trying out new recipes in Fadila's kitchen and, later, working over the accounts.

"It's okay, Fadila," Regan said. "It's going to be okay."

"Okay is good," but the fine, dark eyes continued to move about restlessly, and she continued talking as though she could control the situation with words.

Fadila was the family banker. Although she did not participate in the decision-making, which was the privilege of her menfolk, she had a genius with figures, and the family trusted her financial management. Still she would not be present when Regan was taken before the elders. Both women understood this.

Now with greetings complete Fadila went back inside, inviting Regan to follow. She did, finding herself in a small rectangular kitchen with one unglassed window alive with activity. Three women squatted on the floor chopping vegetables on boards. A fourth women stood at a cast iron sink scrubbing carrots. Another woman, tears in her eyes sat cross-legged on the floor peeling skin from onions. They all took a moment to glance at Regan but did not smile and only murmured a faint greeting.

Fadila tipped her head at an interior door.

Edging through the crammed kitchen, trying not to disturb anyone and skirt well clear of the cutting boards, Regan stepped into the next room, trailed by the nose-twisting odor of sliced onions. She was in a narrow, windowless space. Painted concrete floors were partially covered by red and white woven Berber carpets. Concrete block walls sported brilliant reds on two sides faced by bright azure on the others. European-styled, doily-decorated couches sat against the long walls. A coffee table sporting a lace runner and an arrangement of artificial flowers in a glass bowl was conveniently close to one of them; small tables separated the others. Beyond a high arch, a long table covered with a cut-work cloth ran down the center of the next room. There, at least ten places were set, and glasses and bottles of water waited. Overhead, single bulbs suspended on cords lit the two rooms with a harsh, blue light.

Three elderly, heavily bearded men sat on the couch behind the coffee table. They all wore European slacks and shirts under dark brown burnouses, their hoods lying folded against their backs.

"Madame," Daud led her to the three men who did not rise. She was not given their names although Daud presented her to them. Automatically, she did the polite and expected thing and reached forward toward the closest of the three to shake hands, having to lean awkwardly across the coffee table to do so. He ignored her. They all did. Not by looking away, but by looking through her, denying her presence.

Someone dropped a pan in the kitchen.

The men didn't seem to have heard.

Turning back toward Daud, she saw he had walked into the dining area, his footsteps loud as his shoes slammed against concrete. As she watched, he returned holding a chair. For her, obviously. He put it down at the far end of the coffee table.

"Thank you," she began to say, taking a step in that direction just as Daud sat on it.

A clucking from outside said the chicken had yet to lose its head. Women's voices came as a murmur from the kitchen. A lower wash of sound meant the sea continued eating at the shore. Neither Daud nor any of the three men said anything. She stood with her hands heavy at her sides, weighing down her shoulders. School children called before the principal for disciplinary action must feel this way. It was a new sensation. Novel. Not an experience she would want to repeat.

There was the vacant couch behind her. It was a low divan with a deep seat, placed an uncomfortable distance from the coffee table and the gathered men. Clearly, they expected her to make a choice—stand or sit. Either way she'd be at a disadvantage.

Was there really any good reason why she'd come here? Why wasn't she on a plane to Washington? Or Tunis, for that matter?

Dropping the backpack she'd been carrying, she wheeled around and strode across the room, feeling her widely flared pants swirling around her legs. The woven carpet muffled her footfalls until she reached bare concrete. There her sneakers squeaked ... two, three squeaks and she was back on a carpet. She selected a chair from the side of the dining table, picked it up in both hands and carried it back to place it; not opposite the men or Daud but on a corner next to her backpack where she could see all four without turning her head. Seated, she folded her arms over her chest and waited. This was their ball game and their nickel. They'd called. She'd come.

Daud sat erect, his hands lay in his lap, his expression impassive, his eyes aimed at some point over her head. What was his position here? This Daud was a stranger, as different from the polite, affable head of household she knew as acid from rain water. For that matter, where was the stepper on scorpions?

There was no silence here. Not with the endless muttering of the sea and the chatter of women, but the room felt quiet, as though the thick robes the men wore absorbed sound. Or, it might have been the men, themselves, who did so ... who deadened the air with their mere presence.

Her throat wanted to make a noise, felt clogged as though she should clear it, urged her to say something. What would that something be? Good question. Think about her options instead. Learn something from the old men.

The elder at the far end of the couch from her bore quite a resemblance to Daud. In fact, take away the beards and she'd bet they were all close family members. Perhaps Daud's father and uncles? Or they might all be uncles. The body types were the same, too. How about their ways of thinking? They were of an older generation, would be more traditional. But it'd be more than simple generational and cultural differences. They'd perhaps suffered during the aborted Libyan invasion. There would've been other attitude-shaping events about which she knew little or nothing—prejudice in the general population against them, police harassment, exclusion, hatred.

The three had faces lined with age above well-trimmed beards, all nicely rounded and approximately the same length, as though each had been barbered by the same hand. It was disconcerting.

Should she be—

The central elder nodded at Daud.

"Madame Regan," he said. "These elders wish you to speak of what you want with us, and why you put our people in Tunis in danger." Daud's face gave no hint that he had full knowledge of what she wanted from the clan in Tunis and what had happened at the Cité.

And what was she supposed to say?

"Madame?" Daud prompted.

Daud might be cock of the roost in Tunis. But ... . The grammar school analogy returned. Here he seemed a recalcitrant schoolboy; she his naughty accomplice. Both of them had been called on the carpet to be reprimanded.

The elder near Daud jiggled his knee at her continued silence or, possibly, not that but something else. What? He would be accustomed to silent women, but his silent women came with downcast eyes. His silent women wouldn't stare and assess.

They'd all stopped looking through her when she collected the chair. Now their eyes, narrowed with disapproval, seemed to have found something interesting elsewhere.

Center man was looking at Daud. He would be the clan head unless these three were a triumvirate. Which wasn't likely. A tongue flicked inside jiggly knee's beard. The boss sat impassive, seemingly indifferent to her silence.

Jiggly man said, "Well. We are waiting to hear what you have to say to excuse your irresponsibility."

Enough was enough. She stood up and spoke formally in French. "It seems we are all wasting our time. My organization and my president assumed we were dealing with men who weighed risks against gains and acted accordingly. Obviously, this may well involve danger. You, however, seem not to know that there will always be men like the al-Salan pigs and the need to act with courage and initiative as Daud and his people did." She turned to Daud. "My apologies for creating this embarrassment for you. It was not my intention, and I can now see that this situation will best be resolved by my departure and the severing of our arrangements. If you could arrange for someone to take me to Zarzis, I'll trouble you no more."

Daud's hands gripped the edges of his chair, holding himself in place.

Jiggly knee's tongue disappeared. The man in the center stood and said something in their local dialect to Daud, concluding with a sweeping gesture that dislodged his burnoose from his right shoulder and sent the fabric sliding down his arm. In French he declaimed, "Take her away. We are finished here."

And so must Moses have looked when he commanded the waters to part.

"Wait," Daud said. He was now on his feet, his face flushed, while outside the murmur of the sea seemed to have grown louder, the sound entering the room in a way it hadn't earlier.

Regan waited. Under other circumstances she might have felt sorry for him, but now? What a mess. This is what came of following your own advice. Weigh the risks against the gains, she'd said. And that's exactly what she'd done; was the reason she was here. Well. Sometimes you win. This wasn't one of them. She'd walked into a tribal power struggle, was a pawn in another game. As such, she couldn't win. But once she and Daud were back in Tunis? Perhaps something could be worked out … privately and quietly.

The outside sounds resolved into the distinct rumble of a truck's engine or, possibly, several engines. She heard vehicle doors slam and male voices calling to each other. That explained the number of places set in the dining area.

Daud had begun talking, again in dialect.

Women's voices rose in the kitchen and mingled with male ones. The elders and Daud paid no attention. All three of the older men were on their feet now, all trying to make themselves heard. The boss shouted, his arm swept out again to point at Regan and, again, his burnoose slipped but his opposite hand was ready and caught it leaving him looking like a portrait of an orating Roman senator.

That was Regan's last sight of him. She picked up her backpack and left the room. If necessary, she'd walk to Zarzis, but she suspected that wouldn't happen. She'd recognized Bashir's voice among the new arrivals.

A moment later she found him sampling his mother's cooking. She edged inside the kitchen which had seemed crowded before but was now crammed by the addition of five younger people.

"Ah, Madame." Bashir put down the spoon amidst a chorus of greetings as his cousins spotted Regan. She recognized the short, compact shape of Razid Mohammed and the taller, lean wolfish face of Saleen Reza. Bashir's younger sister, Fatima, was near the door, dressed as usual in blue jeans and an embroidered jean jacket. The fifth person was an attractive woman wearing a long skirt and a yellow and green teeshirt sporting an Oregon duck and a big O. She was introduced as Mina Kanoun, Fatima's classmate at the University of Tunis whose family came from Sfax.

"So," Bashir nodded toward the sitting room after the exchanges had ended. "Are the old bastards up to their tricks? What did my uncle have to say about it?"

Fadila slammed a lid onto a pot. Everyone looked at her, but she'd said what she had to say with the pot lid and busied herself with a basting ladle. The other women followed her lead, all suddenly fully occupied.

"I could use a ride into Zarzis," Regan said.

"You'll need someone to drive you at least as far as Gabés if you think to fly to Tunis," Fatima said.

There was a chorus of agreement from her brother and cousins, all obviously relieved with the change of subject and the practicalities of travel in difficult times. Jerba airport was impossible. The road into Zarzis was impossible. The refugee problem was impossible. People were starving and dying along the road. The entire situation was impossible.

"But," Bashir said, his voice rising above the general. "But there are no flights from Gabés to Tunis until tomorrow. But, we return to Tunis by car this evening, and we are thinking you will return with us."

"Good. How soon can we leave?"

Fatima laughed. "We've only just come, and I want my dinner."

This sparked a variety of other comments and exchanges about when the meal would be ready and who else would be coming. The son of an uncle's wife's sister would not be present because he was building cots for a refugee relief group. A schoolmate of Razid Mohammed's, who everyone had hoped to see, was down at the border selling cigarettes that, it seemed, had been smuggled in from Algeria. And what was that all about? The cigarette traffic had been going the other way. Hadn't it?

Within moments, Regan was forgotten. She made her way through the press of bodies and out the kitchen door. The chicken had disappeared.

Had she really screwed this up? The 'old bastards up to their tricks?' And Daud? His nephew, Bashir? A generational struggle? The old against the young? Fatima and her jeans, while her mother ran family finances from well behind the scenes.

A clacking palm at the side of the house carried on a one-sided conversation about wind and humidity. The sun had passed its zenith. She followed a path around the house to the top of a dune where she could look out over the ruffled face of the sea and a low shroud of mist that obscured the horizon. The breeze soothed her skin and, once she'd removed her scarf, it tangled her hair. Turning, she walked along the dune until it ended at a gravel scree. Inland another seventy feet the trees of a well-tended olive grove offered shade. She found a rock next to a twisted trunk with a view of the sea and sat. Around her, the trees whispered an accompaniment to the surf.

Nothing in her experience or background had prepared her for the encounter. Cultural shock, yes. Cultural sensitivity, yes. The need to understand the local culture? Well, of course. But how do you do that? How can you ever do that without being born and bred to it, without a fluent grasp of the language and dialect?

"Well. Moving right along." Regan said aloud and almost smiled. The words were her grandmother's, were her response to unanswerable questions or unresolvable dilemmas. And she had much more pressing matters to handle.

In a way, though, she'd done well to delay her return to Tunis and to separate herself from the Hayburner problems. It'd given her time to consider, to let all the things she knew and suspected settle into place. She'd told Craig that Hayburner needed to be destroyed, but she was beginning to wonder.

Unzipping a pocket in the backpack, she removed a cell phone and consulted a number in Washington state that Mitch had provided from Fould's phone. She entered it, hoping for but not expecting a response. Hope was rewarded. The voice that answered sounded wide awake despite the time difference.

After an initial exchange explaining who she was, Regan said, "You've heard what happened in Libya?"

Anna Comfort Rose had, indeed, heard and voiced her indifference. That part of her life was over. She had done what no one else could do and she'd done it well. Now, she had new interests and new challenges.

For all of that, Anna Comfort was helpful. When Regan hung up, she had answers to a number of questions. First, the computers stolen from Saharan did run on a first generation Cumulus system, its artificial intelligence trained to work within the Saharan complex and its context. Taken outside it, the AI would need to be retrained and given access to huge amounts of memory before it could again function properly and, even then, it might never regain its former abilities. Moreover, it wouldn't be enough to simply return the stolen elements and hook them back up. Cumulus was an AI-driven system which in this case meant its experiences in the past few weeks had been the equivalent of negative training. Someone, namely Anna herself, would have to reverse the process before it could again become useful.

"Anyone else?" Regan had asked.

"You could try Jerry McCormack," was the answer.

Hair blew in her face and tangled in the phone as she took it from her ear. The waves beat an irregular rhythm. Regan found herself smiling for the first time since landing on Djerba. The conversation with Anna had been exactly what she'd wanted—useful for her and perfect listening for the DGSE. And what she planned to do next would certainly make their ears perk up.

She set the phone on her lap and used the Hermes scarf as a tie to keep her hair away from her face, then she called a Frankfurt number. Before she'd finished talking, she'd had to find her credit card and read off its numbers.

Finally she contacted a Lebanese businessman who kept a sleek, deep-sea fishing boat tied up at the Sidi Bou marina and asked if she might borrow it for a few days.

"I will send someone to stock the galley," the man in Tunis said as footfalls crunching gravel came from behind her.

Bashir appeared, "And here you are. I told Fatima you would come to the olive grove but she thought you might decide to walk to Zarzis." His face held a wide grin.

She held up a hand.

Bashir dropped onto another rock while she finished talking to the Lebanese boat owner.

"Now," she said, disconnecting from a call that, combined with the content of the call to Spanaway, Washington, should well and truly put a fox in the DGSE hen house. "Are we ready to go?"

"First, we must eat. My mother tells me to find you even if I must walk to Zarzis to do it. But not to fear. The old men and my uncle Daud do not stay. My uncle goes to the house of another uncle. The old men go to tell others of how this modern world is destroying the family values."

"Is it?"

"Probably," he agreed, his tone cheerful. "But it is our world, is it not? We have had our Jasmine Revolution. Is this not so?"

"In that case," she said and laughed. "Let's eat. I'm famished, and your mother is an excellent cook."

Shadows had begun to lengthen under the olives when they finally got into Bashir's car and started the long drive to Tunis, Fatima and the other younger people having decided to remain behind to try to track down their friends.

Regan was asleep before they pulled out on the highway. Some time later they passed Gabés where a little black Fiat swung in behind them. Bashir ignored it.

■ ■ ■
CHAPTER TWENTY-EIGHT
Habib Bourguiba Airport, Tunisia

Regan and Bashir reached Habib Bourguiba Airport half an hour before a leased aircraft carrying the CIA computer engineer, Jerry McCormack, touched down. They met him in a small terminal reserved for VIPs and private flights.

McCormack's round face wore a pair of glasses with gold wire rims. They were set above a long nose and a trimmed mustache that almost hid permanently up-turned lips. Jerry, despite his lack of humor, lived with a perpetual smile. "God's little joke," he called it.

This evening he was dressed in a polo shirt belted under the waistband of khaki pants, his clothing accentuating his thick middle and wide hips. He carried a small duffle bag. Bashir took charge of the man's diplomatic passport, found the rest of his luggage—one footlocker-sized locked metal case, two aluminum-sided suitcases, and one small tag-along bag—and handled the airport formalities.

Regan waited with McCormack, trading inconsequential social comments about mutual friends. Jerry had been in Paris when Regan had been stationed there, had headed up the station's cyber program, had coordinated a brilliant operation in tandem with the French, and had been responsible for the CIA contracts both Anna Comfort and George Tendale had had in Paris. From there he'd returned to Headquarters to run the cyber contract office before getting his dream job in Frankfurt.

Bashir reappeared, handing McCormack his passport. "We can depart when you wish," he said to Regan.

They moved outside into a chill night, the temperature modified by parking lots filled with cars that had soaked up the sun during the day and now radiated it back. Bashir's car was parked near the door. The American fell into the back seat as Regan and Bashir manhandled his heavy luggage into the trunk and tied it down with a bungee cord.

"So this little brain teaser of George's you mentioned?" Jerry said as Regan got into the back seat with him. "Something embroiled in politics I imagine. I'm betting your problem came out of George's idea for smart viral blueprints. It's a neat concept that's been around for the last three years at least and ... ."

Regan paid no attention but watched to be sure the DGSE surveillance vehicles that had joined them at Sfax were still on their tail.

Jerry liked to talk. She let him do it, got out an office cellphone, selected an encrypted channel and called Chance.

"I'm back," she said when he picked up. To Jerry she said, "Go on, I'm listening."

Chance said, "You need to get to the office. Right now. The goose is still here. Worse, she's hired a lawyer who's involved her congressman. The ambassador's having a fit ... well, not exactly, but he says he's not going to let us hold her. Keeps talking about civil rights and political realities. Plus he's gotten instructions from D.C. that he's to make a demarche to the government about some equipment the State Department says the DGSE inadvertently got its hands on but belongs to us. Which came as news to me. So I called Sam Brannigan who said he'd get back to me and wanted to know where in the hell you are. Plus –"

McCormack was looking out the window.

Regan cut her deputy off. "I understand. Tell the ambassador I'll brief him as soon as I can."

Chance raised his voice and repeated, "Plus I've been on the phone to the Office of Security. One minute they're sending an escort to take the goose home. The next they're sounding like the damn ambassador and saying I've got to be careful about her civil and legal rights. And it isn't just Sam. Everyone wants to know where you are."

Regan couldn't deal with Tiffany right now. "Anything else?"

Chance said, "In case you don't remember my saying so, I'm not cut out to do this sort of shit, and I'm not getting paid the big bucks to do so. I told you before, and I'll tell you again, you should've insisted on getting a deputy assigned here. But since you didn't, it's on you. So get your ass in here. You deal with the ambassador and the congressman and Headquarters. And you've got to get the goose out of here. The rest of the staff ... the ones who haven't already left ... say she goes or they do. Get it? Come back or you're not going to have a station to come back to."

"Soon," she soothed. It was already too late to do anything about the ambassador's problems today. It was too late to talk to what remained of her staff. Chance was right, though. Tomorrow ... . No. The next day.

She changed phones and tried calling Craig. His new desk was where the buck was supposed to stop. Let him take care of the Tiffany hot potato. The device at her ear rang and rang, finally going to voicemail. He wasn't answering. On purpose? Had he just looked at his caller ID and decided not to answer?

The car had left the Roman baths behind. Now the walls of the presidential palace slid past, floodlights making them bright and white.

Jerry had taken out a notepad and seemed engrossed in whatever was on its screen. He must've modified it to receive 4G. That was the advantage to knowing your way around an operating system. Not her forte.

She stared out the window as they passed the drive—more like an alley—that led to the American ambassador's residence. But what was her strength? She'd thought she had a talent for espionage, believed she was making a true contribution to U.S. security. But as the Tiffany situation just demonstrated, no one with a talent for self-deception could consider themselves worth much as a spy.

Except ... .

She reopened her phone and tapped out a text for Craig, finishing as Bashir skillfully maneuvered up the hill to stop the car on the cobbled pavings outside Regan's gate and almost alongside a boxy and battered delivery van. Rabi Baralguiba rolled down the driver's window and beamed at them, tipping his fingers at his forehead in a small salute. Cigarette smoke drifted out the open window. Fakir Baralguiba leaned forward in the passenger seat to see past his brother. *"Ça va?"* he called. The two men were short but burly housepainters, who sometimes helped out on surveillance jobs.

The theme music of a popular Egyptian sitcom came through the kitchen windows of the Turkish ambassador's house. The elderly night guard stepped through his postern, looked at Regan, and returned to unlock and open the large iron-hinged gates. Bashir released the clutch and rolled through to stop in the courtyard.

Rabi got out of the van and followed on foot. He exchanged a few words with Bashir, then, without any sign of effort, hefted McCormack's trunk to one shoulder. Bashir took the two suitcases. McCormack rolled his small bag.

"God," McCormack said, looking around at the dim gas jets flaring in glass containers alongside the gate and flanking the doors to the three homes opening off the courtyard's thick and ancient walls. "This is positively medieval."

"In here," Regan said, "Go on through to the kitchen … Bashir will show you … and make yourself comfortable. I'll be along in a minute. Just want to have a word."

The 'word' in question was for Rabi and Fakir Baralguiba. She wanted to know who'd sent them up here. Neither answered when she asked, just said how glad she was back and that they'd seen a government Mercedes earlier. It'd stopped and the driver had talked to the gate guard. They had nothing else to report, Rabi said, his eyes now focused on something over her shoulder.

She looked around, and there was Bashir, striding through the still open courtyard gates.

"I called them," he said without waiting for her question, getting into the back of the van as he spoke. "This is a time for taking care."

"The elders?" Regan asked.

He shrugged. "They are from a different time."

"Your uncle?"

"We hold him in high respect."

"Me, too," Regan said, not sure what exactly any of them were saying but … ? It was significant. She looked at each of them, said,

"Good men," actually using the phrase, *hommes braves*. They smiled. She smiled and turned away.

■ ■ ■ ■ ■

A few minutes later she joined McCormack in Hadija's kitchen, a stone-floored space with vaulted ceilings, great expanses of wood block countertops, and a walk-in fireplace that had been converted into a niche for industrial-sized ovens and burners. McCormack had already started unpacking, the two suitcases sitting open on a countertop.

Without knowing how much room he'd need, but being well aware of the man's habit of eating while he worked ... or just eating ... she'd decided the kitchen was the place. Besides, it had the working space of a small lab with a long trestle table, big stretches of countertops. As an add-on advantage, Hadija stored spare transformers in the pantry. McCormack might need them.

"Make yourself at home," Regan said uselessly. She waited a moment for a reply, got none, then began going through the refrigerator and freezer. No one else was there to make a meal. That left her. She got out a container of Hadija's frozen meat pastries, stuck it in the microwave to thaw and put on a pot of coffee.

Next .... Next what? George Tendale's notepad. She fetched it from her safe and, for his first job, asked McCormack to get through its passwords.

"Impossible," he pronounced, lifting a large monitor out of the footlocker. As he moved a custom-formed layer of foam to reveal another monitor, he added. "George invented the ultimate in computer security. Defeat his system?" He lifted his head to show her his permanent smile. His mustache quivered.

Negatives were McCormack's default setting, so all Regan said was, "I'd appreciate your trying," letting the subject go and transferring thawed pastries to plates and putting them in the toaster oven, her mouth salivating. The room smelled deliciously of Hadija's spices and of brewing coffee. Regan sliced tomatoes then walked through into the pantry and brought out paper plates and cups.

The oven hummed and glowed. Outside, a clank of iron meant the guard had finally closed the gates. She walked over to the windows above the sink to look out at the torch-lit courtyard to check and saw the old man had moved his folding chair and was sitting where he had line of sight into a room of the Turk's house where the Egyptian soap was playing on television.

It was all so normal.

When she looked around, McCormack had settled his bottom on a comfortable cushioned chair, had one hand on a mouse, and faced three monitors which were connected to two gray boxes with some kind of composite sides. He'd fanned out a small dish, perched it atop a black box, and placed both on a window ledge. George's notepad lay on the top of one of the gray boxes, a black wire holding them together.

A ping from the toaster oven refocused her attention on food and her rumbling stomach. The smell … . God, she was hungry. She dished up the food, gave one plate to McCormack and took another and a cup of coffee out to Bashir, who had to be as hungry as she was, checking while she was there to see if Rabi or Fakir wanted food or drink.

"No, Madame," and shaking heads were her answer. They'd eaten, they said.

Bashir added something short and pithy in dialect, then dug into his meal without explaining. None of them was worried about the prospect of one of the DGSE cars showing up and questioning their presence. Bashir was registered with the embassy as a local driver and would say he'd driven Madame home and was waiting for her. As for the cousins, they owned a home improvement business and worked openly for Regan, keeping the ancient house—one she'd purchased privately—functional.

Madame had called them in on a plumbing emergency, they would say, and they were waiting for the water pressure to come back up.

All of them, of course, had been called into the Ministry of Interior and questioned about their employment months earlier and had apparently satisfied the DGSE counterintelligence office that there was no more to the relationship than met the eye. So far.

Back inside, Regan sat down to eat her own meal and found that McCormack had cleaned his plate and started a program he called "Ratlick" for reasons he didn't care to share with her. "Okay," he said, "let's see what Ratlick's neural nets can do for us."

Talking more to himself than to her, he described teaching Ratlick how to defeat both passwords and firewalls. "It's like finding the answer to an obscure clue on a digital crossword puzzle," he said. "You have, say, ten spaces to fill in and a clue that could mean almost anything and you'll trigger a total lockdown if you start just randomly trying numbers and letters. What do you do? You've heard of entropic algorithms?"

Her taste buds enjoying Hadija's delicious meat and mint concoction, she let McCormack's words flow over and around her, had no idea what they meant but felt as though they had a sort of solidity, as though she could lean on them. Certainly, if nothing else, she could rely on him having a lot to say about everything. In a way it was relaxing, knowing nothing was expected of her. He didn't even need her as an audience. She ate the last crumb, closed her eyes, felt her head dropping, and jerked it upright.

"I think I'll take a shower," she said during a moment when McCormack was taking a breath. That would wake her up.

"Ummm," McCormack said, continuing with his current thought. "...offices in the basement of a tenement building with rats as big as—"

She was almost out the door, Jerry's voice following her when he broke off, yipped once, pumped a fist, and said, "Ratlick's in. Damn I'm good."

"Ratlick did it?"

"Shit. I did it. Who do you think trained the damn thing? Now all I have to do is figure out how he's customized this device. George was totally into reconfiguring everything."

She sat back down, closing her ears to McCormack's continued musings about George's habits, remembering how she'd rescued the notepad. She'd meant to email George; meant to send it up to London Station in the diplomatic pouch ... just hadn't done it yet. Maybe that'd been a good thing. Maybe looking at it would be a waste of time. Maybe she was squandering valuable time. So much depended on—

"Okay," McCormack interrupted her thoughts to slide the notepad down the table to her. "You've got clear text for the primary aps. It'll take Ratlick a bit longer to get into the aps with unique passwords."

"I'll let you know," she said and put him to work studying the Hayburner problem while she checked George's email account. It opened, and she began reading.

"This is weird," she said aloud after scanning several messages.

"What?" he muttered, glancing up from his monitor. Pastry crumbs adorned his mustache looking like paper scraps caught in a thorn bush.

"Reading these? He could be alive, just absent. In London or Washington or something." She fumbled for words and rubbed her eyes. "I keep thinking if I tapped out a reply and hit 'send,' he'd get it."

"George would like that. Immortalized by his work."

"Oh, right. Him, too. I meant Arnie Walker. There's a series of emails in George's deleted items file. One dated two days after Arnie died. It must've been in some automatic queue or somet... ."

"Death in the digital age," McCormack said, looking at the tomato stain on his paper plate. "Think of 9-11 and Flight 93. I remember how one of the guys on the plane was talking to his wife and telling her what was happening as the plane was going head-first toward ... ." His words accompanied his fingers. They hit keys and his lips moved.

Regan kept scanning, hearing a few of McCormack's words here and there. "... the normality was stunning ... myself, I think ... wouldn't even feel pressure ... God is a sado-masochist ... torture techniques ... ."

Jerry couldn't eat and talk at the same time, could he? She got up and fetched a bag of cookies she'd taken from the freezer earlier and set them before him. He didn't seem to have noticed but one hand absently dipped into the bag and the talking stopped. Cookies worked.

It still felt like she should be able to punch Arnie's number in her cell's memory and hear his boisterous, "Hey, kiddo. What's up?" She smiled at that thought.

McCormack finished his cookie but remained silent. Maybe the greater part of his large brain was actually needed for this work. The kitchen clock ticked. Beyond the shuttered kitchen window, the night guard opened the gate, said something to the men outside, then closed it. A rooster crowed from a nearby terrace.

The damn bird didn't know night from day, dawn from dusk. And what did he have to crow about anyway. The last of his hens had gone into the stewpot weeks ago.

The rooster crowed again, and Regan's smile faded. Her eyes read and reread one address and one sentence, then the entire paragraph, then the message and date. Her fingers had stiffened and hung poised.

Impossible. No way had this been in a queue. This was no anomaly. Except the alternative meant … . Death in the digital age might not be death at all but transformation. A chuckle burbled up and almost made it out of her mouth. Almost. She could call a dead man. If this was true.

If it was true, George had lied to Karim back at that restaurant meeting. What she'd heard on the tape had been a lie. Craig had lied. Everything was a lie.

But that couldn't be so. She'd seen the casket … at the National Cathedral for God's sake. No one would have the gall to conduct a fake funeral in the National Cathedral. Craig couldn't have carried off that good a masquerade. And why had George so cavalierly dismissed Karim's warnings when he'd known Arnie was alive?

No. She blinked her eyelids and ran her tongue over her lips before doing a search for Arnie's name. A list of six emails appeared. Two before the date of his death. Four afterwards—all with the subject line: **Work at Saharan**.

Arnie had wanted George to temporarily replace Anna, and George had refused repeatedly. Whatever had George been thinking? He might still be alive, if … .

It made sense. Lori. Everything. It made perfect sense. She got to her feet.

"You find something?" McCormack asked.

"No," she said and was grateful that he didn't look up from his monitor.

Arnie Walker, her mentor, was really Arnie Walker, the man in charge at Saharan, the man who paid al-Din and Juriy's salaries, had been Nat Fould's boss. Why? And where did Craig …? And what Mitch had said about the airport … probably had faked ill health, like he'd faked his own death. That was so Arnie!

She put one foot in front of the other, taking herself out of the room, the floor tiles slippery under her shoes, like the quicksilver footings of her life.

Oh, dear God.

Her grandmother liked to say, "A house built on sand will not stand." Liza had used those words when she warned Regan against marrying Craig, against working for Arnie. "I like those boys," she'd said, "They're charming rascals, but counting on them for anything important is like … ." What would she say now? Not "I told you so." That wasn't Liza's way. No. She'd say something like, "God helps those who help themselves." And, "No sense crying over spilt milk." And, "Where there's a will, there's a way."

Her shoes clicked on tile and, alternately, made only a whisper on the carpets. The air had a slightly musty smell, just the way it always did. Everything was familiar.

She wouldn't cry. Not from self-pity or the stupidity of disillusionment and disappointment and betrayal. She'd had a pretty good life. Right? She was good at her profession—maybe not perfect but respected—with her relationships built on a solid foundation of loyalty and friendship. Right?

She took herself to the bathroom, stripped and got into the shower. Her marriage was a failure, her career had bombed, she was homesick and needed her grandmother, and Lori was dead—killed while probably thinking she was protecting the man she loved. Poor, poor Lori.

One hand scraped the sponge down the opposite arm so hard the skin turned red. Hot water beat down on her, and she barely noticed her stinging skin or the way steam shrouded the shower stall creating sweat rivulets on what had been cold tiles of cobalt blue, on the four-inch squares that reminded her of the clarity of the Wyoming skies over Highwinds, over home.

Home.

She leaned back against the spray and let it pour over her head, straightening her hair into long ropes.

"You can always live with the truth," Liza Grant had preached to a much younger Regan. "It's the lies that'll kill you."

Lies. The word wrote itself large against the back of her head. She'd been drawn into a conspiracy by lies, and she needed to recognize the consequences because the truth ... Liza's famous truth ... had completely changed the shape of the world she'd thought she inhabited and altered beyond recognition the Hayburner operation.

The water was cooling noticeably. One of these first days she needed to install a larger hot water tank but that wasn't going to help her right now. Shutting off the tap, she grabbed a towel and stepped out onto tiles as red as the iron-rich hills and buttes at home. The contrast between red floor and deep blue walls should have been garish, but she'd found a slab of granite for the counter that was larded with reds, blues, and greens and had had a throw-rug woven in the same colors. Finally, the north wall held a sliding glass door that led out to a small terrace overlooking the sea. During the day the room glowed with light and color and normally she enjoyed just walking into it. Right now she saw nothing beyond the pictures of her thoughts.

If she'd taken her job seriously instead of mindlessly doing as Arnie asked, she would've realized the whole thing was wrong. She could've stopped him. No. Of course, she couldn't have. But she could've extricated herself and built a firewall between herself and that damn Libyan and Hayburner.

And Craig. Of course, Craig had been up to his eyebrows in the entire charade? What about Sam Brannigan? Who else at Headquarters? And MI-6? That Brit, John Darnley? What did he have to do with it?

"Regan?"

McCormack's voice came from beyond her closed bedroom door. He knocked loudly. "Regan? I've talked to Anna Comfort and got your problem scoped."

She threw on a robe and, water dripping down her legs and onto the tiles, opened the door. "What?"

His moustache quivered. His mouth was bent in a true smile that reached his eyes. "It's what you thought. The computers the Tunisians took? They're like a key. The data center? It's the lock. Put them together and I know how to play with your Hayburner viruses."

CHAPTER TWENTY-NINE
Tunis

The men in black suits came at dawn—two men she'd never seen before. They didn't comment on finding their quarry fully dressed at such an early hour but hustled her and McCormack outside and into her office Peugeot which was parked in the courtyard. The fact that they let her take her own car was a good sign. A police auto led the way. Two more followed, which she wasn't sure how to interpret. Police motorcycles flanked them but that just meant they were in a hurry.

Jerry McCormack sat in the Peugeot's passenger seat, his seat belt firmly fastened, his hands between his knees, his shoulders hunched. "This wasn't part of my plans for today." His tone was dry, and Regan realized he was scared. So scared he'd actually tried to use humor. It didn't work.

"Cheer up." She pushed her sunglasses up on her nose. Earlier, they'd segued from questions of how to explore and destroy the Hayburner viral complex to the Tunisian problem and Cumulus.

"I think," she'd said, "they'll give us everything they took in Cairo. But I can't guarantee they got everything out of that house. Also, they'll want you to show their engineers how to replicate Cumulus."

Then, she'd told him exactly what she wanted, concluding, "You can do both."

"Regan?" Jerry shook his head, using her name as though questioning her sanity. His smile remained as fixed as ever. Then, he added, "I have a bad feeling here."

The new commercial developments along the Lac de Tunis were on their left now—white walls gleaming in the growing light. The tall block that was to have been TenTech was just ahead, rising above its fellow leaders in the high tech industrial park. She nodded in its direction and said to McCormack, "That was George's creation, in a manner of speaking. That's what all the excitement is about on the Tunisian side. That's supposed to be the keystone for a Tunisian Silicon Valley."

"Or not."

"There's a lot of prestige and money riding on Cumulus. Then there's the spin offs ... the remote sensors that Cumulus will manage. They're already manufacturing them, ready for the big hardware/software debut."

"You're not comforting me, Regan. Already I'm regretting this."

"You've got your diplomatic passport." She'd made sure it was in his pocket before they'd left the house. Now she added, "There's no reason not to be totally candid about Cumulus. If they ask questions about anything else ... well, that's when we produce our diplomatic passports and demand to talk to Ruby Watson. She's the Consul General. But it won't come to that." She hoped.

"What about George's notepad?" He patted his pocket.

"Let me have it." She held out a hand and he passed it over. They both knew why. Jerry'd entered the country on a diplomatic passport but without orders, so the immunity Regan enjoyed as a member of the Tunisian Diplomatic Corps was problematic in his case.

Ahead of them the lead motorcycle had set a blistering pace once they'd reached the four-lane highway. Other drivers recognized the black and white bikes and the ubiquitous black vehicles and got out of the way. Regan stayed a comfortable two-car length behind the lead, but the chase cars were right on her rear bumper. A mounted cop's white helmet was only feet from her window. Morning traffic was heavy and, as usual, bumptious and suicidal, but their convoy zipped along as though enclosed in a large bubble of space.

CHAPTER THIRTY
Hammamet, Tunisia

The man who was technically Regan's husband hung up the telephone. He had tried the secure line to Tunis Station only to learn his wife wasn't there. He had repeatedly punched in Regan's number on her mobile STU. Where in the hell was she? He stared past heavy drapes and through the windows of his new downtown office in the Executive Office Building. The view of the White House's West Wing was worth its weight in gold. He ought to be happy.

Where in the hell had the woman got to? She'd tried him multiple times, but he'd been busy. He turned back to his desk, thumbed his intercom and said, "Try Regan's cellphone and tell her to call me on her STU."

While he waited he turned to his desktop monitor, got real-time satellite imaging of the Med from a U.S. Navy program, found the leased freighter. It was well out from land.

MI-6 had moved fast considering it was only thirty-six hours since he'd talked to Kendricks in London and secured British agreement to a limited engagement.

In twelve hours London had assembled a mercenary force large enough to hold the walls of the Saharan compound and had flown its members to an assembly point on Cyprus to rendezvous with the MI-6 leased freighter which was clearly on its way. Now, the British were assembling the manpower, ships, and materials needed to pack and transport massive tons of equipment out of the data center. Those resources would follow. The CIA would pay while, in the future, MI-6 would share control of Hayburner.

That was the deal. Now, if everything else moved as expeditiously, within the next three weeks the first elements from the Saharan data center should be arriving at Quantico where he'd leased a compound of unused warehouses.

His secure phone—one with an imaging program managed by his computer—rang. He minimized the video feed from the British freighter, pushed the small image to a corner of his monitor, and keyed Regan's call. And there she was, staring at him from his computer monitor. He hit a key and said, "Damn it, Regan. Where are you?" Best she should see how truly angry he was.

"It's not as though I didn't try to contact you."

Which wasn't relevant. "I've been looking everywhere for you. Can you imagine the position you've put me in?" He stopped, hearing the querulous tone in his voice. Well. Damn it. He'd barely had any sleep in the last few days.

"Thanks for asking how I'm doing," she said into his silence.

"Why aren't you back here? I've got a lot of containment to do where you're concerned and no time to do it. But at least I got an overnight ruling from Justice about your girl's problems. A U.S. Marshall is on his way to escort back here, and we have a court order to hold her under house arrest in Fairfax County while she's debriefed and we decide if there should be charges."

"Good." He'd actually moved very fast. "And a deputy for my station?"

"A deputy? Screw a deputy. It's going to need a new chief. And why haven't you answered my question. I need you here. Right now. Today."

"You think?" She turned her cellphone to give him a panorama that included the long golden walls of a fortified town and the deep shadows of late afternoon. Beyond a sandy beach was the brilliant blue of sea and sky and close up were men in black fatigues loading two big Zodiacs. He recognized them as 7.3-meter inflatable, Medline 3's with ocean-going deep hulls and knew they'd probably been a gift from the Central Intelligence Agency to the maritime unit of the Tunisian Gendarmerie. He also recognized a round-faced, grinning fat man in a blue polo, a suede jacket, and chinos. Jerry McCormack.

Christ! The Tunisian *Unité*, Zodiacs, McCormack, and the sea. An easy run to Libya. He watched men moving around on the beach while, in his monitor's upper right corner, the British freighter steamed toward the Libyan coast.

He felt a burning sensation just under his heart.

Reaching into a pocket, he pulled out a package of anti-acids, extracted a pill, and popped it into his mouth. A minty flavor flooded his mouth, gave him a moment to think. Why was she doing this? This wasn't Regan. Not the woman he knew. Did he give a good God damn about that or, even, why? The real question was how to stop her.

On another level he felt an odd sense of pride. This wasn't the Tunisians going after their operating system—they must've thought they had it. But Regan had persuaded them they needed more. She was using the Tunisians, but to do what? Clearly, she'd already retrieved the boxes stolen in Cairo.

Now he picked his words carefully. "Sweetheart. I can understand that you wanted to help, but we're working at cross-purposes here."

She'd taken off her sunglasses to rub her eyes as he spoke, and he saw they were rimmed with dark circles and glossed with the pink of the sleep deprived. He had no sympathy. If she'd done what she'd been told she'd have gotten lots of sleep.

He continued. "Listen, sweetheart. The problem in Libya is well in hand. But you can do something else for me as long as you're still in Tunis and … obviously," he nodded at the scene beyond her, "in tight with the Tunisians. Just cancel this thing you've organized. I can detail a C130 to you … it should be big enough and I can have it there within the next couple of hours. The Tunisians want Cumulus? We can guarantee they'll get it. No problem. Just move all the materiel the Tunisians took from Cairo out to the airport and send it back here. Believe me, taking it back to Libya is not only dangerous, it's unnecessary. And you'll have a grateful country's gratitude. Not to mention a happy ambassador and a very relieved acting director. What do you think?"

"What I think?"

A heat register behind his desk came on, stirring the flags standing there, sending ripples of red and white across the window and partially obliterating his view of a sudden and heavy spring snow squall.

When she said no more he continued, "Listen, sweetheart, please just do as I ask. Trust me when I say that we all appreciate you, but right now? You've been under terrible stress and probably you're suffering from the effects of smoke inhalation and maybe even some PTSD. I heard what you went through in Cairo. It was a splendid gesture that almost got you killed. Please don't do that again. Trust me. I'm asking. Okay?"

A white van pulled into the parking lot beyond the rail barrier Regan was using as a seat. Two uniformed Tunisians got out. Two more men trotted up from the beach, opened a side door and began removing equipment.

Craig spoke into Regan's silence, "Listen. Please get aboard here. Be a team player and do as you're asked. This is serious, Regan. So serious that Sam's talking about having to terminate your employment. He can recommend that, and I'd have to do it. Do you understand?"

Regan stared at her video connection, saw the flags fluttering behind Craig's head and came close to laughing at the condescension in his voice ... his talking to the little lady voice. What a joke. And implying her judgment was impaired? This from the man who'd aided and abetted Arnie, who'd stood back and done nothing when Arnie sent his boys on their killing spree?

As for firing her? She almost laughed. If even a hint that he was thinking such a thing leaked to the press, the results would be devastating. For him. Fire his wife? That would set off an investigative frenzy. In fact, given what she now knew, she could dictate terms to him.

Or had that been the problem all along? Dead women cause no trouble. Dead women can't make demands. Arnie no doubt thought exactly that. But Craig ... ? Air escaped from her lungs in a whoosh of sound. No. That way pointed to paranoia.

Hamid walked past her, a huge coil of thick rope balanced on one shoulder. Seeing her with the cellphone in her hand, he tipped a finger to his beret in a sketchy greeting. She smiled back. If he noticed the strain on her face, he said nothing.

To Craig she said, "Is that all? If so, I've got to go."

"No. Let me explain," he said.

She listened as he outlined what he'd arranged for the British to do, concluding, "So, you see. They'll secure and hold the facility while clearing it out. They've put this fellow, John Darnley in charge. Some cousin of Lord Kendrick's ... and isn't that so like the Brits to keep it all in the family. Anyway, you see what this means? You've already got back the crates the Tunisians pulled out of Cairo. Just get them out to the airport. I can have a plane down there in three hours ... four max. We'll reassemble everything at Quantico, and we can keep a very valuable operation going."

She looked at the video feed, "And, what are cousin John's orders if Arnie's ghost shows up at Saharan? My sources tell me a helicopter carrying a bald American landed in that compound this afternoon. What's cousin John going to do about him?"

"This is no time for—" Then, he got it. He understood. A muscle in his jaw ticked and his face hardened. Tone implacable, he said, "Butt out, Regan. And I mean it. Don't be tampering in what you don't understand. You stay away from the British and Saharan Enterprises. And keep the Tunisians out while you're at it. Remember who you work for. You think that bimbo case officer of yours has trouble? It's nothing compared to the hot water you're jumping into."

Her eyes burned, only partly from fatigue and she realized how she must look. Fumbling she found her sunglasses and put them back on. With her eyes hidden she stared at the man who was her husband, who was her director, who she'd spent most of her adult life trying to appease, who was up to his neck in a conspiracy that had come close to killing her. Everything about him looked familiar. She knew his suit had come from Brooks Brothers. She'd probably bought the shirt under it, one of a dozen from Macy's. And the tie? It had been a Christmas gift from her grandmother.

And calling Tiffany a bimbo? A girl who'd let love cloud her judgment was a bimbo?

One of his arms lifted and he rubbed his neck as he went back to pleading. "Regan. Things have changed. I've got an opportunity here. Do you understand? Don't screw this up. Be a team player. You always have before. You, me, Arnie ... . We're a team. Please."

Anger flushed her cheeks. She was a bimbo. Arnie walked on water. Craig would get the data center out of Libya, and, if he could get his hands on the programs and drives contained in the boxes that had just been loaded aboard the Zodiacs, he'd set up Hayburner all over again and—one way or another—Arnie would take charge. She had no idea how he planned to do it, but she had no doubt he'd figured a way.

Behind her, activity began to slow down. Men clustered on the boats and on shore. The van drove off. From beyond the town walls, a horn wailed as a train approached a crossing. It had the tenor of an ancient ram's horn, of the sort that might have called warnings from the city walls in the times of the Turkish Beys or earlier when the Phoenicians lived here. She said, "Good bye, Craig."

"You understand?"

She looked at his face, reduced to the size of a quarter. It was the face of the Acting Director of Central Intelligence, and all she could manage to say was, "I'm tired. I need to pee. I'll call you tomorrow." She clicked off.

The horn wailed again. The sun, a flaming deep red, had moved along its daily path and hung halfway between its crossing of the meridian and a hilltop behind Hammamet. Divorce. No more procrastinating. She understood its reality in the way she knew how dust blown in from the Sahara on the Harmattan winds created the red of the sunset. She had invented a man who didn't exist and in his name had excused Craig's womanizing. Through it all she'd remained infatuated … drawn as much to her image of the man as to the flesh and blood. Now? He'd morphed into a political caricature, a creature who sought to assuage some need she couldn't satisfy in the arms of other women and who treated her life like an inconvenient fact.

And there was the matter of conspiracy.

Her ears seemed plugged up. They rang with tinnitus.

"Regan?" Rafik had approached her, unseen and unheard. She tipped her head up. "You ready to go? Are you well?" He peered at her sunglasses as though he could actually see her eyes beneath the treated glass.

"Fine. But give me a couple of minutes." She gestured toward a hotel facing the parking lot. "I'll just make a quick stop and be right back."

In the hotel guest ladies room, surrounded by dark red marble slabs and mirrors, Regan splashed cold water on her face, thought about the call, about her early morning meeting at the Ministry of Interior, about the conspiracy, and fought the urge to feel sorry for herself. The image that stared back at her looked capable. Strong, if tired, with a hard expression in the reddened green eyes. Arched eyebrows. Straight nose leading to a mouth with lipstick eaten half off. All the features were there and eyeglassless, since she had misplaced her last pair of clear lenses and had yet to buy new. But the overall impression was cold and determined. Even without the academic touch of glasses it gave off the warmth of a showroom put together by a careless decorator. Cold. Determined.

As judgments went, that wasn't bad. Her grandmother had called her 'Regan the Tank.' "Put her in motion, and nothing stops her," Liza had liked to say.

Nothing stops her ... . That wasn't true. She always considered consequences but this time? Did she really want to do this? Did she care if Arnie used Hayburner to screw with history if the price of stopping him was any hope of a future with Craig? Was to put paid to her career? Arnie had sent assassins to kill her. True. So perhaps this was all about revenge? And, at what cost? Spending her next years alone, sidelined into meaningless jobs and boring assignments until she gave up and quit. Because while Craig might not be able to fire her, he sure as hell could sabotage her career.

She lifted a hand. Her long fingers trembled slightly. Fatigue. She used more water, cold water, and scrubbed off the remaining lipstick. She should be feeling some grief for wasted time and broken illusions and the removal of a prop that had held her up for the past decade. Well. She'd made her decision last night. She'd come to the end of a long if one-sided relationship. She'd made her stand, and it was final, now, this failure of young hope and expectations.

And there were the plans. Hers and the Tunisians. She'd laid down her bait, and they'd snapped it up, made their arrangements accordingly. They'd ... . Blood-shot green eyes met reddened green eyes in the mirror, their eyebrows raised. She stared at herself, remembering what Craig had said. This wasn't about her or Craig or Arnie, for that matter.

Eschira.

He'd been prepared for the Unit to fight al-Salan. He'd even thought a firefight with Qadhafi loyalists might be in the cards. But a British force? If he knew what the Brits were doing, he'd want to call his opposite number in London, stake out the Tunisians claim to the operating system used in the data center and arrange for some sort of collaboration. That'd be the smart thing for him to do. And Hayburner would go to Quantico. Arnie would take it over.

If she did the right thing for the Tunisians, she would call Eschira. He'd rescind his orders. Craig would credit her. He might even … .

Motions automatic, Regan reached for the door that would take her to the hotel lobby, then out and back to the Zodiacs. If she didn't call Eschira, she'd have to bear the brunt of his anger, too. If she stepped into that Zodiac, she'd be making a powerful enemy in Tunisia. And Craig would never forgive her.

"*Bon soir, Madame,*" a maid with a scarf over her hair bobbed her head at Regan and continued past her down the corridor.

She passed out onto the hotel porch and stopped. Beyond the parking lot, the men of the *Unité* waited for her, and a small swell sent little waves to lap against the concrete wall guarding the beach. A breeze carried the scent of smoke and damp and a memory of Lori's face only inches from her own. Lori, whose only crime was unswerving loyalty and dedication to one man, had died. That man.

■ ■ ■ ■ ■

Once they were underway with the Zodiacs speeding over the open sea and the coast a thin line separating sea from a red sky, Rafik joined her. He leaned close so she could hear him over the engine noise and the sounds of the wind and the hull slapping waves. "The last update from Tripoli is not good."

"No?"

"These Libyans go crazy. Qadhafi's loyalists seek revenge on anyone they suspect is a rebel. They act like wild animals released from a zoo. There is much looting and burning everywhere."

"In the compound?" The wind shifted a point and Regan got a spray of seawater in her face. She'd put on waterproof pants and jacket but, still, decided to move.

"Merde," Rafik waved her out of the wind and said, "The al-Salan cadres guard the compound walls, so it is not looted yet. But all the people there have left. The expatriates go last week. The locals have returned to their homes."

The Minister of Interior, Suleiman Eschira, had said much the same thing. "They abandon what we understand is a very large data center where the Cumulus system is tested. We understand this from our sometimes Libyan associate, Mustafa Karim. This he tells us." With these words he'd lifted his head to look directly at Regan for confirmation.

She had shrugged.

"Now," he said. "You, our CIA friend, disappear for a time during this evacuation. Next, you reappear near the Libyan border before meeting with a computer engineer who comes with several cases of equipment. You also arrange for the use of a very fast boat with large fuel tanks, and I can only think you intend some activity to close down this Saharan Enterprises to … possibly … destroy what is there before it falls into the hands of Islamic rebels or is taken away by these former terrorists of al-Salan. Your government makes this policy decision not to put 'boots on the ground,' as they say, so they do a clandestine operation." He almost smiled. "With you they can claim no boots, just the shoes of a lady. Am I right?"

"You think like an intelligence officer, Excellency," Regan said, forcing a smile of admiration for the Minister's cleverness.

"You see, Mohammed," Eschira turned his almost delicate features toward his aide, a man Regan had last seen during the take-down exercise and whose work name was Mohammed Abdul-Alim. "You see how she thinks to flatter me so that I do not notice how she evades an answer to my question." He turned back to Regan with an inquiring stare.

"In fact, Excellency," she said. "You put me in an awkward position. Perhaps we can leave part of your question for the moment and discuss another aspect of my orders."

He nodded, backlight from the windows shrouding his face and making his features impossible to read.

She continued, "My government is aware that the death of Mr.

Tendale leaves your development ministry with a problem. As you say we've been testing an early version of his Cumulus system at this facility in Libya. The current problems there … well … as you say. And, obviously, I cannot discuss anything sensitive." She stopped to underscore the delicacy of her position. "And as you surmise, Mr. McCormack and I have been asked to perform a few final functions at that facility. Extracting Cumulus in order to present it to you was not one of them."

"But you would not object to our doing so?"

"I hardly think I'm in a position to object to anything, Excellency."

The minister lifted a fine-boned hand to his head and smoothed an imaginary hair into place. Next to her Jerry McCormack said nothing.

After a long pause, Eschira said, "My people tell me you are a most resourceful woman, Madame, but even you must think twice about entering such a dangerous place as Libya is today. Here is what I am willing to do. We will not stop you from returning to this facility, but you will take some Cumulus-related computers that have fortuitously come into our hands. You will go with our *Unité* and our specialists and you will be under orders of our commander."

Thus began hours of hard negotiating and consultations between McCormack and the Tunisian experts before Eschira finally agreed to paring the mission down—specifically to leaving Tunisian computer engineers behind. The confidence of the Tunisian experts that McCormack could do as well as they or better helped. The argument that a small, highly mobile fighting force might escape attention from either Qadhafi's military or the international community and have the best chance of success clinched the arrangement.

■ ■ ■
CHAPTER THIRTY-ONE
Saharan Compound, Libya

The sea lifted and lowered the otherwise stationary Zodiac. According to the GPS, they'd hit the coast precisely where they'd intended. What they faced was a tall dark mass, the rock outcroppings that they'd seen on overhead photography.

"Pelo One," the radio crackled. "This is Pelo Two."

"Go," Rafik said in French.

"We have eyes on the marina," the voice belonged to Lieutenant Abdul Salim. "Nothing there. But we see lights of several freighters a mile or more offshore. One seems to be hove to. What next?"

"Rejoin command," Rafik instructed hooking the radio back on his belt and lifting a pair of binoculars to train them on the open sea where, indeed, a few lights indicated a moored vessel.

To the east, there were more signs of the coming day while the lights from shore—a line marking beach-front properties and a glow marking both Zuwara and Zawiya seemed fainter. Directly ahead, though, all was darkness. The Saharan compound on its peninsula was hidden behind two-story high rock outcroppings and invisible from their sea-level vantage.

"Maybe a little to the west," Rafik spoke in a low voice. Hamid swung the Zodiac several points west.

"There!" Hamid spoke a bit louder. A moment later they all saw it. The line of rock actually made the outer edge of a hook. *There*, as Hamid had said, was the mouth of a small channel. Four minutes later they swung around and into a tunnel-like opening. Hamid cut the engine. Two of the commandos took paddles. The second Zodiac rejoined them and did the same.

"The al-Salan will have watchers up there," Hamid pointed directly overhead. He spoke so softly his words were almost lost under the wash of the sea and the stirring of a pre-dawn breeze. "Perhaps gun emplacements."

"This reminds me of the grottos of the Algarve." Her tone, too, was hushed.

"And on the Algerian coast I see places like this." Half-drifting, the paddlers mostly steering, the water lifted them closer and closer while the sky lightened and the rocks—now rising directly ahead of them—became walls of black. It was quiet here. Too quiet. The men in the bow reached out with their paddles to push the Zodiac off the port wall and dark descended again. Night vision goggles helped, brought definition to the rock. Ledges paralleled the water on either side.

"*Là-bas*," Hamid whispered and pointed.

Ahead of them the channel widened. Slowly, watching for guards and keeping to the shadows, they drifted into a small lagoon. Overhead, the thread of visible sky had begun to lighten in a definitive way, reflecting on the water and producing a gloom. Regan pulled off her goggles, seeing others doing the same. Yes. There was a boathouse holding what looked like a speedboat, something with a low black hull. Next to the building, a short pier extended out from a rock ledge and into the water.

It would be beautiful in daylight. At this hour there was a feeling of mystery and danger.

Still, there were no signs of watchers—no glow of cigarette butts, no smell of cigarette smoke or food, no voices or the clicking of weapons against rock.

Silently, they continued in—feathers on the water—to brush a piling. Rafik gestured to two of his men to stay as boat guards and the rest climbed onto the pier where they immediately and silently fanned out, guns ready, finding cover against the grotto's walls while scanning the baseball field-sized area. It seemed empty but what might be above them? Armed men? Gun emplacements? Surveillance cameras?

Certainly, at a minimum, surveillance cameras. With her feet on solid ground again and her back against solid rock, Regan pulled out her Agency cellphone and restored its chip. Relieved she saw she had a signal from a CIA-dedicated satellite. While Langley could now pinpoint her location, she would need their communications network before this was over.

Rock stairs rose toward another ledge and continued on to the top of the cliff. The boathouse was to her left. Thirty feet to her right, Rafik had signaled his peloton's four squad leaders. Wordlessly, Lt. Salim, a slender and incongruously blonde officer, and two of the squads went up the stairs to the top of the cliffs to—as previously ordered—scout locations and numbers of al-Salan guards. With a third group, Rafik also took the stairs but only as far as the ledge. Regan stayed with Hamid and the fourth squad. Hamid put two men in the Zodiacs and deployed the remainder of his men as guards on the landing platform before immediately disappearing into the boathouse.

Throughout all of this, Jerry had remained in the Zodiac with his gear.

The world fell silent as even the whispers of boot leather on stone faded. The sun had yet to appear although a warming to the air and a yellow glow on the western wall of the grotto showed that it was above the horizon.

She felt naked and exposed here ... and useless. She should've gone with Rafik or Salim. What if the British had occupied the compound the night before and sent the freighter that brought them back to sea? It'd make sense. They wouldn't want an unidentified freighter sitting visibly in a marina where it didn't belong and alarming either the local rebels or the soldiers on the nearby military installations. She should be with Salim and in a position to head off trouble. She should ... ? But she was worrying over something she couldn't change and that didn't help.

Restless, she went after Hamid and found him in the boathouse staring at the sleek hull of a lovely speedboat.

"*Regardez.*" Hamid's loud whisper had an empty, echoing quality in the dim enclosure. "With this a man could smuggle many tons of drugs and escaping every pursuit." He dropped into the boat's well, then climbed to its bridge cabin which put him on a level with her—the open door showing his big figure leaning over a control panel. "Yes," she heard him say before he turned and waved a set of keys in one huge hand. "Yes. This is what is called spoils of war."

"The Minister says only computers are to be taken," Regan reminded him.

"The boat papers say she comes out of Benghazi but is currently registered in Tunisia to a company owned by a Libyan resident in Sousse." Hamid's voice was muffled as he searched about the cabin. "It must be returned there. Yes? Hamid will be a good person and take charge of this difficult task. Me."

She grasped a ladder handle and stepped onto the boat. Owned by a Libyan resident of Sousse. But why was she surprised? Mustafa Karim. Of course. Blocked by the Tunisians, by her, and stymied in Cairo, what else was left to him? She'd guessed he would return to Libya. But here?

Regan opened the door to the salon. Hamid descended the stairs from the bridge and ran into her back as she stepped down and into the room and stopped abruptly. "Good God almighty." She'd clicked on the lights to reveal the cabin's sybaritic interior—all gold leaf, elaborately carved wood paneling, and plush upholstery. But that wasn't the cause of her reaction. Against a counter separating a tiny galley from the lounge was a stack of small, cardboard boxes. Two of them were open revealing well-packed sheaves of money.

"Good God," she repeated and closed her mouth.

Hamid put a hand on one of her arms and moved her out of the door. Two steps took him to the boxes. He reached in, pulled out a packet and handed it to her. "Euros," he said and jerked open the flap of another box. More money.

■ ■ ■ ■ ■

Ten minutes later Regan had shouldered her backpack and rifle and with Jerry right behind her finished the climb to the intermediate ledge. As she took the last few stairs, the space resolved into a flagstoned terrace about the size of a two-car garage and equipped with several chaise lounges separated by tables sporting closed umbrellas. On three sides waist-high walls of rock defined the terrace exterior. The fourth side, the cliff wall, was inset with a structure of curving metal rods and glass.

Rafik's radio came alive with the lieutenant's voice. The freighter, he said, had entered the marina but had stopped just inside the breakwater. Also, he had scouted the western side of the compound which seemed empty and unguarded. The only thing of interest was a small helicopter on the roof of one of the villas.

A thoughtful look crossed Rafik's face, and he paused before speaking an acknowledgement while Regan watched the men of Hamid's squad carrying boxes. She caught a whiff of smoke.

A door in the glass wall was open revealing a massage table and counters beyond. As she walked inside, a golden line that had been falling down the grotto face reached them and lit up the interior where urns sprouted sprays of flowers. Along one curving wall, tiles made a colorful mosaic of a horse and a naked, spear-wielding man. A glassed-in shower stall and a bath equipped with jets awaited use.

"Anna likes her Comforts," Jerry quipped. "You know this just had to been built to keep our Anna happy."

No one else spoke. They all followed Rafik who led the way toward a narrow doorway that looked like it was part of a bank vault, one set in solid rock several feet thick. The door, itself, stood open letting in cold, damp air. Regan with Hamid right behind closed up on Rafik, stepped through and onto a small, subterranean subway station platform. They fanned out.

More mosaics circled the cavern, brilliant bits of glass gleaming in the artificial light, their ancient themes and art form contrasting sharply with the rails, cars, and a plastic pillar near the edge of the platform holding what looked like a small table inset with a computer monitor. The cars, themselves, had bubble bodies and each contained four upholstered chairs. Two sets of tracks ran into the darkness of a tunnel.

"Good." The word rumbled from Hamid's chest. Hamid added, "Very good. We ride now."

Jerry had stopped in front of the monitor, the curl of his lips twitching his mustache. As Regan joined him, he bellied up to the screen. "George always had to be a showoff," he said. "What we're looking at is obviously a miniaturized but more elaborate version of something George devised and sold to the Frankfurt U-Bahn people."

Rafik had come up behind them. "Show us."

"Let's see." Jerry again used his fingers and the lines on a map began to glow, their intersections and ends illumined as small red dots surrounding white numbers. "Where to first?" He looked around.

"Cool," Regan said. But their immediate problem was not how to work the system but how to secure the tunnel system from outside penetration. They'd just seen that the grotto entrance was wide open, and the map showed twelve points of entry—all of which might be in the same condition. They'd talked about this earlier and knew there wouldn't be time to check the entire system. That's why they'd decided on Plan B.

More boxes were brought up from the Zodiacs. Men were equipped and dispatched with blocks of C-4, timers and detonators. They would block the key rail junctions.

In the meantime Rafik heard from Lieutenant Salim again. He'd begun searching the office building. Outside, the freighter had anchored just inside the breakwater where it'd begun offloading men and materiel. Teams were already ashore, scouting the compound. The latter would find the same situation as the Tunisian party—neither walls nor strong points were manned. Al-Salan had cleared out, perhaps warned of the impending British arrival.

Plan B had assumed the British would control the compound one way or another. The Tunisians would confine their efforts to a fast search, if time allowed, of the office building. Blocking access to the data center and holding a line of retreat through the underground while Jerry made a copy of the basic Cumulus software were their only interests. And they'd arrived first. They could do it.

"We do not fight the British," Rafik had said, "but, perhaps, if it becomes necessary we can deal with them."

The last of Jerry's boxes came up and was loaded into a car, and Rafik signaled Regan and Jerry.

Ten minutes, a ride through a long tunnel and a climb up a flight of stairs later, they went through a door labeled "B Level" and found themselves in a wide hallway floored in large white tiles and stretching into the far distance. A rack holding two bicycles stood against the hall's end wall. Otherwise there was nothing to break the monotony of white floor, white walls, white ceiling.

They were directly under the office bloc, identified on the map as the Walker Building, but some distance from the data center. "There's a train station under the data center," Jerry patted his belly. "I don't walk." He looked at the bicycles. "Or ride bikes."

Rafik didn't argue the point, just glanced at Jerry before consulting the rough floor plans on George's notepad and sending five men on up the stairs with orders to help Salim search the building. "*Vite! Vite!*" He waved them way impatiently. Only then did he turn to Jerry, nod, and detail a man to take the computer engineer back down to Station One and thence to the data center station. The rest of them set off, filling the hallway with a hard but hollow sound as they trotted along at a steady pace.

The soles of Regan's shoes slapped the large tiles in time with men. If she was careful she needn't step on a crack. 'Step on a crack, you break your mother's back.' The childhood rhyme repeated itself over and over in her mind. It didn't matter.

She had broken her mother's back a very long time ago, making herself the next best thing to an orphan long before she'd ever seen a sidewalk. Of course, they'd told her it wasn't her fault. But it'd been her ball, they said, a big red beach ball, and she'd been playing with it when it bounced off the veranda of the Highwinds' ranch house. It'd gathered speed going downhill, careening off rocks, zig-zagging unpredictably to stop against an inside wall of a round pen where her mother had been working a young horse. The animal had spooked as the ball passed, and his third buck had sent Jennifer Grant flying.

Spooks and bucks happen with baby horses; nine falls out of ten produce only minor injuries at the worst. This was the tenth, and it damaged Jennifer's spine. She'd recovered from that but not from a related event. Driving into town to see his hospitalized wife, Jack Grant had hit an icy patch on the upper South Fork road, sending his Suburban careening down a sage-covered slope and into a dry ravine. They didn't find the car until two days later. By then Jack had been long dead.

Jennifer had never ridden a horse again. Nor, after recovering from back injury and a nervous breakdown, had she returned to Highwinds either to visit or to retrieve her daughter. At two years of age Regan had been effectively abandoned to the care of her grandmother.

But thinking about the past was a weakness. Her grandmother always said so.

The lead commandos banged through wide double doors at the end of the corridor, guns ready, jumping to either side, one of them finding a light switch. Overheads came on but otherwise nothing happened. The sound of men breathing seemed loud in the silence.

They were in an employee's lounge—a very large room featuring multiple tables and counters with set-ups for drinks and snacks. There were microwaves and refrigeration units and racks of junk food packets. The walls held framed posters, mostly of sports events, and one was lined with lockers. To their left another set of double doors was open and, although the room beyond was dark, they could make out what looked like a line of computer stations. Across from them, more double doors led to another dark room.

Hamid looked in and pronounced, "Dormitory."

Rafik went through a third set of double doors. They led to a small foyer accessing a stairwell and two sets of elevator doors, one labeled "A - D," the other labeled "E." Almost at the same moment the doors to "A - D" opened revealing Jerry and his escort.

"You see?" Jerry said, not specifying what they'd seen, looked around, and headed across the lounge toward the faintly visible computer stations.

The "E" elevator was locked with a cipher pad. Regan remembered George's notepad had shown "E" was a level marked with hatchmarks, several large elevator shafts, and a single rail line that ran from one of the big freight elevator shafts—a rail line that hadn't appeared on the map in the grotto station. She mentioned this aloud, found the cipher code in the notepad and opened the elevator doors.

"Go down," Rafik instructed Hamid. "Check it out and close off that tunnel."

The big sergeant and one of the commandos entered the elevator while Rafik and Regan crossed the lounge to find Jerry had turned on lights for a large circular room, the walls and floor tiled—more of the hospital white—where they weren't filled with large screens hanging over rows of computer stations. Jerry was in a smaller glass-fronted office just to the right of the main doors.

The American engineer had his jacket draped over the back of a chair, while the oversized man purse he'd carried was upended, its mysterious contents dumped onto the floor. Around him empty computer racks sported nothing but wires. The first of the Cairo boxes came through the door behind them.

"You will plug and play, yes?" Rafik walked in, hooked his thumbs into his belt, leaned back and grinned at Jerry. It was his first smile of the day.

"We will see," Jerry said. "Go away and let me work."

"Very much my pleasure," Rafik said heading for yet another set of big double doors through which they could hear commandos shouting back and forth as they checked for hostiles.

Regan followed, adjusting the Tavor rifle she wore slung over her shoulder. The sling was rubbing through her jacket, but she forgot it as she stepped through the door and into a vast hall filled with equipment racked in long lines from floor to ceiling and separated by four-foot wide aisles. Along the ceiling, itself, more equipment and bundles of wires had been tucked into uniquely configured beams. "Good God," she breathed.

Knowing she had no hope of understanding what she was seeing, Regan stayed behind Rafik who'd picked up the pace and was trotting along one of the aisles to the next set of doors. Here they both stopped. Ahead of them, long florescent lights hung on cables from a vaulted stone roof illuminating a giant cavern filled with eight-foot high equipment racks again separated by four-foot wide aisles. Lights, aisles, and racks marched into the far distance.

"There must be thousands of servers here," Regan said, hearing awe in her voice. "Tens of thousands." And they were all turned off, their faces dark. Rafik didn't reply. Only the occasional and faint sound of commandos giving all clear reports to each other and of boot soles rattling on metal stairs in the far distance broke the silence.

The place was incredible in its immensity.

"So, this is what a data center looks like," Rafik said at last. "How can anyone figure out how these things work? How can anyone make them work?" His voice was so low it almost came out as a whisper.

"It's a mystery to me, but George's sketch maps show two more levels just like this below us," she said in a normal tone and was startled at how loud her comment seemed in the dead, warm air … how almost sacrilegious.

Before she could add anything else, Hamid's voice squeaked through Rafik's radio. "*Capitaine.*"

"*Parlez.*"

"Excuse me, my captain," Hamid said, losing the squeak and bringing his voice under control. He continued in a dialect Regan didn't understand, but his tone was so deliberate she strained to make some sense of the words.

Rafik said, "Stand by," then he looked at Regan. "Would you please locate the "E" level tunnel and tell me which other ones might be near it? Above or below? To the side? Are there any?"

Smothering her questions, Regan pulled out George's notepad and tried to lay a map of the main communication tunnels over the E level spur. Her efforts weren't helped by the fact that George had only made rough sketches of everything and nothing was to scale.

Her cellphone vibrated.

"Okay. The Number 5 Tunnel," she said. "It has a short spur that may actually join the "E" tunnel, but otherwise that "E" line looks like it terminates above ground. Why?"

"Munitions," he said. "An arsenal here. For an army. This is what Hamid finds."

"Yes," she said. "Of course." She'd counted on finding where all the munitions Mac had supplied had been stored. Now, she knew.

Rafik hadn't noticed her reaction, had immediately issued a series of orders. When he finished he turned to her and the lines on his face seemed deeper than usual. "It'd be a pity if we all die today because we trigger a sympathetic explosion in this place while attempting to make ourselves secure. Too much irony there, is it not?"

Then, he fell silent. Instead of his voice she heard Hamid talking, reading from an inventory list while his men searched the level. Regan recognized the names of small arms and heavy weapons, of raw explosives and detonators, of ammunition and other materiel.

He droned on until interrupted by a fresh voice. "The "E" tunnel and the Number 5 are both secure, *mon capitaine*."

Regan leaned against the nearest rack of equipment. She would have to go down there and take a look and the sooner the better.

Next to her Rafik was speaking on his radio again but now to one of the men in the grotto. "Send this message to the Director General. Say ... " and he dictated a report on the armory, the British arrival, the absence of al-Salan, and the likely presence of Mustafa Karim. "Finally, say we have secured the data center, and Monsieur McCormack begins his work. Say, when we can make contact, we will work an arrangement with the Englishers."

As he said "Over," the hushed quiet of the vast space lurched into an indefinite sort of sound. It began as a rattling hum, progressed in seconds to a coughing roar. Lights blinked to life in their tiny thousands along the racks of equipment. The floors hummed in sympathy, sending vibrations up their legs, and the decibel level grew, fast becoming an ear-shattering, head-dominating screech.

They grabbed ear protectors from a box by the door, now knowing why they were there. For the first time Regan understood the expression "too loud to hear yourself think."

"Wow," she said when they were back in the circular room, the doors closed behind them, and she could take off the thick muffs. She yawned to clear her ears.

Around her, even here, everything had changed. The screens on the walls glowed with default pages. Through the glass surrounding the office she could see Jerry seated at the desk, seemingly focused on a monitor.

"Who knew." Her cell vibrated with an incoming text.

"It's time to talk to the British," Rafik said over his shoulder. He was half-way to the lounge.

"Speak of the devil," she said aloud. The text was from John Darnley and read: Our ambassadors in Tunis have received Tunisian agreement for Unité to stand down. Orders follow. Please comply and advise.

She felt her lips compress. Could she ignore this? Wait for Lt. Salim to get the message and pass it along? No. But she needed time. She caught up with the captain at the elevators, said, "It seems the British want to talk to you, too." And showed him the text.

He pushed a button to call an elevator. His face showed nothing.

She said, "How about … ?" and typed. Will meet you main entrance of office bldg. 30 min.

Rafik nodded. "Yes."

What could she do in thirty minutes? She didn't know, but it felt right. She hit 'send.'

The elevator doors opened as Rafik's radio spoke, a voice said. "Shots fired on fifth floor."

CHAPTER THIRTY-TWO
Saharan Compound, Libya

Guns ready, moving in silent mode they snaked out of a stairwell and into the fifth floor corridor. Lt. Salim's squad searching the fourth floor had heard shots fired above them. Now, Salim and his men were behind Rafik and ahead of Regan, their bodies under Kevlar vests were damp with sweat, their eyes were narrowed and determined.

She knew these men. She'd exercised with them and felt confident with them ... or as confident as she could be under the circumstances. This was what they had practiced and trained for, why they had raced through their Michelin buildings and crashed through windows, why they wore Kevlar vests. They were professionals.

The hall was empty—bright with early morning light falling in shafts from skylights. Closed elevator doors faced them. To their right, about thirty feet away, glass doors opened into an anteroom with fireplace, elaborately carved wall and ceiling panels and recessed lighting, a space meant to impress. Regency-style furniture made up a sitting group.

In stark contrast to this quiet elegance, three battered wheeled platforms stacked four-high with cardboard boxes sat in the middle of the room. The boxes were identical to those on the boat. Karim had been here. Karim was here.

Regan had her Tavor off her back and set to semi-automatic fire and, like Rafik and his men, she hugged the wall. What about Knowland and Arnie? In essence the Tunisians had been acting like beaters on a tiger shoot, driving anyone left in the building ahead of them. This ...

A vibrating signal on Rafik's radio warned them, and Hamid and his party slipped quietly through a door in a second hallway visible through more glass doors.

Unlike the other floors that circled and looked down on a central atrium, this floor jutted up from the north side of the roof and had window walls opening on wide external terraces on three sides with these windowless corridors running along the fourth. Here was an exclusive little world of four offices, a reception area, and two spaces George had marked as a gallery and a vault.

Saying nothing, Hamid and his team trotted forward and joined Rafik's group pushing through another set of doors. No one did more than glance at the dollies and their cargo. They were silent except for the rustle of fabric, the snicks of equipment shifting on belts, and the almost quiet of feet sinking into deep carpets. Absent, even, were the usual sounds of an infrastructure going about its business of heating or cooling or switching electrical currents about or managing water and sewage.

Regan trotted at their rear and was the last to enter a large corner office. Early morning light came dimly through two window walls with expansive views of the compound—a stunning array of whitewashed buildings with red tile roofs clustered around a man-made marina and backed by this building. And sure enough, there was a freighter anchored out there, dwarfing a handful of small recreational boats lined up along a floating pier.

The office itself was a near replica of Arnie's office at Langley right down to the clutter on the big, round corner table with comfortable chairs pulled close. There was the wall of books on military history and the almost bare top of the desk which sported several silver-framed photos.

She kept moving, staying just behind a commando named Jaffer Abdulahi. But, then, she caught a glimpse of one of the pictures. Jaffer and his comrades continued on into another hall. It wasn't one of the pictures she expected—the ones of Mary and the twins Arnie had displayed on his desk at Langley. They were there, too, but on this one her own face stared back at her.

"Christ!" Her right hand dropped off the Tavor. He had no right. Without thinking, she swatted the framed photo onto the floor. Then she chased into the hall after the Tunisians.

A door to her left was open. Using care she slipped through to find both groups of Tunisians using what cover they could find, their Tavors all lined up on a partially open vault door.

They were in an art gallery that was equipped with a walnut conference table, comfortable chairs on rollers—mostly now overturned. Track spotlights beamed down on individual paintings. Elaborate frames and the subject matter spoke of Arnie's taste. He'd long wanted to own a collection of Western art and had visited the Grant ranch when he could, primarily so he could enjoy Liza's small collection, then spend more hours in Cody's Whitney Gallery of Western Art absorbing the Remingtons and Russells, the Beirstadts and Catlins, the paintings of Alfred Jacob Miller and Thomas Moran.

Rafik made a sharp gesture.

She did as the commandos did, dropping to the floor behind the conference table. At this level she could see why the vault door was open, why the Tunisians all had their guns trained on the opening. The table had blocked her view. An overturned chair and part of a body—muscular brown calves and bare feet stuck out the bottoms of a pair of blue jeans and were tangled in the legs of the chair.

A bead of sweat rolled down her cheek. The Tavor felt cool and ready in her hands, and gradually she realized she was smelling death—recognized the acrid odor of a gut shot and the pungent scent of emptied bowels. The man was dying or dead. He wasn't Arnie or Richie. Mustafa Karim?

Rafik checked to be sure that everyone was in position, then raised his voice and said in Arabic, "Whoever is in there. Come out with your hands behind your head."

Nothing happened. They waited. Rafik repeated himself in French.

She used her elbows to pull herself forward under the table. She stopped alongside Rafik who was behind another upended chair that he surely knew would do nothing to stop a bullet.

He said, "We have no time for this. Will there be an air supply inside that room?"

The question meant nothing; her brain felt as though it'd been drained of coherent thought and might never function properly again. Arnie Walker had been looking at her picture every day for how long?

She'd been his target. He'd violated her with his eyes and his thoughts, and he'd tried to kill her, and he might be only feet away.

"Close the door and lock it," she hissed.

Rafik gestured to Hamid.

The big man was to the left side of the big door and now got to his knees. Keeping well behind the door's cover, he pulled the chair free of the doorway. The man's body came with it. Blood stained the carpet as the shotgun-mangled carcass—its back blown away—slid toward them.

Standing and still protected by the door, Hamid braced his arms and pushed. The door began moving. In that moment, they all heard English words: "Wait. I come. Do not shoot."

Mustafa Karim hurtled through the gap to land face first on the floor next to the body, his hands over his head. "Do not shoot." The door closed behind him with a loud thunk and to the sound of Karim's voice reciting a *shura* which trailed off as he realized no one was shooting at him.

His handsome features were worn and had the washed-out texture and color of a pecan shell. His shirt and slacks showed signs of hard work, and smudges under his eyes indicated he hadn't slept. As usual and even over the smell of death, his distinctive personal mix of halitosis and stale cigarette smoke came with him.

"Secure your weapons," Rafik commanded.

Karim rose to his feet, tucking his shirt into his pants, smoothing his hair back and brushing off his shoulders, the hand movements growing fluid and assured as they completed his ritual grooming. Then he saw Regan. "I thought it likely you would come, Madame." His eyes moved on. "And, Captain, you are a welcome sight."

He switched to French and pointed at the shoeless body. "This is my cousin, Mahmud, who comes only to help me move what is mine from this place … mine because it is owed plus I inherit from Mr. George Tendale. I can give you the proofs if you allow me."

Hamid was moving the men out. Rafik's face remained impassive. "Who is in there?"

"Sons of dogs. Men whose word is excrement. They are called

Walker and Knowland and they are colleagues of Madame Regan, but they try to kill both of us. One deceives me with a false death. They are evil men who deserve a slow and painful death."

Regan pointed at her watch. Their thirty minutes was up.

Karim saw and said, "Captain. I will need help moving what is mine from here. We need not get what remains in the vault, but there are boxes waiting near the elevator. If you could detail two men to me, that would be sufficient."

Rafik waved at Lt. Salim. "Get his boxes down to the grotto, and I want this one secured. He is to come with us."

To Karim he said, "There is a great deal of money involved, and I wouldn't want you to suddenly disappear on that very elegant boat we see in the grotto."

The sound of Karim's sputtering protests faded as Regan followed Rafik back to the lobby, saying, "We'll take him to Tunis. They can deal with him there."

"You realize that Karim told the truth," she said. "About the men in the vault."

Rafik gave her a look that defied categorization but told her she had nothing to say on the subject that he wanted to hear. His job was complicated enough now without her adding to it. She opened her mouth to explain, then snapped it shut. Nothing would be gained or changed by telling him just who he'd locked up.

In fact no one would want custody of Arnie. No one ... except maybe Craig ... would want him at all. Not alive. No senior government official in America or Tunisia would wish for the embarrassment of an Arnie Walker revived from the dead and making headlines. And Rafik—even though he didn't know it—had found a good way to duck the entire issue: leave him alive or dead for the British or the Libyans to release and handle. Probably alive since Arnie had insisted that vault areas of overseas stations, which were designated safe haven areas, have their own oxygen supply as well as food and water. If he'd followed those rules here, except for boredom, Arnie would be as healthy after a month of incarceration as he was today. But maybe that wasn't saying much. Well, *tant pis*, as they said.

Her cell vibrated. It would be Craig. She welcomed the distraction and made a gesture of apology for the need to take the call before thumbing the connection and saying, "Yes, Craig?"

But it wasn't her husband. It was John Darnley. The sound of his accented voice came like a dash of cold water. His call reminded her that the question of Arnie was a sideshow. She had a situation here.

The exchange with the Englishman was blessedly short. She disconnected after saying, "Someone will let you in. We'll meet at the elevators on the ground floor."

"I heard," Rafik said, using his radio to call down to his men at the main doors. As he did, another call came through on Regan's cellphone. McCormack.

"Yes?" she said.

"The system's up," McCormack skipped a greeting. "And the codes in George's notepad worked."

"Great."

"Not great. Of course they worked. I wouldn't have called to tell you that."

"Well?"

"We have another user on the network. He or she logged in a minute or so ago and walled me off from the system. My terminals have turned into slaves. Worse, the new user has triggered what looks like a self-destruct sequence."

For a moment Regan misunderstood, thought McCormack was just building deniability into her plan. She said, "That's not nec—"

"Listen to me," McCormack said. "I haven't had time to get into the operating system, let alone download its elements. Regan? I'm not kidding."

Rafik had continued walking at a normal pace when she'd slowed down to take the call. He was now some fifteen feet ahead of her.

"Regan?"

Arnie in the damn vault. There'd be a computer in there. Or, and now it occurred to her! Arnie not in the vault. The one in her station had an escape route, a chute through the building's core to a tunnel which came up outside the compound walls. Would Arnie have built the Saharan vault with less?

"Hold on," she said to McCormack and hurried to catch up with Rafik, putting McCormack on speaker and switching to French—their common language. "Okay. The captain's here. Tell him what's happened."

"Self-destruct what? The data center? What?" Rafik asked after hearing a short explanation.

"The—" They heard a crash and a sharp exclamation from the computer engineer before McCormack said, "I've got a new screen. It says ... the monitor says, 'Evacuate compound. This peninsula will be destroyed in thirty minutes. This is not an exercise. Evacuate compound.' That's what it says. Word for word."

As though to emphasize his statement, a claxon outside the building began a long, wailing cry reminiscent of civil defense sirens.

Rafik listened for a moment. "Monsieur Jerry. The only one who could do this thing is locked in a vault. He could not destroy this place without killing himself."

"Well ...," Regan began and explained about the likelihood of an escape route.

Jerry reacted first. "I don't know about you, but I'm getting out of here. I'll meet you at the boats. And I suggest you hurry."

Rafik nodded and pushed through the glass doors. "We evacuate everyone. Now. We take everything we brought plus the money. If this is a hoax, we come back. If not ...," he waved a hand as his radio demanded his attention again. He listened, looking at Regan as he did.

"What?" she asked.

"Your British friend. He wants to know about the sirens."

"No surprise there."

Rafik wasn't listening, had already keyed his radio, answered Darnley's question and begun to issue orders. While speaking, he crossed the reception space and entered the outer hallway where a small group of men and one partially loaded dolly were outside the open doors of a freight elevator. Two dollies were inside it.

Regan checked her watch. Light coming through the skylights had lost its early morning slant.

As they approached, the doors to a passenger elevator opened.

"Ah, good," Hamid said, pushing the third dolly, inside it.

"You'll need the men to transfer boxes to cars and get them down to the boats," Rafik said. "I'll take Monsieur Karim and Madame Regan and these few remaining boxes. Go."

Regan had slipped inside the passenger elevator to hold the door open, only then noticing that Karim had his hands tied in front of his body—tied with strings from his own shoes. What was that about? Rafik gestured Regan up on the cart, pushed Karim ahead of him and into the elevator corner, then squeezed himself in beside the controls.

"How much time?" he asked Regan.

■ ■ ■
CHAPTER THIRTY-THREE
Saharan Compound, Libya

In a quiet way, the elevator eased to a stop on the ground floor. The doors opened to an atrium around which the upper floors rose in tiers of balconies. Nearby, a waterfall splashed from the third floor into a pond where lily pads bumped against stone walls and spray turned the leaves a shiny emerald hue. Foot-long goldfish flashed across the pond, and John Darnley was there, standing in front of the elevator door with legs spread and hands on his hips.

His long unshaven face was set in grim lines. This John Darnley made a sharp contrast to the neat urbane figure Regan had seen at the take-down exercise or the rumpled and confused-looking one at the City of Refuse. This was a soldier—the impression reinforced by fatigues, combat boots, and a black beret and not diminished by the empty pistol and knife holsters on his belt.

Then, surprisingly and incongruously, one eyebrow rose, and his bloodshot eyes crinkled in amusement. As they settled on her, the corners of his mouth twitched in a smile, and he relaxed his stance but only to stick a heavy boot against the open door.

"Ah, it's Miss Grant in the flesh," he said, and, "Captain." He said nothing to Karim, although Regan was sure he had to know him. Darnley had, after all, trailed the man around Tunisia for reasons she still did not understand.

Rafik said in French, "We hurry to leave. You, too, must hurry." The open door bumped impatiently against Darnley's foot, adding urgency to Rafik's words. The Englishman didn't budge.

"We don't have time for this," Regan said. "You need to get back to your men, and we need to get out of here." Regan thumped a box under her in emphasis. "You have what you want. We're leaving. And you should, too."

As she spoke, the power went off. The pumps running the waterfall ceased and the cascade of water slowed to a trickle. Underwater lights in the pond went out, the goldfish disappearing into darkness. Rafik spoke into his radio. Hamid answered. Then, Regan heard Jerry's voice. Next, Lt. Salim said something.

"You should get back to your men and get them out of here," Regan said to Darnley while the radio chatter continued. She gathered that there was emergency lighting in the station under them, and Hamid's men were continuing to load cars, but there was no power to run them. As for Salim, he'd recalled all of his people, most of whom were already in the grotto with Jerry who'd been in the vanguard of those to arrive.

The Englishman said, "My people're reboarding and will be putting out to sea very shortly. Which means I'll need to be begging a way out of here with you." He gave her a long assessing stare, amusement still lurking on his face, then added, "I am assuming you didn't contrive this situation just to put a spanner in our works?"

She didn't bother answering.

Rafik said, speaking into the radio, "We have to get those cars moving."

His words were a reminder. It'd be a long run to the grotto ... a race against the clock that they'd surely lose. The thought brought a tight sensation to her throat. She forgot the Englishman.

"*Eh bien,*" Rafik looked at Regan. "I think it is time ... ."

The whine of elevator power coming on cut him off. A moment later the lights rose as though on a screen set, and the doors tried to close on the Englishman's foot.

He jumped inside, put a foot on the front edge of the dolly and landed beside Regan, the elevator doors closing.

Hamid's voice on the radio said the cars below them had power, that he and his men were on their way to the grotto, and that he'd left a car behind for them.

Darnley said to Regan, "Well, here we are again. Once more in a most unusual and dangerous place. Don't you ever take a moment to do normal things?"

What was he talking about, and who the hell cared. He was sitting so close she could almost imagine she felt his breath on her face. She edged away and said, "This is the legendary British tradition of carrying on and of indifference in the face of danger?"

"Something like that."

Using his radio, Rafik said to Hamid, "Did you see any sign of the Americans? The ones left in the vault?"

Lt. Salim answered, "There is the helicopter we see on a roof. And the number 5 tunnel that serves the area of the villas is not blocked. If they are free, perhaps they think to leave that way."

The elevator came to a stop. Darnley jumped off the boxes and said to Regan, "Walker will be long gone. He won't have had just one way out but two or three. He's that kind of man. Come on, help me push this."

She didn't. She stared at him. "How …?" she started.

He ran his fingers through his hair then rubbed his chin. "This world class fuck-up you call Hayburner has been in my tasking orders for months." The Brit took the cart's handle and began pulling. She got behind to push, their footsteps echoing in the station. Rafik's voice as he continued giving instructions over the radio seemed loud.

Darnley continued, "And here we are … your good little British cousins doing your scut work for you which includes cleaning up this God-benighted mess."

Rafik came over to them and said in English, tapping his watch. "Load this, then we go. No time now."

Time. The governing word was time. She looked at her watch. "Ten minutes. We have just ten minutes."

Darnley said, "Except we're far underground here."

From the other tunnel came a familiar rush of sound. Another empty car sped out of the dark and slowed as it approached them. As instructed, Lt. Salim was returning cars to this station as he finished with them. Karim, his wrists still tied in front of him, said, "*Vite. Vite.*" While they'd all been talking, he'd pushed a loaded cart from the platform to the first car, losing a shoe in the process. He didn't seem to notice, was totally focused on the cart, which had jammed in the car's door. There it had lodged. Karim, cursing now, began bouncing it violently.

"Ah," Darnley nodded at the Libyan. "We may have to ... ."

Rafik said, "*Oui, c'est vrai.*"

It took longer than they could have imagined. It took both of the men to force Karim to release the handles while Regan man-handled the cart to free it.

"No time now," Rafik said. "Leave the money."

"Leave the Libyan, too?" Darnley inquired over Karim's head, which he held by the hair.

"Get real," Regan said.

A moment later they were all inside the car, Karim trying to get out. "My money. My money," he kept saying or Regan thought he was saying. His words were in a dialect she didn't understand.

Rafik had left the job of hanging onto the Libyan to Darnley and was on his radio, checking on his men, the walls of the tunnel were blurring past. The Libyan finally subsided, and John got his radio out to request an update from the freighter captain. As the captain spoke, Regan could hear a claxon horn bellowing in the background and the siren still crying from the compound's walls.

They sped through the dark. Reason said Arnie would stop the countdown. But did reason have anything to do with this? She stared at the digital read-out and began counting seconds—realized she was leaning forward as though that could make the car move faster. But counting, as always, seemed to make it better. Counting occupied the brain and tamed the fear.

One way or the other, the *Unité* would come out of this well. If the place did blow up, they might not bring home Cumulus, but even without the money they'd left behind they would've liberated a great sum. And, perhaps, John might be persuaded to convince his organization to work with the Tunisians on accessing and taking control of Cumulus as Craig had intimated. Perhaps ... .

The walls weren't quite as black. It was suddenly noticeable. Almost there. A few seconds later, the little car slid silently to a stop. Regan jumped to the platform. Rafik pulled Karim out with him. The Libyan's face, one that had once looked handsome, was contorted and ugly, his eyes gleaming ... red-rimmed and red-veined.

That's when it started.

The ground trembled, the way a terrified dog might shake in a thunder storm. In the same moment she heard a sound like the roar of jet engine.

"*Allez vite!*" Rafik grabbed her hand and ran for the stairs, John just behind. The three of them dropped below the edge of the terrace, taking the steps in bounds, driven by the shaking earth. She didn't feel blood pounding in her temples, didn't sense the rush of adrenaline power to her legs or notice her wrist. She could feel the cliff face shuddering, shaking. The ground had a voice, one of agitation and protest. The sound grew, an express train of noise, a monster roaring for release. She flew. Her feet barely touched the rock.

Only one boat waited below—the sleek thing from the boathouse. Hamid stood in the stern well, his mouth open, but what he said was lost, was submerged in the cries of engines and earth. Ahead of her Rafik vaulted into the well and reached a hand back. She grabbed and jumped with John—his hand in her free one—beside her.

Regan's feet hit the deck. She turned to see Karim finish a slide down the railing.

"*Allez vite!*"

He jumped, an incredibly athletic feat considering his bound hands and shoeless foot. His remaining shoe spiraled down and into the water. Hamid slammed the throttle forward. The boat's nose reared up. She fell backwards still holding Rafik's hand on one side and John's on the other. The two men staggered, almost going down with her.

Nose in the air, the vessel roared into the deep shade of the channel. She pulled herself to her feet and stared back and up at the shelf that held the spa and the tunnel entrance. She strained to hear over the engine noise; then she was knocked backwards feeling as though she had just run headfirst into a brick wall, a red-hot wall. It smashed into her, a full body blow knocking her to the deck. Blood trickled over her top lip and into her open mouth. Her last sight of the terrace was of geysers of flame boiling over the spa terrace. Shocked, she gasped in air that had lost its oxygen, that seared the throat.

The channel turned some 30 degrees. They slid around the corner into instant cold. She could breathe. The nose of the boat faced the open sea. Around her men grabbed new handholds. Scrabbling to her feet Regan locked her elbows around the ladder leading up to the bridge, did so just in time to be drenched as a section of rock above but behind them sheared off and fell into the channel, creating a great spume which masked the surface and hid the sight of tons of water seeking someplace to go. Their first warning came too late to change anything. Water climbed the sides of the channel, met rockfalls that were burying the grotto, then took the only other available route and rushed toward the open sea with the explosive power of champagne blowing a cork out of a shaken bottle. They were the cork.

"Hang on!" John grabbed the ladder on either side of Regan and pressed her into it. She'd closed her eyes, was aware of rungs digging into her chest and thighs and of a sense of flying. She thought she heard the engine screaming and may have felt propellers spinning free in the air. Her mouth opened in an involuntary scream even as her ears popped from pressure.

Behind them a pillar of dust and water molecules rose above pillars of flame that shot upwards to be augmented and fed by new explosions. The boat slammed down, plowing back to a stable position and slowing. Shaking, Regan looked back at the pyrotechnics, at the destruction. The man who'd spawned Hayburner and done so much in its name had, after all, killed it with his own two hands.

■ ■ ■ ■ ■

Half an hour later they were sitting idle in a quiet sea as Hamid finished emergency repairs to the propellers and drive shaft.

"We go now," Hamid said, pulling himself over the side. John Darnley who'd gone underwater to assist after radioing for a helicopter to pick him up, heaved himself up behind the sergeant. Rafik restarted the engines and steered toward Hammamet while the two men took off their borrowed face masks and snorkels—the only diving gear they'd been able to find. Behind them small explosions still pocked the horizon below a heavy, dark cloud of debris—a man-made storm of thunder and lightning on an otherwise sunny day.

Rafik had sent the Zodiacs on ahead after their rendezvous and after having them transfer the money boxes they'd carried to Karim's craft. The presence of so many millions pacified the Libyan who sat with them in the main cabin.

As for the British expedition, the freighter had been underway and had cleared the channel when the explosion lifted it and hurtled it into the open sea. There it had been caught broadside by the seismic wave and swept onto its side, bobbing back but damaged. There had been no deaths but many injuries, and it would be hours before they could begin to tally the list of injured, inventory the property lost, and assess the extent of needed repairs.

Regan waited until John's helicopter dropped a rope ladder for him. "Take care of yourself," he yelled in her ear and rode up the bucking rope as easily as though it was an escalator, reminding her of his commando background. With the Brit gone, the boat seemed almost empty. Like Mac and Craig and like Arnie Walker, John Darnley filled space.

Oh, well. She'd likely never see him again. She retired to the head on that oddly disappointing thought to check her bruises, wash up, and consider other matters. Walker had survived and gotten away. That had seemed obvious from reports that a helicopter had been seen rising from the roof of one of the villas and moving away to the west. Where did Arnie think he could go?

But, again, Arnie being Arnie, he would have prepared a bolt hole. She didn't want to think of him. That casual disregard for human life, dooming anyone left in the compound to death? And who could say how far the destruction had spread and how many innocents might've perished. Why had he tried to kill her? Why was her picture on his desk? Hands washed, face cleaned and hair combed, she felt more human and less like a rag picker's reject but had no answers for her questions. Probably never would have.

She returned to the main cabin to find Karim there. He had the advantage of being on his own boat and had changed into clean clothes. One of his feet, lacerated without its shoe, had been cleaned and bandaged by Hamid. Now, both his feet were covered by his own slippers. For him nothing much seemed to have changed. The appearance he presented to the world was again urbane or would have been if he wasn't on the floor in the middle of the wreckage, muttering about his money, sorting and stacking euros and dollars, smoke from a cigarette hanging from his lip swirling out the door. He had placed the boat's microwave next to him and was using it as a quick drying machine. His concentration on this chore was so complete he didn't seem to notice her. She watched as he finished the first box, then, instead of starting another one, he went back and began over all the time muttering about his money. His money.

She went out on deck and lay down on a cushioned bench in a place warmed by the sun and protected from wind and spray. The engines were loud as was the swish of dividing waters but not much louder than they'd been inside the cabin with its broken windows.

What would Arnie have planned as his next move? And what about her? A flight to Washington?

Just before she fell asleep she thought again of Mustafa Karim. Crazy as a bedbug.

CHAPTER THIRTY-FOUR
Tunisia

Regan put Jerry on a flight to Frankfurt then went home to Sidi Bou Said—showered and slept. When she surfaced, her mind was clear, her decisions made. As a first order of business, she called Hadija and told her to close up the Georgetown house and return to Tunisia. She was relatively certain that the threat to her life and, thus, the danger that Hadija could become collateral damage was as close to over as it would ever be. Al-Salan would have its hands full in eastern Libya for the near future, anyway. And the Iraqi MOS had shown no signs of activity in Tunis. The DGSE had the one remaining MOS officer under tight surveillance and would know if they made a move.

As for Arnie Walker, he'd lost his power base and his gunslingers.

And not to forget Richie. In a way she felt sorry for the man even though the adage about 'chickens coming home to roost' certainly applied to him. Still, for a brief moment, he'd seemed to have it all. Then, Walker had made one really bad decision, decided to try setting up shop in Egypt, and it'd all turned to shit.

Richie Knowland's career, built on manipulating complex situations had almost taken him to the top of the Clandestine Service. But it didn't matter anymore. Both men were on a CIA watch list and had their own problems.

Even so, too many people might wish for her demise. While that went with the job, prudence was in order, and she'd decided to have the Baralguibas watch her back.

She drove on to the office where she sent a simple cable to Headquarters saying she'd resumed command and Tiffany would be flying to Washington under escort of two U.S. Marshalls—men who'd just arrived from Paris and she'd found ensconced on the comfortable furniture in front of Dawn's counter and empty desk. In the end, Regan was reasonably certain, the girl would be dismissed from service, helped to find a more suitable line of work, and the internal scandal swept under a carpet.

Craig would handle the Tiffany matter, and he wouldn't repeat his demands that she return to Langley. Having her in D.C. where she could be asked to testify to congress or be interviewed by journalists with a prurient interest in a married acting CIA director with a playboy reputation? Not on a bet.

That said she'd expected a response or some acknowledgement or, at the least, recognition that she was alive. She'd expected a call from Craig. She'd thought someone would request a report on events at Sahara. But there'd been nothing, just the normal, routine exchanges of messages about the post-Tiffany clean-up and on-going operations. Hayburner might never have existed. Headquarters' silence on the subjects that really mattered had been anti-climatic and, oddly, disappointing.

Only one series of personnel decisions signaled an awareness in Washington that something extraordinary had occurred in Tunis Station. It began with a cable announcing her appointment as chief of station, but it said nothing about a promotion. She'd get the title without extra pay. A second cable was more welcome. It heralded the nomination of four new station members. If she agreed, Jack Logan would be her new deputy. Lucy Miller, a single woman nearing retirement age, had agreed to take over the ops support duties. Louis Rumfola, a veteran of three tours in Baghdad, would replace the lost communicator. And, miracle of miracles, a second-tour officer named Ruby Jackson would fill Tiffany's position. In the meantime, a retiree on contract arrived as a temporary replacement, sent to pick up Tiffany's agent case load.

Fighting in Libya continued. The British mercenaries returned to England, and a story appeared about their abortive efforts to rescue a group of expatriates from a compound that had been mined by Qadhafi's military resulting in a narrow escape for the mercs. Briefly, the international community seemed focused totally on Libya and talked of no-fly zones and possible aid to the besieged rebels. An earthquake of horrific proportions in Japan, however, knocked Libya out of the headlines, while Regan plugged along at her own job.

Daud returned from the south and signaled for a meeting. She went, taking the usual children's gifts along with chocolates and salaries for the adults. Nothing was said about the Zarzis confrontation. There was no mention of changing the relationship in any way. But there was a new tension, a wariness that was uncomfortable. Regan found herself drawing back from so much reliance on the clan, concerned with what could happen if one of the losers in the internal clan struggles took his revenge in the easiest possible way— by blowing the CIA connection.

Still, the Baralguiba clan kept tabs on rebel activities in western Libya for her and made it possible to feed a stream of unexciting situation reports to Washington. As she said to Chance, "It pays the bills." It also justified, at least in her own mind, approving the use of official operational funds to reimburse the family for their many expenses on the Hayburner affair rather than paying it out of her own pocket. She did, however, use her own money to purchase—on Daud's advice—a set of silver flatware for Abdul-Mujib's wedding present. That would definitely meet the Djerba policeman's definition of "very generous."

No one from the Tunisian government contacted her, presumably engrossed in their own problems. No one came to visit her. No one asked to debrief her. Even her friends in the Unit were silent, and she decided to let sleeping dogs lie. In a month or two, when things stabilized, she'd drive to Hammamet and join Rafik and Hamid at lunch. They'd pick up where they'd left off—she hoped. Much, of course, would depend on the political situation.

CHAPTER THIRTY-FIVE
Nja Island

Richie used great care setting up the room for the all-important phone call. He'd get one chance to flush Craig Montrose into the open, to separate him from his protective detail, to reach both Craig and his bitch wife.

Arnie Walker watched him from his wheel chair, seemingly indifferent to the preparations. He'd agreed to do what Richie asked. Beyond the old man a window wall looked out across a pool that perfectly reflected the sky and seemed to blend with the sea beyond. Except for the red accents of the terra cotta-tiled terrace, the scene reeked of blue. The view was the reason Richie'd bought ... acquired ... the house.

Hell! He'd had ownership of the whole island transferred to his name via a Hayburner virus located conveniently in a bank's computerized foreclosure file. A few keystrokes had given him a brilliant piece of architecture along with grottos and off-shore reefs and a population of wild boar.

"Okay, old man," Richie said, downloading Craig's personal cellphone number into the sat phone. The call would go through a Paris exchange and look to CIA computers, if Craig ever checked, as though Arnie had phoned from Paris.

"You ready? I want to get this over with."

"Almost." Richie straightened, admiring the clean, modern lines of the lounge and the gleaming white floor tiles. Once he took care of a few last important details ... a week, maybe two ... he would move his family here and take a year off to enjoy life and plot the future.

Those details .... No one was going to profit from his disgrace. No one was going to be left alive to gloat over the shame they'd inflicted on him. To come so close to his ultimate ambition. To actually move his family to Washington and notify everyone in his circle, then ... the humiliation.

"I knew from the beginning that the bitch needed to be killed," he said, attaching an external recording device to the sat phone.

Arnie looked up. "What?"

"Yeah," he said and straightened. He hadn't meant to say the words aloud.

"What're you telling me? Regan? You mean Regan?"

"Bitch," he said. "Christ, old man. I was talking about that mongrel bitch the boys saw out on the south point." But it was true about Regan. All because of her grudge over that misunderstanding in Paris. Even though he'd been the one who'd suffered for it—been lucky she hadn't had done him permanent damage. Women usually fell all over themselves to let him do them. Not her. She'd knocked him flat. Totally unwarranted. Hell. She'd been assigned to give him any help he needed, had said so herself. Well, he'd needed help with an erection. What was so bad about that?

"With wild boar out there, you've got wild dogs?" Arnie said. "I wouldn't have thought it possible."

"Believe what you want."

How many people had she told? How many had laughed at him behind his back? People chortling, "He flashed you, and you decked him?"

And, the Martisen business. And, Craig Montrose raising hell with Human Resources over his promotion afterwards? You couldn't say the two weren't connected. Even so, he'd thought, the Agency was a big enough place. He'd be able to avoid both Montrose and his wife. But it hadn't worked that way. Arnie'd decided to be a king maker and given Montrose the extra boost he'd needed to take over the whole damn agency. Worse, if possible, he'd brought the bitch into Hayburner and given her that damn Libyan to handle—another one with a grudge.

It'd been a perfect storm. He'd realized immediately that they'd positioned themselves to get him. The Libyan and the bitch. It was a no-brainer, and he'd had skilled killers sitting around doing damn-all, killers with their own reasons for wanting both the Libyan and the bitch dead.

"Hand me that notepad," Arnie said. "You're taking so long I might as well read today's news."

"Just another minute."

What were the odds that Nat Fould and four experienced, war-seasoned terrorists couldn't kill one woman and one twenty-first century version of Joseph Mengele? The two of them had even escaped from the Saharan blast. But their luck had just run out.

"Okay," he said aloud. It'd been a pain getting the satellite dish positioned for a clear signal, but he had it now. One call to lure Craig to Tunis. A ruse to force both Craig and Regan into a hotel. A quick call to the Libyan to tell him where to meet them to discuss CIA compensation. It wasn't rocket science. Craig and Regan had a pattern of reconciliations and, by this time, they'd both be dying for an excuse to get back together. Karim, of course, was obsessed with his twenty millions.

Yes. He'd get all three in the same room at the same time without a protective detail and without those Berbers who'd been following Regan around.

He said, "Are you ready? You know what to say."

"No harm will come to Craig and Regan."

"If you don't make the call, you'll find Mary and your girls waiting in hell when you get there."

The old man stiffened, looked like he was having another stroke. Richie stepped over and increased the flow of oxygen from the big tank next to Arnie's chair, saying, "I told you. Water under the bridge. Craig and Regan will be fine. But I have to talk to Craig in person. You understand that, old man? I have to explain things to him. Make sure he understands what happened all those years ago when the system treated Jack so shabbily. You know it wasn't my fault. Do this for me, Arnie. Get him to Tunis, and I'll deliver you back to Paris. It'll all be over."

He waited until Arnie's breathing steadied, then he hit the number he'd just entered on the satphone and handed him the receiver. "Show time," he said to his designated scapegoat.

CHAPTER THIRTY-SIX
Tunis

The possibility of a nuclear meltdown in Japan dominated the headlines when Regan's brief interim of normality ended with the arrival of a cable saying Craig was in Europe for talks on Libya and would fly down to Tunis for a brief visit. He planned to be with her late in the evening.

"Thanks for the advance warning," she'd cabled back, her sarcasm evident. "I'll reserve rooms for you and your party at the Carthage Abou Nawas."

Next she got a phone call.

"Regan." The Turkish ambassador who lived in the house adjoining hers was on the line.

"Bonjour, Excellence," she said.

"Regan. I must tell you. We have called the police because our cook hears loud noises from within your house. You know her kitchen window faces across the courtyard to your kitchen window, and we know Hadija is yet to return to Tunisia."

"Yes," Regan heard the sound of bad news in his voice. "What is it? What's happened?"

"Well, I am sorry to say, but ... ."

She didn't need to hear the rest but had to listen to long expressions of sympathy and offers of help. The police had come, but it was too late to either prevent the destruction of her home or to catch the thieves responsible.

Destruction was the right word.

"Shit," she said when she reached Sidi Bou an hour later and saw what the Turkish ambassador had meant. She said it again. Over and over. She walked through the house, her fingers running over damaged walls and exposed and broken pipes as though her touch could heal the devastation or, at least, make the reality less heartbreaking. She righted pieces of furniture and pushed stuffing back inside upholstery, trying with these little efforts to restore order and control the magnitude of the damage.

John Darnley found her on her terrace overlooking the Sidi Bou Marina, staring at the sea.

"It's not so bad," she said to him, her reddened eyes exposing the lie. She sighed, "They didn't break the windows." After a pause when he said nothing, she added, "But you have to wonder why not?" And, "What're you doing here? No one told me you'd be in Tunis."

"What's missing?" he asked crossing the flagstones to her. "They must've stolen something."

"Possibly. We'll have to see. My valuables were in the safe and that's about the only thing still intact. She didn't have the energy to tell him what she thought obvious—the destruction clearly was a twisted form of revenge. Mustafa Karim was responsible. Stepping gingerly, she walked past the Englishman to go inside, skirting the scarred lid of a Bosendorfer piano which lay on the floor amid the wreckage of sounding board and ivories. John followed, sitting nearby when she slumped to the floor next to the ruins of the once splendid instrument.

She said, "Do you ever wonder about this business?"

"Every day. What in particular?"

"What it does to people. How it twists them."

"If you're thinking to blame our profession for someone's sick brain," his voice sharpened. "You've got a problem."

She'd started picking up piano ivories, some still attached to their striking hammers. They began to fill her lap.

In a softer voice John said, "What're you going to do with those?"

"I don't know. Maybe make a montage for a wall ... ."

"Bloody hell!" John's sympathy disappeared. "Maybe it's time to hang up your spurs. That's if you're going to be putting things on a wall."

She stood up, looked out the unbroken windows, then shook her head and turned back to him. He didn't understand about the piano. Probably no one would. People would see this as a victimless crime and put her agitation down to having had her personal space violated, her house trashed. But that wasn't it or not all of it. Before John had arrived, before she'd gone out to the terrace, she'd been sitting here surrounded by a crazy quilt of pieces of something she'd loved, of something she could trust.

People and pets went away. Every dog, horse, and cat she'd ever loved had died on her. Every person except her grandmother had left or died or distanced themselves—like Craig. But through it all her beautiful piano—an instrument purchased by her great grandfather in Europe, transported to America on a sailing bark and to Montana by rail, then carried south on a buckboard to his mountain-bound ranch—had been a reliable crutch and source of solace. It had survived ocean crossings, the Indian wars, and Wyoming's dry climate. It had always been there, and she'd expected it always would be there. Pianos don't go away. They don't die.

But this one had. She'd lost something priceless, something completely incapable of defending itself, something that gave only pleasure. It was a source of solace and joy, soothing her when she was angry or her nerves were on edge, calming her when upset, energizing her when she was tired. And it had been beautiful. So beautiful.

"I'm sorry," she said again to John and, not caring if he understood but needing to say the words aloud, she added, "The thing is. They killed my piano."

■ ■ ■ ■ ■

The MI-6 man met her that evening in the bar of the Abou Nawas Hotel in Carthage where earlier she'd reserved rooms for Craig and his party. A few hours later she'd moved herself there, as well, planning to live in the hotel until her house could be made habitable again. Beyond open windows, lights along the rock wall dividing garden from beach gave the scene a sense of warmth and security. Tiny lines of white caps ran across the sea, playing hide and seek with the darkness, creating random patterns in the night.

They sipped their drinks while Regan slowly and systematically ripped a paper napkin to shreds. Her eyes felt dry as the paper fragments she was massacring and she barely listened to John talking about Cumulus and the help MI-6 had been giving the TenTech engineers. The program launch, she gathered was to be a big deal with masses of celebrities and blow-out parties. In June? She missed the date.

A group of Indians, the women in brilliant saris, entered the bar. Gold bangles glinted on female wrists. More gold hung against smooth brown necks. Regan watched the party move to a round table and sit down, the women's gauzy silks settling in swirls of magenta and viridian, citron and vermillion, amber and plum, indigo and scarlet. For long moments they were a poem in floating and drifting color before resolving into seated pieces of decorative art alongside the beetle-black clothes of their escorts.

"Everyone's excited," John was saying, "figuring on a huge market launch. There's a massive buzz already. Did you see the article Anna Comfort did for *Bloomberg's?*

Regan hadn't but had heard that Anna had written about this huge American-owned non-profit based in Libya with a compound the size of a small city—powered by a wave-driven power station—all managed by a Cumulus prototype. Cumulus had watched air-conditioning units in offices and private houses, ensuring they kept room temperatures stable. Cumulus turned lights on and off, locked and unlocked doors, handled an underground rail network, and ran massive monitoring systems. Home owners could teach Cumulus their personal preferences on when to turn on coffee makers and ovens, when to run cleaning systems, and how to manage a myriad of other devices. The article went on to describe an ideal community, one doomed by civil war. Saharan, Anna told *Bloomberg* readers, had been evacuated just before a rebel force blew it up, or so Anna claimed.

When John paused for breath, Regan asked, "So, that's what you're doing in Tunis? Something to do with Cumulus?"

"A lot of people are going to make a great deal of money," John said. "You know. I was thinking about that crazy Libyan on the way here. How he was fixated on the money. It's truly ironic, isn't it."

"It is?"

"That Mustafa Karim recognized the potential in both Hayburner and Cumulus, saw himself as the next Bill Gates, then got left outside the gate when the train pulled from the station. You can understand his frustration."

"Perhaps you can. I can't. He's the one that killed my piano."

He raised an eyebrow.

So, she told him about the obscenities Karim had screamed at her when they'd docked in Hammamet after the Saharan raid.

"It was seeing his money go," she said. "He spent the whole trip back to Tunisia drying, stacking and packing money. Every box was taped and labeled. For all I know, he'd even decided how to spend it. But when we reached Hammamet, one of those bank trucks pulled up, and the commandos began passing the boxes to the truck guards. Karim tried to stop them and that's when Rafik had him restrained."

She paused in her paper ripping to look at the Englishman. "Remember how he snapped? Back there? In the grotto?"

"Hmm." While she'd been talking, John had watched her hands. When it seemed she'd said all she had to say, he raised his eyes to hers. "There's more to it, though."

She shrugged and condensed the story of the way Arnie had treated Karim, of the man's fixation on getting twenty million from the Agency. "Now, I'm the one who gets to pay the piper ... I'd guess because that crazy son of a bitch sees me as the face of the CIA—a CIA that betrayed him. So he trashed my house. At least he hasn't come after me with a gun."

"I'm sorry," John laid a hand over hers, stopping her paper shredding.

She eased herself free and said, "Karim has a sadist's instincts, a sixth sense for what matters to others. He knew I loved my house and my piano. The bastard."

John drank his wine, and the silence between them lengthened. Finally, Regan said, "You don't agree? You have some other theory?"

"No. It sounds reasonable." Then, in an apparent change of subject, he added, "You know your Mr. Walker's here? I mean here. Staying in this hotel."

She pushed the pile of paper away.

"Director Montrose," John continued, "has an appointment to see him tomorrow, has agreed to talk to Walker about a deal."

"And you know about this because ... ?" It took her a second to process what she'd heard. "Oh, dear God. You think there's a connection to my house. But what?"

"You said it. Walker cheated Karim. You were caught in the middle. You—"

A shadow fell across the table. *"Bon soir, Monsieur, Madame,"* The hotel manager, Maloof Barsand, stood next to them. He was a very thin middle-aged man with a long, hollow-cheeked face, eyes sunken within a ring of bruised-looking skin and pendulous earlobes. His hair was very black, combed straight back, and jelled into place.

"Monsieur Barsand," Regan said, "Good to see you."

"My condolences on the invasion of your home by thieves," he said, "I have heard of this and have come to tell you we are happy to have you with us as a guest of the hotel and for as long as you care to stay."

"Mille merci," she said. "May I present Monsieur John Darnley from London. Monsieur Darnley is a friend of my husband's."

John had stood. The two exchanged a few pleasantries, then Barsand said to Regan, "Speaking of your husband, Madame, I wish to assure you that we are prepared when his group arrives earlier than anticipated, so it is no problem. Now, we are happy that the members of his party are all in the main dining room enjoying our hospitality."

"That's—" she began.

"That's excellent," John said.

"How—" she started over.

"We would expect no less from such a well-run establishment," John said. "Which is why Madame Montrose-Grant arranges for her husband to stay with you. Now, if you'll excuse us."

"Of course." Barsand took himself away.

"You didn't know?" John asked when he was out of earshot. Without waiting for an answer he crossed the bar to the dining room door and looked through. Regan was behind him, eased him out of her way and continued to a long table covered with food. Before she reached it, one of the nine men there stood, said, "Regan."

Brick Mossbacher, chief of the D/CIA's protective unit, probably played basketball in college and absolutely had served in the Marines. He was in his thirties, was tall and angular with a domed head which he must have shaved daily. Even so, his hair grew so fast that by late afternoon he had a heavy shadow on both face and scalp.

"You know everyone here?" he asked.

She did and went around the table shaking hands, then looking around to see that John Darnley hadn't followed her.

"Will you join us?" one of the group asked, a question that was echoed with "Do have dinner with us," and "I'll get another chair."

She made her apologies, claiming a prior arrangement, but lingering by Brick who'd remained on his feet. As attention at the table turned elsewhere, she looked up at him and spoke softly. "Where's Craig? I didn't even know you were here. And, why are you all eating, and Craig isn't?" Meaning 'what in the hell is going on when a protective detail abandons its job!'

"Geeze, Regan." Brick looked uncomfortable, almost embarrassed.

"Geeze, nothing," she snapped, careful to keep her voice low. "Where's Craig?"

"It was supposed to be a surprise. I mean I don't want to get between ... ." His voice trailed away.

"Say what you have to say." It could hardly be another woman. Even Craig didn't work that fast. Unless he'd brought someone with him, and Craig wouldn't be that crass. Would he?

Brick was saying, "Well, see. When Craig planned to go straight from the airport to your place but then he heard what had happened there, so he thought he'd find your things here. In that bungalow. But he didn't. By this time he's getting a bit frustrated." Brick glanced around the table, but no one was paying attention. "So, he called the desk and found out you'd reserved another room and sent me over there." Regan listened as Brick continued, his eyes now off in the distance somewhere, his face and voice wearing their most impassive, impersonal protective-service manner.

"Which is all to say," she summed it up. "That Craig is in my room."

"That's about it. He instructed us to take the night off, go out on the town or whatever."

"In that case," she said. "Go to it."

"Thanks, Ma'am."

She reached up and patted his upper arm noting that she'd been 'Regan' but was now 'Ma'am.' Oh, well. Walking back across the dining room, she pulled out her cell and punched the shortcut to Craig's cell.

It rang and rang. He could be in the shower, she supposed. That was probably it.

CHAPTER THIRTY-SEVEN
Carthage, Tunisia

"I'm a little worried," she said to John a minute later, finding him waiting for her by the door. "What happened to my house today? Craig without his bodyguards. I don't want to alarm anyone but walk with me, would you?"

Her room was an end unit in a row of ten executive suites facing the sea, their doors opening on terraces framed by heaps of shrubbery and fenced from each other. As they crossed the grounds toward it, she explained some of what Brick had said.

The soft wash of the sea against the beach was almost drowned out by the hum of a generator. Path lights showed the way, an occasional yard light brightening plantings and intersections. These pools of illumination were welcome even though the night was not particularly dark.

They paused on the flagstones outside her door. John held up a hand. They both stared at a small gap between door and frame.

Could Craig have left it that way? He was the Acting D/CIA, for God's sake. Bad enough he'd dismissed his guards for the night, but to leave the door ajar? Her heart thudded.

John pushed her to one side and flattened himself on the other. "Director Montrose?" he called.

The smell. She could smell a familiar sickly sweet odor. "Craig?" she called forcing herself to remain where she was, not to rush inside. "Craig?"

Nothing.

"Craig?" No sounds of water running. No answer, either.

John's eyes held a warning look, telling her he'd take the lead now.

Screw that! A piece of framing pressed into her shoulder. Her mind flipped through the possibilities ... a useless exercise. She kicked the door. It flew inwards. Nothing happened. "Craig?"

From the unit to their right came the sounds of a television playing. Insects chirruped in the night. Music, faint but audible, drifted to them from the live band which still played in the hotel bar.

John was on the open side of the door. He reached a hand around the doorframe, searching for a light switch and found it. A lamp came on. Still they heard nothing from within the unit.

She signaled, and the Englishman took a quick look. His head came back. His eyes found hers. "Wait," he said.

Like that would happen. But he was faster than she and, for a long moment the bulk of his body blocked her view. Then they were both in the room, and she saw. For another moment she stood paralyzed. She was nothing but a pounding heart and a set of words beating against her skull. "Oh, my God. Oh, my God. Oh, my God."

The clothes she'd hung in the closet were visible through open closet doors. Her suitcase sat on a bench. A suitcase she didn't recognize lay open on the bed. The curtains beyond a little sitting group were closed, hiding beach and sea. Light pooled under the lamp and ribboned through the bathroom door and there were two bodies on the floor.

She opened her mouth. Nothing came out although useless words ricocheted around her head. Oh, my God. How could he be so stupid as to get himself shot? How could it be?

It couldn't. She forgot caution and hurled herself forward to collapse on her knees next to one of the two bodies.

Oh, my God. He lay face up on the floor, his feet framed by the bathroom door, his torso partly covered by a bloodied guest bathrobe. A towel lay just beyond one outstretched hand. Blond spikes of hair stood up from a shiny black mat on his head, as though he'd had a partial dye job. But it was blood, and it had soaked the carpet.

"All clear," John said, having finished checking the unit's few hiding places. He leaned over the other body and laid his fingers along the pulse point in the neck. "Nothing. This one's dead. Your Libyan ... ."

He came over to her. "Director Montrose? Is he alive?"

She wasn't sure, having trouble separating the pounding of her own heart from the pulse she thought she felt in Craig's neck. Then his eyes flickered. Regan found his hand and clutched it. "Craig. Stay still. Don't move. Just lie still. We're getting help."

"See ... you," Craig's words were barely audible. "Sur...prise... you," and his eyelids fell. His lips sagged and saliva dribbled down his chin.

"Oh, my God." Regan sat back on her heels and fumbled for her cell with trembling hands. Eschira. The minister had given her his cellphone number. Craig needed help. She needed help. "Oh, my God," she said aloud again. Where were the 'E's' on her contact list? There. She pressed the entry but nothing happened. Too hard. She'd pressed too hard. Get a grip. Get Eschira. Eschira could and would arrange everything, and there would be much for him to do. If the Director of Central Intelligence, acting or otherwise, died in Tunisia under any circumstances, it would prove a huge embarrassment. The Tunisian government would move heaven and earth to make sure that didn't happen. Wouldn't they?

His death at the hands of Mustafa Karim would look particularly bad. Karim who'd broken into her room to kill her and got Craig instead ...

"Please," she said when Eschira's assistant answered. She couldn't remember his name. Didn't matter. Didn't matter that she had to hold the cell with both hands, but she managed to give a lucid summary of the situation and listened as the man promised an immediate response. The tone of his voice said he would do exactly as he said.

The exchange with ... Alam Ali ... was that the name? ... steadied her. Craig's eyes remained closed, but he was still breathing.

"Let me ... ," John said, his hands on her shoulders to move her aside. "I'm a good field medic."

"No. Go away." She elbowed him back and wrapped the towel around Craig's head, seeing the gouge in his scalp and the white of bone. There was nothing she could do about the chest wounds, but at least she could see there was no air bubbling from the wounds. That was a good sign, wasn't it? She grabbed the cover off the bed and put it over him, then found a blanket in the closet and piled it on as well.

John watched her, checking to be sure he couldn't do more before saying, "There's a gun near Karim's body, but it wasn't the one that killed him or shot Craig. This one's a .22 caliber Beretta, a target pistol."

CHAPTER THIRTY-EIGHT
Carthage, Tunisia

Events after Regan's call to the interior minister stacked one on top of the other with startling speed. What seemed like a squad of DGSE men arrived within seconds of an ambulance crew, an emergency medical team and a doctor—all sent from the nearby presidential palace as Regan learned later. Craig's protective detail—men Craig had dismissed earlier so he could have, as he had allegedly said, 'privacy with his wife'—showed up shortly after the DGSE adding an unnecessary layer of confusion. Mustafa Karim's bodyguards arrived almost simultaneously. And just then a helicopter with army markings landed on the lawn. Within minutes the flower beds were reduced to shreds and any evidence that might have been left had vanished.

For the first few minutes no one objected to Regan's presence. She watched from a corner as the room became a medical unit, equipment and people flowing through the doors, moving furniture and setting up shop. Very little was said. After the initial chaos the DGSE men kept out of the way as did the tall, strong men with Marine haircuts who made up Craig's protective detail. The doctor and his people worked on Craig. He had the head wound, of course, but the bullet had only scored the skull without penetrating. More serious were the bullets in his stomach and chest.

She watched and picked at a button on her blouse. The Libyan had a gun and must've shot Craig with it—three times. The gun, itself, was lying near Karim's body. But who had shot Karim? He had a bullet wound in his head fired from far enough away to rule out suicide. More, the bullet had gone straight through his right eye. As for what John had said about the caliber? Forensics would say.

Besides, Craig couldn't have made that kind of shot even if he'd had a gun.

It seemed like seconds. It seemed like hours. Then two large men lifted Craig, now connected to life support systems, onto a gurney. Regan pushed off the wall that had supported her and started to follow.

"Madame."

She did not so much stop as was stopped. A hand held her arm, and the firm voice of an Eschira aide—Mohammed Abdul-Alim, the same Abdul-Alim who had been along on the aircraft hijacking exercise—made it clear that she would not be allowed to go with the medical people.

Abdul-Alim. She hadn't noticed him among the men in suits. But there he was standing next to her, every hair on his head in place despite the hour. The small wave above his forehead was combed to perfection, just as it had been it had been after the disastrous exercise.

"Can you ask the doctor if he will live?" she asked. Her lips trembled on the question.

A deep voice to her right added, "And when she will be able to see him." It was John. He was still here.

Regan nodded. "Yes. And when I can see him."

"As to that," Abdul-Alim said. "No one can yet say. As to survival, Doctor Ashouri says his condition is very serious, but your husband is strong. Carthage orders the helicopter to take him to the military hospital where he will have the best that Tunisia can provide. His Excellency asks me to explain to you that we spare no effort. Now if you will come with me. You cannot stay here."

Abdul-Alim led the way.

He took them back past other hotel units and along the garden paths she and John had followed earlier. Then, the small lights illuminating the paths and hidden in the foliage had made the night seem mysterious. All of that was gone, swallowed by big generator-driven security spots on trailers. They lit the scene as brilliantly as the front lot of a car dealership. Men seemed to be everywhere, their voices professional and guarded, their eyes searching the ground or double-checking marks on doors to make sure each unit had been searched. There was an army at work here—a squandering of time and resources in a sense. But it had to be done.

John Darnley kept pace alongside her, "Can't imagine what they think to accomplish."

"We're meant to see."

"No stone unturned." He gave a small snort. "But, yes. I agree."

"I wonder if they'd let us take a look at the hotel computer ... the registration?"

"More to the point, I wonder if whoever's the lead investigator has?" He didn't ask what name she expected to find, and she didn't say.

Far enough ahead of them not to have heard, Abdul-Alim waited at a side door to the main hotel building. When they caught up, he ushered them down a hall and into a room rich with gold velvet-covered, overstuffed furniture and ivory-inlaid tables. Two large flower arrangements heavy with bird of paradise blossoms adorned a center coffee table and a sideboard, the colors reflected in a mirrored wall. A waiter pushing a rolling serving table came behind ready to offer them drinks and unknown selections from covered trays.

"Refreshments," Abdul-Alim asked in a host's voice, adding in a different tone, "If it pleases you, we need to talk for a moment, then one of my men will come to take your statement. Afterwards you will need to see the investigators."

The prospect of making a statement to the police triggered thoughts of consequences. She'd been focused on whether Craig would live and on the question of who had done it, but there was more involved than a killer. Much more. She said, "We have many people to notify."

"Aah. Some of this we have done for you." Abdul-Alim picked a dome cover off a tray and peered at a stack of sandwiches beneath. His lips twisted slightly as if offended by what he saw. He replaced the lid, smoothed back the wave in his hair, and looked up. "Someone from your embassy will be here soon to assist and to handle communications with Washington. Now," he waved a hand at bottles, trays, glasses and plates, "would you be so kind as to make a selection of these small offerings. You must be both hungry and thirsty." While he spoke, his eyes were on the waiter who stood nearby. In response, the man straightened, one hand uncomfortably tugging at the skirts of his white jacket, trying to adjust the way it lay.

Regan saw this in the mirror wall—the fidgeting junior, the disapproving superior officer—both flanked by reflections of the flower arrangements. The sight almost made her smile, it was such a normal sort of human interaction. And, she'd already noted the obviously borrowed jacket's poor fit and the way it bulged over a concealed weapon.

John entered the scene in the mirror, leaning over to check the selections on the table. He wouldn't say anything about the gun. Much better not. The Tunisians were being discreet in this high-profile case. So far, she and John weren't suspects. Not exactly, and as long as they made no move to depart, the "waiter" would be just that. Otherwise ... . Well, he probably had orders to detain them. Forcibly, if necessary.

"We must concern ourselves with your security, Madame," Abdul-Alim said to her back, reinforcing her judgment that he was no one's fool. "The killer may still be among us."

"Of course," she said.

"We'll have two brandies," John straightened and said to the waiter.

"Orange juice for me," Abdul-Alim said.

When the pseudo-waiter finished pouring, he looked at Abdul-Alim and, in response to a sketchy gesture, gave a stiff small bow and retreated, leaving his cart behind and saying, "I will be outside if I am needed."

She didn't want brandy. She left the drink where the waiter had set it and got herself a bottle of water, not bothering with a glass and downing the bottle's contents almost in one long swig, glad to see that her hands were steady. All the fatigue and stress on top of a day of ... on top of an upsetting day. Well. There's nothing like a true crisis to clear the mind and focus the brain.

"It is a question," Abdul-Alim began, speaking to Regan, "of terrorism. There is no doubt, Madame. Possibly these al-Salan who escaped us in February now seek revenge. Possibly they are in the employ of al-Qaeda or an al-Qaeda affiliate. Whatever it is, we will find them and establish the connection to the attack on our ministers." He paused to give her a chance to respond.

She did but on a different subject. "Before we go further," she said. "Could you call and ask what's happening with my husband. The doctors at the hospital should've had time to examine him by now."

"He'll be in surgery, I would think. But ... ," Abdul-Alim's voice trailed away. He'd seen the expression on her face. Without another word he pulled out a cellphone, punched a number, said a few words, then he clicked off. "They will call us back. Now, Madame. Monsieur. If you could tell me precisely what happened? Why is it you rented both a bungalow and an executive suite? I have many questions." He looked at Regan. "If you would start, Madame."

She didn't bother protesting at having to give the entire story to Abdul-Alim now. And then, clearly, she'd have to go over the entire thing again for his office's records, then again for the investigative team. She might have to repeat herself a dozen or more times in the next few days. She also didn't even think of claiming diplomatic immunity or diplomatic privilege. The ambassador would certainly waive it, this being a capital case. No. In any event she was reasonably certain that all Abdul-Alim wanted from her and John was assurance that they'd go along with his theory of events and cause no trouble or embarrassment.

And, his version—terrorism—was certainly possible. Not probable, but possible.

So, she told an abbreviated story beginning with the break-in at her house, her decision to move into the Abou Nawas until her home could be made habitable again. About Craig needing extra space for his party. As she talked, she could see Craig arriving early, deciding to surprise her ... arrogant to the end. He apparently had decided to "forgive" her for Hayburner's destruction, had presumed his mere presence would overwhelm her one more time, and she'd fall into his arms. So, he'd sent his bodyguards away. Showered and clean and mostly dry he'd come out of the bathroom.

What had happened then?

She didn't conjecture, said only that she'd been unaware of Craig's arrival. Obviously, he'd planned to surprise her. Brick would verify that just as he'd do his best to keep their personal business private. She finished with, "That's all. Monsieur Darnley walked me back to the suite. And we found them. That's all."

While she'd been talking, the Tunisian had seated himself in one of the opulent chairs, his long-fingered, light-skinned hands lying relaxed on its broad arms. The cuffs of his shirt showed white and starched between wrist and a fine silk-wool mix of a suit sleeve. It might be the middle of the night, but he was as perfectly turned out as he would be for a formal call at the embassy.

John offered no comments. Abdul-Alim remained silent for a long minute, a time during which she realized the room was completely sound proof. They should be able to hear the waiter shuffling in the hall or the clatter of dishes from the kitchen or, at a minimum, the sounds of night creatures outside. But there was nothing.

During her recital, she'd been standing. Now, she crossed to sit in a chair opposite John, one of the flower arrangements hiding most of his body from her. In a way they were lucky, she supposed. If not for the need to find a "terrorist" to blame, the Tunisians might have thought she and John conspired to kill both Karim and Craig. They had motives, or so the Tunisians might think, having found the two of them together in her room. The story line would be obvious: lover and wife decide to kill jealous husband and slay a by-stander in the process.

"*Eh bien*, Madame," Abdul-Alim said at last. "There is no doubt. We are certain that the terrorist learned your director was arriving early and would be in your room. We think he must have been waiting, perhaps in the closet. When Monsieur Karim entered, he would've seen his chance to make it look as though Monsieur Karim shot your husband, when in fact it was the terrorist who shot both of them." He paused. "This man Karim has had egregiously bad fortune, has he not? And, now, to simply be in the wrong place at the wrong time and been killed so he could not testify against this terrorist."

Abdul-Alim took a sip of his orange juice. "And, now, Monsieur. Will you please tell me what you are doing here?"

"Consultations at my embassy."

"And tonight?"

"As Madame Montrose-Grant said, we met for a drink. Nothing more."

"*Eh bien.*" He stood up, giving no indication he saw more than a business relationship between the two Westerners. He stood up. "Then, we will ... ." His phone rang, interrupting him.

Regan's heart jumped. It would be the hospital. For the first time she thought that the brandy John had ordered for her was actually a good idea. She stood, walked over to the table where the waiter had left the glass, and took a long swallow. The familiar burn ran down her throat and spread through her system, a good feeling but not particularly helpful. Her heart thumped with anxiety.

In the mirror she watched the Tunisian. He held his cellphone in one hand and smoothed his hair back with the other. He listened but did not speak, and his face showed nothing.

"What'd they say?" She turned and asked as he clicked off from the call. "What'd they say?"

"It is as I thought. They took your husband directly to the operating theater. He is there now, and they anticipate the surgery could last several more hours."

"Then he's still alive." She did not try to hide her relief.

"Yes, Madame. We can build hope on this fact. Now, I must go. There is much more for me to arrange this night." He rose to his feet.

"Is there—?" John began.

Abdul-Karim lifted a hand to his forehead. "Ah, I forget. The hotel manager has moved your things to your bungalow, Madame, and," he looked at John. "There is a room for you, Monsieur. It should have everything you will need before tomorrow. Obviously, it is our duty to be certain you are safe. Here we can protect you. You agree?"

"My embassy will need to know," John said.

"Yes. They have been informed that you are cooperating fully."

"Of course," John managed to keep the sarcasm he must feel out of his voice.

As she'd believed, they were being detained—a form of '*guard en vue*' and in a gilded cage but, still, detained. She said, "I'll want to see my husband as soon as he's out of surgery."

"I will do what I can," Abdul-Alim said. "The man outside who served your drinks will take you to your accommodations when you are ready and remain with you as a precaution. If I am right about the al-Salan connection, this killer expected to shoot you as well as your husband, Madame. While it is unlikely that he would attempt to do so when my men are here in such force, one can never be too careful."

"I'd like to thank the hotel manager," John said. "And apologize for the trouble."

Abdul-Karim went out to stand in the door to the hallway. They heard him speaking to his man there. When he turned, there was a slight smile on his face. "This man will take you to the manager. It is kind for you to think of him and the significant disruption to his business all of this is causing. Now, I must say to you 'good night.' Madame, you have my cellphone number if you need to contact me. Please do not hesitate to use it." He shook hands with each of them and left.

For a long moment after the door closed behind the Tunisian, they looked at each other. But this was no place to talk. The odds that the room was bugged were high—not specifically to record whatever they might say to each other but because this would be a VIP lounge used by visiting dignitaries whose informal chatter to each other might prove useful at the Ministry of Interior. Hence, the soundproofing to eliminate ambient noise.

"Let's have a chat with the manager," John said, rising.

"Okay." She finished her brandy, chased it with more water, and followed him into the hall.

As it turned out, the manager's office was only a few steps away. The security man waited in the hallway. He'd used the time they'd been talking to Abdul-Alim to replace his white waiter's jacket with a black one—the fabric was cheap, but it was actually cut to hide a holstered weapon. She'd seen dozens of similar ones on other security officers, all worn like uniforms … the ubiquitous men in black suits who rode around in little black Fiats.

The manager stood when they entered.

Uninvited, Regan sat down, expressing her regret that such a dreadful event had happened in his hotel. Politely Monsieur Barsand echoed his own regrets and asked if there was anything he could do to help Madame?

She said, "An old friend of my husband's was to arrive tonight. We were to meet him in the lounge tomorrow morning but ... ," she waved a hand. "Obviously that is now out of the question, and he needs to be told, but I don't remember his name and I can't very well ask my husband. I do have good name recognition, though. If I see it, I'll remember it, so I was wondering ... ?"

"Ah, yes," Barsand said. "Your husband inquired about him earlier. He and his care giver are in the Ruby Bungalow."

"A nurse? He's traveling with a nurse?"

"A very capable man. Totally devoted to your husband's friend. Never leaves his side."

"And his name?"

Barsand told her.

Robert A. Knight aka Richard A. Knowland. For a moment she simply wondered why Richie was still with Arnie. Then, she wondered where Richie'd been during the shooting. And then ... .

Richie! Richie, the man who specialized in worming himself into the confidence and affections of his superiors and who pulled their strings until they imploded. Arnie Walker. As much a manipulatee as the manipulator? It didn't seem likely. But neither did the alternative.

"Thank you," she said to Barsand. "And, again, my regrets over this difficult situation."

After a few more polite exchanges, they were again in the corridor.

"What?" John said.

"Wait." She pulled out her cellphone and called Abdul-Alim. "I'm afraid," she said, "that we have more complications. Delicate complications. Do you suppose you could meet us back in the lounge?"

While they waited there, John paced the floor until Abdul-Alim arrived. Then she told both men what she thought had happened, concluding, "If I'm right, Richie won't leave here without at least trying one last time to kill me."

"Then, we must—" John began.

"We must make it possible for him to think he can try." She looked at Abdul-Alim. "You can see, can't you? Otherwise, he'll shoot Arnie and set things up so it looks like Arnie shot Karim and Craig."

"You don't know that," John said.

"We'll do everything we can to keep the sick man safe," Abdul-Alim said. "But we'll have to detain them both."

Up until then, she hadn't said a word about Arnie's masquerade, about who he was. Nor did he know that Richie had, briefly, been D/NCS. She looked at John who shook his head. Of course, from the British perspective it'd be better if Arnie just died and was buried in his alias. No fuss. No scandal. Was that why John was in Tunis? If Richie killed Arnie for them, that'd be regrettable but … . Because MI-6 had learned where Arnie would be and planned to put … ?

"Perhaps I'd better explain further," she said, shutting off the paranoid thoughts.

The Tunisian listened, then allowed himself one twist of the lips of disgust, but he was an exceptionally disciplined man. He poured himself another glass of orange juice and got down to business. "If there is a leak and the press hears that even one of these former CIA deputy directors has tried to kill your current director here in Tunisia, there will be disbelief and no end of theories of conspiracy. It will be a scandal which we cannot afford. No. You are right. I cannot arrest these men. At the same time, I do not see what we are to do. I will have to consult."

John had stopped his pacing, standing with his back to one of the massive flower arrangements, brilliant bird of paradise blooms seeming to sprout from his right shoulder. "If you can disarm and detain them," he said, "my government can provide you with extradition requests in the alias names and get them out of here … I'm thinking of a sanatorium in Sussex. I can have the request here almost immediately, if you can find a judge … ?"

Without considering first, she said, "So that's what Craig had … ." She clamped down on her words, substituting, … "just as a suggestion, the Unit has trained in stealth entries and is known for its discretion … just a suggestion."

Abdul-Alim permitted one eyebrow to rise slightly and said with only a hint of irony, "And I suppose you would have no idea of how long it would take them to deploy?"

CHAPTER THIRTY-NINE
Carthage, Tunisia

Richie had reserved a private bungalow, assuming Craig would be staying in one. "God knows," he'd said, "Regan can afford to pay for a luxurious little love nest for their big reconciliation." Richie'd been wrong about that, too, but Arnie hadn't bothered to say so. His chest felt as though a herd of elephants had walked all over it, and not because of the cancer. What had happened. It was all on him. Hayburner destroyed. Craig dead. Both killed by this monster he'd created.

"Are you awake, old man? It won't be much longer." Richie's whispered question came from the same place as before—some point behind him. He didn't answer.

"Not long now and it'll be all over." Richie might be talking to himself. "More lives than a cat, that Libyan. Do you suppose I should've put a wooden stake through his heart just to be sure?" A pause. "Do you hear me, old man?"

"Ummm," he said. If Richie shut up, he could sleep. Well, he'd get his rest soon enough. Richie had made that quite clear.

"I'm almost home free," Richie chuckled. "You all thought you could treat me like toilet paper and get away with it. But, after tonight ... ." His voice trailed away, then resumed, his tone matter-of-fact as though running an audit. "The Hayburner operation. Dead. Mustafa Karim and his claims. Dead. Craig Montrose, the destroyer of careers. Dead. Just one to go. And, of course, one witness."

Arnie's wheelchair faced across the dark room and through open glass doors at a terrace overlooking a sea wall and the Bay of Tunis. Small lights provided vague illumination for the terrace— lights Richie hadn't figured out how to turn off. Arnie was glad of it, glad they made it possible to discern the dim outlines of the cold fireplace, the side table next to him, the settee to his right, a small table and two chairs in front of the terrace doors. He could even see an arrangement of big, waxy bird of paradise blooms on the mantle and another on an occasional table. It'd be nice if he could smell them, but the oxygen was more important.

Richie .... Richie orchestrated everything, the manipulative bastard. It was his talent. Only he hadn't understood enough about Regan and Craig's relationship. Richie had expected Karim would break into the hotel room, which he'd done. Richie'd thought Karim would find Regan and Craig in each other's arms. He hadn't.

How exactly had it all happened? Richie had described the scene in detail after returning to the bungalow and tying Arnie to his chair. "I can't risk what you might do, old man," he'd said. "Just cooperate and you'll get back to your wife in one piece."

You couldn't trust Richie, though. In the past hours Richie had devised a new plan or a variation on the old plan. If it ever had, the current option did not anticipate Arnie's survival. In fact it was dependent on his death.

Arnie had heard Regan earlier, out there in the dark on the terrace next to his, on the other side of a high brick privacy wall. The words had been indistinct, the sound almost buried under the croaking of frogs, the whisper of a breeze disturbing leaves, and the soft, mesmerizing wash of the sea. He'd opened his mouth to call out to her, but he'd been too late. Richie had shoved a handkerchief into his mouth. Later he'd made a gag.

All the time there'd been a lot of coming and going next door, activity which Richie had monitored, occasionally providing short updates on what he'd seen and heard.

Like, the American ambassador had gone directly to the hospital but sent his DCM, the deputy chief of mission, to get the story from Regan. Chance Norris had arrived and departed with the DCM. "I knew Chance in Stockholm," Richie had said in his college-boy voice. "A total cow. No ambition. No kick ass instincts."

Richie's voice. It was an arrow in his quiver. For how can you either fear or respect someone who sounds like he's about to break into a cheerleader's "Rah, rah, rah. Go team, go?"

Regan's voice rose as she made a point of some sort.

Arnie knew every cadence in the way she talked, just as he knew every expression that had ever crossed her face. For a long time, once, he'd been sure he loved her, but it was only an obsession, unconsummated lust.

Never to be sated now. Would she have come to him if he'd succeeded with Hayburner? Would she ever have realized that Craig could not be the kind of husband she wanted? Probably not. No. Of course not.

A faint hint of a breeze stirred the flower arrangement, and he heard the rustle of Richie's clothing as he stood up, heard his footsteps as he crossed the room and came into view by the French doors. Arnie watched the dark silhouette until it turned and retreated to somewhere behind him, somewhere near the outside door. "It won't be long now," Richie whispered. "Not long before the Englishman leaves. Then, you'll wheel yourself into her bungalow and shoot her in her bed. It'll be easy. You'll see. Of course, afterwards, you'll feel overcome by remorse. You'll write a note expressing your grief at Craig and Regan's betrayal and shoot yourself."

Arnie said, "Uh uh," the sound a negative.

"You think everyone involved won't fall all over themselves to accept the obvious? To hush this up?"

"Uh, uh uh uh!"

Richie gave a derisive-sounding snort but didn't respond further.

Arnie stared out at the night, thought he saw something move. "Ummm ... ," he reacted, then shut up. Wishful thinking. All hope of surviving this night had ended hours earlier when the Tunisians completed their search of the buildings and grounds, apologizing for "the inconvenience" when they examined this bungalow, the manager even sending over the flowers as an apology.

They'd been slightly condescending towards Bobbie Knight, the male nurse, and unctuous toward him—Allen Mapleton Windsor, an ailing man with his own import/export business, credit cards, passport, and bank accounts. They hadn't removed the blanket so they hadn't suspected he was tied to his wheel chair. They hadn't searched the nurse nor noticed that he had a silenced gun under his long, white jacket, one he'd kept aimed at Arnie.

Well. Sooner or later the men in Regan's bungalow would leave, then it would all end.

The truth was: it was his fault. He'd thought he could control Richie. And Regan? He'd dropped her into the Hayburner equation with a vague sense that she'd have a ring-side seat, witness his rise to greatness and finally recognize what she'd been missing for so long.

"What you actually did," Richie had said, "was give her a weapon to use against me and you."

Richie had lied about so much, had such an easy way of twisting reality to suit his own purposes. "You see," Richie had said. They'd been in Arnie's Langley office and had just read one of Regan's contact reports on a Karim meeting. "You can see it, can't you? She's about to recruit that Libyan son of a bitch. If she hasn't done it already. One way or the other, he's under her control."

Another day, Richie'd said, "Face it, old man. She blames you for Craig's philandering, thinks you led him by example. And, if that wasn't enough, Karim's poisoned her thinking with his grievances. She may not know you're still alive, but she does know that Hayburner is your monument to yourself. Now, she's going to use her tame Libyan against Saharan and try to destroy us."

The accusation was so outrageous that Arnie had been almost speechless. "You're out of your mind," he'd said, finally. "Out of your bloody skull."

"Think about it."

"Not a chance." The idea, though, once planted, hadn't gone away.

Later, he'd nodded agreement when Richie said. "It won't hurt to hamstring her, to separate Karim from his power base. We'll expose Karim's thefts to Qadhafi and get rid of him altogether. But watch what happens then. That bastard'll run straight to Regan. If you ever doubted that she controls him, that should convince you."

"It'd be good to get rid of Karim," he'd said.

There was a burst of sound from outside Regan's bungalow. He listened, hearing a radio blare. Someone—a man—yelled and the radio was turned down. A car started. Did that mean the Englishman, Darnley, was finally leaving?

Soon, it would be over. Soon ... .

■ ■ ■ ■ ■

He felt something in the room change. Outside, the noise had stopped. Inside ... ? A soft sound, unidentifiable. He tilted his head, trying to hear. "UmmUmmm...?" He heard himself. "UmmUmm...?" It was as close as he could come to 'Richie?'

Then the overhead lights came on as did a spot illuminating a picture over the mantle. For a moment he was blinded, blinking, at the same time craning his neck, trying to turn his chair with weight shifts, needing to see what was going on. His heart thudded. His throat was clogged. Breathing became difficult even with the oxygen tubes still stuck in his nose.

There were voices ... high, excited, testosterone-driven voices ... inside the room.

Two men in black fatigues, balaclavas and berets trotted past his chair and out onto the terrace, giving 'all clear' shouts. They paid no attention to him at all. How could they have missed seeing him? His hand clenched, not into a fist but definitely clenched. "Umm ... Umm ..."

Other men rushed past him, rolled to the sides of a door leading into a small hall, then burst through heading toward the two bedrooms and bathrooms. They, too, ignored him. Was he invisible? Was he hallucinating? "All clear. All clear." He heard the Arabic, still understood it. Hell! He'd learned it just up the road at the Foreign Service Institute's school. Back in the day. When he was young and brave enough to place a sprig of jasmine behind his ear the way young Tunisian men did.

"Hello, Arnie," her voice said, coming from just behind and above his head. She could be no more than a few feet away.

His mouth opened a fraction under the gag. He felt her hands on his head, and the gag came free. "God damn," he said, his breathing coming easier now. "Get my wrists and ankles," his head nodded down at the blanket.

"For a corpse, you're pretty vocal," she said. Then, his chair was being turned. His eyelids blinked; his eyes teared. The bungalow's front door was open, letting in the night air, and there was Richard Knowland, sprawled in a wing-backed chair, his head tilted sideways, his mouth open and eyes closed. A tall, blonde man stood beside him; more men in black were stationed both inside and outside the door.

"Is he dead? He's the one." He heaved a breath, had a critical question. "Did he really murder Craig? He said so. Is Craig dead?"

She sat down next to him. "Tell me all about it."

"Never thought of you as the cavalry," he said. "But you know I'd never see you hurt, don't you? You believe me, don't you? But how did you figure it out? How did you do this?"

■ ■ ■ ■ ■

How? "Before we can plan anything," John had said earlier while they were in the lounge. "We need to know what's going on in that bungalow. How sick is Walker? Is he the shooter or is Knowland? Or both?"

"We can answer the first question," Abdul-Alim had said and called Barsand who, in turn, summoned the maid who had turned down the bungalow's beds. But it was the waiter who'd carried trays of food out to them who proved most useful. Both said the old man had seemed wheelchair bound and covered with a blanket when they'd seen him. "He does not look strong enough to lift a gun," the waiter had added. "But if you want to know ... ," he'd bent down and muttered something in Abdul-Alim's ear.

"*Mais oui.*" The Tunisian had stood, picked up one of the vases of bird of paradise flowers. "Wrap a ribbon around this," he'd instructed Barsand, put a note with it, and have it delivered to the Ruby Bungalow as apologies for the earlier disturbance.

"Well, well," Regan had said. She'd assume the room had audio/video feed buried in the walls; not built into a flower vase. The implicit revelation was almost enough to bring a smile to her face.

For the next hour they'd watched and listened with Abdul-Alim reporting to Eschira. It was 1:00 a.m. before Abdul-Alim said they had enough evidence of guilt to obtain a court order and a detention warrant. Both came through on the hotel manager's private fax machine at 2:05 a.m. By that time, two Unit squads had arrived, and Rafik had joined their planning team.

The actual entry had been anti-climatic. The surprise had been so great that they'd caught Richie without his gun, which he'd left on a side table. Thirty seconds from the moment they'd unlocked the door with a passkey and eased it open, Richie was unconscious from an injection shoved into him by the Unit's medic. A minute later the bungalow had been cleared and Arnie freed.

Then, while Arnie talked to Regan, the medic checked his vitals, adjusted his oxygen, and suggested sleeping pills.

"No," the old man said, clutching one of Regan's hands with both of his. He'd asked the same thing over and over. "You believe me. Don't you, Regan? It was my fault. I let Richie become a monster, but I didn't intend for any of this to happen. You believe me. Don't you?"

Except for his old man's voice, the bungalow was silent. Drugged, Richie slept in the chair by the door where he'd been found. One of his wrists was hand-cuffed to the chair as an extra precaution. The Unit medic had his kit spread out on a table and was rearranging his supplies. Four other men from the Unit guarded the two outside doors. Abdul-Alim sat opposite Regan, listening. John Darnley stood with his back to the fireplace. Everyone else, on Abdul-Alim's orders, had cleared the room.

"Don't you?" Arnie insisted.

"Yes," she said. "Of course." His hands, once strong and vital, felt like bone cages snapped around her hand. She resisted trying to jerk free, finally standing, saying, "We'll talk more in the morning."

He didn't let go, hanging on to her. "We'll give Craig a real funeral at the National Cathedral, won't we?"

"We'll see," she said.

"Don't you—?" John began.

"No," she cut him off. "Tomorrow is soon enough. When we know."

"What?" Arnie asked, his hands finally dropping from hers. "What will happen tomorrow?" He'd misunderstood.

Tomorrow? They'd decided not to move the two detainees tonight, mostly because they didn't want to take a chance on some jailer or guard blabbing to a journalist. The Unit's paramilitaries would keep the bungalow secure for what was left of the night. A British helicopter would pick the men up just after dawn and remove their embarrassing presence from Tunisia.

"I'm going to get some sleep," Regan said.

"Excellent idea," Abdul-Alim agreed, running a palm over his still immaculately neat hair. "We have time for a few hours rest." He looked at the medic. "You'll help Mr. Walker here to bed?"

■ ■ ■ ■ ■

Not more than twenty minutes later, Regan heard the shout. She'd stripped and fallen into bed without doing more than washing her face and brushing her teeth. For a moment she sat up, not yet asleep but not awake, either. Had she imagined the sound?

Her ears strained in the late night dark. Nothing. Until a door slammed next door.

It took only seconds to leap from bed and into her clothes. Still pulling a sweatshirt over her bra, she ran past the guard outside her own door. "Stay here," she commanded.

The guard who should've been outside the Ruby Bungalow door was missing. She found him inside, standing next to Hamid's oversized form.

"*Rien a faire*," he said to her, clicking off the radio he'd been talking into. "Nothing to be done. But, inshallah, this is for the best."

Every light in the room was on. Richie was still in his chair, the medic leaning over him. Arnie remained in his wheelchair, but it had moved, was now only feet from Richie's legs. Arnie's hands were in his lap, two more members of the Unit looming above him. His oxygen tank with its tubes remained on the far side of the room.

When he saw her, Arnie laughed. She thought it was meant to be a laugh even though it sounded more like a coughing croak. For all of that, he seemed to be breathing just fine.

"I did it," he said. "He won't ever get a chance to hurt you again."

The gun was on the floor, the silencer making it look much bigger than it was. Last seen it'd been on one of the side tables, exactly where Richie had placed it. "We'll have the forensic people in here tomorrow," Abdul-Alim had said. "In the meantime, we'll leave as much untouched as possible." He'd looked at the Ruger. "No doubt we'll find that's the murder weapon."

CHAPTER FORTY
Hammamet

The Peugeot's tires crunched on gravel, then rolled to a stop. Through the open driver's window, Regan could hear the sea grooming the nearby beach and the fronds of banana trees chattering overhead. Several of the outdoor tables were occupied. One had three place settings but just two were in use. The men saw her and stood up.

"Madame," Hamid called.

"Regan," Rafik's voice trailed his sergeant's, so that their voices came to her with a greeting of "Madame Regan."

They met her halfway between the parking lot and their table. Both gave her hugs of greeting and kissed each of her cheeks. "In the Tunisian way," Hamid said. "One kiss for each cheek and one more for luck." Having said that he put his huge arms around her and lifted her off her feet, saying, "It is that we miss you, and I worry you are angry with me."

"No one can be angry with you," Regan said as Hamid put her down.

Rafik added, "Hamid is worried that our friend is no longer thinking to join us for our conversations. But thanks be to God you are here again and come in good time. Today we begin to plan the training schedule for the next months. And what is the program? As usual, our very wonderful Director General wishes us to compete against the European teams. As usual, he tells us we are to place higher. But how are we to do this? Who is to supply the budget?"

"It is in the hands of God, the Director General says," Hamid contributed. "And while God has not appeared, you are here. Perhaps Allah sends you to us."

Rafik pulled out a chair for her. Regan sat down and said, "It's good to be loved for oneself. And one's generous employer."

With a pious look on his long face and a glint in black eyes, Rafik said, "Perhaps it is more reliable to be loved for things one can count."

Regan laughed aloud, the sound putting a grin on both men of the Unit. She said, "*Hamdulillah*, I have a bit of experience there."

They all looked at her left-hand ring finger. It held a very handsome opal set in a silver band shaped like a woman's hand, the fingers holding the opal. Her wedding rings were gone.

She'd not had them on since she'd left Washington, and no longer missed them. But the man they represented? She'd only seen him once since the shootings, had visited him in the hospital and had expected to return the next day. Except that the White House had sent Air Force Two with a hospital unit aboard to fetch Craig back to Walter Reed, and no one had thought it necessary to say anything to her until Craig was hours gone.

So she'd only had the one visit which had been all about Arnie with Craig asking, "Is he okay?"

She'd said, "He's fine. Lord Kendrick's taken charge of him."

The hospital room had been large, the floor squeaky clean under her feet. Perhaps because of its size, it'd seemed incredibly bare although there were the usual post-surgery tubes and monitors. And Craig? She'd tried not to notice how his usually tanned face had paled, how the skin on his neck folded over itself, and how gray his hair had become. Even his eyes seemed to have faded, their usual keen blue, exhausted and worried.

She spoke to the worry in as soothing a tone as she could manage, "It's okay. He's getting the best treatment possible."

"Good," Craig's expression relaxed. He smiled and reached a hand out to touch her face. "Thanks, sweetheart. I'll work out a way to visit him soon. He'll need help after the shock of ... everything."

Craig's eyes drooped, and he seemed to have fallen asleep. Quietly and gently, she replaced his hand on the bed, rose, and slipped her bag over her shoulder. She'd reached the door when she heard him say, "Regan?"

"Yes?" She turned around. His eyes were still closed.

"He ... ." His eyelids fluttered open. He looked at her for a moment, then sighed. "I never saw it. Richie was a piece of work, but I didn't give him enough credit."

"None of us did. But Karim? What happened?"

"Karim had a gun. Came in demanding money. Richie was ... right behind with a gun. Didn't say a word. Just shot Karim. I saw ... gun come around toward me and dove ... .Insane. It was all insane." His eyes closed.

This time she was sure he was sleeping. She whispered, "I'll be back later," and opened the door. She was stepping through it when she heard him say, "I do love you, you know."

She knew it to be true. She said, "I love you, too."

So true. So sad.

■ ■ ■ ■ ■

Rafik had poured her a glass of Tunisian white, while Hamid had bent to his briefcase, extracting a piece of paper. "Here we have the accounting of what we brought back from Libya which I keep to show you. It is money that goes to the Foreign Investment people to help build prosperity. It is this very big amount, as you know, and there is concern in Tunis about the possibility of an American claim to these sums." He meant CIA claims.

"Nothing to worry about," Regan said. Craig had decided to follow a 'deaf, dumb, and blind' policy where anything connected to Saharan was concerned. It might be a fig leaf, but it was his fig leaf, and Tunisia would be the primary benefactor.

She looked at the bottom line on the page. "Surely, since the Unit retrieved this money it should at least get a finder's fee and transportation reimbursement."

Rafik looked at Hamid. Hamid looked back. They both turned to her, their faces bland.

She grinned. They were rascals, the two of them. And she'd have to remember to adjust the budget for the Unit drastically. But that was for discussion another day. She lifted her glass. "I propose a toast to the Unit and its friends. Inshallah, together we can do more great things or, at least, with heroes like Hamid to protect us, we can survive."

"This is a good toast," Hamid lifted his glass.

"And to the end of a very bad affair," Rafik added.

They touched glasses, smiling, the toast reminding her of the notice she'd received earlier in the day. Too bad neither of the men could ever have any idea how appropriate a toast it was.

Thought you'd want to know. Craig, who'd sailed through his confirmation hearings and was now officially D/CIA, had emailed her that morning. *Al Windsor died yesterday in London, shot while walking in the gardens of his hospital. The killer is believed to have ties to al-Salan.*

You probably didn't hear, but Al had decided to forego further treatment, would've entered hospice care soon. Is it too much to say that they did him a favor? Miss you, sweetheart. And, if you're not going to do anything about a divorce, think about coming home on R&R. The D/CIA could use a wife. So could I.

ACKNOWLEGEMENTS

This novel has been a long time in the making and came to fruition only thanks to the contributions and encouragement of many friends and associates, most particularly to Bob Cherry, Buck Johnson, Barbara Colvert, Cheryl Wright, and Annette Chaudet who all helped with editing and comments at various stages of the work. Rosemary Lowther and Marilyn O'Hair were wonderful and supportive first readers as were faculty members at Squaw Valley Community of Writers and the Jackson Writers. A special thanks to my book designer, Tina Fagan, and to other authors, specifically Craig Johnson and Kyle Mills, who were unfailing in their support and backing. My deepest appreciation to you all.

CPSIA information can be obtained at www.ICGtesting.com
Printed in the USA
BVOW02s1108040115

381736BV00002B/29/P